Praise for
GONE TO THE DOGS

"[Emily Carmichael] will have readers wagging
their tails in delight . . . [her] scenic descriptions
of the northern Arizona setting, insider's peek
into the world of therapy pets, and loveable
characters, both human and otherwise, make
this lighthearted romp worth savoring."
—*Publishers Weekly*

Praise for
THE GOOD, THE BAD,
AND THE SEXY

"Humor and warmth pour forth from
marvelously talented Emily Carmichael's books
like warm rain. . . . Loads of fun."
—*Romantic Times*

"A lively, witty and savory story readers will adore."
—*Romance Reviews Today*

Praise for
DIAMOND IN THE RUFF

"Carmichael is a master at delivering fresh
and funny books!" —*Romantic Times*

"Piggy's story is great fun." —*Booklist*

Bantam Books by

EMILY CARMICHAEL

GONE
to the
DOGS

Emily
Carmichael

BANTAM BOOKS

GONE TO THE DOGS
A Bantam Book / January 2004

Published by
Bantam Dell
A Division of Random House, Inc.
New York, New York

ISBN 0-553-58633-5

Manufactured in the United States of America
Published simultaneously in Canada

OPM   10 9 8 7 6 5 4 3 2 1

*T*his book is dedicated to the people and dogs of the Paws for People pet therapy group, who spend so much more time making life just a little more pleasant for patients and staff at the Verde Medical Center, Cottonwood, Arizona.

GONE
to the
DOGS

prologue

NOT MANY people have been to hell and back and lived to tell
about it. I have, though. Okay, maybe the place I went wasn't
exactly hell, but it was close enough.

Just in case you haven't met the semi-famous me, let me introduce myself. Lydia Keane is the name, though there are those
who call me by the less-than-complimentary moniker Piggy. Or
Miss Piggy, if you want to be formal. Not too long ago I lived
quite contentedly in Denver, Colorado. As I look back upon it
now, that life seems nearly perfect. I had a face and figure that
would make a Cosmo model turn green with envy. Add to that
a major party attitude that kept life interesting night and day.
Gorgeous, fun, sophisticated . . . well, you get the picture.

And if I was a bit on the wild side, well, you can't expect a girl
with those attributes to stick to the straight and narrow all
the time. I confess that honor, consideration, and selflessness
weren't my style. Back then I didn't think such things mattered.
But now I've learned that they do. Those of you who've met me
before will be surprised at such a confession. Well, don't get too
syrupy about my reformation. I don't believe in overdoing the
goody-two-shoes bit. Lydia Keane wasn't THAT bad, and my

untimely demise and subsequent humiliation were grossly unfair.

For my new fans who haven't heard my sad story, this is where the hell part comes in. In the prime of luscious life I was unfairly struck down, murdered in a Denver alley during a car robbery. I confess, at the time I was making whoopee with the husband of my best friend Amy, and yes, my life to that point hadn't exactly suffered from an excess of morality. But I didn't deserve to wake up dead in some sort of limbo with a spiritual bean-counter by the name of Stanley droning on and on about what a sorry specimen of humanity I was. Sheesh! The guy takes everything so seriously!

But, to make a long story short, Stan convicted me of having had entirely too much fun in life (though that isn't exactly how he put it) and condemned me to work as sort of do-gooder undercover agent on earth. That in itself wasn't so bad. I welcomed another go-around in life, even if it was working for a humorless, moralizing, celestial stuffed shirt. But the little twerp added a nasty twist to the sentence by sending me back to earth not as the smart and sexy chickadee I truly was. No indeed, I woke up to new life as a frumpy, moth-eaten dog. Not a mutt, mind you, but something even less dignified. I found myself waddling the streets of Denver as a Pembroke Welsh corgi, which isn't nearly as grand as it sounds. Corgis are stumpy-legged, tailless little low-riders that look like foxes on steroids. No glamour. No dignity. Just a nose for trouble and a gift for overeating.

So now you begin to see what a monstrous miscarriage of justice I suffered. Yet just to prove what a good sport I was, I excelled at every task, repeatedly rising to real heroism and showing Stan a thing or two about being clever. On my first assignment, I found my friend Amy a perfect new husband (the old one bit the dust along with me, unfortunately. Besides that, he was far from being Mr. Right). Then, not resting on my laurels, I saved a heroic cop and a lonely heiress from jumping into a marriage definitely not made in heaven, and in my spare time I found them both new partners to spend their lives with. All this while operating under the embarrassing disadvantage of being a stupid-looking dog. Am I good or am I good?

What wonderful reward, you ask, did I get for being such a heroine? Not much, really. A little publicity. A dog biscuit or two. A few hugs that I could have done without. In other words, crap-ola. The best thing that happened after my second stunning success is that Stan left me alone for a few years. I thought that was what I wanted. But frankly, dogs don't have a host of options for turning leisure time into fun.

At first I enjoyed relaxing in my friend Amy's house, eating two squares a day and harassing the other resident dogs, but boredom quickly set in. I almost missed Stanley, and I certainly missed having a bit of romantic mayhem to look forward to each day. Believe it or not, lying around on a couch all day long gets old pretty fast.

Then it happened. The status quo stood up and went. None of what happened was my fault. If Dr. Doofus, Amy's husband, had minded his own business, everything would have been fine. If Molly, the corgi bitch (and I mean that in every sense of the word) who shared our house, had been just a bit more under-standing, then things wouldn't have escalated out of control. They put me in an impossible fix, and I, the innocent victim, had to suffer. Totally unfair.

My life with Amy started to go downhill when that busy-body veterinarian husband of hers decided my figure didn't meet his standards of canine svelte. So out comes the diet food. Now, corgis don't take well to diets, even a corgi who used to be willing to live on broccoli to keep her 36-24-34 figure. That was before I got demoted to dog, and where food is concerned, my dog appetite reigns supreme. The bland, gummy mess Amy called diet dog chow was something no self-respecting corgi could live on.

Don't get me wrong. I ate it. I snarfed down each meal in about three seconds flat. And then I moved on to Drover's (he could stand to lose a little weight), and Molly's (the ensuing battles resulted in stitches for both of us), and the dinner dishes of Dr. Doofus's stupid border collies as well. If I couldn't steal food from the other dogs, I broke into the pantry (closed doors are not an obstacle to a determined Welsh corgi), or mooched off the neighbor kids who hung over the back fence. I did quite well, actually. My diet ended up having a lot more variety than before.

The real problem rested with Molly, who held grudges in a very unsporting manner. She hoards her food, daintily crunching a morsel here, a morsel there, savoring every bite with an uppity snootiness that implied she had better food than any other dog in the household. She certainly enjoyed better food than I got. Amy usually fed Molly behind closed doors, but I sort of made a game of breaking in before she finished her meal. Then, of course, Molly and I would engage in a discussion about who should finish her meal. As I mentioned before, these discussions led to quite a few stitches.

Molly got more and more grumpy about the whole thing, until before I knew it, she started to ambush me around every corner. The fights were all her fault, I swear. I may have jumped her a time or two when she wasn't looking, but only because that uppity bitch needed to be taught some manners.

Anyway, the house turned into a war zone that rivaled the Middle East. And that led to my current situation. Can you believe that Amy, once my best friend, actually sent me away? Not too long ago I saved her life and fixed her up with the man of her dreams (her dreams were not all that spectacular, which you would realize if you met Dr. Doofus). She sent me off to live with a friend at the ends of the earth, a friend who had no other dogs I could steal food from and no neighbor children I could con out of a sandwich. I could hardly believe it. At first I thought Stan the Celestial Slave Driver had something to do with my fate, but from him I heard not a word. Very unlike him. Stan disapproves of fighting and loves to deliver lectures on improving one's behavior. Then I decided my departure was a plot by Amy's husband. We've never seen eye-to-eye, Jeff Berenger and I. He insisted on treating me like a dog, and I liked to treat him like the clueless dork he is.

Whoever was responsible, though, I found myself being loaded onto a plane bound for Arizona. They might as well have sent me straight to hell. Amy cried when I left and kept blubbering something about the exile being for my own good. She probably believed it, the fool.

No one paid any attention to my objections, however, and before I knew it Nell Jordan and I were warily taking each other's measure in the baggage area of Phoenix's Sky Harbor Airport. The indignity of being reduced to baggage didn't improve my mood. The two-hour ride to Nell's place from the airport (I told you she lived at the ends of the earth!) hiked up my crankiness yet another notch. I'd been sold down the river.

My first day in my new home in Cottonwood, Arizona, didn't cheer me at all. Nell lived in what could only be described as a dump: an old single-wide trailer surrounded by what she calls desert landscaping. I call it dirt. A tiny patch of green grass enclosed by a stupid little picket fence offered me only minimal privacy in doing, well, what dogs have to do. One of the biggest disadvantages of being a dog is that the sanitary facilities generally leave a lot to be desired. Think about it. How would you like to attend to very personal and private business in someone's backyard?

To make matters worse, Nell herself was not anyone I would choose for a roommate. Her closet was full of jeans, T-shirts, shorts, old hiking boots, and well-worn athletic shoes. No fashion sense at all, that girl. Her idea of formal wear was khaki pants and a polo shirt. Putting that extra effort into looking nice meant throwing her Wal-Mart tennis shoes into the washing machine. Yikes! And I thought Amy was a fashion dud!

Then there was her less-than-snazzy profession. This is where the connection to Amy came in, I guess, because Amy was a photographer, and Nell scrapes by as a freelance journalist. Sound exciting? Not a bit. This journalist didn't cover political scandals, medical breakthroughs, or even alien landings in New Mexico.

She ditzed around with local color, articles on really important stuff like Mabel's new hair salon business and those special hikes in the Arizona back country. Every once in a while she'd try for a Pulitzer by writing about local nursing home problems or the effort to keep a planned strip mall from going up in a residential area.

You've got the picture by now, right? In all fairness, though, I have to admit that Nell didn't get much of a bargain in me. During my first month in Arizona, I trashed her closet (I was bored), woke her up at five every morning (I was accustomed to a later time zone, you know), and broke into her kitchen cupboards. (So sue me! I'm a corgi!) She kept her edibles in cupboards I couldn't reach (my reputation had preceded me), and that really made me mad. Nell quickly learned that corgis have a much broader definition of edible than people do.

Eventually, we compromised. She didn't leave me alone to get bored, and I put up with living in a dump in the middle of nowhere with a fashion-challenged loser who didn't have a television and thought the latest Disney cartoon was great film entertainment. She did feed me homemade low-fat snacks, though, which made my heart warm to her just a bit. And she did let me sleep on her bed, which is very important. Some dogs belong on the floor. I am not one of them.

Considering these adverse circumstances, my behavior in the following story is not all that bad. I have learned to be considerate, brave, loyal, honest, and true. Really I have. But old habits die hard, and a fun-loving girl like me can't be expected to toe the line all the time. Or even most of the time.

So bear in mind, none of the mischief that follows is my fault. Well, not all of it, at any rate.

chapter 1

NELL JORDAN was used to people bursting into tears when they saw her, but this particular woman rivaled the floodgates at Hoover Dam. But of course, the woman's overflowing eyes fastened not on Nell in her clean white tennies, Wal-Mart khakis, and green polo shirt, but on Piggy in her freshly brushed reddish-brown fur, pointy ears, liquid-brown eyes, and the green doggie vest that announced she was a registered therapy dog.

An older gent across the room from the weeper nudged his wife. "Look, Ethel! It's a dog! Right here in the surgery waiting room! Don't that beat all?"

"My word! Isn't he cute?" Ethel made a clucking noise to get Piggy's attention, and others seated in the uncomfortable waiting room chairs also made bids to be noticed, but Piggy focused on the woman sitting in the corner—the one suffering the waterworks.

A younger version of the distraught woman—a daughter, Nell speculated—tried to comfort her. "Mom, it's okay."

But Piggy knew better what the woman needed. The corgi paddled forward on abbreviated legs, stuck a wet nose beneath the woman's hand, and settled firmly against her leg.

Soft comments from a rapt audience:

"Oh, isn't that just darling!"

"Don't that beat all!"

"What a good dog!"

"What'd they do, cut her legs off at the knee?"

Everyone in the room had the courtesy to stare at the dog, not at the woman making such an emotional scene. People waiting for a loved one in surgery or waiting for their own turn under the knife knew about tears, and they didn't begrudge the distressed woman her release.

"Her name is Piggy," Nell said.

"Piggy," the tearful one quavered, and didn't take her eyes from the dog. Piggy sighed in contentment as the woman found just the right spot behind one of her big ears. "You're a wonderful little dog, Piggy." The tears eased a bit as she dabbed at her face with a handkerchief. "A wonderful dog. I just . . . just, well, you know, there's something about a dog." She sighed and bit her lip, then said in a quiet, broken voice, "Since my mother's accident two days ago I haven't been able to cry. It stayed inside me and just burned and hurt, you know? But I couldn't cry. Until I saw the dog. There's just something about a dog." She shook her head. "And now I can't stop crying. But it almost feels good. I'm sorry to be such a blubberer."

"Not a problem." Nell gave her a warm smile. "It doesn't bother Piggy a bit."

The daughter gave her mother's hand a comforting squeeze. "Gran's going to be just fine, Mom. I know she is." Then she smiled up at Nell. "Is she a guide dog or something?"

"Piggy's a therapy dog who visits here at the hospital."

"Do you take her into patient rooms?" someone across the waiting room asked.

"We go everywhere but obstetrics." Nell smiled. "They don't need our help in there."

That earned a laugh.

"Show them your trick, Piggy." Nell waggled an index finger at the dog.

Piggy gave Nell a disgusted look, but she lifted her stubby front leg in the semblance of a wave. The trick earned her a round of applause and a few chortles, then another ovation when she caught the tiny treat that Nell tossed her way.

"She's a mercenary little soul," Nell explained. "Works for food."

"Don't we all?" said a youngish man in worn cowboy boots and a battered Stetson.

Everyone wanted Piggy's attention, reaching out to touch her and tell her what an extraordinary dog she was. Piggy took the attention with queenly condescension while occasionally darting beneath a chair to grab a cracker crumb or peanut that the housekeeping staff had missed. People in the waiting room often munched on vending machine food, and sometimes they weren't too neat about it. The occasional leavings made the surgery waiting room Piggy's favorite stop in the hospital. Nell had supposedly trained her not to take anything off the floor during their visits, but Piggy had become expert at darting after crumbs when Nell wasn't watching.

"She's a hungry little dude," the guy in the Stetson commented.

"You're right, but she's supposed to be on a diet."

"You mean, she's not supposed to look like a basketball with legs?"

Piggy halted her crumb search long enough to glare at him, but the opening of a door distracted her. From the inner surgery sanctum a nurse wheeled out a teenage girl with a huge bandage on her arm. "Hi there, Piggy," the nurse said in a cheery voice.

Nearly all the staff knew Piggy's name. Few knew Nell's. But that was fine with Nell. Piggy did most of the work during their visits, anyway.

"Hey, dog!" The teenager dropped her good arm beside the chair and wriggled her fingers. Piggy condescended to let her scratch an ear. "I didn't know they let dogs in the hospital."

The nurse laughed. "Only because Piggy's a very special dog. And there's a few other special creatures we let visit."

"Like Dr. Tolliver?"

"Don't let Dr. Tolliver hear you call him a creature." The girl's mother had gathered up the afghan she'd been knitting and joined them. "Not after he fixed you up like new." She gave the nurse an anxious look.

"Good as new," the nurse confirmed. "The doctor will talk to you while I wheel Tiffany out to the entrance. I'll stay with her until you bring up your car."

"Wait!" Tiffany objected as the nurse pushed the wheelchair toward the door. "I have to say 'bye to . . . what's the dog's name?"

"Piggy," Nell supplied.

"Piggy! Oh, man! She looks like one, too. 'Bye, Piggy! 'Bye, Piggy!"

Piggy huffed out an indignant snort as the waiting room door closed behind the girl.

"She's sensitive about her figure," Nell explained with a grin.

Most of the waiting room chuckled, including the woman who had wept so on Piggy's entrance.

"Never seen such a thing," one man observed with a snort. "Next thing you know, they'll be bringing in a whole petting zoo."

OKAY. THIS requires a bit of clarification. Me, Piggy, a therapy dog. I can almost hear you laughing. Just don't get carried away with that snorting and snickering, people, because it's not that funny. I'll admit I'm hardly the type to bring comfort to the sick and distressed. I'm a heartbreaker, not a heart-warmer. At least, Lydia Keane was a heartbreaker, and proud of it. Piggy, on the other hand . . .

Well, let's just say I had trouble ignoring all those dog instincts that came with the fat furry body. Dogs genuinely like people. It's one of their greatest weaknesses. They're born chumps. A friendly word or a pat on the head sends their little canine hearts into somersaults of joy, and they're only too eager to repay the attention by cuddling, kissing, and generally making themselves look foolish.

Of course, as Lydia Keane I did a bit of cuddling and kissing in my time, but Lydia required more foreplay than a pat on the head.

But back to the point. The longer I stayed in the dog suit, the more I found my nature changing to incorporate Dog. Stanley no doubt thought the change was a positive one. He would. In the beginning, losing my sharp edge bothered me. Not to mention the total embarrassment of occasionally getting an urge to sniff dog butts or pounce on anything that resembles a ball. But by the time I arrived in Arizona, I had come to accept my fate with good grace, or what passed for good grace with me. Lydia Keane would have laughed at the idea of spreading a little comfort in a hospital, and the first sight of a bedpan would have sent her running. But Piggy found that bedpans have a certain allure—to the point that Nell had to work hard to keep my nose away from them. And bringing a smile to someone who needed a bit of cheer warmed the doggy part of my heart.

I don't want you to think I had turned into some kind of lame Pollyanna, though. I may have lost some of my edge, but not my smarts. Prancing around the hospital as a therapy dog had certain rewards, especially for a dog on a diet. For instance, in the surgery waiting room is a table generally piled high with Danish rolls. Not that Nell would ever let me grab one (I tried once when I thought she wasn't paying attention. Turns out she was paying attention.) But the people in the waiting room munch on the Danishes and drop crumbs on the chairs and floor. Very enticing. My short little legs place my nose close enough to the carpet that grabbing a crumb or two takes only half a second. The crumbs are in my stomach and I'm looking as innocent as a newborn puppy by the time Nell notices I've even moved.

And the surgery waiting room isn't the only area where an alert corgi can earn a bonus. Patients are always trying to coddle me with crackers from their lunch or maybe a Jell-O cup. (I especially like raspberry.) Nell asks them not to feed me—she can be a real killjoy—but some of the patients are sneaky enough to rival a corgi. Occasionally a piece of breakfast roll finds its way beneath the bedcovers just an inch away from my nose, or a Jell-O cup drifts within reach of my tongue when Nell's eyes are turned somewhere else. People commonly turn up their noses at hospital food, but a corgi doesn't turn a nose up at anything edible.

But, lest you think I don't work hard for these perks, let me clue you in that the hospital is not all fun and games for a therapy dog. We are sensitive creatures—yes, even me. A dog picks up on emotion much faster than a person. And a hospital has emotions ricocheting off the walls like balls in a squash court. Anxiety, love, sadness, grief, joy, boredom—they come at you from all directions. The dog part of me always wants to respond, but the part of me that is still Lydia tries to duck like a kid playing dodge ball. My internal battles get quite interesting, let me tell you. So don't think I didn't earn all those ear scratches, Danish crumbs, and Jell-O cups as I did my Florence Nightingale act. I hope Stanley took note of how hard I worked to bring such special attention to those in need.

For instance, take the day that I did my little tricks in the surgery waiting room (Nell thought they were funny; I found them totally embarrassing) and won the heart of that teenager in the wheelchair. That day I was called upon to rise above and beyond the usual role of a therapy dog, and the reward I got is pretty much what this whole story is about.

There I was in the surgery waiting room, innocently going about the business of being entertaining, when the nurse from CCU walks through the door. For those of you who aren't hospital professionals like me, CCU stands for Critical Care Unit. Yes, we dogs do visit there. Even though most of the patients have inconvenient tubes running from various body parts to beeping and blinking machines, they enjoy a friendly dog as much as anyone else.

As I was saying, though, in walked Stephanie Combs from CCU to give Nell an anxious look.

"I thought you two might be here this time of morning," she said. "Were you planning on coming over to CCU?"

"Our next stop," Nell told her.

"That's good. I wanted to be sure you stopped by, because we have a patient in there who really wants to see you."

"Oh?"

I was a little surprised myself. We had many fans in the hospital, but not often did they want a command performance.

"I'd make it real soon," Stephanie said, which sounded a bit ominous to me.

Nell took Stephanie at her word and waved a friendly so long to the people in the surgery waiting room. "Wave 'bye, Piggy."

Stupid dog tricks. Everyone was amused but me.

CCU was busy that morning. A couple of doctors in green scrubs sat at the nurses' station scribbling on charts. A team of three emergency medical techs in their snappy uniforms were talking to a patient being hooked into a heart monitor. (Yes, even as a dog, I still have an acute eye for fashion, and let me assure you, the EMTs have it all over the docs.) And every room was full. Stephanie escorted us into a room that was dim and stuffy. The drapes were pulled against the bright February sunshine, and the lights were off. Though the air-conditioning busily pumped in fresh air, the room smelled of things you don't want to hear about. Probably no one noticed it but me, but dog noses have a gift for detecting such things.

Stephanie greeted the man in the bed with her professionally cheery voice. "Mr. Cramer, look who's come to see you. It's Piggy."

Frank Cramer. What do you know? I'd barely recognized his scent through all the other odors. I was always glad to see Frank. He was a crotchety old devil, but he had class.

In a whispered aside to Nell, Stephanie explained: "He's in a bad way, and ordinarily we wouldn't allow any visitors but family, but he's been asking specifically to see Piggy and you."

Notice how she put my name first? As it should be.

"Piggy?"

The wispy voice from the bed didn't sound like Frank's usual bellow. But it was him, all right. When Nell lifted me up to the bed I recognized him right off, though he didn't look too good. Once I got settled beside him where I wouldn't step on any important tubes or body parts, I looked in his watery eyes and sensed he was very close to leaving, closer maybe than the medical people knew. I know things like that, because I've been there, done that, and won't soon forget the journey. Dying isn't a bad thing, really, but it's something you remember for a while.

"Piggy." He put his gnarled old hand on my head. "How the hell are you, old girl?"

I laid my head carefully on his chest as he made a feeble effort to pet me. Poor Frank. I'd been visiting him for the last six months in a swank nursing home. As I said, Frank was a crotchety old so-and-so, and I don't think family and friends, if he had any, paid him much mind. Probably because he complained about everything and anything, yelled at people just for the pleasure of yelling, tried to boss everyone around, and generally made himself unpleasant to anyone who ventured near.

With me, though, old Frank was downright friendly. Sometimes it just takes a dog to put a person in a good mood. He was okay with Nell, too, because she was the one who brought me to see him. I never heard him get seriously grumpy with Nell. He would complain some, bend her ear about the bad nursing home food (judging from the occasional morsel he snuck me, it wasn't that bad), sloppy attendants (they weren't really sloppy), bad weather (Arizona sunshine), high taxes (not a concern to dogs), and his uncaring, ungrateful family. Nell always let his whining pass her by. She knew he was talking to hear the sound of his own voice. It was me he really wanted to see, anyway. I lowered his blood pressure and eased his anger at the world, and I worked that miracle simply by lying there with my head on his chest while he stroked me.

But as I said, I liked Frank Cramer all right. I could sympathize with his crankiness. I'd been cranky a time or two in my life—both of my lives, actually. And as I have a highly developed sense of injustice, I could relate to another soul who thought he had gotten a bum deal in this world.

That day I figured Frank was about to keep an appointment with Stanley, or Stanley's counterpart. I hoped Frank had been better behaved in his life than I had been, but his temperament made me doubt it. Stan would probably send him back here as a Chihuahua, just to teach him to be careful who he growled at.

"Piggy," Frank crooned. "You're a sight for these old eyes." Then he scowled mightily at Nurse Stephanie. "Who asked you to come in here? You can just take your damned needles and pills and get out."

Stephanie retreated to the doorway, but that was as far as she went.

"Nell, are you here, too?"

For a moment I thought he was going to chew on Nell also, but he reached out a shaking hand to draw her close.

"Nell, girl." His seamed lips gave a twitch of a smile as Nell took the offered hand. "Sure you're here. In a package with Piggy, aren't you."

"How are you doing, Frank?"

Stupid question, to my mind, but he moved his head in a weak nod. "Doing what people do when they have one foot in the grave. I won't be seeing you and the Pig again, Nell, girl. At least, not from these old eyes."

Nell attempted a smile. "Don't talk nonsense, Frank."

"Don't you start." He gave a contemptuous snort that sent rank old-man breath into my nose. I sneezed. "See, even Piggy can't tolerate all the damned false cheerfulness around here. You think I'm so stupid I don't know the score? It's my body that's going, not my mind."

Stephanie admonished from the door. "Mr. Cramer, take it easy."

"Get lost, woman."

I whined winningly and flicked out my tongue to kiss his chin. He tasted like crusty old man, but it calmed him down. We therapy dogs aren't supposed to give kisses, but sometimes I have to use my own judgment. I knew what the old guy needed.

"Piggy." He kept on stroking my head. "I've been waiting until I could see you, little girl. You've given me some bright moments over the last few months—just about the only bright moments. You, too, Nell, girl. I needed to thank you both before I took off."

This time Nell knew better than to deny the truth. It would only make him cranky again.

He kept Nell's hand in his and managed a croaky chuckle. "I hope I'm someplace where I can see your face after I'm gone, girl. I truly do. Sometimes people can deliver surprises even from six feet under."

"Frank..."

"You wait and see. I've still got a few tricks..." His voice faded to a croak, then an ominous hiss.

"Frank..." An edge of panic crept into Nell's voice. "Stephanie?"

Stephanie rushed forward, but it was too late. Frank had slipped right out of his old body. As Nell lifted me off the bed, I saw him floating up above the heart monitor, which was sounding an unpleasant alarm. Was that old man ever surprised to see who was really in his bed during those last moments! I may be wearing a scruffy little dog suit in the physical world, but my soul is still 36-24-34.

So long, Frank. I wished him better luck with Stanley than I had.

NELL CLUTCHED Piggy in her arms and backed into a corner of the dim room as Stephanie called in a Code Blue. She wanted desperately to leave, to flee to the sunlight, breathe in fresh, clean air, and see living, vigorous people going about their business free of the shadow of death. But she couldn't move, couldn't take her eyes off the body that just seconds ago had been a man that she had talked to, joked with, jollied out of bad moods, and served as the sounding board for complaints about nearly everything in the universe.

He was dead, gone, extinguished. In one small moment she had seen the life drain from him like air flowing from a deflating balloon. The quickness and finality of the transformation left her stunned, unable to catch her breath, unwilling to accept what she had just witnessed.

Medical staff crowded into the room in response to Stephanie's call. They blocked Nell's escape. She backed farther into the corner, an unwilling spectator to efforts to restart the lifeless heart, reanimate the thing that now held no more life than the limp bed sheets. Though the window blinds were still closed, a faint golden glow permeated the room and gave the scene a surreal cast. None of it seemed real, but rather a distorted nightmare. Nell half-expected any moment to wake and find herself in bed at home, suffering from a late-night overload of pizza.

But Nell didn't wake, and the efficient, practiced routine of the medical team had the look of reality. Nell held Piggy close, hoping the dog wouldn't react to the stress in the room. But Piggy seemed unaffected. Her bright eyes happily observed a spot near the ceiling, and her face wore a big corgi smile. The dog commented on the situation with a quiet little woof, just as the barely perceptible glow in the room faded away. The medical team pulled back, defeated. Someone noted the time of death. Someone else wrote something on Frank's chart. Everything seemed so cold, so heartless. Nell was very afraid she might do something stupid like faint.

Stephanie came quickly to her aid. The nurse took her by the arm and quietly urged her from the room.

"Nell, I am *so* sorry. If I'd suspected he was that close, I never would have asked you to visit."

"It's okay."

"It's not okay. Doctors and nurses get used to this sort of thing, and we forget that most people don't deal with death every day. I should have been more careful, but ... but he really did want to see you and Piggy."

Stephanie guided Nell to a conference room across from the nurse's station and led her to a seat. Nell felt numb, as if her mind feared opening the gate to the flood of emotion waiting to pour through.

"I'm not sure it's a good thing that we get so used to death," Stephanie said philosophically as she sat down beside Nell. "But you need to build a wall of some kind, or you'd go crazy in a place like this. Uh ... don't you want to put the dog down?"

Nell remembered that she still clutched Piggy to her chest. Her addled mind had scarcely registered the corgi's considerable weight in her arms. She looked at Piggy, and Piggy looked back in bemused sympathy. Nell shook her head and set the dog on the floor. "I'm being stupid, Steph, and I'm sorry. I've never seen anyone die, and it just caught me off guard. Poor Frank."

"Sometimes death is a kindness," Stephanie said. "Frank was in a lot of discomfort, and he didn't want to be drugged insensible. He wanted to be awake."

Nell nodded. "He would."

"Did you know him well?"

"Not really. Piggy and I visited him every week over at

the Springdale Nursing Home in Sedona. He seemed to like Piggy a lot. I don't know much about him except that he was in some kind of computer business in California before he retired out here. I think he has a daughter in the area, but according to the nursing home staff, she didn't visit often."

"The daughter visited yesterday right after he came in. They didn't seem to get along very well. You'd think if your father is dying, you'd make an effort to put up with him being a jackass. A grandson came, too, for a few minutes, but he mostly just sat in the room and didn't say anything. Mr. Cramer didn't say anything, either."

"How sad," Nell said disconsolately. "Sometimes Frank Cramer was a really nice old guy."

But sometimes not, Nell had to admit. The attendants in the nursing home had nicknamed him Frank the Crank—out of his earshot, of course, because the old man had a way of tearing someone down that didn't let the victim get back up anytime soon. A nurse at the home had told her that the entire facility looked forward to Piggy's weekly visits simply because they mellowed Frank's mood.

Yet at times, Frank could be good company. He was intelligent, well-read, and had a wry insight into people and society that had often made Nell laugh. With Piggy he was always extremely gentle, and when he'd told Nell stories of his own dogs, now long gone, he revealed a tender and affectionate side of his character that probably few people ever saw.

She would miss Frank Cramer, Nell realized, and with that admission, the gate holding back her emotions cracked. Her eyes began to swim with tears.

"I'm going to skip the rest of my visit," she told Stephanie. "I need to go home."

"Sure you do. Go home and take a nap, or a hot bath. Or better yet, write one of your great articles and devote it to Mr. Cramer. I'll bet no one else will have a kind word for him. No one writes 'heartwarming' quite like you do. I read you every week in the *Independent*, and if you don't have anything in the paper that week, I'm always disappointed."

"So is my pocketbook." Nell attempted a smile. Talking about her writing reminded her that she had her own life, that Frank—bless him—had only been a small part of her world. She needed to pull herself together, get real, and get out of there. Standing, she tried to forget that Frank Cramer's body still lay in a room just a few feet away. "I'm going home now. Sorry I was such a wimp. And thanks for your help."

"Hot bath," Steph reminded her.

"That's your prescription?"

"And a glass of wine, maybe. Then write something nice about Mr. Cramer. It'll make you feel better."

Scarcely aware of what she did, Nell walked out of the hospital, went to her car, squeezed Piggy into her harness, and strapped her into the rear-seat safety belt. When Nell finally stopped operating on automatic, she, Piggy, and Mel, her 1974 Volkswagen Superbeetle, were chugging along the highway, headed out of Cottonwood in a direction opposite from home.

"Where the hell are we going?" she asked Piggy.

Piggy woofed a soft comment from the backseat.

Suddenly Nell knew where they were going. She didn't want to be alone. If she was alone, her mind would chew on Frank's death. If she could talk out her feelings, then she could get this horrible morning out of her system. So her subconscious had pointed her toward Mckenna Wright. For all that Mckenna rarely sat still and always seemed to have a hundred things on her mind, she listened well, priding herself on refusing, under any circumstances, to give in to flights of fancy or maudlin sentimentality. Nell could use one of Mckenna's "get over it and get on with it" lectures.

Another two miles passed beneath Mel's spinning tires before Nell remembered that Mckenna would be at work this time of morning, and a high-powered attorney to the rich and famous couldn't just walk out of the office to give a distressed friend a few comforting hugs. Well, she could, and she actually might, but she wouldn't appreciate Nell presuming upon their friendship in such a way. Mckenna took her job very seriously.

"Okay," Nell said to Piggy. "Not Mckenna, then. That leaves Jane."

Just in time, she stepped hard on the brake and swung right onto the road to Jane Connor's place. Jane lived at the boarding-and-training kennel she owned in the little village of Cornville. She was always there, day and night, and Nell could depend upon her for a sympathetic ear. Suddenly, Nell wanted desperately to cry on her shoulder. Even though Jane put up a tough-girl front, she hid a marshmallow heart. With springy red hair and swarming freckles, she looked more like a lady leprechaun than the no-nonsense curmudgeon she tried to project, something that never failed to rile her when Nell mentioned it. The thought almost made Nell smile. Yes, talking to Jane was just the medicine she needed.

Piggy barked sharply as she tried to stay upright through the sudden turn. Her harness held her safely in place, but she objected just the same.

"Hold on," Nell told her. The narrow two-lane road snaked down into the little hidden valley made green by Oak Creek, and there wasn't a single straight stretch for miles. "You can get out and roll in the grass at Jane's."

For the past two years, the three of them—Nell, Mckenna, and Jane—had been the local animal therapy triumvirate. They had started Hearts of Gold, a group of certified therapy teams that visited the medical center, nursing homes, and schools. An odd trio they were—a freelance journalist, a take-no-prisoners attorney, and a dog trainer. They had little in common other than the desire to share the healing love of their animals with those who needed it most. When the hospital had first advertised for animal therapy volunteers, they had all walked in from their different worlds, but over the months they had become fast friends, sharing nearly every aspect of their lives.

Jane and Mckenna had both visited Frank Cramer on occasion, so they would share the sadness of his death. But they hadn't seen him die. They hadn't seen the life drain from his body like air from a balloon, leaving an empty, useless husk where there had been a living, breathing man. The memory plunged Nell back into the dim room with the acrid smells of antiseptic, a stale old body, and death. The finality of it still stunned her. The indignity of it filled her eyes with tears and closed her throat so tightly that breathing required hard labor.

The road in front of her blurred. A sharp curve jumped out at her, along with a steep hillside of rock, scrub grasses, and cactus. Mel jumped the road, bounced into a shallow swale, and with Piggy barking indignant objection from the backseat, came to a sudden, crunching halt against a wall of desert dirt. In the same crunching manner, Nell's head connected with an unyielding portion of Mel's metal frame.

And there they all came to rest.

chapter 2

AS DAN Travis maneuvered his Jeep CJ-7 along the twists and turns of Page Springs Road, he thought of Kristy McMahon. What a piece of work that woman was—gorgeous, smart, rich, and truly an alley cat in a woman's body. She'd discarded three husbands and gotten wealthier with each settlement. Currently she was working on her fourth, who just happened to be smarter than she was. Gavin McMahon had sniffed something rotten in the wind and had hired Dan to dig it out. Always thorough, Dan had gathered enough evidence to send Kristy straight to divorce hell, do not pass GO, do not collect any part of your millionaire husband's fortune.

Poor Kristy, happily cheating on Gavin with not one, not two, but half a dozen young studs, was about to discover the true meaning of the phrase "taken to the cleaners." Her husband, enthroned like some kind of royalty in his seven-acre estate in resort mecca Sedona, wasn't exactly the forgiving type.

The whole thing made Dan a bit queasy. Once upon a time, in his former life as a Los Angeles cop, the ugliest thing he had to put up with was drug-dealing or an occasional nice clean murder. Those were the good old days.

Or not. At least as a shoestring P.I. in the Verde Valley of Arizona, he didn't get shot at. His cases might not be fodder for a new Sam Spade movie, but they at least boasted variety—the rich and famous of Sedona, the quiet retirement villas of Cottonwood, the trailer trash of Camp Verde. Not that Camp Verde was entirely trailer trash. The town boasted a large contingent of the horsey set as well. And cowboys. The cowboys, especially, could be downright entertaining. Camp Verde also boasted the offices of Travis, Inc.—two dark, closet-sized ex-storerooms between George Kade's Sports Den (sports in this case being anything to do with guns or fishing rods) and the Hair Affair House of Beauty. The hounds that kept George company in his store occasionally wandered by to see what Dan and his part-time secretary were up to, and so did the patrons of the hair salon. All in all, the location didn't offer a very private work environment, but since Dan didn't have all that much work, it didn't really matter.

Once Gavin McMahon tossed Kristy out on her buff little butt, Dan was going to have to scratch for business. Either that or come up with some creative ways to buy hamburger and pay the rent. Dan appreciated having the afternoon off on this gorgeous spring day, but he would have appreciated cash in hand even more.

What he would have given for a free weekday afternoon when he'd been with the LAPD. Dan had to smile at the thought. He could have spent the afternoon with his kids at the beach or Disneyland, or better yet, just hung out with the little crumb-snatchers, maybe rented a movie and eaten microwave popcorn in front of the TV.

He'd had no time back then, no time at all to give his kids the attention he'd wanted to give them. Now he had lots of time and no kids to hang with, except every other

weekend and whenever his ex needed a sitter. Rotten luck.
But that was the way the world worked. Get over it.

Home was about three big curves away, which meant he
needed to decide what he would do with the afternoon—
vegetate in front of the tube, finish the Robert Ludlum
novel he'd started the night before, or maybe drive over to
the Cottonwood police station and chew the fat with some
buddies there.

All those not very attractive options flew out of his mind
when he rounded a sharp curve. The rear of a yellow VW
bug blocked half of his already narrow lane. Dan swerved,
cussed the air blue, and careened to a stop on the shoulder
with a spray of dust and gravel. Someone still sat in the little crunched bug, and that someone didn't look good at all.

NELL SWAM out of a cold and dizzy blackness and tried to
remember where she was. Wherever she was, it was damned
uncomfortable. Something pressed against her chest and
made breathing a painful chore. Her head throbbed with
the regular blows of a mallet thudding against her skull,
and a noise rudely assaulted her ears—a squeaky, shrieky
caterwauling combined with an insistent pounding that
could drive a person insane. If she could just go back to
sleep, maybe the head-throbbing and chest pains would go
away. If she could only go back to sleep ...

"Lady, wake up, dammit! Flip up the lock, would you?
Come on, wake up!"

Words. Actual words. Nell contemplated the words
wearily and decided that she still needed to go back to
sleep.

The next words that came were not at all polite. The creative cussing, along with the increased volume of the howls
coming from behind her finally pulled Nell back to her
senses. She remembered the sharp curve, Mel spinning
out of control, the sudden and painful halt against a wall of

dirt and rock. Everything had gone black with a painful thump, which might explain the throbbing in her head.

She cautiously opened her eyes to see a large hand and burly arm snaking through the driver's-side window wing. Alarmed, she bolted upright, which was a mistake.

"Ow! Ooooh! Damn! Ouch!"

"Open the door!"

The arm was gone, replaced by a man's face on the other side of the window.

"Open the door!"

Open the door to a total stranger? A cussing stranger? Like hell. She tried to think through the gray fog in her mind.

A shout of "Open the door!" brought her back. Well, of course she would open the door. She had to get out, didn't she?

Nell pulled at the handle. Nothing. Fuzzily, she contemplated the door. Not until a pounding at the window got her attention and the man outside pointed to the lock did she realize the problem. Of course. How simple. The door was locked.

She unlocked it, then pulled once again at the handle. Still nothing. She pulled again and thrust her shoulder against the door, scarcely noticing the pain in shoulder and chest as panic began to blossom.

"Hey! Whoa! Don't." The man outside made a circular motion with one hand to mimic turning a handle.

Well, sure. Why hadn't she thought of that? She rolled down the window. "Hi," she said a bit giddily. The face that greeted her through the opening had a few years on it, but attractively so. If the line of the mouth wasn't so grim and the brows weren't beetled over those pewter-gray eyes, the face would be a good deal more attractive, Nell mused muzzily.

The hands that belonged to the face had clamped

around the door handle and yanked mightily, but nothing budged. "Stuck." The man let loose a colorful curse.

The mallet pounded away at Nell's head.

"Unfasten your safety belt and climb out the window," the face suggested.

Good idea. Nell fumbled at the seat-belt buckle. For some reason her fingers wouldn't work quite right. "I can't...damn!" Did she smell smoke? Was Mel going to burn, with her inside? That first blossom of panic burgeoned into a vine that twisted to constrict heart and lungs. She couldn't breathe!...

As if sensing her sudden paralysis, the man reached awkwardly inside. "Take it easy. Calm down."

He fumbled blindly for the seat-belt buckle, connecting first with her hip, then with parts unmentionable.

"Eek!"

"Sorry. Oops, sorry again. There it is."

The buckle released. She was free, at least as free as the narrow space between seat and steering wheel allowed.

"Can you climb out?"

She tried to move, but the task proved harder than she thought. Folding her five feet seven inches into the bug always resembled a magic trick. Unwedging it from beneath the steering wheel and threading it out through the window might come close to a miracle. The extra ten pounds she'd been meaning to lose didn't help matters any.

"Can't," she said.

"Yes you can. I'll help."

Before she could protest, the man reached through the window, wrapped his arms around her upper torso, and pulled.

"Ow!"

"Sorry."

She got her head through the opening, then the shoulders squeezed through.

"That's it. Come on."

With the man's help she oozed through the window until her hips stuck. A Volkswagen window just wasn't made as an exit for a healthy, mature woman.

"Ouch!"

"You're going to have to wriggle a little."

She would have given him a baleful glare, but she was too busy. Finally, with her rescuer pulling mightily, the lower half of her popped through the window like a cork shooting out of a bottle. The momentum landed them both in the dirt with matching his and her grunts.

The fellow did not make a good mattress. He was all hard muscle, bone, and . . . other stuff. The intimate tangle of various body parts left little to the imagination.

"Yowch!" was his complaint when she tried to move one knee.

"Sorry!"

"Easy does it. Watch the knee, please."

"Are you all right?"

"Could be better. Careful." His grip moved to her waist, where her polo shirt had slid free of her slacks, leaving bare skin. He lifted gently, but she spoiled the plan by twisting to prevent his thigh becoming even more intimate with her personal parts. The cross purposes tumbled her onto her back with several sharp rocks digging into places she would rather not have dug into.

He rolled with her, his chest brushing her breasts and his broad shoulders blocking the sun. For a moment they froze, eyes locking with unexpected intensity.

She was dreaming, Nell decided. She did occasionally have dreams along this line, tangled up with broad shoulders, brawny arms, and long, strong legs; they generally left her with an unsatisfied ache and sizzle inside that slowly yielded to the reality of waking. Yes, she definitely had to be dreaming.

Then the man moved. The sun hit her in the eyes and the rocks still poked painfully.

"Sorry," he said.

Well then, she wasn't dreaming. Too bad.

"Are you okay?"

"Never better," she groaned.

He helped her sit, then knelt in the dirt beside her, looking at her head, which complained mightily at her every move. But the complaint of Nell's head was nothing compared to the loud complaints still issuing from inside Mel. Nell suddenly remembered that she hadn't been the only occupant of the bug.

"Piggy!"

"Hold still. Let me look at this."

"My dog!"

"We'll get it out in a minute. You've got yourself quite a bump there. Do you feel sick to your stomach?"

"No, I feel just dandy!" Annoyance tinged her voice. "Of course I feel sick to my stomach. I just wrecked my car!"

"Are you dizzy?"

"What are you? Some kind of doctor?"

"Nothing like that."

"I need to get my dog. Let me up."

He offered his hand to pull her to her feet. His clasp was strong and warm, and Nell didn't object when he steadied her on her feet. She was feeling a bit dizzy, to tell the truth. But poor Piggy. The corgi had never been one to suffer adversity in silence.

Nell stumbled to the bug and tugged futilely at the door. It hadn't changed its mind about opening. Even though the little car was upright, the frame was probably bent.

"Let me," the man offered.

He didn't have any better luck.

"We've got to get her out!" Panic began to build again. She stuck her head back through the window with the intent of wedging herself far enough inside to grab Piggy, who was still harnessed into the backseat, barking her displeasure, but firm hands around her waist pulled her back out.

"Let me go!" Nell insisted. "I've got to get her. The car could burn, or explode."

"It's not going to burn."

"Do you smell smoke?"

"No. All I smell in there is dog."

"Piggy doesn't smell."

"Right."

The man smiled patiently and handed her a handkerchief. "Here. Mop the blood off your head, then take yourself over to that rock to sit still. I'll get the dog."

Nell took the offered cloth, just now noticing that blood trickled from her forehead down the side of her face. She suddenly felt sick.

"Sit," he repeated.

She obeyed.

The man stuck his head through the open window to assess the Piggy situation. "I don't see why the stupid dog doesn't just jump up here and out the ... shit! Is it wearing a seat belt?"

"It is a she, and of course she's wearing a seat belt. She deserves to be as safe as any other passenger. Her name is Piggy, by the way."

"A well-deserved name, I see. She's going to have as much trouble coming out this window as you did."

The guy didn't excel at tact, but under the circumstances, Nell could hardly complain.

He tried to crawl farther into the car, but while Nell's shoulders had slipped through the window without leaving skin behind, his didn't have a chance.

The air turned a bit blue as he tugged on the door, but it stubbornly didn't budge. Piggy kept up a running commentary with remarks both loud and indignant.

"I can crawl back in ..."

"Sit. And stay."

Maybe he was a dog trainer. He certainly had the commands down pat.

"I've got tools in my Jeep."

Their rescuer was clever with tools, fortunately, and Mel's door yielded to the persuasion of a screwdriver, wrench, and several less ordinary devices that Nell didn't recognize. She was not good with tools.

"Okay, Piggy," the man said soothingly as he disappeared inside the bug. "Let's get you unfastened."

Sudden, blessed silence, then a woof from Piggy and a laugh from the man. "Are you sure this is a dog? What happened to her legs?"

Nell sighed. "Corgis are supposed to have short legs. And no tail."

They emerged butts first from the car, one backside nicely put together and masculine and the other fuzzy and rather fat. Piggy didn't like her position tucked beneath the man's arm and let the whole county know about it as her rescuer tried to exit Mel without hitting his head on the doorframe. As soon as her rescuer set her on the ground, Piggy shook herself thoroughly, glanced around to take in the situation, then looked up at her savior with a loud bark.

"She didn't appreciate your comments," Nell interpreted. "And she's giving you what-for."

He shook his head. "Typical female."

Both Nell and Piggy responded with a glare.

"So now that you're both okay, what happened here, anyway? Don't you believe speed-limit signs?"

"I wasn't speeding."

He gave her a look that encompassed the bug with its nose crunched against the hillside.

"What are you, a cop?"

"Nope, just a concerned citizen who lives along this road. It's beginning to fry me, seeing folks whiz along here at forty-five when you really can't take these curves at more than thirty, at least not without defying the laws of physics."

Nell sighed disconsolately as she looked at her beloved Mel. "I confess. I wasn't paying attention to what I was doing." Memory rushed back in a depressing wave. "I . . . a friend just died in the hospital, while I was with him, standing right there. It threw me for a loop."

He was immediately apologetic. "Ouch. Sorry. That's rough."

"And now I wrecked my car." Tears burned her eyes, perilously close to falling. After the morning she'd had, anyone with tear ducts would cry. Hot wet drops trickled down her cheeks. Piggy padded over and stuck a little black nose in her face. "Oh, Piggy!" Nell put her arms around the corgi and touched the dog's furry forehead with hers.

"Hey now!" the man said, obviously flustered. "Don't cry. Cars can be fixed. And . . . and . . ."

He was understandably reluctant to mouth comforting words about a dead friend.

"Sorry," Nell sniffled. "I'm usually not such a crybaby."

"I should apologize. I shouldn't have taken after you like that." He took his bloodstained kerchief from her and dabbed gingerly at the cut on her head. "I think we should probably take you to the emergency room."

"No." A fresh flood of tears escaped her eyes.

"It doesn't look that bad, but I still think . . ."

"Forget it. I don't have health insurance. Do you know what an emergency room visit costs?"

"Well, no. You don't have health insurance?"

She grabbed the kerchief and wiped away the tears, miffed by the "how stupid is that?" tone of his voice.

"Have you ever tried to get health insurance when you don't have a group plan?"

"No."

"Well, it costs a fortune. And so do emergency room visits. I'll just go home and . . . shoot!" She fought back fresh tears as she looked at Mel. The bug wasn't going anywhere under its own power.

•   •   •

THE LAST person Dan had heard using "shoot" as an expletive was Andy Griffith on Nick at Nite. He tried to suppress the smile that twitched at his mouth, because the woman looked ready to turn on the waterworks. Like most men, he reacted to a woman's tears with helpless confusion. He surely didn't want her to cry again.

"Hey, buck up. Things could be worse. Both you and the dog are in one piece, and the VW can be repaired, I'll bet."

She gave him a watery sniff.

"Come on. Come sit in my Jeep. You, too, dog."

"Her name is Piggy."

"Right. You, too, Pig. I'll call a tow truck, set out some caution cones so no one will come around the corner and smack your car, and then we'll go to my place and get you cleaned up."

"You carry traffic cones?"

He shrugged. "I believe in being prepared."

She didn't protest when he guided her to the Jeep with a steadying arm around her shoulders. She was not a small woman, nor dainty, but at the moment she seemed fragile enough to break into pieces. So he hated to bring up the subject, but . . .

"I don't suppose you have a roadside assistance service?"

She just looked at him.

"Doesn't matter. I have a friend in the towing business. He'll cut you a deal, and he's reliable. Promise."

Dan called on his cell phone and received assurance from Dirk, a client's cousin, that he would be there in an hour or less.

"My place is just around the corner," he told the woman as he flipped his phone shut. "You'll be a lot more comfortable waiting there. Dirk will buzz us when he gets here."

"You're being awfully nice to a total stranger," she observed.

"I'm a nice guy, sometimes."

"Ah. Wait. Before we go, I'm going to fasten Piggy's harness to the seat belt."

"Don't move. I'll do it." He leaned over the seat and threaded the rear seat belt through the loop in the dog's harness, suffering hot dog breath on his neck while he groped behind the seat for the buckle. This was a lot of trouble for a half-mile ride, but then... "See. I'm a *really* nice guy."

That earned the first smile he'd seen. When this woman smiled, even wearing smudges of dirt and smears of blood, her face lit up like the sun coming from behind a cloud. Impressive.

"Thank you," she said.

"My pleasure."

Okay. He confessed trying to impress her just a bit. She was terrific-looking, even in her current mess. Not that he could afford a woman in his already complicated life. But a man couldn't *not* look at a woman with that sexy Cupid's bow mouth and those emerald-green eyes, not to mention all the best sort of parts where parts were definitely meant to be. His imagination replaced the plain getup she wore with something from the *Sports Illustrated* swimsuit issue, and the very image made him ache.

Yessirree. Men liked to window-shop every bit as much as women did, but men didn't window-shop for anything as boring as clothes.

They pulled into his place only a minute or so after he finished hog-tying the dog. As they cruised down the hill of a driveway, his passenger looked confused.

"This is an RV park."

"Yup. Nice, isn't it? That's Oak Creek over there. Who knew Arizona could grow so many big trees?"

"You live in an RV?"

"Sure. I get a deal on space rent because I do a lot of the maintenance around here." He stopped the Jeep in front of a thirty-four-foot bus-shaped motor home with an awning on one side and a slide-out on the other. Two huge cotton-wood trees provided shade, and a wooden picnic table served as patio furniture.

"Come on in," he invited. "You, too, dog. It's...uh... housebroken, isn't it?"

"She. And yes, she's housebroken. Wow!" she said as he gave her a hand up the steps. "Look at this! You have all the comforts of home—stove, fridge...I didn't know these things were so livable."

"It's comfortable, even though it's about seven years old. I got it used. Sit down. I'll get a washcloth and bandage."

She grimaced. "You don't need to play nurse. I can manage."

"Sit. You're looking puny."

She obeyed. He liked that in a woman. Easy compliance. But he figured this lady probably had more kick to her when she hadn't just cracked her head against a hillside.

"Okay." He pulled up a stool and sat in front of her, legs spread so he could get in close. "Let's take care of you here."

She sat quietly, looking almost embarrassed as he dabbed dirt and blood from the cut on her head, applied antiseptic ointment and butterfly bandages, and gave her aspirin for muscles that, from her posture, were obviously stiffening.

"You want some coffee?" he asked when he finished. "I'd offer whiskey to dull the pain, but I'm fresh out."

She grimaced. "Thanks, but..."

"Coke? Seven-Up? Tea?"

"You have hot tea?"

"In the bag."

"Amazing. Men never have hot tea."

"My mother drinks it on her once-per-year visit. You drink it with milk and sugar?"

"Black."

"Ah. Hard-core tea drinker."

The dog, after dropping her little nose to the floor and

taking a quick cruise around the motor home, had made herself at home on the couch beside her owner. She eyed the small refrigerator with interest.

"Your dog looks hungry."

"She's always hungry."

"Don't you ever feed her?"

"Yes, I feed her. But she's on a diet."

He chuckled. "Not working yet, eh?"

The dog regarded him with a look that sent a chill down his spine. The expression on the little furry face looked uncannily human.

"Okay." So much for that subject. He set water to heat on the stove. "How about you? Could you use something to eat? I have"—he opened the fridge—"hm... stale bread, leftover spaghetti sauce, a brown banana, half a bottle of red wine, grape jelly, packaged salami, and, uh, two donuts."

She smiled politely. "Thanks, but no. I don't have much appetite just now."

He could understand that, given the menu he'd just listed.

With a sigh, she got up and looked out the window. "This park is pretty."

"Yes, it is." He moved close beside her to take in the view. Well, not only to take in the view. "The combination of trees and water is pretty much irresistible for anyone who lives in the desert." And the view wasn't the only thing that approached being irresistible. Dan wondered what she would do if he moved just a bit closer.

"Have you ever seen anyone die?" she asked abruptly.

That was a mood breaker if he'd ever heard one. "Well, uh, yes."

"I never have, until today. I've never even thought much about death and dying. Until today."

"Most people don't when they're young."

"My friend who died was old. Really old. And he wasn't well, so I'm not so upset that he died, actually. It's just that seeing it happen, seeing the life just go out of him as if someone, somewhere flipped a switch from on to off—that hit me."

Dan remembered the first time he'd made death's acquaintance. The memory still gave him a sick feeling inside.

"There was a glow in the room after he died," she said wonderingly. "I keep telling myself that it was my imagination, but I really don't think it was. Piggy saw it, too. I'm sure of it."

"Strange."

She stared out the window with eternity on her mind. He wanted to bring her back.

"I never saw any glow hanging around after a death, but then, the kind of deaths I've seen weren't peaceful passings in a hospital room, and the people dying usually weren't the type to rate a glow of any kind, unless it was a red reflection of hellfire."

At her puzzled look, he explained. "I was a cop in L.A. From traffic accidents to murder scenes, I've made more than a passing acquaintance with the Grim Reaper."

"You must think I'm a terrible wimp."

"I think you're a very nice person with a tender heart."

"I've always thought of myself as rather tough."

"Yeah? Well, even for a tough lady, you've had a pretty rotten morning. So why don't you sit before you fall down. Sure you don't want a donut?"

She laughed a bit at that, and Dan decided he liked the sound of her laughter. She had a gentle, musical laugh that made him want to smile.

Before he could try to make her laugh again, his cell phone tweedled.

"That was Dirk," he told his guest when he had flipped the phone shut. "He's loading your bug and needs to know where you want it towed."

For once he wished that Dirk wasn't so damned efficient.

"I don't even know your name," the woman said when Dan

offered her a ride home. A hint of her usual sparkle crept into her voice. "I need to know who to send a box of thank-you chocolates to for being such a knight in shining armor."

He grinned. "I don't think I've ever had a woman send me chocolate before. And I know that no one has ever called me a knight in shining armor."

"And I would send the candy to? . . ."

"Dan Travis. At your service." He sketched a little bow.

"Well, thank you, Dan. I would be grateful for a ride home. I'm Nell Jordan."

"Nell Jordan. Where have I seen that name?"

"Probably in the local papers. I'm a freelance journalist."

"Okay! I'm impressed."

She chuckled. "Don't be. It sounds fancy, but what it means is I sell stuff for pennies a word while I do contortions to make ends meet. But it's an interesting life. I can't complain, really."

"Well, it apparently bought you that fancy car."

"Fancy? . . . Oh, you mean Mel! Sarcasm." She grimaced.

"Mel?"

"My bug. You should show him more respect. He's over two hundred years old in car years. How many people are still going strong at that age?"

"Car years?"

"Like dog years. Seven for every calendar year. Mel is ancient. But he's cute, and cheap."

"I've been called both ancient and cheap, usually by my kids, and I don't get much respect, either."

"Ah. Kids."

"They live with my ex up in the mountains in Flagstaff," he felt compelled to explain. "You have kids?" he hinted.

"No kids. No husband. Sum total of relatives is one mother down in Sun City."

He felt unreasonable relief.

"My kids are Piggy and Mel, I guess. I just hope poor Mel can be repaired."

Nell ached in every part she possessed as handsome Dan Travis ushered her to his Jeep, strapped Piggy into the backseat, and then helped her in on the passenger side. Every muscle positively creaked, and she moved like an old lady of at least ninety. So she didn't complain when Dan gave her a boost through the door before he went around the Jeep and slipped into the driver's seat. And if Nell wished suddenly that the backside he boosted was just a little more buff— that was the word Mckenna's thirteen-year-old niece used, at least—she told herself to get real. She wasn't trolling for a man, even when presented with a major hunk (another vocabulary contribution from the thirteen-year-old).

Dan Travis certainly had all the premier ingredients of a hunk: carelessly trimmed black hair ruffled in the breeze as he headed the Jeep down the road; clear gray eyes made a cool contrast to skin of warm bronze, a gift of the Arizona sun. Broad shoulders, neatly trimmed nails (Nell found that very important on a man), a nice smile, and willing to rescue damsels in distress. Dogs in distress, too. A made-to-order hunk? Yes indeed.

On the other hand, Mr. Perfect could have a wife or girl-friend tucked away somewhere. Just because he had an ex in Flagstaff didn't mean he had AVAILABLE stamped on his forehead. Or he could be a serial killer with a body cut into tiny pieces and stored in his freezer. She'd seen stranger things in her varied journalistic career.

Except the motor home's freezer wouldn't hold more than a couple of ice trays and a quart of ice cream. So she could dismiss that possibility. And he wasn't wearing a wedding ring. That was something a single woman always noticed, whether or not she was fishing for a man.

The man had rescued her, Nell reminded herself primly. Just to be courteous, she really should show a little interest in him. Get to know him a bit. Just to be nice.

"I saw the camera in the backseat," she began. "Are you a photographer?"

"Of sorts." He smiled. "I like the camera. It can make time stand still."

"I don't think I've ever thought of it that way."

"Well, you photograph a moment in time, don't you? Whatever it is you shoot will never be quite the same again. But because you have that photo, you've preserved it the way it was, for as long as the photo exists. The camera doesn't play favorites, doesn't tell lies, it just shows things the way they were at that moment in time, whether or not you like it."

Nell thought he sounded just a bit sad, with a touch of wry irony. She wondered what he had to be sad about.

They talked of cameras, photography, and local photo-op hot spots. Then they cautiously danced around more personal subjects. Why he liked living in a motor home (you can pull up stakes and leave any time you want). Why she had named her VW Mel (what girl doesn't want to be carried around by Mel Gibson?). His kids. Her philosophy on the importance of dogs in the universe.

They arrived at Nell's place too soon. Talking to Dan Travis was fun. She had even laughed a time or two.

"Here?" He sounded just a bit dubious as they pulled up in front of her house.

She laughed, determined not to be ashamed of where she lived. True, most of the neighborhood was landscaped in junked cars and weeds, and the house next to hers was painted an interesting shade of orange, but her place was very tidy, with desert landscaping in the front—gravel, cactus, and a couple of yucca plants—and a neatly mowed little lawn in back. Mexican pottery filled with colorful flowers decorated the cement slab that passed as a patio, and a freshly painted white picket fence enclosed the front. She had once dated a fellow who worked at Home Depot, and he had built it for her. She had always wanted a white picket fence. The guy from Home Depot left after a few months, but the fence had stayed.

"Nice place," Dan commented.

Nell could tell he was trying not to look at the orange house next door. But he couldn't say much, after all. He lived in a house that had wheels attached.

They sat there on the street while the atmosphere got a bit awkward.

"Uh . . . listen," he finally said. "You might have a concussion, you know. Is there someone you can call if you start feeling puny?"

"Oh yes. I have scads of friends." Well, two, at least.

"Or you could call me," he offered with a casual shrug. "I'll give you my number." He searched his pockets for something to write on and came up with an old grocery-store receipt.

"Oh hell!" he grumbled after scribbling his number. "I'll just cut to the chase. You want to go out sometime? Do something more fun than attend a car wreck?"

She would be a fool to say no. How many hunks were there in the Verde Valley?

"Call me," Nell invited with a smile. "Nell Jordan. I'm in the book. And thanks for everything."

She and Piggy watched him drive down the street as they stood together on their sorry excuse for a patio.

"He seems to be a nice guy," Nell said to the dog, as if she needed to defend her decision to go out.

Piggy gave her a skeptical look.

"Don't be that way, just because he said rude things about your figure. Besides, I'm not getting all romantic about one little date. I'm a mature, realistic, very well adjusted single woman. Sort of."

With uncaring disdain, Piggy snorted and headed for the door.

As soon as Nell stepped inside her little single-wide trailer, the phone rang. She expected a call from the Volkswagen mechanic in nearby Clarkdale—someone to whom she gave entirely too much business. But the voice on the line was unfamiliar.

"Ms. Jordan?"

"Yes?"

"This is Catherine Lewis, at Johansen, Taylor, and Leibowitz. Mr. Johansen represents the late Mr. Frank Cramer. Were you aware that Mr. Cramer has passed away?"

Boy, was she!

"Ms. Jordan?"

"Uh . . . yes. I know he passed away. It was just this morning."

"Correct. Mr. Johansen would like to talk to you sometime after the funeral service."

"There's already a date for the service?"

"Friday morning. At Chapel of the Red Rocks in Sedona. Could we set an appointment for Friday afternoon?"

She was supposed to be interviewing the director of a new day-care center on Friday. "Sorry, I'm tied up."

"The next opening I have is Tuesday morning at ten."

"Why does Mr. Johansen want to see me?"

"You'll have to ask Mr. Johansen that question, ma'am. Is Tuesday all right?"

"Tuesday is fine."

"We'll see you then. Thank you."

Baffled, Nell set down the phone. Then she remembered the old book of poetry that Frank had given her to read a month or so back. It was an antique. Maybe valuable. Probably his family thought they needed an attorney to get it back.

She grimaced at Piggy, who watched her from the couch. "No one in this country can do anything without an attorney these days."

Maybe she should write an article about that. It was worth a thought.

chapter 3

NELL HATED funerals. Sending someone into the afterlife with a dirge and tears, with black-clad friends squirming in the chapel pews and wishing they could be anywhere else, seemed a lousy way to say good-bye. The Frank Cramer she knew would have wanted to be sent off in a grander way, maybe on a burning boat with prized possessions piled around him, or shot in a rocket toward the stars, there to orbit forever looking down upon the earth with a superior smirk.

"You're looking gloomy again," Mckenna complained.

Friday had come, and the three of them were riding to Frank's service in Jane's van, which smelled somewhat of dogs and dog food, with just a hint of the sheep she had transported a few months ago. The van was aromatic enough for them to leave the windows down, even though the air was chilly. But Mckenna's BMW sports convertible only rode two, and Mel still languished in the shop.

"I'm not gloomy," Nell replied. "Just . . . contemplative. One should be contemplative when attending a funeral."

Jane agreed with Mckenna. "You're gloomy."

"You got way too involved with Frank," Mckenna said. "You always do that, Nell. Like that kid with the heart problem that you organized all those fund-raisers for—"

"Or old Birdie who you used to drive to the grocery store every week," Jane reminded her.

"If you would put more energy into your work and less into being everyone's personal savior—"

"I'm nobody's personal savior," Nell denied.

Mckenna continued as if she hadn't heard her. "As I was saying, if you put as much energy into your work, you'd end up with a Pulitzer."

"I don't think they give a Pulitzer for the local junk Nell writes," Jane said.

"But she's so good at it."

"Doesn't matter."

Nell's gloom lifted a bit, which, as she well knew, was the point of this nonsense banter. All three of them had visited Frank occasionally, Mckenna with her "therapy cat" Nefertiti and Jane with her wonderful border collie Idaho, but Nell and Piggy had made him a project of sorts, and Nell was the one most affected by his death. Upon hearing her account of the old man's passing, Mckenna and Jane had refused to let her endure the funeral alone.

Having such caring friends was what made living worthwhile. Nell doubted that Frank had possessed a friend in the world. No one had been around for his decline into helplessness and death, not even his family. The thought made her gloomy once again. No one deserved to end life alone and unloved, even a crotchety old soul like Frank.

The Chapel of the Red Rocks just outside Sedona was not a large church, but the sanctuary wasn't even a quarter full when the three women walked in and slipped into an empty pew. Nell recognized several attendants from the Springdale Nursing Home where Frank had spent the last three years of his life, along with the director of that upscale institution. A scattering of older folks might have been one-time cronies of the old man, but Nell had never seen them visit or heard Frank speak a word of friends. Near the front of the chapel was a good-looking man of middle years and sober expression. His suit was dark gray and tailored in a way that simply oozed dignity. With him was a short, plump woman whose black-and-white checked dress nearly matched her black-and-silver frosted hair.

Mckenna nudged Nell. "Attorney," she informed her. "Jared Johansen is his name. Does a lot of estate and contract law. Very well thought of. The woman's his secretary."

Trust Mckenna to know every attorney in the state, and their secretaries, too. But Nell was curious to see the man who had commanded her appearance.

Jane leaned over and whispered. "I'll bet those two women in the front pew are Frank's family."

"One of them must be his daughter," Mckenna speculated. "Frank mentioned her once."

He'd mentioned her to Nell also, and the old man hadn't had a kind word to say about the woman. According to Frank, his daughter was careless, misguided, hardhearted, unwomanly, weak-spined, and just downright irresponsible, but an undertone in his biting comments made her think he harbored a great deal of affection he wouldn't admit.

Poor woman, Nell thought as she looked at the slender figure in black who sat stiffly facing Frank's coffin. Now she would never settle things with her father. Frank could not have been easy to tolerate as a parent. She wondered if the younger woman in the pew was Frank's granddaughter. Had she gotten on with the cranky old guy more easily than the daughter?

Not that Frank's family soap opera was any of Nell's business. But the journalist in her manifested as incurable nosiness, and in a way, she had been very fond of the old crocodile. She would have liked his story to have a happy ending, like in fifties movies, where all is forgiven and forgotten at someone's bedside to allow death to come in peace.

Real life didn't get wrapped in such a tidy package, though. Beginnings, middles, and endings—they were usually pretty messy. Her own life was nothing to brag about, after all. She had endured a few endings that didn't make her proud.

The service began with the pastor talking about life and death in worn clichés. His comments about Frank were mostly generalities. Possibly he didn't really know much about the man beyond a sketchy history that would have been provided by the family. But he did his best to assure family and friends—what few of them attended—that Everlasting Mercy included even Frank, and the old man probably was busy trying on a new set of wings.

Then a gray and somewhat wasted gentleman took the podium and described himself as a longtime friend of the "old bugger." He described a Frank Nell had never known, a hard-hitting, hardworking businessman who played as intensely as he worked, a Frank who liked to gamble both in business and in Vegas. Apparently he won big in both venues.

"Not many folks appreciated Frank's sense of humor," the eulogizer admitted.

Jane whispered an aside. "That's for sure."

"But he did have one. He liked to keep people jumping, keep people guessing, and our Frank always had to have the last word. But in the end, it's always God and his angels who have their way. I hope they appreciate what they've got in Frank, because he was a fine man, a real man, and I'll miss him."

Nell blinked. The glow was back. Maybe she needed her eyes examined, or her head, but a diffuse pale glow gathered near the ceiling above the speaker's head.

"Do you see that?" she whispered to Mckenna. "Just above the guy up there."

"See what?" Mckenna hissed back.

"That light."

"What light?"

Jane shushed them with a frown, the same frown that controlled a class of beginning dogs and trainers at her kennel.

The light wasn't her imagination, Nell swore. It moved slowly now, drifting from the front of the chapel, where the eulogizer held forth on the number of times Frank had beaten him at golf back in the days when they both could still play. Closer and closer it moved, passing slowly overhead. Nell wanted to turn around and look for it in the rear of the church, but Jane fixed her with a quelling eye. Jane expected the same decorum from her friends as from her dogs, and her dogs were probably the best behaved in the county. So Nell kept facing forward like a good girl and listened to the speaker.

Suddenly she had a very clear vision of a younger Frank, a Frank who thrived on competition on the golf course as well as in the business world. This Frank had thick brown hair and a face unlined by hard years. He stood straight, tall, and strong. The bitter twist no longer pulled at his mouth. The laugh had lost its cynical edge.

What a contrast! Unaccountably, Nell knew for sure that this image was the Frank Cramer the man at the podium remembered. How sad that such a man had become the Frank she and her friends had known. Where was justice in a universe where a vigorous life ended in such a plaintive whimper? The thought made the sunshine streaming through the stained-glass windows seem a bit dimmer.

Then came a soft and surreptitious brush against her hair, like a hand reaching out to touch her in silent comfort. Startled out of her gloomy thoughts, she glanced quickly around her. Jane sat focused on the speaker, and such gestures were not Mckenna's style. And how could anyone have known at that moment she had been sliding down the slope into gloom once again?

With a little chill racing down her spine, she twisted to look behind her. The glow was gone. The entire chapel within her view was totally innocent of apparitions that might be floating about touching overly impressionable journalists. Her imagination was running away with her. That was the price of being a writer. Her mind was always on overload. Likely she should be writing ghost stories instead of local color.

Mckenna nudged her. "You have ants in your pants?"

"Sorry," Nell whispered back. "Crick in my neck."

At long last the service was over. Frank was gone. They had paid their last respects. Now she should get over it, Nell told herself. She watched the two women from the front speak to the pastor. The granddaughter kept dabbing at wet eyes, and her mother looked unhappy and... "conflicted" was the only word Nell could think of to describe her manner. The woman was attractive, with aristocratic features and deep brown hair fashioned into a smooth, chin-length bob. Her slender figure could inspire envy in a twenty-year-old. But the line of tension between her brows and the set of her mouth ruined the overall effect.

Get over it, she reminded herself. She had been only an occasional visitor in Frank Cramer's life. His family wasn't her business.

"Let's go get lunch at Oaxaca," Mckenna suggested as they headed for the door. "As long as I've taken the day off, I might as well enjoy myself."

"I'm always up for Mexican food," Jane agreed.

"Sure," Nell said. "My hips can use another couple of inches."

"Well, no one twists your arm to make you order the sour cream enchilada," Mckenna told her primly.

Life headed back to normal, Nell told herself. No more

strange glows. No more ghostly fingers touching her hair. A sour cream enchilada was a surefire cure for a case of the weirds.

As they climbed into Jane's van, Nell thought she saw a familiar face. Was that Dan Travis disappearing around the corner of the chapel? Tall, black hair, good shoulders—just like Dan. No, she decided. What would Dan be doing at Frank Cramer's funeral? Taking photos? Of course not. Even a freelance photographer wouldn't be that crass. Imagination overcharged again. Four days had passed and her very attractive rescuer hadn't called yet. Typical.

"What are you staring at?" Jane asked.

"Nothing," Nell said. "Absolutely nothing."

Jane gave her a look that could have come straight from her mother. "Get in the van, then. You obviously need your blood sugar recharged."

DAN PUNCHED the accelerator of the Jeep and burned rubber out of the church parking lot. She had been at his grandfather's funeral. Nell, the woman with the fat dog. The woman with the bright green eyes and a pixie smile that matched her short and curly blonde hair.

Not that she'd been smiling that much when he'd pulled her out of that tin can of a Volkswagen. So . . . his grandfather had been the "friend" whose death she had witnessed in the hospital, whose death had so upset her that she'd driven her car into a hillside. Small world. Small, contrary world. He'd spent the days since Monday trying not to think about her, and here she had showed up where he would have least expected to see her.

His grandfather would have laughed at that, but it wouldn't have been a nice laugh. Frank Cramer was seldom nice about anything, and he had always enjoyed throwing a monkey wrench into the works of anyone's life. If Frank did someone a favor, that favor always came with enough strings to tie up an elephant.

The old man would have been amused if Dan fell for a woman like Nell. He had not been fond of Dan's ex-wife Cathy, and when they had divorced, the old man had pelted him with suggestions about finding a "better woman." He wondered if Nell would have been a "better woman" in Frank's book.

Dan turned right onto the highway out of Sedona. The road traversed some of the most spectacular scenery in the world: rock monuments and castles of the deepest red rising against a sky so blue it dazzled the spirit. Cutting a swath through the sandstone landscape, the new, clear spring green of Oak Creek reminded him of the color of Nell's eyes. Eyes so vivid didn't come along every day.

Is that why he had asked her for a date, because she was pretty? Pretty girls were a dime a dozen. They were part of the landscape. So why *had* he wanted to call her?

Because she had a spark, Dan decided. She and her quirky dog and putt-putt car made him smile. But he hadn't called. He had been tempted a time or two, but good sense had won in the end. He didn't need to get involved with some soft-hearted female who was into puppies and good deeds. Forgetting the momentary attraction would be doing her a favor, because he wasn't the kind of man a tender-hearted woman should allow in her life. He wasn't a politically correct, sensitive, twenty-first century kind of guy. Cathy had called him a Neanderthal. He didn't think he was quite that bad, but maybe from her point of view, he had been.

He swung south onto Interstate 17 and let the speed climb up to seventy-five. The battering of the wind in the open Jeep felt good, felt real, while several other things about this day didn't. His grandfather ... well, he didn't want to think about his grandfather. They'd had a knack of making each other furious, and Dan wasn't going to pretend an emotion he didn't feel. But his mind still hadn't quite gotten around the idea that the old bastard was gone. Nell would probably think he was heartless. Nell Jordan. How had a girl like her become friends with a warty old dragon like Frank Cramer?

Well, he wasn't going to call and ask her. He wasn't going to call at all, despite that quicksilver smile of hers and the way the sun made spun gold of her hair.

The spun gold doubtless came from a bottle, he told himself. He was definitely not going to call.

He exited the freeway at Camp Verde, drove through McDonald's to get a Coke and hamburger, then took the back streets to his office. George Kade and one of his hounds lounged on the porch of the Sports Den next door. George had his nose buried in the newspaper, the hound entertained himself with a bone.

"Hey, Dan."

"Hey, George. Business slow?"

"Could say that."

The office was empty. BJ, his part-time help, had class at NAU in Flagstaff on Fridays. Just as well. He didn't want to talk to anyone this afternoon, and BJ could talk a man's arm off. He would get some work done for a change, tie up some loose ends on old cases, maybe write up a new ad for the classifieds.

He went through BJ's closet-sized anteroom into his own closet-sized office and sat down at his desk. The phone beckoned. He would not call Nell Jordan, Dan told himself. There were good reasons not to call, and he wouldn't.

But the phone smirked at him in return.

He got out the McMahon file and tried to focus on writing a report for Gavin. The phone still smirked.

Somehow, the right words to tell Gavin McMahon that his wife Kristy was a cheating, lying bitch wouldn't come. He wondered why rich men with potbellies and graying hair married young, curvaceous sexpots and insisted on believing the girls married them for love. Idiots.

The phone sat there, waiting.

Dan shoved aside the file and cursed. To hell with it. He reached for the receiver.

She answered on the second ring with a wary hello.

"Nell?"

"Yes?"

"This is Dan."

A hesitation. "Dan. Oh, Dan!" As if she momentarily hadn't remembered who he was. So much for the white knight. "Who is Travis, Inc.?"

"Cheater. You have caller ID."

"Keeps the salesmen at bay."

"The only thing I'm selling is myself. Travis, Inc. is just my feeble attempt to sound important. You remember me?"

"Of course I remember you."

"We talked about going out."

"We did."

He liked the sound of her voice. It was friendly, not flirty. She was cute. A nice lady. Not calling her after he'd already asked her out would have been an insult, he told himself as an excuse.

"So . . . Where would you like to go?"

One date. Just one. One date wasn't much more than window-shopping. Trying on clothes for size didn't mean you had to buy.

"Where would *you* like to go?" she countered.

"You choose."

A fancy dinner in Sedona, maybe. He'd have to spend some bucks. But he'd get to look at that sexy Cupid's bow mouth all evening.

"How about a nice hike?"

A hike? She wanted to go on a goddamned hike?

"We could go up West Fork."

Did women consider hiking a date?

"The weather next week is supposed to be lovely. Perfect for being outdoors."

"Uh ... sure. A hike. Next week." He glanced at his appointment calendar, which was mostly blank. "I could go Tuesday."

"I have an appointment that day. How about Thursday?"

"Great. I'll pick you up."

"This will be fun."

He agreed. He wasn't much of a hiker, but following that shapely backside up a trail couldn't be all bad.

NATALIE DONNER gripped the phone so tightly that her knuckles turned white. Children, she decided, were put on this earth to be a pain in the ass to their mothers. Even grown children. Just as the true role of mothers was to be a nuisance to their kids.

Fathers, too. But Natalie didn't want to think about her father. Frank Cramer was dead, now just so much ash in an urn. Yet his image remained large as life in her brain.

She didn't want to think about it.

The line was ringing, finally. For the past ten minutes she had heard only a busy signal. After only one ring, her son picked up with a businesslike "Travis, Inc."

"Daniel Travis, this is your mother."

"And you're pissed at me, aren't you?"

"Yes."

"The 'Travis' tipped me off. You only call me Travis when you're mad. And the full 'Daniel Travis' means you're in a real lather."

"An unflattering image, but yes, I'm upset. You're behaving like a Travis, which isn't good. Your father was a jackass, but that's no excuse for you to act like a jackass."

"Ouch! What did I do this time?"

"You didn't go to your grandfather's funeral today. How

could you not go to your own grandfather's funeral? I know you two didn't get along. Your sister and I didn't get along with him, either, and we went. That old man was your flesh and blood, and you owed him at least a show of—"

"Mom, I went."

"You didn't. I didn't see you."

"Because you don't have eyes in the back of your head."

Natalie's eyes narrowed. "Where were you?"

"In the very back. I didn't want people looking at me and expecting red eyes and sobbing."

"Your sister and I were not crying."

"You were, Mom. I could tell even looking at your back. Besides, Emma cries when a parakeet dies. Do you think she's going to get through the old buzzard's funeral and not turn on the waterworks?"

"Your disrespect is uncalled for, Daniel. In spite of how difficult he was, my father was family, and family members love one another," she said stiffly. Years past—many years past—love for her father had been real emotion, not just an obligation. She remembered her sixteenth birthday. He had taken her to San Francisco for dinner at the Top of the Marc, just Natalie and her dad celebrating at a very fancy restaurant in a very fancy hotel. He'd been pleased with her because she'd made perfect marks on her report card in school, and on top of that, her boss at Cramer Business Machines, where she worked part-time to learn the "family business," had given her glowing praise. She had hated every hour she put in at the plant, but pleasing her father had been worth the boredom.

That was back when she still thought she could please her dad, before she admitted that nothing she could ever do would make him think she was worth his love.

Dan's voice cut into her memories. "Mom, okay, I'm kind of sorry the old guy is gone. I'm sorry he was a jackass who drove his whole family away from him."

"Daniel..."

"I'm being honest. You should know by now that tact isn't my strong suit. I can't work up much serious emotion over a guy who didn't have a kind word for anyone, who whined like a kid when he didn't get his way, who used money like a club to get people to do what he wanted them to do. And I can't imagine that you can be in serious mourning any more than I am."

"He was my father, Dan."

"And we all went to the service and paid our last respects. Mom, don't obsess over this. Let it go. He's gone. You don't have to deal with him anymore."

Natalie wished with all her heart that was true, thinking with a grimace about her visit to Jared Johansen's office after the funeral. Her father knew how to deal out humiliation even from the grave. Humiliation and embarrassment. Acknowledging out loud what the old coot had done made her stomach churn. But if she wanted Dan's help, she had to tell him. "Son, it's not quite true that I don't have to deal with your grandfather now that he's gone. Dad got in a last punch, I'm afraid. And I need your help in putting things right."

NELL SPECULATED all through the weekend about her mysterious appointment with Frank Cramer's attorney, and when Tuesday finally arrived, she was curious as a cat. In contrast to his appearance at the funeral, today Jared Johansen didn't look particularly attorneylike. Jeans, a casual sweater, and walking boots made him look more like one of Sedona's Jeep tour guides than a lawyer. His hair was a bit ruffled, giving him a look of just having come in out of the breeze. It was brushed with gray at the temples, and his pleasant face had seen considerable wear, but youth shone from his eyes.

He held out his hand for Nell to shake. "Miss Jordan, I'm glad you could come in."

She sat in the chair he indicated, a comfortably upholstered armchair facing his desk. "Call me Nell, please.

"Ah. Nell, then. Hope you don't mind the . . ." A sweep of
his hand indicated the jeans and sweater. "I have a long-
standing habit of going hiking with a group of friends on
Tuesday afternoons, so Tuesday mornings the staff and
clients have to put up with me in the rough, so to speak."

Nell smiled. "It's a nice day for hiking."

"Beautiful. You must do a lot of hiking yourself. I read
your stuff in the *Red Rock News*, especially the "Backcoun-
try Adventures" pieces. Very informative. Your trail ratings
are right on, by the way. I like the idea of using a ten point
scale for difficulty and a similar scale for scenery."

"I'm glad you get some use from them."

"Yes, well, down to business, I suppose."

"If this is about the book . . ."

"The book?"

"The old book of poems that Frank loaned me. It's very
old, and I'm sure it's valuable. I brought it with me." She
reached into the tote bag beside the chair.

"This isn't about a book, Nell. No one has mentioned a
book."

"Oh."

"Yes, this is . . . Did you bring your dog, by the way?"

"I brought her. She's in your reception area with the
friend who drove me here. I'm . . . uh . . . temporarily without a car."

"Ah. Well, Frank specifically requested that Piggy be
present for this meeting. He must have been very attached
to her."

Curiouser and curiouser, Nell thought.

She fetched Piggy from where Mckenna sat with her in
the reception area. Mckenna had ducked out of work—very
unusual for her—to give Nell a ride.

"Friends don't abandon friends to killer attorneys,"
Mckenna had said when she swung by Nell's house.

"Killer attorney?" had been Nell's amused inquiry. "This is about a book of poetry, not some capital offense."

"Never assume. Johansen has a rep as a tough, take-no-prisoners kind of guy. People hire him when they want something difficult pushed through the legal system. There's only one better attorney in this part of the state."

"And that would be you, of course."

Mckenna had grinned. "Who else? If you need help with Johansen and whatever Frank's relatives have cooked up, I'm your gal."

"It's just about the book." Nell had held up the ancient little volume. "And no offense, girlfriend, but I don't think you're that tough. I've seen you and Titi at work in the hospital."

Mckenna had shrugged, as she always did when one of her friends suggested she harbored an actual heart beneath the hard-as-nails image. "Even killer attorneys have a soft underbelly somewhere. Mine happens to be cats and sick people." Then she had showed her teeth in a shark's grin. "But other attorneys—and their clients—get no mercy."

So Mckenna looked up with narrowed eyes when Nell came into the lobby. "Mr. Johansen is charming," Nell assured her, taking Piggy's leash.

Mckenna snorted. "We lawyers are at our most dangerous when we're charming. Just look at me."

Nell just smiled and led Piggy away.

In Johansen's office, Piggy immediately put her nose to the floor to sniff for crumbs. In Piggy's furry little mind, every floor had potential to yield up crumbs.

"This is Piggy, is it?" The lawyer's mouth slanted with humor. "Interesting-looking dog."

"She's a Welsh corgi. They're supposed to look like that."

"No kidding? Well, Piggy, if I could have your attention?"

Piggy deigned to glance his way.

"I have something here that might be of interest to you."

Nell noted the twinkle in the attorney's eye. This was getting stranger by the minute.

"We have a rather unusual situation here, Nell, and friend Piggy. You might want to sit down, Nell."

"Are you going to tell me what's going on?"

"Indeed. You know I am Frank Cramer's attorney."

"Yes. Of course."

"I asked you to come here—with the dog—because Frank mentioned Piggy in his will, and Frank thought it was appropriate that Piggy get the news firsthand. He must have been quite fond of her, and in fact, he seemed to consider her a person as much as you or I."

"Frank and Piggy took to each other." Nell smiled. "He used to slip her Lorna Doone cookies when he thought I wasn't looking. That made him first-rate in Piggy's book."

"Well, he's slipping her more than Lorna Doones now. In fact, Frank set up a trust fund for her care and maintenance, naming you as her guardian and me as his executor of the fund."

Piggy's ears perked up, and Nell's heart jumped. "Oh my! How generous of him."

Gently, the attorney asked, "Nell, do you have any idea how much Frank Cramer was worth?"

"No. I assume he was fairly well off. Springdale Nursing Center is a very upscale nursing home."

"He was very wealthy indeed."

"At the risk of sounding greedy ... uh ... Mr. Johansen ..." Nell suffered a sudden difficulty in breathing. "Just ... just how much did Frank think Piggy needed for care and maintenance?"

The attorney grinned. "Roughly twelve million dollars."

Piggy's gasp sounded very human as she wilted into a very well-timed swoon.

chapter 4

RICH! I was RICH! Rich rich rich rich rich rich rich rich rich
RICH! Money! Money money money! All of it MINE. I
couldn't believe my good fortune. Literally a fortune! Loads of
money! Tons of money! All for me! Every single little darling
greenback. All for Piggy!

Piggy. Aaaaagh! That was the catch, of course. I was still
Piggy. Four stumpy legs, big ears, a shedding problem, and not
allowed to open a bank account, much less write a check.

There's always, always a catch. It's grossly unfair. When I
was walking around the earth on feet instead of paws, money
crowned the head of my priority list. I didn't have a big bank
account, but I admired people that did. Admired and envied. I
always intended to marry money, or at least marry someone
with the potential for money, like a lawyer or stockbroker or
such. With my looks and charm, I could have carried it off, but
I bit the dust before it happened. Now I had tons of money,
money enough for everything I'd always wanted. Lucky me,
rich as Midas, and still trapped in a dog suit.

Oh my, what I would have given to be human once again.
The things I could do with Frank's fortune! I'd start with a

Mercedes sports model—no, maybe a Jaguar. I could just imagine the Lydia Keane of old, cruising down the highway in a Jag. How terrific she would look! And clothes! Oh, the clothes I could buy! All designer stuff. Slinky and sexy, trendy and tight, with strappy designer high heels to make my legs look like a million dollars. It might cost a million dollars, but what would I care?

Of course, at the end of a wonderful shopping day I would go home to my very modern, very posh showplace of a house. No more living in a creaky old Victorian, as I'd done in Denver. No more living in a trashy trailer, like Nell's digs in Cottonwood. I would move to a ritzy part of California, or maybe to Seattle to keep Bill Gates company. My very upscale place would have servants, of course. No washing or dusting or picking up for me! A maid for each floor, a cook, a gardener, and a head housekeeper to keep them all in line.

No dog, though. Definitely no dogs. No critters crapping up the yard, leaving hair on the furniture and paw prints on the floor. I was tired of dogs! I was tired of being a dog! Every day I lost more of myself to being a DOG, and I'd just about had enough!

But all those images were merely dreams—seductive, tempting, wonderful dreams. Reality, on the other hand, sucked, because this poor little rich corgi wouldn't enjoy a single penny without the consent of Miss Never-Give-A-Dog-A-Cookie Nell Jordan.

Nell. Yes, Nell. My "guardian," my caretaker, who didn't seem to care about clothes, cars, money, or the finer things in life. Nell the Girl Scout. Nell the Do-Gooder. Nell the Drab, the Unimaginative, the Boring.

The situation had to be one of Stanley's tricks. It was just like his twisted sense of humor.

Unfair, unfair, unfair!

•   •   •

SHOCK WAVES still reverberated inside Nell's head as she lifted Piggy into the tiny jump seat of Mckenna's BMW and strapped her in.

"You've got to be kidding," Mckenna said after she regained control of her jaw, which had dropped halfway to the parking lot pavement. "You are joking, aren't you?"

"Do I look as if I'm joking?"

"You look as if someone just hit you with a bat."

"That about sums it up."

"Twelve million dollars? Twelve million? For a dog?" Mckenna laughed out loud. "Oh, lord! Why couldn't that old man have fallen in love with my cat?"

Nell melted into the passenger seat and pressed her palms to her temples, which had begun to throb. "It's all very complicated, but Mr. Johansen said in Arizona it's perfectly legal to set up a trust fund for the care and maintenance of a pet. The fund's capital is twelve million, give or take a few hundred thousand." An urge to collapse into hysterical laughter seized her. A few hundred thousand—pocket change, scarcely counted in the sum total. Oh my, oh my!

"You need to get a copy of the trust documents and give them to me for review," Mckenna said in her official attorney voice.

Nell laughed. "You're hired! What do you know? I can afford an attorney."

"Oh, sweetie! This one's for free. It comes under the category of 'this I gotta see!' "

"He told me all the details, but honestly, Mckenna, after we picked poor Piggy off the carpet, my brain just stayed in neutral. And Piggy—the way she reacted, you'd think she totally understood. The timing of her little swoon was perfect. Mr. Johansen just about freaked out."

Mckenna glanced back at their furry passenger before starting the car. "She seems all right now."

"Perfectly. But maybe I should take her to the vet anyway."

"Oh by all means, get her the best of care." Mckenna's mouth lifted in a wry smile. "Piggy has to live a long, long time."

They sped away from the offices of Johansen, Taylor, and Leibowitz and onto the streets of Sedona. Every side street and shop was familiar to Nell's eye, but in spite of that, the world had changed, and she felt the change like a bubble swelling inside her, uncomfortable and at the same time exciting. For the past three years she had lived hand to mouth after leaving a high-powered journalistic career that left her disillusioned and sad. At the young age of twenty-five she had discovered that living where you wanted to live and doing what you enjoyed more than made up for a steady paycheck—most days. Climbing the ladder of conventional success had its moments, but so did peace of mind. In Chicago, Nell had been a square peg in a round hole. She didn't like urban life, big-city journalism, or the nastiness that went along with them. And the city most definitely had not liked her. Nell winced at the memories of how her short career in Chicago had ended.

She had put all that behind her, though, trading city life and city money for the quiet life in rural Arizona among the scrub brush, cactus, and spectacular scenery. She did what she wanted to do—write. And she woke up each morning to fresh, clean air and a view of the world that gave her soul wings. Never mind that she woke up each morning in a single-wide, thirty-year-old trailer house in a neighborhood where weeds and junked cars were the most popular landscaping.

And now? . . . Now her simple life had tipped upside down. This was going to be horribly complicated, Nell just knew it. Part of her floated on Cloud 9, but another part feared there might be a catch hidden in this lovely package of money.

"Hey!" Mckenna nudged her with an elbow. "Smile, sweetie! You're filthy rich."

"Piggy is filthy rich."

"And I have no doubt Piggy wants all the things you want, too. Clothes, a new car, a new house, a better haircut."

In the back, Piggy's ears snapped to the alert position.

Nell leaned back, closed her eyes, and let herself dwell, just for a moment, on all the lovely possibilities. Then she sighed. "I don't think I could justify any of that as care and maintenance of a dog."

The ears dropped down again, deflated.

"Of course you can justify it. Piggy would enjoy the good life! Besides, I can't believe that Frank didn't make some provision for you as the little darling's guardian." Mckenna tossed her sculpted, glossy black hair. "And if he didn't, you've got a very good lawyer."

"He did," Nell admitted. "I get a salary. Two hundred thousand a year. Do you believe that?"

Mckenna harrumphed. "Compared to millions?"

"And I can use the interest from the trust fund for anything remotely connected to Piggy. That amounts to a little over a million a year. Then when Piggy dies, the capital in the fund goes to an heir that will be named at that time." She shook her head in bemusement. "Mr. Johansen said Frank didn't want anyone taking potshots at poor Piggy. He put that right in the will, the old devil."

"Wise man, Frank," Mckenna said with a nod. "When millions are involved, most people wouldn't hesitate to knock off a dog."

Piggy woofed indignantly, and Mckenna chuckled. "Don't worry, Piggy, old girl. We're going to guard you well. You're going to live a long, long life. And we're going to set up an investment plan so that your mother here never has to worry about money."

"What a wonderful thought. With all that money, I could write just for the fun of it and never have to worry about deadlines. That would be heaven. I could travel. Oh yes. I feel a cruise coming on. Do you think Piggy might need a cruise?"

"I definitely think Piggy would enjoy a cruise. Especially the buffet. But she also needs to think about money management with some sound, safe investments. I know a very competent broker."

"There's a payable-upon-death account of five hundred thousand that doesn't have to go through probate. Frank said in his will that I was to use it for incidentals."

Mckenna laughed. "Excellent! A house could be an incidental."

"Oh, Mckenna! I can't help but think this is too good to be true."

Mckenna didn't answer. She just slammed on the BMW's brakes and swung the little convertible into the parking lot of a strip mall.

"Why are we stopping?" Nell asked.

"Piggy wants to shop." Mckenna gestured to the sign above the store in front of them. Sedona Pet Supply.

I LIKED Mckenna, even though she was a cat person. She and I had very similar priorities, except for food. Her idea of a fun meal was a BLT without the bread and without the bacon.

Ah well, I was like that once, when I had a figure to worry about. The skin-and-bones look gives a girl a boost in both the business and social world. Back in the days when I was a hot babe, my figure edged out my appetite all the time. And well worth it, too. You should have seen the heads turn when I walked down the street. Nowadays, when heads turn to look at me, laughter usually follows.

But back to our story. As I said, Mckenna and I could have been soul sisters. Witness that she homed in on the first good shopping place she saw. Very considerate of her, I thought. The woman knows what money is for—to buy stuff.

Sedona Pet Supply, doing business in an upscale town like

Sedona, has everything an upscale dog could want. And I had just become very, very upscale. I trotted through the doorway as if I owned the place, which I could have, if my money could be pried loose from you know who.

"You have to loosen up," Mckenna told Nell as I homed in on the squeaky toys. "Put a little green into your thinking, sweetie. As in the color of money."

How true, how true. Go to it! I urged Mckenna silently. Then the rawhide display captured my attention. Chews of all sizes tempted from various bins. Big rawhides, small rawhides, rolls and chips, basted and plain. I could have them all if I wanted. What a lovely thought.

"Look at her," Mckenna said, and I thought I detected admiration in her tone—one world-class consumer admiring the superior technique of another. "She knows exactly what she wants."

"She probably wants everything in the store," Nell replied. "You'd think from her attitude that she actually knows she's now a very rich dog."

"She does, I'm sure," Nell told Mckenna. "That little corgi scares me sometimes, she's so close to being human."

If she only knew! But wait! Was that a whole pile of stuffed toys over there? It was! Stuffed ducks, stuffed puppies, stuffed octopi, stuffed balls. I selected a duck and pulled it delicately from the pile. When my jaws clamped down, it quacked. I mean, it really quacked. No cute little squeak, but a hearty "Quack, quack, quack!" so real you'd have thought it had just waddled in from the closest pond (which, this being the desert, was maybe a hundred miles away). My little corgi heart swelled with adoration. "Quack, quack, quack, quack, quack, quack, quack!" I chomped away, enjoying the sound.

"Oh, that's what I want to be hearing all day!" Nell said with a sigh.

"Don't be a killjoy. Buy it for her."

That was why I liked Mckenna.

Nell bought it for me, along with a bag of rawhides, a

gummy bone, a new collar (I wanted rhinestones, but she insisted upon a teddy-bear motif. I told you she was dull), a new brush, and a comfy dog bed to replace my old one, which had been chewed upon, clawed, and suffered other indignities you don't want to know about.

"That ought to do the princess for a while," Nell concluded.

"For a while." Mckenna's expression became acquisitive. I know that look well, having worn it many times when I was human. "Now we need to think about you. A shopping spree would do you good, you know."

"I don't need anything right this minute," Nell objected.

"Hello? Get real, sweetie. Look at your shoes. And all you ever wear is jeans."

"I like jeans."

"Okay. Now you can wear designer jeans."

Wait a minute! I thought. Mckenna needed to remember whose money she was spending. My money. Mine, mine, mine.

And then an awful possibility dawned upon me. This could be a test. It would be just like Stanley to think up something like this—throw a ton of money at poor Piggy to see if she's really learned selflessness, generosity, and restraint. Sneaky Stanley. Obviously, I had to be very careful.

"I suppose I could use a new jacket," Nell told Mckenna as we left the pet supply store. "Did I tell you I have an actual date later this week with the guy who pulled me out of the bug when I smashed it?"

A date with the hunk? Hubba, hubba! I didn't think the girl had it in her!

"We're going hiking up West Fork."

Hiking? Oh, no! That means they'll expect the poor dog to go with them.

"Hiking!" Mckenna gushed. "Perfect! Not only a new jacket, but new boots, too, and there's a great outfitter's shop right over there. They carry the very best stuff."

"Hiking boots are expensive!"

"You don't have to worry about that anymore, sweetie. Get used to it."

I tugged Nell toward the car. After all, I had to use my own naked feet. Why should I buy her new boots?

"Piggy can't go into the store, and she'll throw a fit alone in the car," Nell told McKenna.

"Of course she can go into the store! One thing you've got to learn, sweetie. If you have money, you can do anything and go anywhere you want."

A SPIFFY new leather jacket kept Nell warm and top-of-the-line hiking boots cradled her feet on Thursday morning as she stood on her front cement slab—euphemistically called a patio—to watch Dan pull his Jeep to a stop in front of her fence. The jacket cost more than a month's groceries, including dog food, and the boots should have been made of gold, considering the price. Nell's conscience smarted at the extravagance. On the other hand, she did feel rather like a fashion plate—in an outdoorsy sort of way—standing there in her designer duds. Very cool.

Dan waved. Nell waved back. Then suddenly she didn't feel so cool.

"Shoot!" she muttered to Piggy as Dan climbed out of the Jeep. For the first time she noticed he moved with a slight limp. "I invited the guy on a hike, and he's a cripple!" "Disabled" was the more politically correct term, but however correctly one put it, Dan Travis probably didn't enjoy scrambling over rocks and over rushing streams. "How did I miss that? Duh!"

Piggy nailed her with a look and turned to waddle back through the front door, but Nell stopped her with a quiet hiss. "Get back here, you little deserter. You're not leaving me alone to face him."

With a martyred sigh, the corgi plopped down beside her. Nell tried to put on a smile, but it felt more like a nervous grimace. The patio and trailer were both about six feet above street level, and Nell winced at every step the man had to climb. On the other hand, running to greet him at the fence didn't seem like a good idea—way too eager for this stage of their relationship. If they had a relationship.

"Hi there," he greeted her, having overcome the steps with no trouble. "Ready to go?"

"Uh...I...listen, we don't have to go hiking if you'd rather do something else."

He looked puzzled, then chuckled. "Don't worry. The gimp doesn't slow me down much."

Nell's face heated. "Are you sure? I'm such an idiot, suggesting a hike. I didn't notice, when we first met, that... uh..."

"I limp," he finished for her, then shrugged. "I'll bet you didn't notice the chipped tooth on the upper left, or the way my pinkie"—he held up the offending finger—"grows a little crooked on the end."

Nell gave in to a smile. "Actually, I did. Are you sure you wouldn't rather take in a movie?"

"Is the dog going hiking?"

"Well, yes, she was—"

"Then we'd better keep her company. If a pudgy little thing with two-inch legs can do the hike, I think I can."

"Her legs are much longer than two inches."

"Three inches, then." A sweep of pewter eyes took in the jacket. "Nice. What'd you do, rob a bank?"

How rude. But she smiled. "First National."

"Uh-huh. Looks good, though, sweetheart."

The endearment had an edge. Nell had looked forward to telling Dan about her good fortune, but something in his tone of voice held her back. She had no reason to feel guilty about Frank Cramer's generosity, Nell told herself, but just the same...

Once on the highway, they lapsed into an awkward silence. The strange camaraderie that had sprung from their first meeting had collapsed. Dan Travis radiated a tension Nell didn't quite understand. Gamely, she tried to fill the silence with trivia.

"I love the drive between Cottonwood and Sedona. The most beautiful fifteen miles in the world, I'd bet."

"It's a corker," he agreed.

Sedona's spectacular vermilion spires rose in front of them, and to either side the Verde Valley stretched away in rugged, brush-covered bluffs, mesas, and ravines. The beauty of the land was both stark and soul-stirring—always a safe topic of conversation.

"Have you lived in this area long?" she asked.

"Three years or so. I'm from California, but my whole family seems to have migrated here."

"Big family?"

"Not really. My mother grew up in Phoenix before marrying my dad and moving to L.A. I have . . . had . . . a grandfather here."

He slid her an appraising glance that Nell found rather odd.

"My grandfather moved here from San Francisco."

"One of my favorite cities, San Francisco."

"Yeah. Then, of course, there's the ex in Flagstaff. She moved here from California, too. And the kids."

"I'd say that's a lot of family."

"I guess so."

They chatted aimlessly, like two strangers, through Sedona and into the lower reaches of Oak Creek Canyon. The cliffs closed about them in shades of red, ocher, and white, and the stream tumbled beside the highway in cheerful, splashing abandon. They *were* strangers, Nell told herself. She had no reason to expect an instant rapport just because they had somehow drawn close during a crisis. Emergencies had a way of destroying barriers between people. But when the emergency ends, the barriers snap back into place as strong as ever.

This, she thought as they turned into the trailhead parking area, could turn into a very long day.

Dan loosened up a bit once they unloaded their gear from the Jeep and prepared to start up the trail. He insisted upon carrying the daypack Nell had brought, since he didn't have a pack himself.

"I know the ladies are into pulling their own weight these days, but I'm not going to be seen waltzing up the trail free and easy while my date shoulders the—carumba! What do you have in here?"

"Lunch for both of us. Camera. Extra socks. Extra tennies. Water. And a water bowl for Piggy."

"She can't drink from the stream?"

"Oh, no. Not Piggy. She's not much into getting back to nature."

"Is that why she's still in the Jeep?"

"She's not much into exercise, either, but it's good for her."

He cracked a smile, and for a moment the white knight who had pulled her from Mel shined through. "I'll make you a deal. You get Miss Couch Potato out of the backseat and drag her up the trail, and I'll manage the three-hundred-pound pack."

"Not even thirty pounds," she denied.

"It feels like three hundred."

"Well, I figured you'd want a big lunch. So it's partly your fault. Where's your camera, by the way? We can stick it in the pack."

"Camera?"

"You didn't bring a camera? What kind of photographer are you?"

"Uh . . . one who doesn't want to carry a ten-pound camera up a mountain."

"Tch! Well, if you see a shot you just can't resist, you can use mine."

A few minutes later, Nell had pried Piggy from the Jeep

and the three of them wandered up the trail as it followed Oak Creek toward the mouth of West Fork Canyon. This was not a trail on which hikers labored to cover as many miles and gain as much height as possible. Rather, the trail inspired explorers to take their time, with eyes taking in the marvels of blue sky, sheer canyon walls, and the lush green foliage that made Oak Creek Canyon and its tributaries a hidden paradise in the desert.

"I can't believe I've never been up here," Dan admitted. "It's really close."

"It's one of my favorite walks. There's nothing like a good dose of Mother Nature at her finest to remind a person of the truly important things in life."

For that she got a pointed look. "What do you think are the truly important things in life?"

"That's a deep question for such a gorgeous day."

He shrugged, but the pewter-gray eyes had turned into tempered steel. "Just curious."

"Well, let's see. The most important things . . . Health, of course. Security." She smiled at Piggy, who trudged behind at the limit of her leash. "A good dog for companionship."

"Better than a man, eh?"

"Don't be insulted. Dogs take up less room in the bed."

"That would depend on the dog."

She laughed. "Okay. What do you think are life's most important things?"

"I don't know as I really ever gave the matter serious thought. Things always seem to arrange themselves in order of importance rather than consulting my opinion about the matter."

"Oh, that's a depressing way to look at life."

"Well"—again a smile cracked his armor—"maybe I should get out to places like this more often. There's more than one person in this world who thinks my attitude needs mending."

Add her to the list, Nell mused privately. Dan Travis,

though he could apparently turn on the charm when he wanted to, was way too serious. Way, way too serious. She would be doing a public service by taking him in hand and convincing him to lighten up and enjoy life.

She still couldn't believe that a professional photographer could hike through all this spectacular scenery without a camera in his hand.

DAN WAS cranky. Cranky and annoyed. For many reasons.

First, he was enterprising enough to get a date with a good-looking, interesting, sweet, sexy woman, and then the woman turns out to be a money-grubbing, con-artist bimbo who sidled her way into his grandfather's affections and made off with the family millions. That made him cranky.

Second, the con-artist bimbo had her act down so perfectly that she still seemed like an interesting, sweet, sexy woman whose bright green eyes and cheery smile made a man want to just give her a bear hug, and then a good deal more. Dan had dealt with all sorts of sleazy characters, both as an L.A. cop and a hick private eye. You would think he could see through this little gold digger's performance, but he couldn't. If his mom hadn't told him about Nell Jordan duping the old man, Dan would be walking along this trail dizzy with the very charm of her. That made him even more cranky.

He hadn't seen eye-to-eye with his grandfather. He and the old man had gotten on each other's nerves from the time Dan was a kid. But that didn't mean he wanted to see some predatory female take advantage of the cantankerous old bastard when he was too decrepit to resist her false charisma. And really, how could the old goat have resisted her? She was pretty, she was perky—her smile could light up this whole canyon, much less the sterile halls of a nursing home.

The woman was dangerous. Dan had half a mind to give in to his mom's demand that he dig into the bimbo's past and find something that would allow the family to challenge Frank's will. The other half of his mind, however, wanted to push her up against the nearest tree trunk and kiss the living daylights out of her.

A conflict like that would make any man cranky.

They came to the tumbledown ruins of a guest resort that had stood by Oak Creek in the early twentieth century, and Little Miss Innocent had to explore. One would think, as she dug out her camera and started snapping shots of the old stone walls and chimneys rising from the rubble, that she didn't have a mercenary bone in her entire delicious body, that such simple entertainments always delighted her, that duping a dying old man out of his fortune would never cross her mind.

Of course, she hadn't wasted any time going on a spending spree with Frank's money. That jacket cost a pretty penny. The boots, too. So new they didn't have a scuff on them. Once probate was through, would the little rich girl be wearing diamonds and gold?

But damn, she had a good act. Warm, genuine smile— with dimples, even. Honest, straightforward eyes. And so damned likeable. It annoyed the hell out of him. If there was anything worse than an evildoer, it was a cheerful, sweet, likeable evildoer.

"Isn't it fascinating to imagine people moving in and out of these old cabins?" she gushed. "People have been enjoying themselves here for a century, just as we're enjoying it."

Enjoying themselves. She should speak for herself. For his part, his bad knee ached, the pack she had brought dragged at his shoulders, and Nell Jordan's strange little dog was getting on his nerves with her sullen looks and martyred sighs.

"Let's get moving, okay?"

For a moment Nell looked miffed, but then the bright,

easygoing smile came back. "Sure thing. It just gets prettier from here forward. Come on, Piggy, you lazy girl."

Piggy gave Dan a sour look as Nell pried her off the bed of leaves where she'd settled, as if this hike was all his fault! The dog was really beginning to piss him off.

The trail soon left the main canyon and turned to follow West Fork, a tributary that tumbled from higher country three thousand feet above. Smaller than Oak Creek, the stream burbled cheerfully between sheer rock walls. The streambed was rocky and in places choked by fallen pines and boulders as big as Nell's Volkswagen, but the Forest Service carefully maintained the trail.

"Oops!" Nell said happily. "This is where we get our feet wet."

Bridges, apparently, weren't high Forest Service priorities. The trail ended abruptly against a jutting canyon wall and appeared again on the other side of the stream, where the banks provided more room. A treacherous path of slippery-looking rocks barely emerged from the rushing water to form a rough path of stepping stones across the stream.

"Actually, this is just the first crossing," Nell told Dan. "From here on up, the trail crisscrosses the stream about a dozen times."

"And so the extra socks and shoes in your pack."

She gave him an apologetic grimace. "I should have warned you. I just assumed that anyone who lived in this area had been up here."

"Wet feet aren't going to kill me."

"Well, you only get wet if you fall in."

He snorted.

"We could turn around," she said amiably. "There's a great little cafe at the Junipine Resort down the highway. We could have coffee on the porch."

Her very reasonable attitude grated. "We came to hike up the canyon. Let's hike."

The crossing wasn't as tricky as it looked. Nell ventured out first, jumping from rock to rock with a light-footed grace that would have done a fairy credit. Dan's bad knee robbed him of any pretense to grace, but he managed to reach the opposite side of the stream without dunking his sneakers.

"Oh shoot!" Nell said just as he put a foot on dry land.

"What?"

"Piggy."

Nell had dropped Piggy's leash so the corgi would be free to find a route that would accommodate her stubby legs, but apparently the dog had decided that her best option was simply to plunk her broad butt into the dirt and watch them from the other side.

"I should have known." Nell chuckled ruefully. "Come on, Piggy," she cajoled.

"If she were a person, I'd say she's giving you the finger."

"The little snot. Piggy!" she shouted. "Don't make me come get you!"

The corgi yawned.

"I can see I'm going to have to play the hero here. I'll get the little fur bag."

"Don't . . ." she began, but fell silent when he held up a hand.

"It's the manly thing to do."

Holding on to his annoyance with this woman was proving to be tough. For a self-proclaimed hard case like him to allow himself to fall under a scheming female's spell—well, what was the world coming to?

The cursed dog gave him a knowing look as he made his ungraceful way across the stream, stumbled onto the bank, and marched toward her.

"Come on, you bag of dog fat. Up you go."

He grunted as he tucked Piggy beneath one arm. "Yikes! What a load!"

"She's just a little corgi."

" 'Little' my everlovin' foot!"

But when he managed to lurch back across the stream, he had to laugh. Much as he hated to admit it, he was having a good time. "So much for dry feet!" He set the dog on her own four paws, only to suffer her almost humanly indignant glare.

Nell colored with embarrassment. "I'm sorry. I've never really taken Piggy hiking before. I had no idea she would be so stubborn."

He laughed again. "Is she female?"

That coaxed a smile from her. "That's a low blow. Oh, look at that. She got mud all over you, the little snot."

She made a swipe at wiping it off his shirt, and Dan's heart—and several other parts—gave a start at the sudden, unexpected contact. Nell froze, as if only then realizing the intimacy of the gesture. But her hand stayed where it was, as if glued to his chest.

Almost instinctively his hands went to her shoulders to hold her there. Her eyes jumped up to meet his, and beneath that crown of silky golden curls her face warmed to another rosy blush. They both swayed forward. Almost... almost... and then no. Nell came unglued, both the hand resting on his chest and the mouth that had just about been his. In a flustered fluttering of words, she backed off.

"Oh goodness, what is Piggy into now? Piggy, you twit, what is that in your mouth? Dirt?" And on she went, chattering to the dog, pretending she hadn't very nearly kissed him, that he hadn't very nearly kissed her.

He attempted to get his breath back. How long had it been since the simple touch of a woman sent his blood racing?

Yes indeed. He was starting to have a good time, whether or not he should.

WELL, WASN'T this just dandy! Fast on the uptake, Mr. Studly was, already plotting a way through Nell's heart to MY money. Somehow he had found out that I was worth a fortune.

How did I know this, you ask? Obvious. He was a studmuffin in spite of the limp. Actually, the limp added an attractive bit of contrast to his hunkiness. A true connoisseur of men appreciates these things. But back to the point. Dan Travis was a studmuffin, and Nell was, well, she was okay, but not exactly a Cosmo cover model, if you know what I mean. What was this prime catch of manliness doing tromping through these godawful woods, carting muddy corgis across rushing rivers, and then almost planting one on Little Miss Girl Scout?

Trying to get a finger in the pie of my trust fund, that's what!

What Mr. Fortune Hunter didn't realize, though, was that however easy Nell might be, I wasn't! That was MY money. Mine! A girl can't be too careful when she's rich, you know, because men will line up to take her to the cleaners. I knew how these things went. After all, I was once a fox on the prowl, and I wouldn't have hesitated to do the same thing Dan was trying to do.

Studly Dan was definitely a predator on the loose.

But he hadn't reckoned on a smart corgi with an attitude. There would be no studmuffins for Nell. No, no, no! Not if this little Piggy had anything to say about it.

chapter 5

THE COFFEE Pot Restaurant always saw a good lunch crowd. They boasted one hundred and one types of omelets, and served them morning, noon, and night along with good sandwiches, soups, salads, and anything else a hungry customer might fancy. This Thursday was no exception. People stood in the entryway, sniffing the tantalizing aromas while waiting for a table to become available.

Natalie Donner had arrived early for just that reason. She sat at the polished wooden table for two, nursing a menu and a cup of coffee. Lunch didn't really interest her. In fact, putting anything other than coffee in her stomach might inspire her to throw up. She nervously tapped a manicured fingernail on the menu and tried to look as if she had her wits about her. Which she didn't. How ridiculous was this? A mature, accomplished woman of fifty-five, she owned her own hugely successful business, presided over the Sedona Chamber of Commerce, had just been appointed to the board of the Sedona Medical Center, and was now serving her third term on the town planning and zoning commission. Not only that, this year she reigned as person in charge of the annual Saint Patrick's Day parade. Obviously, Natalie Donner was someone to be reckoned with.

So why was she sitting here all twitterpated and shaky just because she had a luncheon appointment with a man whose role in her life was long past? Natalie Donner, the mature and accomplished matron, should be above such silliness.

Then the main course on the plate of her afternoon came through the door, spotted her, and waved cheerily. Jared Johansen. No man nearing sixty should be allowed to look so good.

Damn, the man looked better than when they'd been an "item" more than thirty years ago at Northern Arizona University, back when he'd been a political science star and she an English literature introvert. The silver that brushed his dark brown hair added dignity rather than age. Lines etched into his face by passing years gave him a comfortable, lived-in look, but robbed him of none of the vigor that had always been his hallmark.

"Natalie, it's good to see you. I'm glad you suggested lunch."

"Jared, you're looking well. Thank you for breaking into what I'm sure is a very busy schedule."

"For you, anytime."

His smile was genuine and warm, the same smile that had seduced her more than three decades ago.

"All these years I've been trying to take you out, ever since William left. What is it, ten years now?"

"Fifteen," Natalie admitted. Her chest still tightened at the thought of her husband's abandonment. As usual, Jared didn't dance around subjects for the sake of tact.

"Fifteen. Well, at least for ten of those years, ever since Sara passed on, I've been pestering you to at least have coffee with me, and it takes a death to get us sitting at the same table again."

She grimaced, and he raised a brow. "I did assume that you wanted to talk about Frank's will."

"Yes, I . . . I apologize for getting so upset when we met right after the funeral, Jared."

"It was a bad time to meet. I should have known better."

"That's no excuse. I was rude. It wasn't you who dictated the terms of the will." She gave him a sharp look. "Though how was it that my father happened to choose you as his representative? It's an interesting coincidence."

Jared chuckled. "Frank and I didn't break up when you and I broke up, Natalie. We were always friends. Whenever he was out here from California we would play golf, then almost every week when he moved here full-time. Until he had to give up the game."

"But I thought he used Gilmore and Barnes for his legal affairs."

"About nine months back they had a falling out."

She blew out a disgusted breath. "Now why doesn't that surprise me?"

The lawyer smiled. "Your father could be hard to get along with."

"Like I didn't know that?"

"But down deep he was a decent man, Natalie. He lived in an older world, where men were kings in their own families."

"He never adjusted to the twentieth century, much less the twenty-first."

Jared chuckled.

A jeans-clad waitress bustled up to their table, refilled Natalie's coffee, filled Jared's, then stood with pencil poised. "Orders?"

"Avocado-bacon omelet, hash browns done crisp, whole wheat toast with honey."

Natalie grimaced at the audacious cholesterol of Jared's order. "Chef salad. Oil and vinegar on the side."

The waitress gathered their menus and hustled off,

leaving a silence that neither of them broke. Finally, Natalie decided to borrow Jared's penchant for straight talk. "Jared, Dad's will is ridiculous."

"I wouldn't say that, Natalie. I don't expect you like it. That's understandable. Frank didn't expect you to like it."

Natalie suspected that Jared understated. She pictured her father's glee at thinking of yet another way to demonstrate just how little he cared for his daughter, for his whole family. "I'll bet he was tickled pink every minute he worked at hatching this ridiculous scheme," she said bitterly.

"Natalie, I don't think Frank made that will as a slap in the face to you."

"Didn't he?"

"No. I think for the last months of his life, Nell Jordan's visits were the highlight of his existence. He wanted to make a gesture of appreciation."

Her laugh was sudden and sharp. "Some appreciation!"

"It is only while the dog lives, you know."

"Right. And then the next mysterious heir is named. Who do you think it will be this time? The Model T Club for the care and maintenance of their old jalopies? Or maybe the Society for the Preservation of the House Finch? I'm sure the little birds outside his window must have given the old man a lot of entertainment while he was in Springdale."

"Natalie . . ."

Jared's voice urged calm. Calm was his trademark—always reasonable, equitable, composed. When Natalie had been twenty, she had loved that about him. Right now, those qualities made her furious.

"Natalie, be reasonable?" she queried in razor tones. "Natalie, be calm, be gracious, be understanding? Well, bullshit! Jared, how could you let my father leave his entire fortune to some Barbie-doll little hustler who slithered her way into his affections solely to get to his money? How could you?" She had more on the tip of her tongue, but his calmly lifted hand motioned her to silence, and she obeyed. She didn't possess the kind of forceful personality that could stand against the likes of Jared Johansen, just as she couldn't make a stand against her father beyond simply avoiding being anywhere near him, where he could bully her with his scowls and cutting words.

"Natalie, you've jumped to some pretty broad conclusions. From what I can tell, Nell Jordan was the most surprised of anyone about the will. She's certainly not the hustler type. And the money was left to her dog, after all, not to her."

He smiled in a way that invited her to find humor in the bizarre situation, but Natalie wanted no part of it.

"He left it to her dog!" she growled. "As if that makes everything all right."

Natalie pulled in her claws and smiled blandly as the waitress came with their food. The salad was fresh, crisp, and colorful, but it held as much appeal to her as a pile of straw.

She lowered her voice when the waitress left, but the intensity of it came from a dark and bitter hurt. "My father disowned me for a dog, Jared. How do you think that makes me feel?"

"Frank didn't disown you. He left you his house, which is worth about a million and a half on Sedona's real estate market. What's more, you don't need Frank's money. You're a very successful businesswoman in your own right. Frank knew that. Perhaps he wanted to give a helping hand to someone who really needed it."

"My father never offered a helping hand to anyone unless it would somehow bring him a profit."

Jared regarded her with a hint of sadness in his expression. "Maybe," he suggested, "you didn't know Frank as well as you think you did."

"I knew him all right. He was my father, after all." She sighed. The hope which had led her to call Jared dwindled.

"What he did just isn't right. I was hoping you would tell me that this ridiculous will can be challenged in court, but I can tell that you're on That Woman's side."

"I'm on Frank's side. That's why he named me personal representative in the will, because he had faith that I would carry out his wishes. Natalie, we go back a long way, and I've never known you to be less than fair and honest. But in this case, I think your judgment is clouded. You say these things because this is such an emotional issue."

"Of course it's an emotional issue!" she nearly hissed. "Frank was my father. We didn't get along well, and I didn't haunt his doorstep—like some others—to get my hands on his money. But he was my father. It was bad enough when William walked out, cleaned out our accounts, and left me with two teenage kids and a mountain of bills. It's far worse when a father ... well, a father is supposed to love you no matter what."

He admonished her with a fork laden with hash browns. "Frank loved you, Natalie. I have no doubt about it."

When she made a contemptuous sound, he shook his head. "Love is a strange thing, sometimes difficult to see, and sometimes even more difficult to express. If Frank had left his entire fortune to you, that wouldn't have meant that he loved you. And his setting up a trust fund for Nell Jordan's dog doesn't mean that he didn't love you. Love isn't money, Natalie."

"I have to concede that you're more of an expert on love than I am." Jared had enjoyed a rare and lasting affection with his wife. Natalie had been shamefully jealous of their happiness until a car accident had killed Sara Johansen and turned that happiness to ashes. But at least Jared had known the joy of Sara's love. Perhaps if a person is granted at least one source of love in life, rebuffs from other directions didn't hurt so much.

For half her life, Natalie had tried to earn her father's love. For the other half she had tried to understand why she failed. And then William had poured salt on the open wound. The two men who, of all the men in the world, were supposed to love her, had stomped on her heart before handing it back to her. And now her father's will had re-opened old wounds.

Maybe she was overreacting, as Jared thought. But the hurt of this final rejection drove away any desire to be un-derstanding. Still, she labored for a calm, reasonable tone. But firm. Very firm.

"Jared, with all due respect, I think I'm more of an expert on my father than you are. I think he was duped and mis-used, and I'm going to break that damned will. Just see if I don't."

ONE WOULD think that suddenly coming into possession of a very large amount of money would drastically change a person's life, Nell mused. So far, however, little had changed for her—other than nights spent lying awake al-ternately fantasizing about what the money could do and then panicking about the same thing.

Of course, in her former penurious life, she never would have rented a car to buzz around town while Mel was being fixed. True, she had taken an economy car—a cute little Plymouth Neon—instead of a bigger, flashier, more expen-sive model. But a person had to ease into being rich. Other-wise the amounts showing on the credit card bill could cause a heart attack.

Feeling rather flashy in her royal-blue Neon, Nell buzzed into the medical center parking lot and swung into the nearest parking spot. In the backseat, Piggy huffed out a loud sigh.

Nell turned around and tickled one of the corgi's big ears. "Come on, Lazybutt. Time to get to work."

Ten minutes later, after Piggy had endured being stuffed into her little green therapy dog vest and had dutifully trotted onto the grass and done what dogs do on grass, Nell signed them in on the volunteer roster.

"Hey, Piggy." A "pink lady"—volunteers other than the animal therapy people wore a pink smock that would have driven any fashion-conscious woman for cover—came down the hallway and stopped to give Piggy a scratch. "You're looking very Irish this morning in your bright green vest."

"She got a new vest for St. Paddy's Day," Nell said. "Her old one was positively faded."

"Well, she deserves a new vest. Ta, ta, little girl."

Before Nell finished signing in, one of the social services workers greeted Piggy as well.

"Here she is! The celebrity!"

"You heard, did you?"

"Of course! Everybody's heard! You and Piggy have more people here talking than the newest version of *Survivor*. How many millions is this dog worth?"

"It's a trust fund, so she just gets the interest."

"Enough to keep you both in dog biscuits, I'd wager."

Social services left with a laugh, and Piggy looked at Nell with a pained expression.

"Enjoy the attention while you can," Nell advised. "Tomorrow you'll just be yesterday's news."

In CCU, everything settled back to normal. Celebrity dogs didn't cut much ice with the staff responsible for the fragile patients there, but therapy dogs did. A new nurse in the unit exclaimed when she saw them.

"I didn't know you guys came in here."

"Every week," Nell told her. "This is Piggy. You'll be seeing a lot of her."

On hearing Nell's voice, two other nurses looked up from their patient charts to smile at her. One came around the desk to kneel down and rub Piggy's ears. The corgi sighed with contentment, slowly melting to the floor to present her furry tummy for similar attention.

"Can any of the patients have a visit?" Nell asked.

"Stay away from room four," the new nurse warned. "That guy will bite your head off."

One of the older nurses chuckled. "Nah, let Piggy visit the old grouch. Maybe she'll improve his mood."

The infamous patient in room four, Nell discovered a few minutes later, suffered an army of tubes leading from various body parts to several intimidating machines. She mused that anyone would be testy in such a state.

She stuck her head through the doorway. "Would you like to say hi to the hospital visiting dog?"

After a short while, Nell and a smug Piggy came out of room four. Piggy had reason to be smug.

"I see Piggy worked another minor miracle," Stephanie said, glancing at the nurse's station monitor. "His pulse is down from one-sixty to one-twenty. Good job, Fuzzbutt."

"He's a nice old guy," Nell said.

The nurse snorted. "For you, maybe." Stephanie gave her a keen-eyed look. "So, did you drive up in a Cadillac today? I hear our Piggy's a rich girl, now."

Nell chuckled. "So now she's *our* Piggy, is she?"

"Girl, old Frank Cramer's money would buy a lot of liver crunchies. Piggy might have enough in petty cash to buy her Aunt Stephanie a new truck."

Okay, so even in CCU things were not quite back to normal.

On the second floor was the largest patient area in the hospital. A nurse's station served as hub for a wheel where room after room housed patients suffering from all kinds of ailments. The hallways bustled with medical staff, visiting family, and a few brave patients taking their IV bottles out for a walk.

The nurses here were much too busy to take much notice of Nell and her heiress dog, for which Nell was grateful. They simply gave her a thumbs-up, which meant that all the patients were able to visit with Piggy if they so desired.

Piggy did her rounds in a workmanlike manner. She might be funny-looking and at times condescending (how a dog could pull off condescending was beyond Nell's understanding, but Piggy could do it), but with all that, she was still a friendly face and a warm furry body. Those attributes were all most patients required.

Midway through their visit, a nurse stopped Nell in the hallway. "There's a baby in two-fourteen. She could probably use a dog fix."

The baby could certainly use something, Nell decided as they approached two-fourteen. Infant wails could be heard all the way down the hall. When she stuck her head through the door, she saw a distraught mom wearing a path in the floor with a very unhappy one-year-old in her arms.

"Uh . . . hi. Would the attention of a friendly dog be of help?"

Mom gave her a tired look. She had no energy to be surprised at the appearance of a dog instead of a nurse. "She's had three shots today, poor thing. The last one really hurt, and she's just fed up."

Piggy's ears had perked up at the sound of infant wailing, and now her little nose quivered to take in the kid's scent. Almost all corgis adored children, and Piggy, for all her eccentricities, was no exception.

"I don't know if she'll even notice," Mom said, collapsing into a chair with her precious, noisy burden.

Piggy trotted up, stretched upward to touch Mom's knee with her nose, and called attention to herself with a soft, inquisitive woof.

The wailing faltered, then stopped as the baby's teary eyes met Piggy's.

"Gaaaa?"

Piggy politely nosed a tiny bare toe.

"Gaaaa!" Then a squeal of laughter.

Assured of Piggy's gentle manners, Mom placed the baby on a blanket on the floor, where Piggy happily endured the kid's clumsy petting. Both Nell and Mom stayed close to make sure neither of the parties in the little love fest got too rowdy.

"Oh, thank you," Mom said to Nell. "I didn't think she would ever stop crying. I'm sure everyone else around here had their ears stuffed with cotton."

"Tomorrow there will be a cat here to visit," Nell promised. "Does she like kitties?"

"She loves all animals."

"I'll leave word at the nurse's station to make sure McKenna brings Nefertiti to visit your room."

When she left the room, Nell turned back to smile at the baby, who still happily cooed and gurgled, so when she looked up and suddenly found a photographer getting ready to snap a shot, she squeaked in surprise.

"Hi, Nell! You don't mind if we do a few photos, do you?"

"Yes, I do."

The flash exploded in her face. "I'm from the *Valley News.*"

"This is a hospital, for crying out—"

"Yeah, yeah. I know. Smile. Look rich."

Flash.

"Would you quit!"

"That's the dog, right? What's her name?"

"Hey there!" A male nurse hurried up. "What are you doing? Do you have an ID badge or a pass?"

Nell slipped down the hall and let the staff hustle the guy away. This money thing was going to be more of an annoyance than she thought.

SATURDAY TURNED out to be a perfect day for Sedona's St. Patrick's Day parade. The morning was just a bit chilly when Nell, Mckenna, and Jane met at the staging area, animals in tow.

Mckenna, never at her best on early mornings, grumbled. "Remind me again—why do we march in this stupid parade?"

Jane answered primly. "Public education. We need more volunteers for our group. Besides, it doesn't hurt to remind people that pets can behave, given a little bit of effort on the owner's part."

"There speaks the dog trainer," said Marsha Torres as she walked up with Taco, her Chihuahua. Marsha and Taco were newcomers to the Hearts of Gold group. "I think marching in a parade will be a gas."

"It wouldn't be so bad if they didn't insist we show up at the crack of dawn," Mckenna said.

"The sun's been up a good hour," Jane pointed out. "Quit your whining. I gave up two obedience trials in California to be here—where, by the way, Idaho might have finished his obedience championship. So if I can be cheerful about that, you can be cheerful about dragging your butt out of bed before the sun rises."

Mckenna chuckled. "Cranky, cranky."

"Come on, Jane," Nell admonished. "You don't really want Idaho to finish, do you? Then what would you do to scratch your competitive itch?"

"I'll think of something."

All in all, the entire Hearts of Gold band numbered seven people, five dogs, a cat, and an African Grey parrot. The parrot, understandably, had taken a pass on the parade, but the rest of the crew showed up. They were quite possibly the smallest group there, and certainly not the most interesting—even with Nefertiti the cat riding in a wagon pulled by Idaho the border collie.

Also taking their places in the lineup were an antique fire engine pulled by a team of spectacular Belgians, two boy scout troops, the Dancing Grannies in their spangly fringed costumes with matching top hats, a choir group from a local New Age commune, a wagonload of 4-H kids, and a multitude of classic cars sporting ads for local merchants. Not to mention a rodeo queen from Flagstaff and her entourage, the local quarter-horse fanciers group, the Yavapai Sheriff's Posse, and a green crepe paper-festooned ambulance from Sedona Ambulance Service.

Mckenna elbowed Nell. "Hey, sweetie. I hear you had a hot date on Thursday."

"Nell went out on a date?" several of the group exclaimed in unison.

"Hey! It's not *that* unusual," Nell said in her own defense.

"Now that she's a rich woman," Marsha said, "men will be flocking to her."

"Too true," Norma Collins said. Bandit, her mixed-breed terrier, sneezed in agreement. "But this is the Verde Valley. What kind of men are going to be flocking?"

"Cowboys," Jane said.

"Lonely retired guys," Marsha added.

"New Age gurus in homespun tunics and hemp sandals." This from Mckenna with a wicked grin.

Nell made a face. "Quit, you guys. This was a perfectly normal guy." Then with a sly grin, "And a hunk besides."

"A hunk! Whoo-hoo! Did sparks fly?" Marsha demanded.

"Uh, well, none of your business. He's the guy who pulled me out of Mel when I drove into a hillside."

"A hero!" Norma nodded approvingly.

Jane snorted. "If you get a real man in your life, you won't have to pretend your car is Mel Gibson."

"No ordinary man can displace Mel Gibson," Marsha admonished.

"Tom Cruise could," Norma opined.

Marsha arched one brow. "Not even close."

While her friends bantered to pass the time, Nell drifted back to West Fork trail and how the sun had shot sparks off Dan Travis's glossy black hair. A hero? Maybe. A hunk?

Definitely. Had sparks flown? Well, the jury was still out on that one. There had been something electric in the air, but it stung as often as it excited. He had nearly kissed her. But nearly wasn't the same thing as a kiss. He had also blown hot and cold more often than a heat pump.

What was up with that? When she had crashed Mel, Dan Travis had been a knight in shining armor, riding to the rescue and seeing her safely home. Ten days later, his armor tarnished a bit as he bounced from prickly one moment to smiling the next.

Had he heard about Piggy's windfall? she wondered. The thought of all that money could do strange things to people, as she had lately discovered.

Norma poked Nell in the back. "Earth to Nell! We're moving."

Nell came back to the present with a jolt. Just in front of them, the Dancing Grannies trotted out to the street, spangles flying and tap shoes tapping. Hearts of Gold was next.

"Sorry," Nell said. "Daydreaming."

Norma laughed. "I should have so much to daydream about!"

One by one the groups moved out to march a route that wound through town. The streets overflowed with Sedona citizenry and tourists, everything from infants to graybeards. Parents waved frantically at children in the Scouts or 4-H or the high school marching band. Kids squealed in delight as the Hearts of Gold dogs did little tricks, waving their paws at the crowd, bowing, dancing, spinning, and generally having a good time. Mckenna had dressed poor long-suffering Nefertiti in a cat-sized nurse costume, and the wagon that bore her, pulled by Jane's border collie, boasted a banner that announced HEARTS OF GOLD THERAPY ANIMALS: CELEBRATE THE HUMAN-ANIMAL BOND. Below that was Jane's motto: *Obedience training is a dog's best friend.*

In front of them a tape player blared music for the Dancing Grannies, while the ladies went into a tap routine.

"I think we should wear sequins, too," jested Midge Carter, who had Fred the golden retriever on the end of her leash. "And those short little skirts."

"You'd give the cardiac patients a heart attack for sure," Marsha said with a laugh. She caught a wrapped piece of hard candy that pelted them from the 4-H wagon behind them, then caught another and offered it up for grabs.

"No thanks!" Mckenna said with a grimace. "If I ate all the candy that's being thrown, I'd gain forty pounds at least."

"Then you might look normal," Jane cracked, only half-jesting.

"A woman dealing with million-dollar clients has to look like a million dollars herself."

"Are we talking about Nell's money again?" Marsha asked.

"No," Nell said firmly. "We aren't."

"If someone gave me that kind of money," Norma said. "I wouldn't mind talking about it."

"Or spending it," Jane added with a laugh.

They turned a corner to face an even bigger crowd. The dogs were getting tired. Marsha picked up Taco and let him ride in her arms. Fred's tongue hung from his mouth, and Piggy maneuvered to stay in Fred's shade.

"Look!" Jane pointed ahead. "There's the Desert Acres gang."

Indeed, lined up on the sidewalk, some sitting in wheelchairs and others in folding chairs, were a group of seasoned ladies and gents from the Desert Acres care facility. Their attendant had set up a canopy to protect his charges from the warm spring sun.

"There they are!" Old Maisie waved both arms at Hearts of Gold in extravagant greeting. "There's my Fred!"

Maisie liked to claim that beautiful Fred was really her

dog and was simply living with Midge until Maisie could go back home.

"Line up!" Jane called out.

Four dogs—Piggy, Fred, Taco, and Bandit—lined up to perform for their fans, while Idaho patiently brought the "cat wagon" to a halt. In unison, the canine line waved to the Desert Acres oldsters. At least the wave was intended to be in unison. Fred and Taco managed to lift their paws at the same time. Bandit got distracted by a kid down the street who was waving a hot dog in the air. When Norma managed to remind him of his performing duties, he did a spin instead of a wave. Piggy, on the other hand, just looked disgusted with the very idea.

"Piggy..." Nell prompted, pulling a small sliver of homemade corgi cookie from her pocket.

Piggy's ears pricked up, and looking somewhat embarrassed, she lifted a front paw.

"That's a five-point-eight," Maude called from her wheelchair. She never gave up trying to teach Bandit to play checkers with her.

"You nincompoop," her roommate Carolyn growled. "It's a perfect six-point-oh if I've ever seen one."

"Hey, Nell!" Maude called out, ignoring Carolyn's critique. "Hear you hit the jackpot!"

"Lookin' good, rich lady!" Carolyn joined in.

"Take care, honey! Easy come, easy go!"

"And watch out for the IRS!"

Nell sighed as the troupe moved on. "Does everybody know?"

"Probably the East Coast hasn't heard yet," Jane said with a chuckle. "Unless *The New York Times* got hold of the story."

From the pushy trio of reporters that greeted the group at the parade's end, Nell guessed that the *Times* couldn't be far behind. There was nowhere to run and no handy nurses to tell the reporters to take their cameras and get lost.

"Nell Jordan?" Flash! "Did you know that Frank Cramer planned to name you in his will?"

"Nell! Why do you think he left the money to the dog and not to you?"

"Do you think he was sane?"

"Is the family fighting the will?"

"What do you plan to do with the money?"

"What does the dog plan to do with the money?" A braying laugh.

Within moments the commotion began to attract the parade spectators, so if anyone in the town of Sedona didn't know about the odd circumstances of Nell's good fortune, they soon would.

Jane and Mckenna both waded in and started swinging, metaphorically speaking.

From Jane: "Bug off, guys."

"Before we call the cops," Mckenna added.

Jane dealt with rottweilers and pit bulls every day. A few reporters didn't intimidate her. And Mckenna didn't back down from anyone.

But the reporters smelled a story, and they surged right back.

"Is that fat little thing the rich dog?"

"How 'bout an interview? You know, the heartwarming, human interest sort of thing?"

Nell tried to be polite. "Really, I don't think that—"

"Party's over, fellas!"

Out of the crowd came a familiar face, broad shoulders, crisp black hair, and pewter eyes that snapped with determination. Dan Travis. He took two of the reporters by the shoulder, wedged the third in between them, and pointed them all three in the other direction.

"Go get an interview with the rodeo queen, boys. Nell Jordan and her money are all mine."

chapter 6

"SO YOU'RE the fellow who rescued Nell from a hideous death inside that stupid bug of hers." Mckenna regarded Dan with razor-sharp eyes. No one got past Mckenna without being weighed, measured, dissected, analyzed, scrutinized, and otherwise assessed for overall worth and character. Most ordinary human beings—particularly men—she found lacking and simply discarded. It was one of her less endearing qualities.

"I was not headed for a hideous death, Mckenna. And Mel is not stupid."

"Whatever. This is the fellow, though?"

"I'm the fellow," Dan admitted with perfect composure.

Nell had to admire his cool. Most men crumpled under Mckenna's scrutiny.

The four of them sat stuffing their faces—or in Mckenna's case, sipping coffee—at the little hamburger and ice cream stand in Sedona's Uptown Mall, a small plaza that rated the title "mall" only in some developer's overambitious imagination. A postparade lunch here had become a tradition. The food was good, the outdoor tables nicely shaded, and

the animals could sit with them, enjoying the passing specta-
cle of Sedona tourists. Shops in the plaza offered everything
from New Age vortex tours and crystal therapy to fine Southwestern artwork and jewelry. On a second-floor balcony
across from them, a woman enjoyed a chair massage while
her partner read to her from a brochure about a Humvee
tour. A man sitting beside the plaza fountain played a haunt-
ing melody on the Native American flute. A rack close by
displayed his CDs for sale.

"I like the music," Jane commented. "He hasn't been
here before."

"I'm thinking of buying a CD," Nell said.

But Mckenna refused to shift focus. "Just what is it you
do, Dan?"

"Dan's a photographer," Nell supplied.

"Uh . . . yeah. But I'm beginning to dabble in freelance
journalism."

"Just like Nell, eh? What a coincidence."

Nell regarded him in surprise. "You didn't tell me that."

He just smiled. "Small world."

"Isn't it?" Mckenna remarked sharply.

"Mckenna, spare the poor man the third degree. She's a
lawyer," Nell explained to Dan. "For her, interrogation is instinct."

"Not a problem," Dan said. "I've been in the court hot
seat a few times, and believe me, she's a lot gentler than
some of the lawyers I've had work me over."

Mckenna's brow arched upward in sharp question.

"He used to be a cop, Mckenna, not a criminal."

"A cop?" Jane echoed, looking impressed. "That's where
you got your crowd-control training."

Indeed, Dan Travis had been a godsend in the Attack of
the Reporters—Nell had begun to think of it in capital letters—and the subsequent surge of curious parade spectators. He had a natural authority, holding back the crowd
with a smile, but still holding them back. While Nell still

reeled from the barrage of unwelcome attention, Jane had invited Dan to lunch with them. He had slid into their little group as slick as butter onto a cracker.

"A cop, eh?" Mckenna relaxed a bit. "Where?"

A man wearing worn cowboy boots, faded Levis, and a much-used Stetson interrupted Mckenna's third degree.

"Well hello, Mckenna," he greeted her, walking up to their table. "I thought that was you dragging this poor cat through the parade."

Mckenna gave the newcomer an arch look. "Tom. Hello."

Tom flashed Mckenna a grin that had the wattage of a nuclear power plant, and Mckenna's cheeks flushed. Nell couldn't remember Mckenna ever reacting so visibly to a man, but then, this guy, with a devil's smile and Tom Selleck looks, deserved female reaction.

"Everybody, this is Tom Markham. He's a new hire at Bradner, Kelly, and Bolin."

"An attorney?" Jane failed to hide her surprise.

"Tom used to be a cowboy," Mckenna explained in a mock cowboy drawl.

Tom, Nell noted, endured Mckenna's sarcasm with good humor.

"He did the rodeo circuit."

"No kidding?" Nell's ears perked up. "How interesting! I'll bet you have a million stories you could tell."

"There goes Nell's journalistic radar," Jane warned. "Watch out or she'll be writing an article about you. Why don't you grab that empty chair at the next table and sit down?"

The cowboy lawyer accepted the invite without hesitation, despite the little pucker of a scowl that marred Mckenna's perfect brows. As he sat down, she pointedly turned back to Dan.

"So, you're a cop."

"Was a cop. Past tense."

"Where?"

"L.A."

"Hard duty. Is that where you got the limp?"

"Mckenna!" Nell objected.

Dan didn't seem to mind. "Bullet to the knee. I had a good surgeon, though."

"Lucky you. Must have put an end to your jogging days, though."

His smile flattened. "It put an end to more than that."

Even Mckenna wasn't bold enough to pursue that opening.

"Mckenna is harassing poor Dan," Nell explained to Tom, "because he had the temerity to rescue me from a car wreck the other day."

Tom lifted one brow. "No kidding! He's got nerve."

"And after the parade today, he chased away some obnoxious reporters."

"Worse yet."

Mckenna sniffed indignantly. "What Nell isn't telling you is that she recently came into a ton of money, and every, Dan, Dick, and Harry"—she gave Dan a pointed look—"knows she's an easy mark."

Nell gave Dan high marks for putting up with the harassment. If Mckenna had been running with a wolf pack, she definitely would have been the alpha bitch.

"Mckenna, you make me sound like a patsy who would fall for any con man's line."

"You're more naive than you realize. It's a big, bad world out there, filled with very clever people."

Tom lightened the mood by chuckling. "And no one knows that better than a lawyer." That earned him a glare from Mckenna, but he ignored it as well as Dan disregarded her harassment. The two men exchanged the universal "men who are put upon by women" look.

"Do you have a dog?" Jane tactfully changed the subject. She was always on the lookout for new recruits, both for her training classes and as candidates for therapy certification.

"No dog," Dan admitted.

"A cat," Tom confessed.

Mckenna looked surprised. "A cowboy with a cat?"

"A lawyer with a cat."

"Well, at least you have good taste. What's your excuse, Dan?"

Dan shrugged. "Uh . . . I'm not much of a pet person."

He was in the wrong company to admit such a thing, and the look on the three feminine faces at the table made him backtrack.

"Not that I don't like animals. But, uh . . ."

"Think fast," Nell prompted sternly.

"I don't have a yard, and sometimes I don't get home until late at night. That would hardly be fair to a dog. Or a cat, either."

"I guess we can accept that excuse," Jane allowed.

"It won't get you points with Nell," Mckenna warned.

"Mckenna!" Nell's face heated. She breathed a sigh of relief when yet another interruption spared her the need for comment.

"Hey there!" A middle-aged woman in an embroidered tunic, earth-mother skirt, and sandals—Nell concluded she was a local—stopped by the table. "You all did so well in the parade!" she exclaimed. "I think the work you do at the hospital and old folks' homes is just inspired. But where's the cat? Oh," she answered herself, "curled up on your lap like a cat should be. She was so cute sitting in the wagon."

"Thank you," Mckenna said politely.

"And aren't you the one I read about in the *Red Rock News*?" she asked Nell. "Is that cute little thing the dog who got all the money? Aren't you a sweetie?" She squatted down to make google eyes at Piggy, who looked up at Nell as if to ask, "Can't you do something about this?"

"Such short little legs! Is she a dachshund mix?"

"She's a Pembroke Welsh corgi."

"Such a big name for a little dog! What is she going to do with all that money?"

"Buy dog cookies, if I know Piggy," Jane offered wryly.

"You know, dear," the woman advised in a sage voice, "you should stop down at our place on Highway 179, the New Age Center. We have a couple of really tuned-in psychics doing readings there. A reading might help you decide where that money belongs."

"I might do that," Nell lied.

The woman went on her way, but Dan echoed her question. "Yes, Nell, what are you going to do with all that money?"

His tone had sharpened.

Nell grimaced. "You're miffed because I didn't tell you last Thursday," she concluded.

"I read about it in the *Red Rock News*," he replied blandly.

Tom chimed in. "You're the one whose dog inherited all that money?"

Nell sighed. "I feel kind of funny talking about it. People react in such peculiar ways."

"She'll get used to it," Jane predicted.

"And she is going to have no trouble putting that money to good use," Mckenna declared. "For Piggy's sake, of course."

"Of course," Dan agreed with a smile.

It seemed to Nell, though, that the smile didn't quite reach those pewter eyes.

"Piggy needs a better house and a decent car, to start with," Jane said.

"I like my car," Nell objected. "And he'll be fixed tomorrow."

Mckenna ignored her. "And Piggy's mom needs a decent wardrobe. And when we get the small stuff out of the way, then we can look into some investments."

Nell smiled wryly. "Who would have thought that having money would be so much work?"

Dan gave her an enigmatic look. "Yeah. Some kinda work."

"It is work! For years I thought if I just had money, I'd never worry again. No worries about the mortgage, or repair bills on the car, or my tennies growing holes and no money to get another pair. But now that I have money, I worry more than I ever have, reporters hound me, people I don't know feel free to play a game of twenty questions with my personal life, and next thing you know, every charity in the world will be knocking at my door."

"That will happen," Mckenna agreed.

"If the money's too much of a burden," Dan suggested blandly, "you could always give it away. I'm sure the old geezer's family would be glad to get their hands on it."

Three pairs of cold female eyes fastened upon him simultaneously, and he backed off with, "Just joking, ladies."

Jane still nursed indignation as she explained to Tom. "Frank Cramer's family hardly gave the poor man the time of day all the time he was in Springdale They forced him to look to strangers and a dog as his only friends."

Dan's mouth flattened to a hard line.

"All the same," Nell said in a placating tone, "I'm sure they feel entitled to Frank's estate."

Mckenna sniffed. "Frank wanted Piggy to have that money. Piggy and you, Nell. You didn't persuade him to write that will, and you don't have a thing to feel guilty about."

"Why would she feel guilty?" Dan asked. "No one would ever suspect Nell of anything underhanded. How could they?"

Nell suffered a momentary thrill of alarm. Something in his tone rang with a dark note. Or was she just oversensitive?

"But," he continued smoothly, "everyone is going to bug

you for the juicy details. Hell, you're a real soap opera plunked down upon their doorstep like a gift from Hollywood. The local media will milk this until the cow runs dry."

"Hm." Mckenna's eyes narrowed. "Maybe Nell should hire protection for a while." She glanced at Tom. "Know any tough cowboy types who could intimidate pests?"

Dan didn't wait for Tom's answer. "How about a not-so-tough photographer?"

All eyes swung his way.

"Give me an exclusive on your story. When I told those reporters out there that you belonged to me, did you see them back off?"

Mckenna smiled slyly. "And here I put an entirely different meaning on those words."

Dan refused to be distracted. "You *should* give me an exclusive, Nell. I could keep those nasty reporters and nosy busybodies away."

Mckenna said coldly. "And who will protect her from you?"

"Me?" Dan gave Jane a blank look. "Nell doesn't need protection from me. I'm harmless as a little lamb."

"Right," Mckenna replied. "You look harmless."

"I think it's a good idea, Nell." Jane regarded Dan appraisingly. "At least you'll have only one pest to deal with."

"Wait a minute, ladies! I save your bacon out there on the streets of Sedona and—"

"Chasing away a troop of reporters hardly qualifies as saving our bacon," Nell told him.

"As I was saying," he continued, "before the rude interruption, I save your bacon, or at least make myself useful, out there on the dangerous streets of Sedona, and suddenly I'm reduced to the status of 'pest'?"

Nell patted his hand, and noticed suddenly how much she liked Dan's hands. They were big, square, and competent-looking. In fact, Nell decided, she liked Dan. Not just his hands. All of him. Up until this moment she hadn't been quite sure of her feelings on the subject, and she still found his occasional sharp thrusts confusing. But she did like him. If he had a bit of the mystery about him, getting to the bottom of it might be fun. "I don't think you're a pest, Dan, and if you want an exclusive on this silliness, you can have it. But," she qualified quickly, "I get to read everything before you send it out."

"You'll let me stick with you for however long it takes?"

Nell felt another blush coming on, because a certain spark in his eyes seemed to inject the words with a double meaning. "Within reason," she promised. "And you'll keep everyone else away?"

"You can be sure of that." His smile was beatific. "I'm a very territorial sort of guy. I don't let others horn in on what I've staked out for myself."

Piggy underscored his bold statement with a quiet growl, but no one noticed the low rumble coming from beneath the table.

THE THREE friends sat in the plaza for a while after Dan and Tom had both gone. They enjoyed the sunshine, the laziness of simply sitting and doing nothing, and the quiet company of their animals.

But most of all, Mckenna and Jane wanted to grill Nell about Dan Travis.

"He is a hunk," Jane declared. "I wonder how he stays so fit with that bad knee of his."

"He told me that he swims and works out at a gym,"

Mckenna jumped on it. "So you two got to talking about personal stuff, as in how he maintains his washboard abs?"

"We didn't get that personal. And how do you know he has washboard abs?"

"I'm assuming from the rest of him. You're blushing," Mckenna noted.

Jane gave her leprechaun's grin. "Nell blushes about

everything, but if I had a date with Dan Travis, I would get personal real fast."

"You're hardly the one to talk!" Nell scoffed. "You won't take time enough from your training and competing to date!"

She shrugged. "Someday I might find a man who's worth more than a good obedience trial dog. It's not impossible."

Nell and Jane both laughed. "If Mckenna gets to grill me about Dan," Nell said, "I think it's only fair that she answer some questions about her good-looking cowboy."

Mckenna looked momentarily discomposed. But only momentarily. "He's not *my* cowboy. Not my type at all."

Jane's knowing grin stretched her freckles to the breaking point. "Don't give us that line. We saw you look at him."

"Honestly, you guys!" Mckenna hastily turned the subject back to Dan. "Nell, be serious. What do you know about this Dan fellow?"

"I know he's an ex-cop with an ex-wife and two kids, and he pulled me out of Mel when I crashed him, which means he has certain admirable qualities. He lives in a motor home in Page Springs. He hikes well, even with the limp. He was gentleman enough to carry Piggy across the creek when she wouldn't walk herself—several creeks, in fact. And he's a photographer who has some ambition to be a journalist."

"And he's a hunk," Jane reminded her.

Nell smiled. "Yes, there is that."

"You need to be careful about men, now, you know," Mckenna warned. "I mean it. A woman with money never knows whether a man is attracted to her or her cash. Unless, of course, the man is richer than you are. Which Dan Travis doesn't seem to be. The guy lives in a motor home?" She made a face.

"Come on, Mckenna. The guy asked me out the very day Frank Cramer died, long before I became an overpaid guardian to a filthy rich dog."

"Yes," Mckenna said, "but now that he knows you have money, he's sticking to you like a leech."

"Oh shoot! This is not a big deal. On our one and only date, he didn't exactly turn somersaults trying to impress me. He's kind of moody, actually. Nice, but moody. I'm still trying to figure out the mixed messages."

With a soft woof, Piggy added her two cents.

"What's wrong, Piggy girl?" Nell asked.

"She probably wants the remnants of your hamburger." Jane spoke Dog, or fancied that she did.

"Yeah, well, a nice hunk of rare beef would go great on those hips of hers."

"Poor Piggy," Jane sympathized.

"I think she's telling you to be careful," Mckenna said. "After all, it's her money."

"Well then, Dan should be putting the moves on Piggy if he's interested in money."

Mckenna laughed. "You did say he carried Piggy across the creek, didn't you?"

WHILE NELL and company enjoyed lunch, Natalie Donner showed off Sedona to new clients, Hiram and Delia Bradley, who had just retired to Arizona from Minnesota. She had invited the Bradleys to the parade—since she was in charge of the thing, she couldn't very well dodge that responsibility—and they had happily stood curbside and watched. Then she had bought them lunch at the Heartline Cafe—very small, very good, and very expensive (when rubbing elbows with the wealthy, it never hurt to demonstrate your own financial success)—and now, finally, they were cruising the galleries for artwork to grace their new home in the red bluffs above the town.

Except that Delia kept getting distracted by jewelry and gewgaws. Now what had caught her eye?

"Look, Hi." Delia pointed at a sign touting the "spiritual"

experience of a Humvee tour of the local "holy places." Sedona was supposedly chock full of New Age holy places. Delia pulled her husband through the entrance archway of the Uptown Mall to take a closer look. Normally Natalie didn't frequent the little plaza. With its vortex tours, chair massages, aromatherapy shops, and of all things, a Christmas store, she considered it one of the tackier places in the town. It became all the more tacky when Natalie noticed the woman sitting at one of the shaded tables adjoining the hamburger stand.

Natalie had seen Nell Jordan and her overstuffed sausage of a dog in the parade, marching along with her troupe as if she were some kind of nurturing angel to the sick and aged. Therapy animals, indeed! Nell Jordan had used her little dog—and heaven only knew what else—to wedge herself into the affections of Natalie's father. The man had been a cranky old pain in the ass, but he deserved better than to be prey to a scheming, cold-hearted bitch. And Natalie wasn't referring to the dog.

"This town is just one of the most fascinating places I've ever been," Delia Bradley gushed. "I'm so glad we decided to move here. Have you ever taken one of these vortex tours, Natalie?"

"No, I haven't. But many tourists enjoy them. If you and Hiram will excuse me for just a few moments, I've just spied someone I need to have a word with."

As Natalie approached the laughing trio at the table, a slow burn ate at her gut. Normally she loathed confrontations. Confrontations with her father had driven her from his company for the past few years, despite her onetime determination to be a dutiful daughter. Confrontations, in fact, made her physically ill.

But at some point a person simply had to draw a line and then step over it.

"Good afternoon," she greeted the women politely. "I'd

like to introduce myself. Natalie Donner." She paused a moment for effect. "My maiden name is Cramer."

Natalie dropped her name like a bombshell into the midst of the three friends, and the smile on Nell Jordan's face faded.

"I'm Frank Cramer's daughter," Natalie added unnecessarily. Their expressions told her that they knew exactly who she was.

"Mrs. Donner," Nell said, "I'm so sorry about your father."

Brazen woman, acting as if her conscience was clean as new snow.

Natalie glanced at the other two, one a plain sort of girl with kinky red hair and the other a sleek, dark-haired Barbie doll with "predator" written all over her. "If you ladies would excuse us for a moment, I have a few private words to say to Ms. Jordan."

The Barbie doll surveyed her cannily and answered with a cold little smile. "I don't think so. What do you think, Jane?"

The plain girl shook her head. "Nope. We'll stick."

Rude. But then, what did Natalie expect?

"Ms. Jordan doesn't need your protection, I assure you. I merely came to say that I'm aware of how you manipulated my father, and you're not going to get away with this travesty. People who take advantage of others for their own profit eventually come up against someone who won't stand for it, and this time, you have."

"Mrs. Donner—"

"Save your protestations of innocence, Ms. Jordan. I am the wrong gender to be susceptible to your charms." Anger flared, making her voice rise a notch. With difficulty she kept herself under control. "No doubt you feel that you're set for life. But don't start counting your money, because I'm going to make sure you don't profit from taking advantage of an old man. You are a predator, and you have violated every ethical standard there is, along with a sick old man's trust."

"WOW!" JANE said as they watched Natalie Donner march stiffly away. "Do you suppose she wears that rod up her ass every day?"

Nell felt a bit stunned—stunned and mortified. "Heavens, with family like that, no wonder Frank left his money to a dog." She immediately clapped a hand to her mouth. "I'm becoming a bitch."

Jane laughed. "Speaking of bitches, look at Piggy staring at that woman. If looks could maim, we'd have a bloody mess on our hands."

"Go to it, Piggy." Mckenna smiled cynically. "I don't suppose all that righteous indignation had anything to do with money rather than with her poor violated father, could it?"

Nell toyed dejectedly with the remnants of her hamburger. "I just assumed that Frank had told his family what he planned, and they approved."

Mckenna laughed. "Frank? Consult his family? Oh please!"

Nell made a face.

"Come on, Nell, don't let the witch get to you. Ignore it. The will is legal, and Frank had a right to give Piggy—and you—the money if he wanted to. Not to say you shouldn't tell Jared Johansen about this little encounter first thing Monday, and from now on, I'm officially your attorney. If Natalie Donner wants to mess with someone, she can mess with me."

Jane chuckled. "A challenge always brings out the pit bull in Mckenna."

Nell attempted a smile, but it was a weak one.

Mckenna poked a finger at her. "Get with the program, Nell. And don't lose sleep over that woman. You have other things to lose sleep over. Like upgrading your life and thinking about some investments. You can't let all that money hang around without using it. That's a sin against the Gods of Finance."

"The will has to go through probate, and it sounds as if the family is going to challenge it."

"They have to find grounds first," Mckenna said. "And they won't. Besides, didn't you say Frank set up a payable-upon-death account for you?"

"Five hundred thousand." Nell shook her head. The thought of even that amount made her dizzy.

"That's enough for a good beginning. We need to get organized, ladies."

"Just hold on." Nell folded Mckenna's admonishing finger back toward its owner. "Mckenna, you're morphing into a bulldozer."

Mckenna shrugged.

"I've been thinking about this," Nell said

"Thinking can be a danger," Jane warned.

Nell merely gave her a face. "Here's what I think. I think Piggy and I should put this windfall to good use."

"A new car would be a good use," Jane reminded her.

Mckenna grinned. "And I'm sure Piggy could use one of those fancy air beds with an individualized hardness or softness number. A king-sized one, so you can keep her company on it."

Nell laughed. "Get serious, guys."

"We are serious," Mckenna insisted.

"Well listen to this, then, seriously, because it involves you. I want to use Frank's money to fund an animal therapy network in northern Arizona. The southern part of the state has plenty of programs working, in Phoenix and Tucson, but up here we have hardly anything. The Verde Valley has us, and there's a program in Flagstaff, but a lot of places don't have anyone. How about Williams, Page, Prescott, even Camp Verde, in our own backyard? They may not have big hospitals, but nursing homes, schools, eldercare centers—we could be helping there. And there's training available to people with therapy animals to assist in disasters and emergencies. With money available for expenses and fees, maybe we could get someone to do a training course here."

Jane nodded. "We could use the training room at the kennel to do some seminars."

"Right!" Nell's enthusiasm grew. "And how about financial help for people wanting to certify their dog to do therapy? Doggy scholarships, sort of."

"Not a bad idea," Mckenna conceded. "And we could arrange for it to be tax deductible."

"It's a great idea," Jane agreed.

"We could set up programs in every health care and nursing facility who will have us. Frank would have liked that, don't you think?" Nell asked hopefully.

"He would have," Jane assured her.

Mckenna grinned. "And you'll still have plenty left over for a car, a house, and how about we check out the new shopping mall in Prescott?"

THAT FANCY air bed sounded like heaven after marching in that cursed parade. I liked the way Mckenna thought. She knew the importance of material acquisition, and her taste ran to expensive. Why couldn't I have ended up living with someone like her, someone who shared my priorities and values? The answer, of course, is that Stanley didn't want me comfortable. Yes, indeed, the strait-laced little bean-counter upstairs was perfectly capable of using the lovely prospect of all this money to test my ethical reflexes. Ethics is one of Stanley's favorite things, and I was supposed to be nurturing a set of them while stuck in this dog suit.

No one, you say, could be that cruel, that perverse? You don't know Stanley.

I was sure I could deal with old Stan when the time came,

though. I always do. So I was grateful to Mckenna for prodding my "guardian" along the shopping lines. Houses, cars, more dog toys—bring them on. I dreamed of a new house that had a special room just for Piggy, with plush carpeting, one of those beanbag dog beds upholstered in velvet, and a private door leading into a walled, grassy yard for my own private retreat. Oh yes, and how about a weekly massage by an official dog masseuse (yes, they really do exist), a warehouse full of rawhide chews, and my own pizza place? And an endless supply of knuckle bones loaded with fat. To hell with the diet, I decided. I was rich. They can do doggy liposuction, can't they?

I'm sure Mckenna would have applauded all those things, because after all, Frank had intended that money for my welfare. Right? I should get to shop. Nell, on the other hand, had work in mind, not fun and shopping. What a dweeb! A good cause is all very well and good, but all work and no play makes Piggy a dull little corgi. And we wouldn't want that, would we?

And speaking of play, how about Studly Dan and his party crashing? Mckenna was suspicious of the guy the minute he showed up. She knows the score with men and money as well as I do. The hunk might think Nell is kind of cute, but believe me, his eye is fixed on the bank account. Been there, done that, and I know how the game is played. Journalist? I don't think so. Wanting the story of how Nell handles her new wealth? Dull reading, if you ask me.

I needed to dust off my matchbusting skills—matchmaking in reverse. Piggy to the rescue—again.

chapter 7

ON MONDAY, Nell's mailbox produced the usual drabble of bills and glossy invitations to indebt herself to various credit card companies. As Nell stood in front of her street-side mailbox and sorted through the pile, she decided that today she might actually look at those credit card invites. She could picture herself strolling into the local bike shop, pointing to the mountain bike she wanted, and blithely handing the clerk her platinum credit card. "Charge it!" she would say, and happily ride home on her brand-new twenty-one speed.

How nice! And next time she went to the mall in Prescott, she and her credit card could march into Dillard's and march back out again with new jeans, sweaters, and underwear with elastic that didn't sag at the waist. On further thought, forget the mall department store. She could take her credit card to Prescott's little town square, where all the trendy shops offered everything from artwork and jewelry to hiking boots and cargo pants. Maybe she would splurge and get an outfit that would knock everyone's socks right off their feet. Something—maybe not quite slinky, but definitely sexy in a subtle sort of way. Something sophisticated, expensive, and absolutely shouting good taste. She could wear it to the next Desert Writers' conference in Phoenix.

Or better still, she could wear it for Dan Travis.

Nell warned herself away from such a thought. That road led to trouble. Still, she wondered what Dan would think if she put on such a display. Would his eyes pop out of his head? The desired reaction, certainly. Or would he laugh, the more probable result? Nell wasn't exactly the sort of woman one expected to see in silks and lace. She was much more the sweatshirt and sneakers type.

Piggy greeted her with a hopeful little woof as Nell came through the front door with the mail. The corgi lay on the kitchen floor in front of the pantry that locked away her dog food.

"Give it up," Nell advised. "You've already been fed. Hours ago."

Piggy sighed.

Besides credit card invitations, the pile of mail included a volunteer newsletter from the hospital, a notice of dues from the American Journalists Association, an electric bill, and five solicitations from charities.

"How do they sniff out money so fast?" she asked the corgi. "Look at this—kids starving in Africa. Sheesh! And suddenly my alma mater, good old NAU, needs my financial help to continue offering quality education. Right. And this one—my money can help fight the good fight to preserve these tiny little birds in their natural habitat. What are they?" She showed the picture to Piggy. "Have you ever seen a sillier-looking bird? And what's this strange-looking letter from . . . Fuzzy Cridler? It's addressed to you, Piggy, supposedly from a dog whose family could sure use a handout so they could buy dog food and pay the electric bill.

Shoot! How does a person read stuff like this and not feel
guilty?"

She picked up the last letter and froze, and almost
dropped the envelope. "Omigod! It's a letter from Frank
Cramer."

Piggy perked her ears.

A chill crawled up Nell's spine. Not every day did a girl
get mail from a dead man. She looked at the postmark. The
letter had been mailed two days before Frank died, more
than two weeks ago. The Pony Express could have delivered
it faster.

"This is why we pay a small fortune for a first-class
stamp," she told Piggy.

But the stab at the U. S. Postal Service didn't make the situation any less eerie. She sat down at the kitchen table, gingerly opened the envelope, and smoothed out the folded
stationery. Unexpectedly, her eyes sprouted a crop of tears.

" *'Dear Nell and Piggy,'* " she read out loud. "Listen up,
Piggy. This is for you, too."

Piggy had joined her, sitting attentively at her feet with a
corgi smile on her face.

" *'Dear Nell and Piggy,*

*"Knowing our local mail service, by the time you get
this letter you will have long since learned that I
arranged a token of thanks for the kindness you and
Piggy showed me during these last months. You must be
wondering if I was insane, and since I know you quite
well by now, I predict that you're feeling rather awkward
as well. Probably my daughter shrieked to the high
heavens when Johansen told her. I'm wondering if I'll be
able to hear her where I'm going. Don't let it bother you,
girl. Natalie can be a feisty one, but she's not out-and-
out mean. Not like her old man in that way. She'll get
over it.*

" 'The rest of the family will just curse my memory for

a few minutes and then forget it. They're used to me
being a contrary old so-and-so. You are not to worry
about them, girl. They'll be taken care of in good time,
when Piggy's time is up. But for now, Piggy and you
deserve to have a little fun. If you are smart, you'll fix
things up so that you won't ever again need to live in a
broken-down trailer house in a seedy neighborhood full
of deadbeats.

" 'Yes, girl, I had you investigated.' "

"Well, that old jackass!" Nell huffed indignantly, then read on.

" 'A dying old man needs some entertainment in his life,
and nosing around in other people's lives fills the bill. I can
picture your face as you read this, your nose wrinkled in
dismay and eyebrows puckered up in a frown. Yes, I know
about that little ruckus at the Chicago newspaper, but I
don't believe for one minute you're that kind of person.
Everything else I know, along with my gut instinct, tells me
that you are a good sort, and smart besides. You and that
stupid-looking little dog of yours made my day every time
you came by, and you're the only person in years who has
had nerve enough to play poker with me—even if we were
only playing for pennies.' "

He had always won those games, and not because Nell had
let him. Nell had to chuckle at the memory.

" 'You won the pot this time, Nell. What you've got
now isn't pennies. See that you use this money for
Piggy's benefit, and your own. I'll be watching.' "

Nell smiled. Somehow she didn't mind the idea of Frank
watching her from the other side. She wished he could give
her some advice on how to handle Piggy's new wealth.
Life had gotten very complicated.

• • •

DAN STOPPED his Jeep in front of Nell's place and surveyed the rather run-down neighborhood. Cottonwood
didn't have what anyone could call a slum, but this street
came about as close as anything else in town. The dwellings
were a mix of small, shoddy houses and mobile homes—
not mobile in the way his RV was mobile. In Dan's opinion,
RVs had class. They were the high-tech version of the colorful gypsy wagons of centuries past. But these old tin cans
that people plunked down on a piece of dirt and then
dressed up in a pathetic attempt to look like a house—
those had no class at all.

Compared to most other places in the neighborhood,
though, Nell's trailer wasn't all that bad. Everything was
neat and tidy, rather like Nell herself. But he could understand someone being so desperate to get out that they
might sweet-talk an old man out of his money.

He was not the right man to investigate Nell Jordan, Dan
told himself for the hundredth time. The obvious emotional tie to the case killed any chance at impartiality, and
his very male reaction to the woman guaranteed so many
internal battles that he might as well declare war on himself. What she had done (so much for impartiality!) made
him furious, but her smile made his heart beat faster and
his brain go soft.

Yet he didn't want anyone else prying into this dirty
business, and if he had told his mother not only no, but
hell no, as he had wanted to, she would have hired some
other sleazy private eye to look into the matter. Dan felt his
temper rise at the thought of some other guy sneaking
around to get the lowdown on Nell. If there was sneaking
around to be done, Dan Travis was the man for the job.

Besides, he did admit that the task of wooing Nell Jordan, even if it was only to get the goods on the little gold
digger, filled him with a certain anticipation.

The noise coming from inside the trailer house told Dan that Piggy, at least, had heard him drive up. This was a surprise visit. Nothing kept a woman off balance more than surprises.

By the time he climbed out of the Jeep and had opened the silly little white picket gate, Nell had stuck her head out the front door.

"Dan!"

"In the flesh."

"What a surprise!"

"I was in town, so I decided to stop by and offer you a ride to pick up your car. You mentioned yesterday that it would be ready today."

"Well, yes. Mel is supposed to be ready today. That's very nice of you."

Her gratitude didn't seem to be shared by Piggy, who ambled out the front door, sniffed his ankles—the stumpy-legged little hairball couldn't reach much higher—and then glared up at him.

"Come in while I save what I'm working on. The mechanic is over in Clarkdale, you know? Do you mind going that far?"

"Nah, the extra time will just give me a chance to pry into your secrets."

She gave him a mildly startled glance.

"For my story. You do remember that I get to be privy to everything about you for the next few weeks."

"Was that the deal?"

"Yup. Do you have any secrets worth telling?"

She hesitated just a moment. "Not a one. I'm the least interesting person you'll ever meet."

That hesitation set off instinctive alarms that had served Dan well during his years dealing with scuzzbags. Little Mary Sunshine, Dan decided, did indeed have secrets.

The inside of the trailer home wasn't quite as neat as the outside. A shabby sofa showed evidence that the dog spent more time there than Nell did. The kitchen table barely peeked through a pile of mail and miscellaneous papers. And the carpet was worn enough to show the backing in many spots.

"I'll be just a minute," Nell told him.

He let her go while he wandered around the little living room in search of he didn't know what—anything that might give him a clue about who Nell Jordan really was. Anything, frankly, that could be used against her. Such tidbits rarely appeared easily, but one never knew.

Glancing down the dark, narrow little hallway to make sure Nell was out of sight, Dan took a quick look at the mail on the table. Right away he recognized Frank's very shaky handwriting. He picked up the letter from his grandfather, dated a couple of days before the old man had died.

"I'll be damned." He scowled. What was this "ruckus" his granddad had discovered and then discounted? But before he could ponder the implications, a mastiff-sized growl alerted him to trouble. He looked up to find himself skewered on the stilettos of the corgi's intent brown eyes. The dog obviously didn't like him prowling through Nell's mail. Picturing his ankle ripped to the bone, Dan dropped the letter and eased into the little hallway that had swallowed Nell. He found her in a small bedroom—little more than a closet, really—that she apparently used as an office.

"Hi there," he said.

She looked up from where she sat at the computer.

"I just had to finish this paragraph. You know how it is."

He didn't. Dan hated to write anything longer than a grocery list.

Every bit of wall space not taken up by the computer desk was covered with bookshelves; books, magazines, and file boxes overflowed onto the floor. And Dan had thought *his* office was small. He would have casually sauntered in and gotten a peek at the computer screen, but the pesky dog had stationed herself in front of his feet like a concrete barrier.

"What are you working on?" he ventured.

Nell clicked the screen into blankness. "I'm doing a piece on Walnut Canyon National Monument. You know, the cliff dwellings outside of Flagstaff. I wish that I'd known you a month ago. I would have asked you to do the photography. With all the light and shade up there, getting good photos is tricky."

"Still working, eh? Even though you're rich?"

She laughed. "Birds gotta fly, fish gotta swim, I gotta write. Besides, somehow, that money just doesn't seem real."

As they left, Dan glanced toward the letter on the table. *The plot thickens.*

"It's going to be great having Mel again," Nell told him as they pulled onto the highway. "That shiny little Neon is nice, but there's nothing quite like a vintage VW. And now he's going to have all new paint and a new windshield and hood. He's going to look like new."

"Then he won't exactly be 'vintage' anymore, will he?"

"Sure he will. They don't make new parts for those little bugs. He'll still be old, just old with a facelift. Which means he'll be just as lovable."

"Until you replace him. Every man's complaint."

"Replace Mel? Oh no. I couldn't do that."

"Every guy should have a woman so loyal." He snorted. "Mel Gibson. Doesn't do a thing for me."

"You're the wrong gender to have the proper appreciation."

"Ha!" He chortled. "That's true."

"My mother agrees with you, though. She's says I'm infantile. But every girl is entitled to be infantile in at least one area of her life."

"What does she think of her *nouveau riche* daughter?"

"Oh, I haven't told her. We haven't talked much since I

gave up gainful employment back East and came out here to be what she calls a 'glorified bum.' "

"Then she'd probably be pleased to know you're now rolling in dough."

She shrugged and flashed him a glance, looking somewhat uncertain. "It just feels very strange, all this. I still don't know what to think." Those green eyes, he noted, changed color with her mercurial moods—spring-green when she was happy, warm hazel when she appeared ready to weep, and all the shades in between. The dark shade of bruised grass seemed to be the color of uncertainty, of vulnerability.

A warmth rose in him, a need to reassure, to comfort. Don't be a chump, he told himself. She's a good actress, an expert manipulator. You're too tough to fall for false charm and innocence.

"Think about the things you can buy," he said with a wry smile. "You can buy another car to keep Mel company. A lady car, this time. That should make the little old bug happy. And with your money, you should make the next car bigger than a postage stamp. You are a rich woman, after all."

"No. I'm a woman with a rich dog." She smiled happily. Apparently with Nell Jordan, uncertainty and vulnerability didn't last long. "But maybe Piggy does need a car of her own. A minivan with plenty of room for a nice big safe portable kennel."

"Maybe Piggy needs a Caribbean cruise as well. Or maybe a trip to one of those big dog shows in Europe with a couple of side trips to the jet-setting hot spots."

Nell laughed. "That's right. I can just see me and Piggy on the Côte d'Azur."

"Every woman's dream."

"Or touring the Mediterranean."

"Just the ticket."

She laughed. "Dan Travis, you're an instigator."

"Is that a writer's fancy word for 'troublemaker'?"

"It is."

"I might have to confess to that," he admitted. "Maybe I'll come along on these luxury trips as Piggy's official photographer."

"There's an idea."

Then her bright smile flowed like quicksilver into a dubious frown. "Are you going to include photos in this so-called story of yours?"

" 'So-called'? I'm hurt. And yes. What's a story about a lovely heiress without photos?"

"I get veto power on the photos, just like I get to read the text."

He prodded her with a grin. "Afraid I won't catch your good side?"

"If I have a good side, I haven't found it." She grimaced comically. "I'm not very photogenic."

Charming. Modest. Just a hint of feminine vanity. Nell Jordan seemed to be just the opposite of what one would expect in a fortune hunter. If she had shown the least bit of gloating over her new wealth, he could have more easily believed his mother had a case. If she had been seriously cataloging the things she wanted to buy and wanted to do, instead of kidding about it, he could have mentally slapped a label of GOLD DIGGER onto her flawless forehead.

But Nell Jordan wasn't going to make the job easy by being an obvious bimbo. She certainly didn't seem the type to deliberately take advantage of an old man. Could she be that good at camouflage? And what the hell was the "ruckus" in Frank's letter? He had to get his act together and start digging for that. Damn. Why couldn't this be simple? Black or white. No gray.

He had a suspicion that Nell Jordan didn't fit into black or white, but might pull all the colors of the rainbow down upon his head.

•   •   •

NATALIE'S SHOWROOM occupied a quiet nook in old Sedona among the upscale shops, galleries, and boutiques nestled in earth-tone adobe buildings. Sedona was a shopper's paradise. From one shop to another, the Southwestern aficionado could find fine art, jewelry, sculpture, and Native American crafts as well as the usual tourist knick-knacks and memorabilia. The town boasted several fine interior design shops, to be sure, but Natalie had built hers into the most prestigious, not to mention the most expensive. The expense went with the status.

In contrast to the elegant showroom, her office in the back overflowed with clutter—fabric swatches, catalogs, books, correspondence. Her desk and computer seemed to cringe against the flood that threatened to overwhelm them.

Still, Natalie was comfortable in her little workspace. In spite of the seeming mess, she could lay hands on everything she needed without a second's thought. More than her condo, even, her office was her private place. In this little cubicle she did what she did best, seldom interrupted, never uncertain. Confident. In charge.

"Hello?"

Startled, Natalie stood, sending a cascade of forms to the floor. Jared Johansen leaned his tall frame against the doorframe.

"Jared!"

"So this is where you keep yourself. It's against city code to have an office without windows, you know. A criminal waste of all the lovely scenery."

"Pish!"

She knelt to pick up the paperwork she had dropped. He moved into the office and helped her. Inevitably, their faces came close enough for Natalie to smell the faint, clean odor of aftershave and feel the warmth of him press upon her own personal space. Hastily she backed into her chair. "I...I..." Where did all her confidence go when this man walked into sight? What happened to her hard-won composure and self-esteem? What about Jared Johansen turned her into a bumbleheaded nincompoop? "I...goodness, Jared! Leave that mess be. Whatever are you doing here?"

"What kind of welcome is that?"

"That didn't come out quite right. I...I just didn't expect to see your face popping into my doorway."

"Now you make me sound like a jack-in-the-box."

She had to laugh. "You're not making this easy!"

"That's what we attorneys do best—complicate matters. So..." He surveyed the clutter with appreciative eyes. "This is where you hide out. I always knew there was a secret part of you that was disorganized and sloppy."

"I beg your pardon! This is not disorganized. I know where every single thing in this office is to be found. Sloppy, perhaps. But that's because I'm too busy to put everything away."

"Don't get defensive, my lady. I find this little chink in your perfection quite endearing, really."

"Perfection? Oh my, Jared. You have forgotten over the years, haven't you?"

"I haven't forgotten much," he said with a warm smile. "You were always my idea of perfection."

"Oh pish!"

"It's true." His smile turned quite wicked. "Of course, I was young and callow. Didn't know much back in those days."

"I'd venture that you're not much wiser as a gray-haired old fogey."

He brushed casual fingers through his thick hair, still rich brown for the most part. "The gray doesn't bother me. I consider it a badge of honor for having survived this long."

Natalie's eyes followed the sweep of his fingers, longing suddenly to comb through that thick mane and feel it curl around her own fingers. Such silliness. A woman her age should be past such fancies.

"Why is it that a little dignified gray on a man is a badge of honor, and on a woman it's something to be hidden at all costs?"

He shrugged. "We live in an unjust world."

"How true. As much as I'm enjoying this strange conversation, Jared, I am rather busy this afternoon. . . ."

"That's exactly why I dropped by. You work much too hard. I've come to take you on a walk. It's a beautiful day, and you live in the most gorgeous place on God's green earth. You need to take some time to enjoy it."

"Really. That's very nice of you, but—"

"No buts. You can spare fifteen minutes for an old friend."

She really wanted to refuse. An afternoon stroll with Jared Johansen spelled danger. The very idea seduced her with possibilities, dangerous possibilities of her losing her good sense, of him sneaking past her painfully erected defenses and finding his way once again to her heart. That, she wouldn't allow. A woman her age just didn't let herself get giddy over an old flame with a flattering tongue.

But the standard brush-off wouldn't work with Jared. He always had pushed persistence to the limits.

"All right, Jared. Fifteen minutes. Fifteen minutes only. And you get that just because something tells me you're after more than a conversation about old times."

"You accuse me of having ulterior motives?" he asked, feigning hurt.

She took her Anne Klein jacket from the antique hat tree crowded into one corner and motioned him out the door.

"You won't need a jacket. I tell you it's beautiful."

"It's part of the outfit, Jared. The look, you know?"

"The look?" He chuckled. "Of course I don't know. I'm a man."

"Don't sound so proud of it."

As they walked through the shop, Natalie told her clerk she was going out. "Fifteen minutes," she assured the woman. "Then I'll be back."

Jared just smiled.

They walked out into sunshine that bathed the town in a warm spring balm, just as the man had promised. The sycamores and cottonwoods along Oak Creek sported a hint of green, and planters of spring flowers decorated the sidewalk. Crimson castles and minarets rose above them, etching a sky so blue it nearly hurt the eyes.

As always, tourists swarmed the walkways and stores. A Japanese family, each laden with a camera, chattered about a bronze eagle displayed in the window of the Turquoise Bear Gallery. A middle-aged couple in matching Virginia Tech T-shirts strolled hand in hand while enjoying ice cream cones. In Sedona, visitors were part of the landscape. Natalie enjoyed the crowds. They made the town thrive. And not even throngs of people detracted from the imposing and somehow spiritual splendor that surrounded them.

"You're right," Natalie admitted. "I should get out of my cubbyhole more often. It might keep me more sane."

"Everyone needs a sanity break now and then."

She smiled wryly. "Some more than others, you're thinking."

"Am I?"

"Probably." She sighed. "I'm not the person you remember, Jared."

He looked thoughtful. "Yes, well, you've added some layers to that girl. But life does that to a person. What kind of creatures would we be if we didn't grow and change?"

She commented only with silence.

"I still see the girl you were inside the woman you've

become. I'll bet you have the same laugh. I'll bet you put on the same tough act that anyone who knows you can see right through."

For a breath-stopping moment, she wanted desperately to be twenty again, to let her toughness be just an act instead of a hard shell built up by life's battering. How nice it would be just to let everything go, betrayals and hurts just rolling past her like a wave that tilts a boat, then moves on.

"You're right." Jared's voice distracted her from her musing.

"Uh . . . naturally." She allowed herself a smile. "What am I right about this time?"

"I do have a minor agenda in dropping by to see you."

"Of course you do."

"I got a call this morning from Nell Jordan."

The woman's name struck a sour note that nearly spoiled the beauty of the day.

"You and she had a little conversation yesterday after the parade?"

"I'd hardly call it a conversation." Natalie tried to squash a twinge of guilt.

"Ah yes. That's right. Nell did mention that you did most of the talking."

"I guess I'm not surprised she complained."

"She didn't complain, exactly. But she sounded concerned. You came as a bit of a surprise to her, I think. Nell, for some reason, assumed that Frank had discussed his financial arrangements with his family and that they approved."

Natalie burst out with a "Ha!" that was half laughter, half derision. "So you're here to order me to back off, are you?"

Jared sighed patiently. "What I'm here for—besides really wanting to take you for a walk on this lovely afternoon—is to ask you to leave Nell Jordan alone. Approaching her in that manner doesn't help anyone."

"I thought I was quite polite, given the circumstances."

"Natalie, I know you. You can do quietly and politely what most people need a set of knives to accomplish."

She simply raised a brow.

"Let it go, Natalie. Nell Jordan is a sweet girl, and Frank wanted to show his appreciation to both her and her little dog. The only way he knew to communicate was through money. Besides which, it's only a temporary arrangement."

"Yes, and God only knows who my father named as next in line after the dog." She dared a glance up at his face. "But then, I suppose you know, don't you?"

He just smiled.

"And of course, being the Boy Scout that you are, you're going to abide by the letter of that ridiculous will and keep mum until that little dog kicks off."

"I'm Frank's attorney, Natalie. I have to do what he directed me to do."

"You know if any of the local hit men take contracts on dogs?"

Jared chuckled mildly. "I could ask around."

She looked up at him in alarm, then glared when he laughed.

"Just how many stray dogs did you take in when you lived in that wretched little apartment by the university?" he reminded her. "Four in all, wasn't it?"

"Six. But none of them made off with the bulk of my father's estate."

He kept on laughing.

To dispel his mistaken notion that she lacked the determination to do whatever it took, she let him have it.

"I've asked Dan to dig into Nell Jordan's past, and present, and anywhere else he finds something to prove that the woman is a sleaze who took my father for a ride. I mean business, Jared. That woman is not going to get away with taking advantage of my father."

"If he turns up nothing, will you let it go?"

She hesitated.

"Natalie?" He gave her a look.

"If he turns up nothing, I'll let it go. Satisfied, Counselor?"

"Satisfied."

"If ever I decide to commit murder, remind me to hire you as my defense attorney. Sheesh!"

To make up for the scolding, Jared bought her an ice cream cone at the Black Cow. They sat on a bench outside, to enjoy the treat.

"Speaking of wretched places to live," Jared said, "are you planning on moving from your condo to Frank's house on the hill?"

She smiled. "The mausoleum?" So they had named it more than thirty years ago when they had been friends—and lovers.

"We have some memories in that house," he reminded her.

Before Natalie's father had retired, he had occupied the big house only during holidays. But he had given his daughter a key. Natalie and Jared had spent some good days, and better nights, in Frank Cramer's Southwestern palace.

She admitted to that with a nod. The memories were still vivid, even though she hadn't dragged them from the back of her mind for years. Her experience with William, her husband, had taught her that love is a pleasant fantasy that usually has an unpleasant ending, and she didn't care to wallow in her past delusions of romance.

Jared's next question proved that he also thought of old times. "Why did we break up, Natalie? Do you remember?"

"I moved to Phoenix to live with my mother and go to graduate school. You wanted to stay in Flagstaff with your fresh air and hiking trails and dreams of reinventing Arizona politics. I didn't want to spend my life in the sticks."

"Ah yes." He shook his head. "The dreams of youth. Ironic, isn't it, that I wound up in the big-city pollution and traffic shortly thereafter? I aimed to reform the world, but I guess the world ended up reforming me."

"We were so young." Natalie contemplated the remnant of her cone, wondering how her life would have gone if she had stayed with Jared, had never escaped to Phoenix, had never met and fallen in love with William. But she had. And mistake or not, those decisions had brought her the life she had now, which was a good life. Speculation never accomplished anything.

"We were young," Jared agreed. "We had things to do in life. Things to get out of the way. And here we both are—not back in Flagstaff, but close." He grinned. "Still in the sticks, full of fresh air and hiking trails. An hour from the pines and snow-capped peaks. I've decided that certain things are supposed to happen in a person's life. You might take detours now and then. You might think you're getting off on another road entirely, but you always end up back where you're supposed to be."

"How philosophical."

"It is, isn't it? Do you know that you're the first woman I ever slept with?"

That little tidbit took her aback. "You're kidding!"

"Why would I kid about such a thing?"

"You didn't seem like..." Her face heated a bit. "I mean... you seemed... very knowledgeable at the time." Oh, lord, could she sound any more lame?

"And I wanted to be the last man you slept with."

"Jared, don't. Please."

"Did William make you happy until he decided to take off?"

"No one needs to make me happy," she said firmly. "A person's happiness is their own responsibility."

"And are you making yourself happy now?"

"I'm very content, thank you."

He laughed a little. "Natalie, you have a lot of starch. I've always liked that about you."

The nerve of the man, intruding into her life once again just because her father had made him his attorney. Yet another trick played by the old man? He had always liked Jared.

But she was not going to stand for her old flame picking up where they had left off thirty-five years before, just because now he had an excuse to talk to her. Talk to her, eat lunch with her, take her on pleasant walks in the Sedona sunshine. But how did she extinguish the tiny part of her—okay, more than a tiny part—that wanted to stay there in the sunshine with him, eating ice cream, arguing about everything from philosophy to the past to her father to Nell Jordan? Jared Johansen made her feel alive. He always had.

"Oh pish! Look at the time!"

Her fifteen minutes had expired over an hour ago. She hoped that was the only resolution Jared Johansen made her break.

chapter 8

DAN SQUEEZED his Jeep into a tiny parking space a half-mile from the university and walked to the campus feeling lucky to find a space that close. Cars without a student or faculty sticker on the window rarely managed to park at NAU, and the narrow side streets surrounding the university were clogged as well.

He didn't mind walking so much, though he could do without the wet snow that turned the sidewalks and streets to slush. In Sedona, thirty minutes away and three thousand feet lower, flowers bloomed and duffers whacked golf balls in the warm sunny afternoon, but in Flagstaff, at the base of the snowy and wind-whipped San Francisco Peaks, Dan's breath made frost in the air as his feet slogged through Mother Nature's latest winter offering. Spring came late at an elevation of seven thousand feet.

Nell Jordan had endured four winters in this town, studying for a degree in journalism. So Dan's research told him. Unfortunately, digging through records at a remote computer terminal in the warm Verde Valley only gave him the bare-bones facts, not what her profs and acquaintances had thought of her. So being a thorough sort of guy, and knowing his mother would give him the third degree about his progress picking Nell apart, he had donned his heavy parka and made the trip up the mountain.

Ten minutes of slush-skiing put him on campus, a crazy-quilt combination of old red sandstone buildings and modern edifices built of glass and concrete. Finding the communications building, Dan thought, might take all day. He should have packed a lunch.

The thought reminded him of his own brown-bagging university days at UCLA, where he'd suffered through pre-law. Not that he had suffered that much. He had loved school, loved the challenge, the constant discovery, the endless demand to stretch the brain as an athlete might stretch a muscle. His grades had gotten him into law school with no problem, but that endeavor hadn't lasted long. He might have finished with honors if he hadn't been such a goddamned fool. But he had been a fool, had mistaken lust for love, beauty for character.

Okay, that characterization of his marriage was harsh, Dan admitted to himself. He had loved Cathy, and probably she had loved him. But love hadn't stood the test for long. The fact that she'd grown tired of marriage, tired of him, didn't mean Cathy didn't have character as well as spectacular looks. It just meant she had better things to do than stick around when their life together started to slip from her predetermined mold. Maybe Cathy was simply smarter than he was.

But he shouldn't be thinking about Cathy; he had driven up the mountain to learn more about Nell Jordan. The two women resided at opposite poles of the feminine spectrum. Cathy was drop-dead gorgeous—Nell was cute. Sexy. Charming at times. Funny. But not gorgeous. Cathy loved designer stuff—designer clothes, designer shoes, designer homes, designer cars, designer everything. If piss pots came in designer brands, she would want one of those, too. Nell lived in a beat-up trailer, wore T-shirts sporting slogans like CORGIS RULE!, and drove an old VW bug. That kind of ruled out any pretension at designer taste.

How could the man who had fallen head over heels for Cathy turn around and pant after the likes of Nell? It was a mystery. Monday, after driving her to pick up her silly little car, Dan had seduced her away from her work long enough to have lunch, where he had further slipped his way into her trust by being his charming, witty self. She had sat in the booth at McDonald's, laughing at his stupid jokes, falling for his stupid charm, and all the while those green eyes had warmed every smile, that strawberry-blonde hair had artlessly caught every ray of sunlight and scattered it into gold.

"You're very nice to take me to pick up Mel," she'd said, giving him one of her dynamite smiles.

He wasn't nice; he was sneaky and underhanded, wooing her for the purpose of flying beneath her radar and dropping a few bombs on her future. Her cheerful trust made him feel dingy.

"I've been thinking about your photography business," she continued.

"Uh . . . yeah?"

"I think all the Hearts of Gold animals should get together at your studio and you could do a group shot—for flyers and Christmas cards. Something formal with a backdrop. What do you think?"

Shit! "Uh . . ." You'd think a private eye would be able to think faster. "My studio. Well, sure. We'll set it up. But . . . right now my best camera is being serviced. It does the best portrait work."

The little frown that creased her brow told him that lying wasn't one of his talents. But she let it go. "We'll wait, then."

Sooner or later Nell was going to find him out, and then all hell would break loose. For reasons that had nothing to do with his lame investigation, Dan didn't like the prospect of her inevitable disillusionment.

But what the hell about *his* disillusionment when he got the real dope on her?

Damn, but he had gotten himself in way over his head. Every time he was with her, she freshened that fascination that made him indulge in extravagant dreams that woke him up nights, sweating and grinning. He'd last seen the woman on Monday, three days ago, and he still smiled whenever he thought of her, which was often.

The woman had to be the world's best actress. If Cathy had ended up in Frank Cramer's will, Dan would have readily believed that she had plotted and schemed for the old man's dough. But Nell, with her rattletrap bug, her fat, very un-designer dog, her leaky little trailer home—well, she had motive enough to go after a fortune, but did she have the balls? Nell Jordan's idea of lunch out was a booth at Mickey D's. Her notion of a hot date—a hike up West Fork with ham sandwiches by the creek. The woman seemed to have more fun being poor than most rich people had being rich.

Somewhere in that squeaky clean, cheerful image had to be a crack. He needed to concentrate on the woman who had run out and splurged a good chunk of his grandfather's money on an expensive leather jacket and boots, dancing the happy retail dance when Frank Cramer had barely warmed up his grave.

Dan Travis needed to remember he was an investigator. Yes indeed, Dan decided. He would focus on who Nell Jordan really was, and when he found her out, he would probably feel like knocking his own head against a brick wall for falling for all that bright, green-eyed charm.

He finally located the communications building with the help of the radio towers sprouting from the front lawn and roof. In the 1960s, the building might have been considered modern. In the twenty-first century it just looked worn down and old. Inside, yellow-beige walls and institutional green asbestos tile served as decor. On bulletin boards along the walls, ads for roommates, book sales, rooms for rent, and bicycles for sale mixed with flyers about a protest rally against the latest intervention in the Middle East, an ad for civil disobedience training, and a notice of a meeting of the Society of Environmental Communicators.

Not being the shy sort, Dan poked around until he found someone home in a faculty office.

"Hi there," he said, sticking his head into the rather musty cubicle. "Could I bother you for a few words?"

A slight, balding fellow sporting a poor excuse for a mustache, Assistant Professor Donald Eastwood looked up from his book and blinked at Dan. "What can I do for you?"

Dan pulled out his story about being a freelance journalist. Perhaps this was not the place to try to get away with that particular ruse, but hey, no guts, no glory.

"Nell Jordan?" Eastwood frowned.

"She graduated from NAU in journalism five years ago. So happens she's worked herself into the public interest by inheriting a rather large sum of money. Or rather—and this is the twist that makes it interesting—her dog inherited the money. Anyway, she's allowing me an exclusive on writing about her."

"Nell Jordan, eh?"

"Tallish. Short blonde hair. Good-looking. Laughs a lot."

"Oh, I remember Nell. I only had her in one class, I think. When she was a junior. Pete Revere could tell you more than I can. He was Nell's academic adviser. But I remember her, all right. Talented girl. Hard worker. Was a reporter on the university newspaper."

And off he went, talking about Nell. For having had the girl in only one class, Assistant Professor Eastwood seemed to know her quite well. Nell Jordan made an impression upon people.

Pete Revere, whom Dan cornered in the department secretary's office, knew her even better.

"Nell's still in this area? I'll be! That's a surprise. We all thought she was headed for the big time in the big city. As I remember it, she took a job in Chicago right after graduation."

Chicago. Ah yes, the site of the mystery ruckus. "Hear anything about her work in Chicago?"

"No. Lost touch with her after she graduated. I'm sure she did fine, though. She was a good student," her old adviser said. "Ambitious. Almost a perfectionist. She's in the money, now, eh? More power to her."

Eastwood and Revere were the only two profs in the department who had known Nell. In five years' time, half the faculty had gone their own way, to be replaced by others who hadn't known her. Two of the old-timers found her in their old records but didn't remember anything about her.

How did a man forget Nell Jordan? Dan wondered.

Dan's next errand in Flagstaff was bittersweet—lunch with his ex. She had promised to bring the kids, who were off from school for a teacher in-service day. That was the sweet part.

They met at Buster's, just south of the university campus. The four of them—his ex, the two kids, and their nanny, waited for him in their usual booth. Cathy still outshone every other woman in the room, but mere beauty paled beside the welcoming smiles of Marta and James. At eight and six, they were, in their father's opinion, the world's most precocious kids.

"Dad!" little James squealed. Almost everything he said was a squeal.

"Father." Two years her brother's senior, Marta was already a little drama queen. Probably she had a future in movies—or writing romance novels.

"How's my best kids?" Dan gave each a hearty squeeze.

Cathy and Jana, the children's nanny, merely got a smile. "Hi, Cathy."

"Dan."

"This is *our* weekend with you," Marta reminded him. "What are we going to do?"

"What do you want to do?"

"Go to Disneyland!" James let the whole restaurant know.

"Well, boy-o'-mine, that's a ways off. We don't live in California anymore, you know?"

James probably couldn't even remember when they had all lived together in L.A., because shortly after his birth, Cathy had taken him and his sister and moved to Arizona, leaving California, and her husband, behind.

"I want to go horseback riding," Marta said solemnly.

"That might be arranged." Dan had a buddy with horses. For a few beers, he might be persuaded.

"Dan," Cathy objected. "That's so dangerous."

"It's not dangerous. It's fun, eh, big guy?"

"Fun!" James agreed.

Cathy pursed her mouth in a way that made her look almost unattractive, if that was possible. "Jana," she said, "would you please take the kids outside to stretch their legs a bit? Dan and I have a few things to talk about."

"It's cold out there!" Marta objected.

"Then bundle up in your jacket, pumpkin." Cathy tweaked her daughter's nose. "You wanted to build a snowman, didn't you? There's a wonderful pile of snow behind the restaurant."

Dan watched them go, longing tugging at his heart. After leaving the police force, he had moved from California back to his native Arizona to be close to his kids. They were the most important things in his life. He still didn't get to see nearly enough of them.

"Are you sure that you trust that girl Jana?"

"Of course I do."

"You can't be too careful. Kids are a prime target these days, and you and Mike have quite a stash of money."

"Oh, get real, Dan. Jana is Mike's niece, and she doesn't have enough brains to concoct a scheme to kidnap the kids. She's too busy 'finding herself.'"

"It might not hurt to do a background check on her."

Cathy made a disgusted sound. "You're paranoid. That's what comes of dealing with scumbags for a living. You know what you ought to do, Dan? You ought to go back to law school. Then at least you'd get paid big bucks for dealing with scumbags."

Cathy had suffered a big disappointment in their marriage—or in him, to be more precise—when Dan had quit law school during the first year to take a job with the LAPD. She had thought he quit because he didn't want to put the effort into studying. The fact was that a new baby and the expenses of running a household had made staying in school an impossibility. But she had really wanted to be the wife of a lawyer, not the wife of a cop. Now she was the wife of a millionaire car dealer in Flagstaff.

She raised an artfully plucked brow. "I can see that suggestion went over like a lead balloon. You really ought to try to make something of yourself, you know. If not for yourself, then so your kids can be proud of you."

"Don't go there, Cathy. Not all of us are as hung up on status as you are. The kids should learn that any honest work is honorable."

Cathy rolled her eyes, but didn't persist. "Have it your way. You always did. But listen, that's water under the bridge. I'm glad you came by today. I was going to call you. Mike and I are going to England for a couple of weeks in May, after school is out. I was hoping you could take the kids while we're gone."

His day brightened. "Of course I'll take the kids."

"Good. That's settled, then. Oh, by the way, I was sorry to hear about your grandfather. I know you and he didn't get along all that well, but it's still hard—especially when he screwed your whole family out of big money."

"I didn't want any part of my grandfather's money," Dan said sharply.

"I know you didn't. I remember when he offered to finance your way through law school. You should have taken him up on it, you know. You'd be writing your own ticket now."

"My grandfather's largesse always had strings attached."

"Of course it did. He was a smart old fellow. But wow! Who would have guessed the old geezer would have it in him to take up with some hot honey at his age!"

A flash of resentment surprised Dan with its intensity.

"Nell Jordan isn't exactly the kind of woman you would describe as a 'hot honey.'"

Cathy's brows shot up. "Is that so?"

"Yeah."

"You actually know this woman?"

"Yeah," he admitted with a touch of belligerence.

Cathy's brows lifted higher.

Dan didn't really want to say anymore about it. Confessing to snooping around Nell's past felt sleazy. Ironic that he felt like defending her. He, after all, was supposed to be proving the woman was exactly what Cathy had labeled her.

Not only did he feel like defending Nell's reputation to his ex-wife, he felt a strong desire to make a run for his Jeep, point the front end southward, and drive until he ended up at Nell's house.

Sometimes, life just wasn't sane.

A VISIT with Piggy to the medical center usually lifted Nell's spirits. Making people smile made a day worthwhile, and not many patients or staff could resist a smile at the sight of Piggy waddling about the hospital. But today both

Piggy and Nell dragged home with long faces and low moods.

McKenna waited for them by the front door of the trailer as Nell pulled Mel into the little carport. Her presence scotched Nell's plans to change into sweats and watch the midday soaps while eating a whole bag of Cheetos. Bad moods affected her that way.

"About time you showed up," Mckenna scolded. "Did you forget we were supposed to go over the therapy network ideas?"

"I got delayed at the hospital." Nell lifted Piggy from Mel's backseat, set her on the ground, and took off the corgi's little therapy vest.

"Uh-oh. You're down in the mouth, aren't you? I hear it in your voice."

Nell shrugged.

"How can someone who just came into a huge sum of money be depressed?"

Nell grimaced. "Do you know that every day now my mailbox is stuffed full of pleas from charities, promos from brokerage firms, and even sob stories from people who want a handout? One of those local news stories printed my address, the jackasses."

Mckenna dismissed such things with a casual wave of the hand. "That's why you have a garbage can, sweetie."

"But those charities are all worthwhile! And so many people could use a hand up. How can you ignore things?"

"Nell, you can't save the whole world. You're putting this money to good use. If all those things keep you awake nights, either throw them in the garbage unopened or hire someone to screen your phone calls and mail."

"You can hire people for stuff like that?"

"When you have money, you can hire people for anything. Now, what else happened? It's not just the mail that has you in the dumps, is it?"

Nell avoided Mckenna's eyes as she opened the front door. "Mr. Zachary died."

Mckenna's face fell. "Oh. That sucks."

"You're right. That sucks."

Jane, Mckenna, and Nell had all visited Mr. Zachary, a stroke victim, in both the hospital and the nursing home. He had seemed to be doing well, but he had died unexpectedly the night before. Stephanie in Critical Care had told Nell on her visit to the unit that morning.

"You can't let it get to you, sweetie," Mckenna advised. Though she looked none too happy herself. "You give your heart to sick people, some of them are going to die on you."

Before Nell could answer, the phone rang.

"Nell?" said the voice on the line

"Dan!" Nell's mood shot upward. She had to remind herself not to sound too happy. The poor guy would think she was picking out china patterns.

"I'm in Flagstaff. It's snowing."

"Yes. It looks bad up there in the mountains."

"Yeah. Snow everywhere." A short silence. "Uh . . . and cold."

Nell smiled. She suspected, from the hemming and hawing, that Dan had called simply to call, because he wanted to talk to her. How sweet.

"It's really nice down here." If he wanted to talk about inane things just to be talking, she would oblige him.

"Uh . . . listen. Why don't I come by tonight and we could talk? For my story, you know. Or I could take you to dinner."

Nell was beginning to think "The Story" was a ruse to keep her company rather than anything she would ever see in print. She found the notion flattering.

"Or better still," he continued, "you could take me to dinner. After all, you're the one with all the money."

"That sounds like a plan."

"Great. And I didn't mean it about the money. My treat."

"No, you're right. I'll take you to dinner."

"Now you're embarrassing me. I don't go around letting women take me to dinner."

"This time you should."

"We'll discuss it."

Nell's smile grew broader. The macho image again. With most guys that sort of thing annoyed her. With Dan—well, Dan didn't annoy her.

"The hunk?" Mckenna asked when Nell hung up the phone.

"The very same. We're going to dinner tonight. Maybe we should go to a place in Sedona. I could afford Sedona now. What a thought! I could get used to having money."

"You came in with a frown dragging the ground, and now suddenly you're all aglow. I think I'll bring by a prenuptial contract and let you look it over."

"Get off! You're being silly."

"Oh?"

"We're just going to dinner."

"Uh-huh." Mckenna tapped a toe against the worn carpeting. "But, funny thing, sweetie. I see a look in your eye that I haven't seen before. Don't forget that you have to be careful now that you've actually got a bank account."

"You're beginning to sound like a broken record. What do you want me to do, swear off men forever?"

"What a thought! No. I just want you to cast your eyes upward to the guys in the same financial strata that you will soon enjoy."

Nell gave her an impish smile. "But I like this one."

"Piggy won't be pleased if you lose any of her money to a fast-talking, good-looking charmer. In fact . . ."

Piggy looked up at them with a worried corgi frown.

". . . she doesn't look too happy about this fellow of yours. Doesn't Jane say we should always trust a dog's intuition about people?"

Nell laughed. "Mckenna, Mckenna! And here you pretend to be Miss Cynical, Miss Pragmatic, Miss Get-Real-And-Get-

Over-It! Wasn't it you who once told me only sentimental fools ascribed human emotions to animals? And listen to you now."

Mckenna sniffed. "Piggy's different."

"That's for sure," Nell agreed. "Piggy is different."

Piggy's comment was a disdainful sniff as she turned and stalked toward the kitchen.

"SO, WHAT interesting things did you do with your ill-gotten gains today?" Dan asked Nell.

"Piggy's ill-gotten gains." Then she frowned. "What makes you call them ill-gotten?"

They had just parked the Jeep behind Oaxaca in the only parking space left—or so it seemed—in all of Sedona, and Dan had opened Nell's door before she could do the job herself, just like an old-fashioned gentleman.

"According to some, all riches are ill-gotten. Class envy and all that."

"Are you a socialist?" she asked with mock horror.

"Just a journalist trying to cover all aspects of an interesting story."

"Is that so?" She lifted a suspicious brow. "Have you written anything yet that I might like to read?"

"I . . . believe in gathering all the facts in a story before setting pen to paper."

"Or fingers to keyboard?"

"That, too."

"I think you have all the relevant facts."

"Hell, no. I need to know you much better. I'm a very thorough kind of guy."

"I'm not that interesting, Dan. What you see is pretty much what you get."

He took her arm as they walked down the steep walkway to the restaurant. "I think you're interesting. You caught my interest."

.

A typical date-progressing-toward-romance flirtation, but there was that thing in his tone, that little zing Nell couldn't quite place. Or perhaps she imagined it. She liked Dan Travis a lot. The night before, she had even dreamed about him, the kind of sensual, achy, sweat-right-through-the-sheets kind of dream she hadn't had for a long time.

But out-of-kilter details nagged at her mind. Evasiveness mixed with his charm to make him a confusing mystery. Not to mention that occasional little zing.

They got a table by one of Oaxaca's big view windows that looked out over the main thoroughfare and beyond, to imposing castles of sheer rock. A Budweiser appeared on the table in front of Dan as if by magic. Apparently the proprietors knew him well.

"Speaking of interesting heiresses," Dan said as they lit into the homemade chips and salsa, "I'm surprised the Princess Corgi didn't join us tonight." He grinned. "She seems to go everywhere else with you."

"That's because she doesn't behave when left to her own devices. She's spending the evening with my friend Jane—the one who trains dogs and owns a kennel. No dog gets away with anything while Jane is watching."

Dan chuckled. "Poor Piggy."

"It was either that or stay home in her dog crate. I can't help it that she's a troublemaker."

His grin twisted into a roguish slant. "That will look good in print. 'Heiress dog languishes behind kennel bars while guardian takes cash and steps out on the town.'"

She punched him playfully in the arm. "You wouldn't!"

"That's good, don't you think? I could work for a tabloid."

Nell caught her breath as her heart jumped. Was that an innocent remark, or could he have learned? No. She was oversensitive about that past stupidity. Her former employer, *The Chicago World News*, couldn't be classified as a tabloid, even though it wasn't exactly *The New York Times*.

She tried to keep her voice light. "I think maybe you should stick to photography."

He gave her a smile that could have stood in for a flash-bulb. "Too late, sweetheart. You already promised."

The "sweetheart" caught her by surprise, warming her insides more than the spicy salsa. "I guess I'll have to put up with you for a while, then. But don't you dare submit anything for print until I read it. I know how you journalists are—sensationalists, every one of you."

He lifted his beer in salute. "You ought to know."

She searched his expression, but didn't find anything there to support the sudden sink of her stomach. Get over it, she chided herself. Get over those doubts Mckenna had planted in her brain. The worst Dan Travis might have done—and even that was just speculation—was hand her a line to string her along on a few dates. *Get over it.*

After filling up on green chili enchiladas, they strolled down Sedona's main thoroughfare. Most of the shops had closed over an hour earlier, but they certainly weren't the only ones window-shopping. Tourists thronged the side-walks, enjoying the slightly nippy spring night and the lit displays in the shop windows.

"How does it feel, knowing you could buy almost anything you see here?" Dan asked Nell.

She looked away from a dazzling exhibit of turquoise set in gold. "Frankly, it spoils the window-shopping experience. There's a certain fun in futile longing."

He laughed. "I'm going to have to use that line. You've got to be the only woman I've ever met who isn't into power shopping."

"Yes, well, power shopping is much more of a challenge when you have to figure out where the money will come from. Not that I'm complaining. I totally enjoy the thought of all that money. It just takes some getting used to."

"Let me ask you a personal question," he said as they moved on to a pottery shop.

Her heart stepped up a pace. "How personal?"

"You seem to regard money as more of a hassle than a blessing. Why did you let Frank Cramer set all this up?"

That certainly wasn't the question she had hoped for. She stared at him in surprise. "You think I *knew* Frank planned to set up that fund for Piggy?"

"Hard to believe the old man would do it without asking."

"Ha! If you had known Frank Cramer, that wouldn't have surprised you."

That earned her a peculiar look.

"What?" she asked.

"Nothing," he replied hastily. "Nothing at all."

Nell decided that Dan Travis wasn't mysterious or dangerous; he was simply a bit peculiar.

SEEING NELL Jordan just a few hours after keeping company with his ex might have been a mistake, Dan admitted to himself. The contrast between the two women strengthened the impression that Nell was a breath of fresh air wafting from the world of women. If she acted a part, then she deserved an Academy Award. He couldn't break through her facade, not with charm, not with a frontal attack.

The whole situation made him angry. Her innocent act angered him. His failure to detect a flaw angered him. His mother's determination to believe the worst angered him. His grandfather's twisted sense of humor angered him. His own contentment to be walking the tourist beat in Sedona with Nell Jordan by his side angered him. The heat that fired inside him when she moved, spoke, smiled, frowned—that angered him.

She was a fake. She had to be. And he was a fool. Why hadn't he stayed with the safe life of an L.A. cop?

"Do you see that bronze sculpture over there?" She pointed to a piece of life-sized art in front of a plaza of shops. "It's my very favorite in the world. When I look at it, it just sort of makes me smile."

Damn her, it so happened that the sculpture was one of his favorites also. Caught in the rich patina of bronze, a little girl rode a rope swing close to the pool of a fountain, where her perfect, lifelike fingers reached out to brush the water. The work was full of movement, freedom, and a wild, joyful innocence that most people left behind with their childhood. Like Nell, Dan smiled whenever he looked at it.

Except Nell could have bought the thing if she'd wanted—with his grandfather's money.

"I think we should head back to the Jeep," he said in stilted tones.

"Oh?"

She was baffled. He tried not to care.

"It . . . well, it's almost nine."

"Of course. You're right."

When they reached the ill-lit restaurant parking lot, his control dissolved. Temptation beckoned, and the edge of his anger prodded him to take up the challenge. Nell uttered a surprised little cry when he pulled her toward him and clamped both hands on her shoulders. He lowered his mouth toward hers, but then waited a bit, half-hoping she would cry out an objection that would bring him to his senses.

She didn't. Instead, after her initial surprise, she melted into him, turning her face upward in unreserved invitation. What man could resist?

His mouth came down upon hers in a hard seeking, and when she didn't pull away, he deepened the kiss to intemperate passion. Passion or possession, one and the same. Her heart pounded against his chest through the sweet swell of her breasts. He could almost feel the rush of blood in her veins—warming quickly under the searing heat of his building desire.

He threaded fingers through her soft, short curls. Everything about her was soft. Hair of silk. Skin of warm velvet. The scent of roses and baby powder. Baby powder. Oh, God! Dan nearly lost himself.

Finally they parted, breathing hard, his hands still cradling her head, her arms still wrapped around his waist. Seconds of silence passed as they slowly drew apart.

"What are you angry about?" Nell asked shakily.

"What?" he croaked.

"You kissed me as if you were angry."

He could have spit. "I kissed you because you're damned near irresistible."

Her eyes opened wide in surprise. "I am?"

No. No. Don't go there, Dan warned himself, but he could feel his insides warming. "You are," he breathed. "And don't get that fuzzy look on your face, woman. Someone like you, someone with money, has to be careful about getting involved with charming fellows like me."

She seemed to recover a bit, drew herself up straighter, and gave him a wry smile. "You're a charmer, all right, Dan Travis. But if you were after Piggy's money, I doubt you would give me fair warning. Villains rarely play by the rules."

Did she know that because she was a villain herself? He didn't want to think about that right now.

"You would be surprised at how sneaky some people can be. Don't let yourself be fooled by a kiss."

He softened the comment with a smile, and at the same time told himself he should heed his own warning. He really should.

chapter 9

ON HIS way into his office, Dan stopped to scratch the old hound sprawled on the porch. He wondered if BJ was in yet. Dan's assistant sometimes strolled over to the Hair Affaire to hit up Helga and her girls for a manicure. The fact that BJ was a man added even more color to the place. Cheerfully gay in a very redneck community, he loved to chat with the ladies when Dan didn't have enough work to keep him busy, which was most of the time.

This being a Monday, however, BJ had more than enough to keep him busy. Every other Monday at Travis, Inc. was bill day. Bills to be sent. Bills to be paid. Somehow, the amount owed always more than wiped out the amount coming in, partly because P.I.s seemed to be lowest on everyone's payment priority list, somewhere below divorce attorneys and the charities that send address labels designed to guilt people into writing them checks.

When Dan stomped into the office, he brought with him a truly Monday mood. He hated bill Monday, hated signing all those checks, hated getting back to the grind of a job he didn't really like. This Monday was worse than some because he'd spent his nights since Thursday thinking about Nell Jordan instead of sleeping. He felt like knocking his head against the wall for kissing her. What a stupid thing to do. Stupid, stupid, stupid. What had gotten into him? Was he some thirteen-year-old with runaway hormones? Didn't he think things were complicated enough without him mixing a little passion into the situation?

So he hadn't slept. He had forbidden himself to call Nell, which didn't improve his mood one bit. And now it was bill-paying Monday.

"Good morning!" BJ called cheerfully as Dan blew through his assistant's little office. "Checks are on your desk."

"Thanks loads," Dan snapped.

"Well look who got up with a case of the grumps this morning."

"Don't push it, BJ."

"I'm shivering in my boots," the assistant assured him airily. "And by the way, there's a message on your desk, Grumpy. From a woman named Nell. Very nice voice. Young, I'd guess. Pretty. Nice smile. Cheerful little person."

"She's not little," Dan grumbled. "And how the hell can you tell so much from a voice, anyway?"

"I'm very intuitive."

"Then intuit your way into finishing that report for Mr. Briggs on what his daughter's been up to, and then call the paper and update our ads. Next month's bills are looming, and clients aren't exactly lining up at the door."

"Oh my! We are grumbly."

Dan merely growled and shut his office door behind him.

Yes, indeed, there on his desk sat a message from Nell Jordan. Of course she would call. Coyness wouldn't be her style. He'd wined her, dined her, kissed her, and then nothing. She would want to know why.

He would have to lie, of course. He couldn't tell her that she heated his dreams to the point of conflagration, or that he felt guilty for his deception, or that he struggled against liking her. More than liking her. He couldn't tell her that he feared doing his job, because sooner or later, some piece of sleaze, of reality, would show up to tarnish the image of Nell Jordan that shone in his mind in spite of his best efforts at cynicism. If he didn't watch out, the woman would have him believing in love and romance and all that crap.

You got yourself into this, Dan told himself. *So grit your teeth and carry on. You stupid ass.*

He picked up the phone and called. When she answered, he took a deep breath.

"Hi there. It's Dan."

"Oh. Hi."

She sounded uncertain, and why wouldn't she? He had practically sucked her lungs out through her mouth and then had done a silent act all the way back to Cottonwood.

"Hey listen. I...I meant to call this weekend..." Here came the lies. "But I got swamped...." in feeling sorry for himself.

"That's all right. I was very busy myself. Mckenna had me talking to investment brokers all Friday. And this weekend we gave a demo up at Flagstaff to some of the hospital staff—how to utilize therapy animals to motivate physical therapy patients."

"Oh. Interesting. Though Piggy looks like she could use a bit of physical therapy herself."

"I'll tell her you said that, cruel man." A hesitation, then, "How are you coming on my story?"

"Your story? Oh. The Story. Yes. Fine. Never better. It's pretty much writing itself. But of course, it's not nearly finished. I want to put in the whole experience."

"How whole?"

"Well, whole. You know."

"Until the happily ever after."

"You got it." Dan just wished.

"Well then, you're in luck, because that's why I called. I

did promise you could tag along just about everywhere. Mckenna and Jane are dragging me house-hunting on Thursday."

"Excellent." Didn't take her long to get used to spending.

"So if you want to tag along, you're welcome."

At least if her two imposing duennas were along, he wouldn't be tempted to toss Nell on her back. "What time?"

"About two, I think."

"Great. I'll take you out afterwards."

"Well . . ." Then she chuckled, and the sound had just a tinge of ominous. "Okay. But let me take you out. I'll treat you to a surprise."

"A surprise?" His eyes narrowed.

"You do want to know your subject, right? In the best journalistic traditions?"

"Uh . . . sure."

"Then I'll see you Thursday."

And that was that. He looked up to see BJ lounging in the door between their offices, openly eavesdropping.

"Another hot date, is it? You have really become the stud about town."

"BJ," Dan warned. "I'm not in the mood."

The younger man chuckled. "Isn't that supposed to be her line?"

"Don't you have a class to go to up at NAU?"

"Not today. Today I'm all yours."

"Wonderful."

Uninvited, BJ took a seat on the metal folding chair that served as Dan's office furniture. "I must say, Dan, that you're very lucky to have me around as watchdog, because you have a tendency to get so involved with what you're doing that you lose all objectivity."

"Watchdog?" Dan hooted. "I need a watchdog, you think?"

"Don't thank me. You know I'm always happy to be of help."

Dan sighed.

"To the point, though, I really think you need to give some thought to the ethics of your relationship with Nell Jordan." He fended off Dan's predictable outburst with an upraised hand. "Now mind your temper, Dan. It was you who told me that getting personally involved with an investigative subject is a no-no."

Dan had half a mind to show his assistant a real "no-no" and physically toss his skinny butt into the next office with orders to mind his own business. But he restrained himself. He liked BJ—usually. When Dan had first hung up the Travis, Inc. sign on his door, BJ had come to him and offered to work cheap. A part-time student at NAU and a wanna-be writer of mystery novels, he had wanted to learn the ins and outs of real investigative work. Actually, the kid had employed more colorful terms. Something like prowling through the back alleys of investigation. BJ should shift his ambitions to journalism, Dan decided. He never ran out of words, and he specialized in butting into other people's lives.

But Dan liked him. He was a good kid. Different, but good.

"Listen, BJ. Rather than launching you out of my office as you deserve, I'm going to explain."

"It's good that we can have a conversation about this."

"No conversation. I am going to explain to *you*. Nell Jordan is the subject of a—let's call it a background investigation."

"So I've gathered."

"And it's true I am personally involved, because it's sort of a family thing."

"Difficult, to be sure."

"A man of my experience is capable of being objective in these circumstances." Which was a total load of crap. "If she took advantage of an old man in order to weasel him out of a fortune, then she deserves whatever she gets."

"That's objective?"

"Shut up and let me finish. On the other hand, if she didn't, then my prowling into her past and her character will prove her innocent. Which is a good thing for her, isn't it? Hell, she should be paying me."

"A novel viewpoint. You know, Dan, someday I should base a character on you. I really should."

Dan didn't know whether to preen or frown.

"But does prowling around her past and her character including romancing the poor girl?"

The frown won. "I'm not romancing her."

BJ grinned. "I saw the credit card receipt for Oaxaca. And did that include a moonlight stroll down the lane?"

"The main street of Sedona is hardly a romantic lane," Dan growled.

BJ tsked. "Dan, my man, what are we going to do with you?"

"Dammit, BJ, just shut up. I'm conducting an investigation here. And in this case I need to get to know the subject. She thinks I'm doing some sort of newspaper or magazine story on her."

"Oh that's clever, since you can't write your way out of a paper bag. Marvelous!"

The idea bulb lit up in Dan's brain. He grinned wickedly. "Good point, BJ. But a good investigator always finds a way out of a corner. I can't write, but I know someone who can."

It was BJ's turn to frown.

"I'll give you my notes, and you write something that will impress the lady. Something journalistic and intelligent." He smiled serenely. "Get cracking, kid."

SEVEN DAYS had passed, but Nell still stood in the parking lot of the Oaxaca restaurant in Sedona. At least her mind did, still riveted there by Dan's kiss.

You would think, Nell chided herself, that something as simple as a kiss wouldn't dominate the mind of a mature and experienced woman such as herself. In these days, when people seemed to jump into bed with each other at the blink of an eye, a kiss was nothing. Well, almost nothing. Very minor. Nearly inconsequential. Close to meaningless. A kiss certainly had no right to dominate her dreams at night and seduce her into wandering the byways of imagination during the day.

Only two things poked holes in Nell's reasoned approach to getting that kiss off her mind. She couldn't really boast about her maturity and experience, because her heart still operated on a junior-high level. And The Kiss—by now it had earned capital letters—had been delivered in a manner far from simple. No mistake about it. Dan Travis really knew how to kiss, how to send a lightning bolt of heat straight to a woman's most vulnerable parts. Even now, seven days later, Nell sighed at the vivid memory. Her heart still beat faster. Her blood was still heated. Her mouth still tingled. Her insides still turned to mush. The Kiss had been everything a kiss was supposed to be.

Or maybe The Kiss possessed no more pizzazz than any ordinary kiss. Maybe the man who had delivered it made it special.

"Don't go there," Nell told herself out loud.

Piggy gave her a quelling look from where the corgi sat beside her on the front stoop of their trailer house.

"Okay," Nell conceded. "I'm talking to myself. You would, too, if you'd ever been kissed like that."

The corgi made a noise that would have qualified as sheer contempt if she'd been human. Nell interpreted it as indigestion. Piggy had managed to get into a box of Cheerios that morning. Fortunately, the box had been only a third full.

"The problem is," she explained to Piggy, "he's divorced. With kids. Probably burned out on relationships and marriage. He's footloose and fancy-free, probably doesn't want to be tied down. And I'm getting to the point where I'd like to be tied down." She made a face and scratched her chin thoughtfully. "Not to mention that a couple of things about that man don't quite add up. Usually I'm not the suspicious type, but well, maybe I ought to be the suspicious type."

Piggy growled.

"So why did I ask him on this house-hunt today? I did promise him the story, you know. And I am a sucker for those steely gray eyes and that mysterious half-smile of his."

Piggy huffed in a way that was anything but sympathetic. "Do *you* think he's the type of man who would be tempted by our money?"

An insistent bark said the corgi felt strongly about that one, but strongly which way, Nell couldn't interpret.

"I just can't think he is. He's too independent. Besides, if he wanted to court the money, he could be doing a better job of it, don't you think? After all, I had to call him about this little house-hunting jaunt. For all I know, he would have left me with The Kiss and never called again."

The Kiss again. Nell grimaced. She really had to grow up one of these days.

The sound of Dan's Jeep coming up the street quashed any further speculation.

They met Jane and Mckenna at the real estate office. Mckenna, always the organizer, had taken upon herself the task of selecting an agent and explaining the requirements of the house search. Nell didn't mind. She liked the idea of new digs for herself and Piggy, but would much rather spend her time working up a marketing plan for their expanded Hearts of Gold program than deal with the details of a house-hunt. Mckenna, on the other hand, possessed the acquisitory nature that reveled in that sort of thing.

"Hello, hello!" Sheila, the lucky real estate agent who had won Mckenna's approval, greeted them in the lobby area of Valley Properties. She accepted Piggy's presence with admirable composure. "So this is the little canine heiress! Aren't you the lucky dog!"

Piggy seemed unimpressed by her gushing. But then, Piggy wasn't impressed by much in life.

"And you must be Nell," Sheila continued with a broad smile, which got broader when she turned to Dan. "And? . . ." she prompted.

"This is Dan," Nell supplied. "He's a . . . a friend."

"The more the merrier!"

Mckenna introduced herself with a businesslike handshake, and likewise identified Jane as the resident expert on canine comfort. But not more expert than Piggy herself, who jumped onto the lobby couch to peruse photographs of properties for sale. A corgi grin split her face as she enjoyed the display.

"Oh my!" Sheila gingerly patted Piggy's head. "You'd think she understood all this, wouldn't you?"

Jane chuckled. "Don't sell that little girl short. She's as smart as they come."

"Notice," Mckenna pointed out, "that she's sticking pretty much to houses priced above three hundred thousand."

Sheila totally approved. "Obviously a pooch with excellent taste. Well, here we go. Come along. I believe we can all fit into my minivan, dog included."

In the parking lot, the agent walked along with Dan, chatting about rising property prices. Following behind with Nell and Piggy, Mckenna and Jane eyed Dan dubiously.

"You don't need to look at him like that," Nell chided in a whisper.

"We're just looking out for your interests," Mckenna assured her.

"He seems very persistent," Jane noted. Then she smiled. "I rather like that in a man."

"I do, too," Nell agreed. "And I'm especially beginning to like this man, so both of you behave today."

"Behave?" Mckenna sounded shocked.

"Us?" Jane chortled.

"You're expecting a lot."

As they drove off toward the first prospective house, Mckenna blithely ignored Nell's plea. "Hold on to your hat, Dan. You know there's nothing more dangerous than a group of women out shopping—no matter what they're shopping for. Everything Nell latches onto needs to be perfect, as far as we're concerned."

"You mean the house," Dan said.

"Of course the house." Nell glared at her friends.

His wry smile showed he knew very well what Mckenna meant.

The first house the agent showed sat on two acres outside Sedona. Red Rock State Park was only a stone's throw up the road, and every direction boasted views of crimson cathedrals and spires. Downslope from the house, a line of cottonwood trees marked the path of Oak Creek.

"Beautiful!" Mckenna exclaimed.

"Wow!" was Jane's reaction.

Nell prowled through the three thousand square feet of exquisitely decorated tile and stone, trying to imagine living in such magnificence. The master bedroom boasted huge windows that swept the eye toward breathtaking views. The master bath came complete with a Jacuzzi and a tile walk-in shower big enough to play soccer in. And the kitchen—oh the kitchen! If one lived in this house, cooking would be a necessity. Gourmet cooking. A person could probably be sent up for life for letting such a kitchen go to waste.

"Piggy seems to like the kitchen," Sheila commented cheerfully. The corgi's nose investigated every corner and available surface, her nails tap-tapping on the tile floor as she made the rounds from counter to counter.

"Crumb hunting," Jane told her. "She never misses an opportunity. You'd want to put in a dog door and fence in a grassed area beyond the patio," she suggested to Nell.

"Small change," Mckenna commented.

Nell felt Dan's eyes follow her as she prowled the place. "What do you think?" she asked him.

"It's really something, and I guess you can afford it, eh?"

"Affording something doesn't mean you have to buy it."

He lifted one brow. "Now there's a novel concept."

They drove on to the next house, a three-year-old ranch-style house on a hill overlooking the Verde River in Camp Verde. The attached three-car garage was big enough to hold one of Jane's obedience classes. A tiered back patio looked out over the river, the mountains, and the other homes that occupied one of the choicest neighborhoods in town.

"The place next door has sheep," Jane noted. "Cool!"

"Plenty of room for Piggy to run off that extra weight," Mckenna said.

"You absolutely must see the master bedroom," Sheila told Nell. "The walk-in closet has the space every woman wants. And it has its very own fireplace!"

"The closet has a fireplace?" Dan asked wryly.

Sheila sighed. "You're a kidder, aren't you."

She took both Nell and Dan by the arm and pulled them into the master bedroom, as if assuming they would be using it together. "Isn't this just the thing?"

The room was big and light. A set of French doors opened to a private little courtyard where plum and pear trees flowered in perfumed extravagance. A fireplace set into one wall burned either gas or wood, and a large arched opening led into a big dressing area. In the middle of all this splendor sat a king-sized bed with a lush red satin-looking quilt.

The images that leaped into Nell's head made her face heat to the color of the quilt.

Piggy saved the day, however, by springing onto the bed and curling into a little brown ball in the geographic center of all that softness.

"Piggy!" Nell scolded. "Get off!"

"That's quite all right," Sheila assured her. "The owners have long since moved. They just left the furniture for show, and it's available with the house for a very fair price." She chuckled with satisfaction. "She seems to have made herself right at home, hasn't she? The courtyard through the French doors is completely fenced with a four-foot adobe wall to keep the little dog safe, and the rest of the acreage you could keep free of dog damage, if you know what I mean. The landscaping is gorgeous, and the patio is a perfect setup for entertaining."

Nell made appropriate sounds of appreciation, still thinking about that huge bed.

Sheila smiled like a fairy godmother who has just waved her magic wand. "I'll just leave you two alone to prowl around."

Dan sat down on the bed and bounced. "Nice," he concluded, and patted the bed beside him. Before Nell could take him up on the invitation, however, Piggy came in from behind, putting paws to his shoulder blades and a very cold nose to the back of his neck. He sprang up with a "Yikes!"

"Piggy!" Nell chided.

Dan laughed. "I guess she thinks it's her bed."

"Really! She's usually not so rude. You know better, you little snot!"

The corgi sent a triumphant woof Dan's way and stalked back to the center of the bed.

Then Jane poked her head through the doorway. "You've got to see the backyard, Nell! Someone spent a fortune making this a showplace."

Nell followed her out, leaving the bedroom behind. Just as well.

They looked at three more houses. Modern and beautifully decorated, they could have popped from the pages of *House and Garden* magazine. Gourmet kitchens, Jacuzzi bathrooms, walk-in closets the size of Nell's current bedroom all fuzzed together in her mind. Nothing sparked inside her, though. Dan walked through every home with her and watched her examine the luxuries offered, listened to Mckenna's exclamations at the quality, and Jane's outright awe. He watched but seldom offered a comment. He watched to the point that Nell felt him watch, and about midway through the afternoon the watching began to weigh on her mind. She felt as if he waited for her reactions, testing her in some way.

"Shouldn't you be taking notes or something?" she asked as they looked at the kitchen in the fourth house. "For your story?"

A hint of expression flashed across his features. Guilt? Chagrin? But in a mere second the hint was gone and a lethal smile took its place. He tapped his head. "Up here. Maybe I'll subtitle this part of the story 'From cave to castle.'"

"My trailer house is not a cave." She sighed and leaned against the granite-topped kitchen island that held a huge porcelain sink and a top-of-the-line dishwasher. "But these certainly are castles. Do you suppose a person could ever get used to living like this?"

"I think expectations, like spending, expand with income. Places like these are the American dream. You set your sights on having money, and this is one of the things you get with it."

"I don't remember ever consciously setting my sights on having money."

He gave her a puzzled frown. "You know, I'm beginning to believe you."

"Why on earth wouldn't you believe me?" Nell asked, baffled.

"Everyone wants money, and most people will go to great lengths to get it."

"Meaning people will lie, cheat, steal, and scheme?"

"A lot of them will."

"You're a cynic, aren't you?"

"Maybe I am. It's hard to work as a cop and maintain much faith in human nature."

"Are you like that, then? Would you go to great lengths to get money? Lie, cheat, scheme, or whatever?"

Again a hint of uneasiness flickered in his eyes. "Money isn't much of a motivator for me. Other things, well—" He shrugged and grinned a hand-in-the-cookie-jar grin. The atmosphere seemed much lighter, as if he'd shrugged a weight off his shoulders. "Maybe."

"Other things besides money? What other things?" she said, teasing.

"That's for me to know and you to find out."

"You're no more grown-up than I am, you know that?"

Just then Jane came around the corner into the kitchen. Her kinky red hair drooped from the confines of her pony-tail, and the set of her mouth hinted that the parade of homes had lost its charm. "Are you going to buy this place?"

"Nope," Nell answered.

"Well then," she said with a sigh, "let's move on to the next one."

By the time they finished with the seventh house of the afternoon, Sheila the Realtor had lost her perky cheerfulness. In truth, the poor woman was slipping into a state of frazzled frustration.

"I always say"—she attempted a brave smile—"that I prefer to work with choosy buyers, because once they find something that suits, they're so much happier than the buyer who simply settles."

"Like marriage," Jane said.

Sheila tittered. "Of course."

"You've driven everyone to a case of punch-drunk," Dan told Nell.

"House-drunk," Mckenna added.

Nell defended herself. "I'm just looking for something that looks like home."

"Of course, dear," Sheila said. "But we've nearly run out of houses." She consulted her list and pursed her lips. "All right. There is one more I could show you."

Sheila apologized for the "one more" on her list. "It's just come on the market, and the sellers can't be out until the last part of May. The house isn't quite up to the standard of the others we've seen, but the situation is lovely, don't you think?"

Nell got out of the minivan and fell in love at once. A circa 1970s stucco home sat on a fenced, irrigated acre in Cottonwood's Verde River greenbelt. A wealth of trees sprouted new spring green and a hedge of roses showed the results of someone's loving, careful tending.

"This is wonderful!" she exclaimed. "Look! A wraparound covered porch. I've always wanted a porch swing where I could sit and drink iced tea in the summer."

Compared to the other homes they had seen, this one was small. But someone had remodeled with an eye to efficiency and good taste. The master bedroom was light and airy, with glass doors opening into the huge, grassy backyard. The kitchen had updated appliances, tons of cupboard space, and a walk-in pantry. A pellet stove in the corner of the living room would keep the place warm and cozy on chilly January days.

"I really like it," she told Dan as they surveyed the place from the vantage of the backyard. "What do you think?"

"I think it's a fine house, but not exactly the sort of place a rich woman dreams of."

She laughed. "How would you know? Have you ever been a rich woman?"

"You got me there."

"A two-story detached garage with a guest room upstairs," she noted. "Classic."

"You could give Piggy the garage room. Keep her out of your hair."

"I don't think that would make her too happy."

"She doesn't look too happy anyway."

It was true. Piggy had trundled through the house with a sour look on her face. Now she sat in the middle of the big backyard staring at them.

"Piggy certainly doesn't seem smitten with me," Dan ventured.

"She's just tired."

"No, I really don't think she likes me. Wouldn't you think she would be grateful to the hero who pulled her furry little butt out of a car wreck?"

Nell slipped her arm through his. "I'm grateful. Does that count?"

His smile seemed more relaxed than before as he folded her hand in his. "I'll let you make up for the rude dog."

"All right, you two!" Mckenna called from the back door. "Cut the PDA and get with the program. Sheila found us another house to look at."

Nell suddenly felt very lighthearted. She hadn't been admonished for a public display of affection since high school. "No more house-hunting. I'm buying this one."

Mckenna marched out the door with Jane not far behind her. "You what?"

"I'd like to buy this one."

"You could have a mansion, and you want to buy *this*?"

"It's homey."

"A mansion could be homey," Mckenna declared.

Nell got distracted by a squeeze of Dan's hand, that big, warm hand that enveloped hers. Strange that something so simple could make her feel light-headed.

"The place does need some work," Jane told her.

"I'll hire someone."

"But you can afford to buy a house that doesn't need work," Mckenna reminded her.

"With more room," Jane said.

"A real Taj Mahal," Dan joined with a grin. But he didn't release her hand.

Nell snorted happily. "What do you all know? Mckenna, you live in a slick condo that only sees you when you're sleeping. Jane, you live in a kennel, for pity's sake. And Dan here lives in a motor home. None of you knows twaddle about real homes."

"All that money is making her think she can run her own life," Jane noted with a smile.

Nell laughed. "Piggy and I will get the place entirely spiffed up. You'll see."

As if summoned, Piggy appeared, wedging herself between Nell and Dan with an energy she seldom displayed. They moved apart to accommodate her.

"I told you that dog doesn't like me," Dan said with a chuckle.

Nell's heart warmed, though, because in spite of the fat little wedge between them, not to mention a needlelike glare from corgi eyes and more subtle but equally pointed looks from her friends, Dan still held on to her hand.

Life was good.

chapter 10

DO YOU believe that Nell passed up hot tubs, gourmet kitchens, native stone fireplaces, and built-in stereo systems for that dump?

Okay, okay, the house isn't really a dump. But a cute little stucco bungalow with a quaint wraparound porch is not my idea of where an heiress should live. An heiress should live in elegance. Big, roomy elegance with cushy carpets and a gourmet chef to go with a gourmet kitchen.

This house—sheesh! Elegant? No. Roomy? Well, it beats Nell's trailer, but it's not exactly palatial. And across the street a whole herd of smelly ugly cows did their best to perfume the whole neighborhood. I know the corgi's original purpose in life was to herd cattle, and I'll admit that some buried instinct perked up its ears at the sight of Bossy and her crew. But now that I had money, I was more determined than ever to leave those dog things behind.

Don't you think that I should have been consulted about what kind of house I wanted? Indeed, I should have had more say in the matter than anyone else, seeing that my money— MY MONEY—bought the place. It's very sad—don't you *think?*—that the winner in life's financial lottery couldn't even apply for a credit card. Not only that, but I had to sit there mute while others decided what to do with my fortune. I wanted to demand a luxury home, soft dog beds (note the plural!), crunchy dog cookies, and perhaps a hot, sexy car, or at least a car that has more comfortable accommodations for the dog passenger.

And speaking of hot and sexy, it was past time for Nell to give the studmuffin the old heave-ho. The man tagged along on our house-hunt just as if he belonged. Okay, Nell invited him, so I can't really blame the guy for taking advantage of the come hither. But it looked as if Studly Dan intended a serious effort with Nell, and not incidentally, my money. My efforts so far to nix the romance obviously hadn't worked. The guy couldn't take a polite hint. Too bad, because impolite displays of disapproval have rather harsh consequences. Biting dogs are frowned upon by the local authorities, both down here and in Stanley's realm. And somehow I thought that with Dan Travis, even biting might not drive him away.

No worries, though. I had a Plan B that didn't include biting. Or at least I would as soon as inspiration hit me.

That evening cemented the need to come up with a match-breaking plan fast. Like, yesterday. Dan had wanted to step out on the town that night, if you recall, and Nell had countered the offer with the promise of a surprise. Some surprise. For most guys, that would have been the end. Totally the end. My problem solved. But the studmuffin showed his colors as a very determined trooper in going after my money. He didn't run. He didn't so much as grimace, which shows how savvy he had become in knowing what would warm Nell's heart. Sneaky, clever man. He had the guts to act cheerful when, after a quick burger at McDonald's, Nell dragged him off to obedience school.

Obedience training has never been my favorite pastime. Every method of behavior modification and operant conditioning has been tried on me, ad nauseam, by experts far more determined than Nell Jordan and her friends, though Jane had a steely-eyed competence that told me no dog should mess with her. Jane and her suck-up border collie Idaho regularly walk away from obedience and herding trials with top honors. Such overachievement is an obsession I don't understand, but then, border collies are that way. And Jane is a kissing cousin to a border collie, if you ask me. Nell, fortunately, accepted that I was above such things as obedience. After all, I was a corgi. While many corgis pretend to obey, they all have an agenda. Even corgis who were actually born corgis are not ordinary dogs. We are highly evolved little creatures who can think for ourselves.

Since Nell wisely contented herself with a minimum of obedience on my part, when I attended obedience class, I watched from a superior position atop one of the spectator seats. Actually, I gloated, because I didn't have to practice those silly little exercises like "sit," "down," "stay," "come," "fetch," and all that nonsense.

Anyway, Nell regularly assisted Jane in teaching at the kennel, so on the evening after Nell found her "dream house" (insert a sarcastic sneer, please), she dragged Dan to watch the very first session of Jane's new beginner class. I almost felt sorry for the man. Not quite, but almost.

Men, as a rule, do not take their dogs to obedience class, though they might if they realized how many single women drag their pooches through such silliness. Actually, the world might be a better place if someone came up with an obedience class strictly for men. For the men themselves, not their dogs. All of the techniques trainers use on those poor unsuspecting dogs can just as effectively be used on boyfriends and husbands, you know. And they are, I'm sure. All the top obedience competitors in the sport—most of whom are women—you don't see their husbands and or boyfriends giving them any grief, do you? They travel around to shows and competitions, leaving the menfolk behind, and the menfolk just wag their tails while eating leftovers and microwave dinners without complaint. I wish that I had discovered obedience training when I was active on the dating scene. Of course, I never had much trouble getting men to do my bidding. They didn't necessarily behave, you understand. But they misbehaved in a way I liked.

Anyway, sitting there watching class, I envisioned some training techniques I might use on Dan Travis. Most of them involved chains and shock collars. But right then, I had to be satisfied with sitting on my chair sending negative vibrations into his skull. Such things supposedly work for the New Age gurus in Sedona, so I hoped it might work for me.

I didn't appreciate my concentration being broken by Nell, who wanted to use me to demonstrate teaching the "sit." I really wasn't in the mood.

"Come on, Piggy," she cajoled uselessly. "Let's look alive."

She could look alive. I had other things to do.

There was no help for it, though, so I followed her into the middle of a ring of wide-eyed beginning trainers and their dopey dogs.

"What'd you do?" one moron asked. "Cut off the legs at the knee?"

"She's so cute," an elderly lady gushed. She probably would have pinched my cheeks had she been close enough.

"What is that? A wiener dog mix?"

Patiently, Jane shushed the students and explained the steps of teaching the "sit." A treat appeared in Nell's hand, waved temptingly in front of my nose, then traveled up and back over my head. The theory, I knew, said that I would lift my nose to follow the treat, and my butt would just naturally plunk down upon the ground in a sit. I knew the routine, but as I said before, I just wasn't in the mood. So instead of letting my tushy drop, I sprang off the ground with my short front legs and grabbed the treat from Nell's hand.

"That," Jane said as I swallowed the tidbit of tuna-garlic flavored cookie, "is the 'how not to train' exercise."

I gave Nell a corgi smile. From the cheap seats, Dan guffawed and Mckenna—who comes to these sessions but doesn't *even pretend to know how to train a dog—laughed. Nell was not pleased, I could tell.*

"Titi is more trainable than Piggy," Mckenna chortled. Her silly cat Titi had passed her therapy cat test only because she doesn't have enough ambition to do anything but lie around like an inanimate bag of fur.

"Try again?" Jane suggested with a sigh.

This time I cooperated. It was the only way I would be allowed back on my chair. As I executed a perfect sit, I couldn't help sending a superior glance toward Titi, who vegetated in Mckenna's lap.

Cats, you know, are virtually untrainable, which, though this hurts to admit, shows that they have one up on dogs. Fortunately, the slinky creatures understand English better than most of the kids in the public school system, so they know everything that goes on around them. They just don't let on. Sneaky creatures, cats.

As I jumped up once again on my chair, Dan gave me a wary glance, then turned his attention back to watching Nell with curious intensity.

Cats are not the only sneaky creatures in this story.

GOOSE BUMPS prickled Dan's bare arms from the chill evening air, but his heart basked in warmth. Ridiculous, really—a wary ex-cop, tough private eye, and all-around cynic turning to mush just because of a woman.

But there it was. He had watched Nell all day as they went from house to house and trudged through enough architectural luxury to make Frank Lloyd Wright blush. She had tried to act interested for the sake of her friends and the very patient real estate agent, but her acting stunk. Those mansions of tile and glass left her cold. She didn't care for ostentation. Luxury for the sake of luxury baffled her.

Hardly the attitude of a scheming bitch who plotted to

wrest a fortune from an old and dying man. In fact, right then, sitting with goose bumps in Jane Connor's training yard, Dan was willing to bet that Nell didn't have an ounce of scheming bitch in her whole delightful body. The conviction had grown gradually during the day, or maybe it had been growing gradually over the past few weeks, since the day he had walked with her up the West Fork trail, trying to understand how someone who seemed so ingenuous could be so venal.

Nell wasn't venal. She was real. Genuine gold shinning in a corrupt world.

The moment Dan had surrendered to that conviction, a ton of weight had lifted from his shoulders. His mouth seemed stuck in a smile. Sunshine had gotten at least two shades brighter and night two shades softer. Because Nell Jordan was exactly what she seemed.

That didn't end it, of course. A good investigator didn't end an investigation because of a warm feeling inside. His mother wouldn't be convinced of Nell's innocence by anything short of a miracle. What he needed was hard evidence that Nell was one of the good guys. And he still needed to ferret out the mystery "ruckus." He now had confidence enough in Nell to be sure that it couldn't be that bad.

But Dan didn't have to decide right that instant what to do about those sticky problems. Right that instant, he wanted to enjoy watching Nell. Some silly little dog class wouldn't be his first choice in how to spend an evening, but this one proved downright entertaining.

"This is dog obedience, is it?" he said to Mckenna, who sat next to him on the plastic patio chairs bordering the training area.

"Calling it obedience at this stage is an exaggeration."

The mink-colored cat in her lap, paws folded neatly beneath her, watched the canine shenanigans with contemptuous yellow eyes.

"This is a beginning class," Mckenna explained, "and

only their first meeting. They'll get better in a few weeks. Jane is an excellent teacher, and Nell isn't bad."

Indeed. Nell wasn't bad at all, he thought with a grin.

"And you come to these classes with a cat because? . . ."

Mckenna gave him a minimal smile. "It reminds me how blessed I am to have a cat."

"Ah."

The keenness of her eyes set off a warning tingle inside. "Dog people, you know, tend to be trusting and open, accepting, generous, and sometimes not too wise in their affections. Cat people, on the other hand—" She paused, one perfectly plucked brow lifted in emphasis. "Cat people are more wary, with sharp insight and sharp claws. Like cats, they see through to a person's soul. It's hard to deceive a cat, and even harder to fool a true cat person."

He nodded, trying to look innocent. "Nice to know."

The warning continued. "Nell's a good friend of mine."

"Nell seems to be a friend to a lot of people."

A clever deflection, Dan thought, but Mckenna's little smile grew no less chilly. His mother didn't stand alone as an obstacle to solving the problem of Nell Jordan.

The rest of the evening passed without subtle threats or warnings from either the cat or its mistress, so Dan settled down to watch the entertainment, congratulating himself that he possessed the good sense not to own a dog. The dogs appeared to be in control: bouncing, barking, drooling, licking themselves in embarrassingly personal places, lunging, pulling, yowling, and in the case of one mountain-sized mastiff, plunking down in an attitude of total boredom rather than pay attention to anything the woman on the other end of his leash might do. Jane and Nell worked hard to keep order, and eventually, they herded all the canine students and their supposed masters and mistresses into a rough line with the dogs under semi-control. Only one dog had a man on the other end of the leash, and the poor guy seemed totally at sea.

Then came the practice of the "sit." Some dogs actually sat when a little cookie tempted their noses upward and their butts downward. Others made a play for the cookie without doing the work. The mastiff continued to lie down, and any minute Dan expected to hear a mastiff-sized snore. And a white, arctic-looking dog by the name of Snowball appeared to have fallen in love with Nell. Snowball made his amour graphically obvious.

Dan sympathized. He felt poor Snowball's frustration.

NELL HAD been full of doubts when this adventure began, but as spring slid into the balmy days of April, she had to admit that life had never been so good. Money made a difference. Soon she and Piggy would be living in a wonderful house with plenty of elbowroom for anything they wanted to do. The daily worry about paying bills had faded into the past. Her tennies no longer sported holes, and she had just bought a new—actually brand-new, not used, not demo, but new—minivan that was clean and roomy and had that wonderful new car smell. At the dealership, a yellow Fiat had momentarily tempted her. Such a sexy little car. So hot. And so impractical. In the end, functional won out.

Of course, even with a shiny new minivan parked in front of her house, Mel remained Nell's favorite. One person certainly didn't need two vehicles, but Nell couldn't break Mel's heart by selling him. Parts of her old penurious life, chiefly Mel, had to stay.

As the advantages of money became clearer, the hassles of being wealthy grew fewer. Upon Mckenna's advice, Nell hired an answering service to deflect the influx of calls from charities and individuals who felt Piggy should toss some of the wealth their way. She made large donations to a few selected charities, chief among which were several children's foundations and the AKC Canine Health Foundation. Again on Mckenna's recommendation, Nell engaged a competent financial adviser to explore safe investments that would ensure the future stayed as golden as her present. The good things she wanted to fund—scholarships for people wanting to train their dogs as assistance dogs, financial help for handlers wanting to attend Delta Society conferences and classes, and perhaps a little training center right in the Verde Valley—would have financial needs long after Piggy left this world, and so would Nell. After getting used to having money, not having money wouldn't be fun at all. As soon as Frank's will passed probate, much of the interest from Piggy's trust fund, plus a large percentage of Nell's salary as "guardian," would go right into building stability for the future.

The good new life hinged not solely on money, however. Not even mostly on money. After a rather rocky start, Dan Travis moved in to fill a hole in Nell's life that she'd scarcely noticed before he arrived. Dan provided friendship, a well of warmth that seemed reserved specifically for her, and sometimes, she thought, an anchor to sanity. He endured teasing from her friends, hostility from her dog, and emotional ups and downs from her without flinching. The occasional sharp thrusts stopped, making Nell wonder if she had imagined them—a creation of her own insecurities. Dan served willingly as her safe haven. His smile could bring her back from a blue funk. A lift of his brow headed off spells of craziness. And a kiss—oh my! His kiss seemed to make everything else in the world unimportant.

Nell wished those kisses served as preludes to something more intense, but so far, Dan's restraint held firm with annoying steadiness. Nell knew his blood could run hot when they were together. The evidence couldn't be mistaken. But some wall stood between them—something he wasn't telling her. A few times he had tried, or so it seemed to her, but his jaw had snapped shut on whatever words attempted an escape. Nell wished he would just spit it out and get it over with, whatever it was.

Time would tell, she kept assuring herself. He couldn't hold out forever. Certainly she couldn't.

But she had vowed at the beginning of this beautiful Friday not to think about frustrations and puzzlements. She, Jane, and Dan sped along I-40 toward the little pine-clad town of Williams. Nell and Jane had an appointment to give animal therapy presentations to a nursing facility, the staff of an elementary school, and the urgent care center. Dan tagged along simply to tag along, supposedly to further his research into the changing life of Nell Jordan, accidental heiress.

This hypothetical article of his, Nell reflected, must be the longest story in the known universe. If he truly wanted to try his hand at journalism, he had to churn out words with a bit more speed. Still, he had delivered the peace that he'd promised. Her answering service referred all calls from the media to him, and he took care of them some way or another. Nell didn't inquire into his methods. An ex-L.A. cop might be a little more enthusiastic about "discouragement" than she wanted to think about.

"Your friend Jane is a speed demon," Dan commented.

Because Jane planned to attend a training seminar the next morning in Flagstaff, they had brought separate cars. Nell and Dan rode in the minivan, and Jane led the way in her van. Jane didn't believe in being a turtle on the road. When she went somewhere, she really went somewhere.

"Makes me wish I had a siren and red lights on this puppy." He patted the dashboard of Nell's new Dodge Caravan.

"You miss being a police officer?" Nell asked.

He thought a moment. "Not as much as I once thought I would. If my knee hadn't made me retire, I would have gotten fed up with the life sooner or later.

She smiled. "You just miss it when the car in front of you is doing eighty-five?"

"Hell yes. I did a chase once at one-twenty-five. Now that was a chase!"

Nell just shook her head and laughed. "I don't think you're going to get that out of Jane."

The town of Williams, sprawled along I-40 at the foot of Bill Williams Mountain, attracted the tourist trade by making the most of its Wild West heritage. During the summer, the town was a natural playground, high up in the cool pines where Arizona's summer heat couldn't reach. In the winter, the surrounding countryside sparkled with snow and clear, frosty days.

Every morning at ten, the Grand Canyon Railway chugged out of Williams to make the sixty-mile north-bound trip to the south rim of the Grand Canyon, and at six in the evening, the same train disgorged a load of passengers eager to avail themselves of the town's hotels, restaurants, and bars.

Yes indeed, Williams was a thriving little town, catering both to the tourists and the growing population of people who willingly traded the conveniences of the city for fresh air and no traffic. But one thing the town didn't have was an active animal therapy program. Enter Nell and Jane, armed with facts, figures, research, and, hopefully, winning words to convince the local authorities that Williams needed to go to the dogs.

Their first call was at the elementary school, where Nell, Jane, Piggy, and Idaho presented their "Safety Around Animals" program to a gym full of eight-, nine-, and ten-year-olds—a challenge in anyone's book. Dan willingly acted the fool when he demonstrated how not to approach a dog, then cracked up the room in standing-like-a-tree and making-like-a-rock to avoid the unfriendly attentions of a "scary" dog—Idaho, in this case, who snarled convincingly while poor Dan protected his head and chest by curling up in a "rock" ball and practically kissed the gym floor. The kids giggled in delight and willingly imitated him when

Idaho and Piggy strolled down the rows of youngsters, sniffing, kissing, and teasing them with cold noses.

Nell's heart warmed to Dan for his silly yet effective performance. How many men would willingly throw aside their macho image to cavort on the floor with children and dogs? The better she got to know the man, the more certain she was that he was a keeper. If she could only persuade him to be kept.

They left the school with assurances from the faculty that they would welcome other certified therapy dogs working with the pupils. A counselor even ventured forth with the idea of testing his pooch so that he could bring it to work.

"The kids will talk more freely with a dog in the office," he explained to the principal. "And they're better behaved. No kid wants to look like a jackass in front of a dog. In front of us, sure. But not in front of a dog."

The principal agreed.

Next they visited Alpine Eldercare, where the dogs worked the room like politicians, giving doggie smiles and canine kisses, or just laying a furry head in a lap and looking into age-worn faces with loving eyes. Short-legged Piggy didn't have enough height for the head-in-lap ploy, so she simply got on the patient's level by making herself comfortable on the couch alongside. It was a natural move. Piggy had always considered sofas and chairs to be little more than elevated dog beds.

"I don't think I've ever seen Piggy so friendly," Dan commented wryly after a very wizened little woman had given the corgi a big, camphor-scented hug—and almost done the same to Nell and Dan.

"She especially likes older people," Nell told him. "Sometimes I swear she almost talks to them."

Jane chuckled. "Don't let that little corgi smile fool you. She's cruising the room for another trust fund."

Dan almost choked.

"Piggy wouldn't do that," Nell denied. Then with a wicked smile, "She already has more money than she can spend."

Dan hesitated, then laughed. "She does, doesn't she?"

There it was again, Nell noted—a flash of... of something in his eyes, in a momentary subtle grimace. She couldn't quite identify it. After the work of the day was done, Nell decided, she was going to get down and pry. No more Mister Nice Guy, or in this case, Miss Nice Girl.

"This is such a treat," the activities director told Nell. "Look at those faces light up."

"We're going to be recruiting people and dogs in Williams to train for this service," Nell told her. "Our goal is to provide you with a dog to visit twice or three times a week."

The director sighed. "Our budget is a bit limited."

Nell chuckled. "No, no. This is all volunteer. And we have funds to defray the cost of training for any qualified therapy teams who would like to go for it."

The day went so well that Nell almost felt Frank Cramer looked down from wherever he resided and nodded his head in approval at her plans for his money. She could pay to advertise therapy dog training without worrying about the expense. She could pay the expenses of a licensed instructor to come to Williams and teach the class. She could even give promising applicants scholarships to defray the cost of certifying their dogs. What's more, she could do the same in every town in northern Arizona that had facilities to use their services—and still have plenty left for a new house, new car, and those designer tennies that had caught her eye in a Sedona boutique. Amazing how a person's tastes elevated right along with income. She thought Frank would approve of Piggy's new house—in a few weeks they would be moving in. He would like the new car as well. Once he had grumbled about learning too late in life that money existed to be enjoyed.

"Now here I am stuck in this goddamned bed!" he'd complained. "I worked hard all my life to earn a fortune so that it could rot in the bank. Don't you let that happen to you, girl," he'd said to Nell.

Since she'd had no prospects for ever having much money, Nell hadn't thought much of his comment. Even back then, she now realized, he had been planning to leave Piggy that hard-earned fortune.

"Have we spread enough cheer for one day?" Dan asked as they left Alpine Eldercare behind.

Nell elbowed him. "You were the one who wanted to come along."

"I'm gathering journalistic color."

Walking with them, Jane laughed. "Have you seen anything on paper from that man?" she asked Nell.

"No," Nell snorted.

"I'm a perfectionist," Dan told them in a lofty tone. "No one sees my rough drafts. When it's finished and perfect, you'll see it."

"Yeah. Right."

Their last visit of the day hit a snag in the person of the Williams Urgent Care Center's infection control officer. The man sat patiently through Jane and Nell's facts, figures, and anecdotes about animals lowering blood pressure, alleviating depression, and speeding the healing process. While the medical director and several nurses smiled and nodded, Mr. Infection Control questioned:

"What about asthmatics? We have quite a few who pass through here. And parasites. Fleas. And what about the dirt and crap they'll bring in on their feet?"

Jane and Nell had good answers for all the questions, but Mr. I.C. didn't soften. When they left ten minutes later, Nell's balloon of contentment had been thoroughly deflated. "I don't think any facts, figures, or anything else convinced that guy," Nell moaned.

Dan put an arm around Nell. "You're just tired. I'll buy

you dinner at the Frey Marcos. That'll perk you up. Jane, you up for dinner?"

Jane had plans to meet a friend in Flagstaff, so Nell found herself alone with Dan at a table in the upscale Frey Marcos dining room. The historical hotel next to the Grand Canyon Railway station was known throughout northern Arizona for its food. Its prices weren't exactly plebian, either.

"You'd better let me buy," Nell ventured.

"Nope. My treat. Got paid yesterday."

"Sell a photograph?"

For a moment he hesitated, then smiled. "A whole ton of photos, as a matter of fact."

"You're looking mysterious again."

"What?"

"Mysterious. You get this look every once in a while. What is it that you're not telling me?"

His expression confirmed her suspicions.

"You're married, aren't you?"

"Divorced. I told you."

"Okay, then . . . you're committed to another woman."

"Yeah. Marta, my eight-year-old daughter."

"You're . . . running from the law?"

"I am the law, or at least I was the law."

"Okay, that was a reach. But you're hiding something."

"What is this, woman's intuition?"

"Yes. Don't you believe in such things?"

"What I believe is that you're tired after a long day. You really take this dog therapy thing seriously, don't you?"

He had neatly changed the subject, but Nell was tired, so she didn't press the issue. Sooner or later he would come clean.

She hoped.

• • •

DAN APPRECIATED the silence as they drove homeward along I-40. Nell wasn't a woman who constantly chattered, and she didn't regard silences as threatening. He liked that about her. He liked any number of things about her. The trouble was, he knew that Nell and he together, as a couple, had disaster written all over it. He had gotten into this relationship by accident, continued it through deception, and now found himself so twisted up inside by conflicting commitments that he didn't know whether he was coming or going.

He almost wished that Nell Jordan had turned out to be a scheming bimbo, someone he could despise and resent. Life would have been so much easier. Less fun, but a lot easier.

"Stop! Oh stop!"

Police reflexes still honed, Dan swung onto the shoulder and screeched to a halt on a cindered turnout, sorely testing the minivan's brakes. "What? What's wrong?"

"Nothing's wrong. The moon is rising."

"What?"

"The full moon is rising. One of my favorite shows."

"Better than Mel Gibson?"

For that crack, Nell punched his shoulder. "No, it's not better than Mel. But almost as good."

Nell got out of the car and stood in the cold night air, arms clutched around her body for warmth. Dan joined her. A milky glow in the east outlined the San Francisco Peaks. Against the inky blackness of the spring night, the moon's pregame show was eerily luminous.

"This is the perfect place to watch." She leaned against the car, intent on nature's display.

Dan saw his chance—it was just too good to pass up— and braced her from behind, wrapping his arms around her. "Are you cold?"

"Not now I'm not."

He heard the smile in her voice and figured he'd made a

first down. He might be a bit confused as to which team he played for, but he refused to be benched.

Together they watched as the moon's bright orb rose over the Peaks, spilling moonlight over the landscape in a milky flood. Long moon shadows gave the pine-clad mountains and valleys an unearthly look, so different from day. So different, actually, from anything Dan had ever seen. He'd spent many a black night on the streets of L.A., but in L.A. one couldn't see the moon for the smog, and even if such a sight appeared, a cop gaping at the night scenery was likely to get his ass killed.

No indeed, Dan had never thought of standing out in the freezing night watching the moon rise as an evening's entertainment, but it was worth it. The flood of elation that warmed his blood amazed him. He enjoyed the cold night, enjoyed the glowing moon, and enjoyed Nell.

"Isn't it beautiful!" Nell sighed. "Watching the moon rise is one of my absolute favorite things. It reminds me what a gorgeous, blessed place I live in."

It was beautiful, but not as beautiful as Nell when the moonlight set her face aglow. She was alabaster, pure and perfect. But not cold. That face could never be cold.

With predictable speed, the warmth of elation pulsing in Dan's blood turned to a different sort of heat. He closed his eyes on the night's majesty, to better focus on the sensation of having Nell in his arms, her scent in his nostrils, her hair tickling his cheek, her sweetly curved backside cuddled warmly into his groin. Scarcely thinking about what he did, he turned her in his arms.

A smile lit her face more brightly than the moonlight. If Dan's life had depended upon it, he couldn't have resisted the indulgence of a kiss. Her mouth invited him so warmly, her eyes alight with the spark of shared passion.

He met no resistance when he tangled his fingers in her hair and lowered his mouth to hers. So soft. So fresh. So much a woman that she made his pulse pound and his whole body want to surrender to desire, to climb back into the minivan and take advantage of all that roominess for something that would leave them both breathless and sated. When her tongue tentatively answered his gentle probes, he thought his bones would melt. When she fitted herself to him so that every curve cuddled into corresponding nooks and crannies of his own physique, he thought he would disgrace himself right then and there, like some pimply junior high kid popping a peek into the girls' locker room.

But he didn't. He'd left junior high far behind, and the woman in his arms was Nell, not some strutting cheerleader. Nell, the woman he would vote most unlikely to be a scheming bimbo. Nell, who couldn't deceive anyone. Nell, who, when he got up the courage to tell her who he was and what he had been doing these past few weeks, was going to kick him into the next county.

chapter 11

DAN FINALLY showed up at his office around eleven the next morning. After watching the moon rise and ... other things ... he had gotten home late. Then he had trouble falling asleep. Once asleep, he really hadn't wanted to wake up. And once awake, he hadn't especially wanted to trudge into the office.

But duty called. Plus, unlike some very well-paid dog guardians he could name, Dan still needed to make a living.

BJ lounged behind his desk with one of George Kade's hounds at his feet. "Well, look who dragged himself into work? Hard night, hm?"

Dan growled in a way that made the hound raise his head and give him a wary look.

"You had a new client waiting in your office, a very unpleasant woman who wants you to follow her husband and take photos of his infidelity. That should be fun."

"Crap! What a business!"

"She waited about twenty minutes, then left in a huff. But she'll be back. She seemed very determined, and after all, you're just about the only P.I. in town."

"Great. I'll look forward to it."

"Whatever happened to the idea of a beautiful, mysterious woman engaging a down-and-out P.I. to find some exotic missing item? Hm?"

Dan poured himself a cup of gut-acid coffee from the pot on top of the filing cabinet. "You live in Fantasyland, BJ."

"Well, in my opinion, the world would be much more interesting if it started spicing up reality with some concepts from commercial fiction and TV. A person might have something to look forward to each morning if he had a chance of stumbling into Diagon Alley. Or strolling the streets of San Francisco and meeting Kirk and Spock after they've flown through a time warp to do something or other. Or rounding a corner and running into Sam Spade or Ellery Queen." He paused with a wicked smile. "And speaking of beautiful, mysterious women, how did it go in Williams?"

"None of your business," Dan told him amiably. Now that he had strong coffee in his hand, his mood had improved.

"Everyone's business is a writer's business. How do you think we get plot ideas?"

"I don't know. Have you ever really come up with a plausible plot, BJ?"

BJ smirked. "How about this, Mister Smart Guy? Private investigator sets out to get the goods on a clever, scheming, but sexy dame, and ends up falling for the object of his investigation. The woman twists him around her little finger, leading him down dark alleys of lust and depravity while giving the finger to the forces of justice and truth. Sexually wrung out, not to mention disgraced and shamed, the P.I. is aced out by his brilliant and faithful assistant, who has the brains—not to mention the sexual orientation—to see through the hussy's charms and blow the case wide-open, thus earning himself fame and a ton of rich clients. In the end, he generously pays for his former boss's psychiatric rehab."

"Agatha Christie, move over."

BJ lifted a warning brow. "You laugh now—"

"And speaking of writing," Dan interrupted. "Have you put anything on paper that might pass as a story about Nell?"

BJ threw up his hands dramatically. "How can I? I've never met the woman. Your notes need an Egyptologist to decipher them, and they're not exactly overflowing with description."

"Nell isn't easy to describe."

"Well, Romeo, try."

"She's tall and blonde."

"Bottle blonde?"

Dan pictured the cropped shining curls with the hint of red highlighting the gold. "That color could never come from a bottle."

BJ gave him a canny look. "Fashionably thin?"

"Hardly. But not fat. This lady has curves where a woman should have curves. And she's not one of these females who think a Big Mac with cheese is going to kill her. Man, the way she looks—like nature intended a woman to look, I tell you."

"Interesting. Cute?"

Dan smiled. "A face like an angel."

"Oh give me a break!"

"She does! An angel with an imp's eyes. She has humor and perspective, and a great talent for having a good time with the simplest things."

"Sounds as if you're really making progress proving what a louse she is," BJ chortled. "You mother should be pleased."

That brought Dan down to earth like a meteor plunging from orbit.

"And by the way, your mom is going to meet you for

lunch at Dahl and DiLuca in Sedona. She said not to be late."

The meteor hit the ocean and plummeted to the cold depths. "Great. Just great. Just what I need."

"Make her pay," BJ suggested. "I hear Dahl and DiLuca has truly Sedona prices."

"If I had any guts at all I'd tell her that Nell Jordan is without a doubt one of the nicest women I've ever met and that she should just back off."

"And what was that you were saying earlier?" BJ prodded. "About your investigation doing the saintly Nell a favor by convincing folks of her sterling character?"

Dan sighed.

BJ had the nerve to laugh. "How is it, my man, that such a tough-guy cop and Sam Spade clone is afraid of his own mother?"

"I'm not afraid of my mother," Dan snapped, then reconsidered during a swallow of coffee. "I'm just cautious is all. My mother is a bulldozer with a hundred-dollar hairdo."

BJ snickered. "More like two hundred, friend. You're obviously out of touch with Sedona prices."

Dan poured another cup of coffee. His gut would regret it, but if he had to lunch with his mother, then he needed the caffeine. "Besides, BJ, I keep telling you that I wasn't that tough a cop."

"Then why does the local fuzz think of you as some kind of hero for that spectacular hostage rescue that got your knee trashed? How many medals got pinned on your manly chest?"

"Give it a rest," Dan warned.

"The Camp Verde cop who gave you that speeding ticket the other day said our local keepers of the peace wouldn't mind you running for sheriff."

"Oh that's what I need. Local politics. I'd rather run for dogcatcher."

BJ tsked. "Cranky, cranky."

"BJ, go stick your nosy head in a septic tank—after you write something I can show Nell. Meanwhile, I'm going to hell."

"Don't you mean lunch?"

"Same thing."

DAHL AND DiLuca's Italian food was as tasteful as the decor. The clients typified a Sedona mix—a smattering of tourists, a gaggle of older, well-dressed folks sporting a ton of turquoise jewelry, a few business people treating themselves to an expensive lunch, and in the corner, a real estate agent trying to impress a well-heeled couple with stories of Sedona grandeur.

"Mother, I enjoy having lunch with you, but can't you ever come over to Camp Verde to eat?"

Natalie indulged in a ladylike snort. "Camp Verde!" Her tone made Camp Verde sound like the seventh level of hell.

"Camp Verde's great place. Down-home cooking. Interesting local color. We could eat someday at Crusty's Pizza."

"Please!"

"Crusty's has great pizza. Cheap. Or the BBQ Corral."

"Don't be ridiculous, Dan. Camp Verde is a cowboy town with cowboy tastes, and I'm definitely not a cowboy sort of person. If you had to go into this wretched profession, why couldn't you at least have set up shop in Sedona? There's much more money here, and probably a lot more sinning going on. Your business would skyrocket."

Dan had to chuckle. "I don't know, Mom. There's quite a bit of sinning going on in Camp Verde, too. All those high-living cowboys, you know."

"I shudder to think of it."

"If I had to pay Sedona rent, I'd go belly-up the first month."

"Well, then you could get a real job."

Dan could have told her that he might actually make

quite a bit of money if he would just get off his duff and beat the bushes for business, but his heart wasn't in it. He had moved to this area to be near his kids, and he liked the place, with all its variety and quirks. But he couldn't get enthusiastic about following cheaters and philanderers with camera in hand, looking for delinquent runaway kids, or doing a stakeout to solve the mystery of which of the neighbor children was teasing the family dog after school. It was a living, but Dan wouldn't call it a profession.

But he couldn't tell that to his mother, who would offer him half her business or pull strings to find him a suit-and-tie job in the blink of an eye. A bulldozer she might be, but his mother wrote the book on giving family the shirt off her back—or the silk blouse, in this case. She would never understand that he didn't want half her business and he certainly didn't want to get dressed every morning in a tie.

"But as long as you *are* in your dubious profession," she continued. "I'm not above taking advantage of it. I have hired an attorney in the matter of your grandfather's estate."

"Another attorney? What about Johansen? He's a good man, or so I've heard."

"He's named personal representative in the will, so he has to be impartial. I want someone who's on my side, willing to take no prisoners." She gave him a pointed look. "Besides, unless I miss my guess, Jared has been taken in by Nell Jordan just like everyone else. That Jordan woman puts on a squeaky clean act and convinces every gullible fool, especially every gullible *male* fool, that she's Saint Theresa. Disgusting."

"I . . . uh . . . wouldn't say she was Saint Theresa."

"Of course she's not Saint Theresa! Anything but. The point is, Dan, the attorney tells me we need something very solid to make a judge consider setting the will aside. Something definite that will point to her low character. Something glaring that will prove a pattern of scamming money." She looked at him hopefully.

Dan thought of the Nell Jordan he knew—her smile, her laugh, the stupid new minivan she regarded as the height of luxury, the way she touched the folks in the eldercare center they had visited. The dogs didn't do all the "therapy."

"Dan," Natalie prompted. "This is the point in our conversation when you're supposed to fill me in on what you've found out about our little schemer."

Dan shook his head. "Mother, have you ever stopped to think that Nell Jordan's squeaky clean act isn't an act?"

She blinked. "What?"

"You heard me. Because Granddad set up that crazy trust fund, you just assume that she somehow scammed him into doing it. Maybe you should consider the possibility that he wanted to do it because he liked the dog and he liked the woman. Not as some kind of bimbo, but as a friend who brought him a little warmth during the last months of his life."

Her expression grew dark. "Don't tell me that you've been taken in as well. I thought that you, of all people, could see through her. Honestly, Dan! As a cop you dealt with every sort of human trash under the sun, and now you're a P.I., which amounts to the same thing. I'd think that you'd be smarter about people."

He sighed. His mother was a very intelligent woman, but once she got emotionally involved with an issue, her inflexibility rivaled steel. What she needed to be the truth *was* the truth, and that was that.

"Mom, on the pretext of writing a story about all this garbage, I've shadowed this woman almost everywhere she's gone since Granddad died. I've gone house-hunting with her. You know what she bought with Granddad's money?"

Natalie snorted. "I can imagine."

"She passed up a whole raft of star-quality mansions to

buy a cute little bungalow that any working-class slob could afford—because her dog and her friends' dogs could run and play in the big backyard."

"Then she's a fool. But that doesn't make her innocent."

"I've visited schools and old folks' homes with her. And while she might not be even close to sainthood, those old folks think she is. Her and that fat little dog of hers."

"Yes, well, that's the problem, isn't it? Any of them start rewriting their wills?"

Dan remembered the joke about Piggy trolling the room for money and smiled.

"What else?" Natalie asked in a sour voice.

"I went up to NAU to talk to her old profs. She was a hardworking student. Smart. Ambitious."

"Obviously."

"Ambitious as a journalist. She went to Chicago to take a job after she graduated."

"And? . . ."

"And nothing."

"You didn't follow up the lead about Chicago?"

Here he felt a bit uncomfortable, because more than one lead still dangled loose ends. "It wasn't exactly a lead."

She harrumphed—in a ladylike way, of course. "I'm disappointed, Dan. I thought you'd have more commitment. You might find this girl charming just because you're at, shall we say, a gender disadvantage? But you just ignore those hormones and get back to work. BJ tells me you don't have much else to do right now. If you have expenses, I'll reimburse you."

Dan closed his eyes and sighed. He had known this wasn't going to go well from the beginning.

"Now don't look like that, son. I know your heart is in the right place. But I think I'm seeing more clearly on this than you are. That woman might be enjoying the cash in Frank's payable-upon-death account—I know there's not much we can do about that. But by God, she's not going to get her mitts on the rest of it. Not if I have anything to say about it."

"HEY, STRANGER." Mckenna's voice greeted Nell when she picked up the phone. "Where have you been keeping yourself? Jane and I missed you at dinner last night."

Nell smiled to herself. "I had a date."

"I know. Jane told me you stood us up for the hunk. She also said that at Williams—when was that? A couple of weeks ago?—you two seemed pretty cozy."

Cozy. Ah yes. Kissing cozy. Nell had been dancing on Cloud 9 ever since.

"Jane is imagining things," Nell lied.

"I doubt it, sweetie. Our Jane is not prone to letting her imagination off the leash. She worries about you, and so do I."

"Worry? Stop worrying. Why are you so convinced that Dan's up to no good?"

"Nothing specific. But let's face it, sweetie, you're an easy mark for anyone with good pecs. You don't have much experience with men."

Nell took exception. "I have tons of experience."

"Besides the disaster in Chicago, you mean?"

A low blow. Chicago, where she had thought herself grown-up enough to play with the big boys. One big boy had chewed her up and spit her out, showing her how very naive, unsophisticated, and downright stupid she could be. That particular smudge on her conscience wouldn't go away anytime soon.

"Okay, I was stupid in Chicago. But that certainly isn't my only brush with romance."

"Really?" Mckenna used her stern-mother voice.

"I had a boyfriend in junior high."

"Very exciting, I'm sure."

"And in high school."

"Not in the same league, kid."

"College. That was serious. I even lived with him."

"For how long?"

"A week," Nell admitted. "Spring break, actually."

"And all that experience," Mckenna said wryly, "didn't give you the smarts to avoid Mr. Bad News in Chicago."

She had a point, Nell admitted. But Dan wasn't Oliver Jones. Dan was...or could be...maybe...Mr. Right? "Mckenna, this is different. Don't dis Dan. It's been three years since Chicago, and since then I've had a big neon VACANCY sign on my heart. Then along comes Dan, a great guy who finds me even though I'm in the official Middle of Nowhere, the Timbuktu of the singles scene. It's like Fate. With a capital F."

"There's a capital F in fool as well." A pause. "You really are falling, aren't you?"

"Well, not totally."

"Right. I'm hearing 'totally.' Listen, sweetie. I just want you to have your trouble antenna up until probate is over, all right? And I'm going to do you a big favor and have someone look into this Mr. Right. Okay. Just a little investigation."

"No! Mckenna, I forbid it. That is so sleazy!"

"Sensible. Not sleazy."

"Really, Mckenna. I mean it. That's a horrible invasion of someone's privacy. If Dan found out...well, it might ruin everything."

"You're being unreasonable."

"If I am, then I am. Don't you dare sic one of your hounds on him."

"Let's go to lunch and I'll talk some sense into you. Or you can try to convince me this guy walks head and shoulders above the common everyday man."

"Uh...can't. I have a date."

Mckenna's sigh sounded like a hiss. "Dan, right?"

"Of course Dan."

"Middle of the day? This really is getting serious. Just go slow, okay? No rose-colored glasses?"

"I never wear rose-colored glasses. They clash with my skin tone."

"Very funny. Just be careful."

"Good-bye, Mckenna."

"Okay. I get the hint."

"I'll keep you posted."

"You'd better. So good-bye. Take care."

The phone line clicked in Nell's ear. Go slow. Be careful. No rose-colored glasses. Nell could do that. After Chicago and Oliver, she should be able to spot trouble a mile away. Her conscience still smarted from that stupid mistake, and it would for a long time to come. Oh yes, she knew what trouble looked like. She'd been there, done that. Didn't like it.

But who could worry on a beautiful April day when she had a date with a guy who wanted to go clothes shopping, of all things?

An hour later, she peered into a shop window at the outlet mall in the Village of Oak Creek. Of the small communities sharing the Verde Valley—Cottonwood, Sedona, Camp Verde, and Village of Oak Creek—VOC, as it was known, was the only one with anything resembling a shopping mall.

"I've never met a man who wanted to shop for clothes," she told Dan. "Most guys could care less."

"I have a good friend who cares a lot about clothes, but he's gay."

"See?"

"As for me, I just want to see you modeling some of these slinky styles."

She whacked him lightly with her handbag.

"We tough guys don't do clothes," he said with a grin, rubbing the shoulder where her industrial-sized shoulder bag had connected. "We do the women inside the clothes."

Nimbly, he sidestepped another attack.

"And even someone clothes-clueless like me would know that you need new clothes."

Usually Nell found shopping boring. But nothing done with Dan was boring.

You really aren't that much past junior high, she chided herself.

"The problem is," she confided to him, "that I never really have occasion to wear, say, a drop-dead gorgeous outfit like that one."

The ensemble graced a display dummy in the window of Anne Klein. Sleek black trousers of some shimmery material bloused gracefully over the hips and narrowed toward tailored cuffs and the ankle. A short, bolero style jacket dovetailed from padded shoulders to a narrow waist. Wide lapels parted to reveal a bold scarlet insert that gave the outfit its only splash of color.

"I could never wear shoulder pads," Nell said ruefully. "I already have the shoulders of a linebacker."

"If you were a linebacker, the other team would line up to get tackled."

She wrinkled her nose. "Dan Travis, you are so full of blarney."

"Charm, not blarney."

"Blarney."

"Why don't you just go in and try it on?"

What woman could resist such an invitation, even if the top did have padded shoulders?

The black pants outfit, Dan declared, would get her wolf whistles walking down any city street. Not in Sedona, of course. Sedona was much too politically correct for that sort of thing. But in any normal town, she wouldn't dare walk past a construction site, he assured her.

She laughed at the very idea of being whistle bait. And the laughter inspired her to try on yet another creation, a short, straight leather skirt topped by a ribbed turtleneck and matching leather vest.

"Oh no," she said when she looked in the mirror, even before she walked out of the dressing room.

"Come out," Dan urged.

"Not a chance."

"Come on! How bad could it be?"

She screwed up her courage, steeled her jaw, and left the shelter of the fitting room. If she didn't, Nell knew, Dan would be teasing her for the rest of the day.

His brows shot upward when she came into sight.

"Don't you dare say anything."

"Any comment would be entirely complimentary."

"Right. On the rack," she complained, "it looked like the top tucked into the skirt."

"How clever of it not to."

She huffed, embarrassed. "Well, I know it's all the rage, but I'm a bit too old to have my navel hanging out for everyone to gape at." She grimaced into a full-length mirror. "Good grief! Who over fifteen could wear this sort of thing and actually look good?"

His answer rang with certainty. "You, Nell."

The third try brought success. Nell felt quite at home in a narrow khaki skirt and soft cotton blouse that buttoned up the back. A green silky scarf with tiny red ladybugs draped around her neck for a bit of color.

"What do you think?"

"You look like you stepped right out of L. L. Bean."

"Don't let Anne Klein hear you say that."

He twisted his face speculatively. "Something's wrong."

"What? You're still stuck on my navel hanging out?"

He circled around her. "You have it buttoned wrong in back."

"They shouldn't make things that button in back. Women don't have ladies' maids anymore."

"I can be a ladies' maid." Without asking, he deftly

unbuttoned, rebuttoned, and even conquered the hook-and-eye.

A tingly shiver traveled down Nell's spine at the light touch of his fingers, the warmth of his big hands so close to bare skin with only a fragile drape of cotton between them. She tried not to shiver. Shivering at his touch would be way too obvious.

"You're awfully good with women's clothes, aren't you?" she chided lightly.

"Hell, yes, I am. For three long years I was married to a woman who couldn't dress herself to save her life. Now there's a woman who needs a whatchamacallit, a ladies' maid. I probably deserve a master's degree in buttons, hooks, and jewelry clasps."

She whirled away and struck a pose. "Ta-dah! What do you think."

"It's you. Buy it. Even though it hides your navel."

She laughed, thoroughly enjoying herself. But they walked out of the store with no packages under their arms.

Dan thought to himself that even his mother might have been convinced if she had been there. No woman who rated the title of bimbo ever walked into a designer outlet store with money in her hand and walked out without needing a pack mule to carry the packages.

THE DAYS passed a bit uneasily for Dan, who liked to think of himself as a realist. He generally faced mountains head on, admitting that not all mountains could be climbed. But he excelled at dynamiting those he couldn't scramble over. His problem-solving techniques lacked subtlety, but they generally worked.

Nell, however, seemed to blind him to reality. A huge mountain loomed between them. Dan doubted he could climb it. Once Nell understood the truth, she likely would cut him off at the pass with a stick of dynamite in her hand.

The tough-guy approach to the problem wouldn't work. Hearts and flowers wouldn't work. Nothing that Dan could think of had much chance of saving his neck. Nell would kill him, plead justifiable homicide, and any jury of women would let her off the hook in a heartbeat.

So instead of gritting his teeth and taking his medicine, as he usually did in such a situation, Dan postponed the inevitable. Maybe within a few weeks someone would come up with a cure for acting like an incredible jackass. Jerry Lewis could do a telethon.

While he could, though, Dan enjoyed himself. If a certain cloud of doom didn't lurk on the dark horizon, he would have enjoyed himself more. He wouldn't have contented himself with kisses and flirtation, that's for sure. But somehow, taking that final step when he knew what he knew and she didn't know that he knew, and so forth, stretched his ethics just a little too thin. He had stretched them to the limits already. A guy needed to preserve at least a little self-respect.

If he could.

Except Dan wasn't sure that he could. Especially when such a ripe opportunity came knocking, escorted by Nell herself.

It happened in a nursing home—no surprise, given Nell's propensity for dragging poor Piggy, and now Dan as well, to such places. This day they were visiting a care facility in Camp Verde: Desert Acres by name. The Hearts of Gold Performing Players presented "Christmas in May," an off-season frolic requested by some of the Desert Acres residents.

"We've done this program before," Nell told Dan as they waited in the lobby with the rest of the Hearts of Gold circus. "Christmastime is their favorite, and quite a few of them, I'm afraid, won't last until then, so we're doing the program now."

The concept made Dan a bit queasy. Violent death once

had been a commonplace part of his life, and he'd thought the senseless shootings, the traffic deaths, the drug overdoses represented grim reality at its worst. But the idea of these old folks sitting in their wheelchairs on the home's fancy leather sofas, simply waiting for the Grim Reaper to beckon—somehow that image was as sad as anything he'd seen in the streets of L.A.

When they went into the big day room and greeted the folks there, however, the atmosphere rang with Christmas cheer, even though outside, the trees wore new foliage of green and the temperature hovered in the nineties.

"Merry Christmas!" Jane shouted to the eager inmates. "Welcome to Christmas in May! Come along with us now as we mangle a fine poem by Major Henry Livingston Jr." And with great ceremony, she pulled out an edited copy of 'Twas the Night Before Christmas, edited so that the little Hearts of Gold circus of seven dogs, one cat, and an African Grey parrot could perform a drama to rival the Muppets' version of Charles Dickens's A Christmas Carol.

Dan perched on the arm of a sofa to watch. The tiny, birdlike little lady seated there patted his knee and looked up. "Are you new here?" she quavered.

"You might say that," Dan replied with a smile.

Her eyes narrowed suspiciously. "I saw you come in with Nell. Are you courting her, young man? You'd better behave yourself. Our Nell isn't one of these gadabout girls you can play fast and loose with. She's a nice girl, and she's got friends, you know."

"I wouldn't dream of playing fast and loose," Dan assured her patiently. "I'm not that kind of guy."

She sniffed. "You look like that kind of guy."

Heaven help anyone who tried to put anything over on this old girl. Dan was grateful when Jane called for silence. The room obeyed, just like a class of obedience training students. Having gained everyone's attention, she cleared her throat and read.

" ' 'Twas the night before Christmas,
When all through the house . . .' "

In came a cardboard construction resembling the front of a
redbrick house with huge windows.

" 'Not a creature was stirring,
Not even a mouse.' "

Enter Taco the Chihuahua, the tiniest Hearts of Gold
player, dressed appropriately in a mouse-colored
Chihuahua-sized T-shirt and sporting a set of mouse-ears
on his head. At Marsha Torres's urging, he sniffed the cardboard house, then sat up on his hind legs and waved to the
audience with a tiny front paw. As he jumped through the
window of the house, everyone laughed.

" 'The children were nestled
All snug in their beds,
While visions of dog biscuits
Danced in their heads.' "

The stage crew—Nell and Mckenna—put two small dog
beds beside the house, and with a great sense of drama,
Piggy and Nefertiti, both decked in cut-down T-shirts pro-
claiming "I believe in Santa Claus," took their places.
Above the beds dangled a child's mobile of tiny dog biscuits
and cat treats, which kept the actors' attention riveted.

An old gent in the audience raised a thin arm and
pointed at Piggy. "She's gonna get that biscuit!"

He called the shot right, for Piggy had gauged the distance to the lowest biscuit and jumped for it. The recreation therapist, who had volunteered to hold the mobile,
dropped it in surprise, and both Piggy and Nefertiti moved
in for a feast.

The rest of the performance degenerated into a farce

that had the Desert Acres residents in stitches. "And Mamma in her 'Kerchief, and I in my cap," called forth Fred the golden retriever and Bandit the terrier, both dressed appropriately, and Santa's sleigh was towed in by none other than Idaho the border collie, wearing felt reindeer antlers and a sled-dog harness decorated with jingle bells. Inside the sleigh rode Santa's "elf," an African Grey parrot who shouted "Merry Christmas" to the audience. As parrots will, he shouted other things as well, but "Merry Christmas" at least came out the loudest.

Dan could only shake his head as the "performance" ended and the animals and handlers scattered to accept the kudos of the residents. "You guys are insane, you know that?" he said to Nell, whose smile sparkled in a manner that made his heart absolutely hurt with what might have been.

"It's a good kind of insane, though, isn't it?" she countered.

He had to smile. "And you want to spread this sort of silliness all over northern Arizona with the help of Piggy's money."

"Well, we don't do skits in hospitals."

"Okay. Silliness in nursing homes and turning your dogs into candy stripers in hospitals."

She refused to be teased. "Wonderful idea, isn't it? And I have great news. The Director of Volunteers at the hospital here called a friend at the medical center in Page, and they want a presentation on how they might utilize therapy dogs both to visit patients and—this is what makes it *so* wonderful—in their physical therapy program."

Dan's first thought was fond amusement at what strange things set Nell aglow, and then it hit him. The golden opportunity nearly knocked Dan off his feet, a setup so perfect that a saint would have had trouble resisting. Dan had never claimed to be a saint. Without hesitation or remorse he jumped in with both feet.

"What a coincidence. I happen to have a friend who has a houseboat on Lake Powell. He keeps it at a marina in Page."

"Lucky man!"

"He's always telling me that I can use it whenever I want."

She got the implication right away, and from the slight tremor in her smile, he guessed that she knew as well as he did that cruising Lake Powell together in a houseboat called for a lot more than recreational kisses.

Yes indeed, it was a perfect setup.

chapter 12

NELL THOUGHT she handled the situation like a pro. Well, not a pro—in the context of dating, "professional" calls up a rather unflattering image. Rather, she handled the situation like a sophisticated woman of experience, which she wasn't. Having been raised by old-fashioned parents and believing in, if not marriage, at least some kind of emotional commitment before cavorting, Nell's time logged in unchaste activities didn't add up to much. Yet here she was, driving with Dan to Lake Powell, Arizona's water playground, for four long, lovely days of fun in the sun. Fun and cavorting. Definitely unchaste.

Was she nervous? Not really. Did she blush and giggle? A few blushes maybe. With her, blushing was almost as normal as breathing. No giggles though. A giggle or two might have bubbled to the surface, but Nell firmly refused to let them slip out. She was a mature, soon-to-be experienced woman, after all. Mature women did not giggle.

They didn't talk all that much as Dan drove the minivan up through Flagstaff and then north on Highway 89 through the land of pines and cinder cones and then down into a desert that was as spectacular as it was stark.

"You're sure that you actually have to talk to these people at the hospital?" Dan asked for the third time.

Nell laughed indulgently. "You are so bad! Of course I do. That's the reason I'm going to Page, remember?"

"Ah. That's right." His smile wrapped around certainty that the hospital had become her excuse for going to Page, not her reason. "You know, since we got started before the sun rose, we'll be getting to Page in plenty of time to get in a lot of cruising under this beautiful sun. Unless your meeting lasts a long time, that is."

She laughed again. "Temptation, get thee behind me."

He grinned. "Temptation, am I? I kinda like that."

They ate the lunch that Nell had packed at a roadside picnic table surrounded by the colorful beauty of the Painted Desert. The bleak landscape of rounded hillocks and gullies could have been imported from some foreign, lifeless planet, but bright bands of blue, gray, pink, beige, and ocher saved it from being dull as well as bleak. The life that survived there—snakes, scorpions, birds, insects, and lizards all holed up in dens and nests sheltered from the midday sun—left the place to Nell and Dan and Piggy.

Piggy had come with them, of course. Nell hoped that a change of scenery and activity would do the corgi good. The dog had been sulking lately, enthroning herself on the sofa for hours and giving Nell the hairy eyeball every chance she got.

"Something is bothering the little twit," Nell had explained to Dan as they had packed the car early that morning. "She's acting like a sullen teenager."

"And that's different?" he had asked.

Nell had smiled. "More sullen than usual."

He hadn't objected to bringing the dog along. "After all," he had said cheerfully, "how much trouble can one little dog cause?"

The one little dog had regarded him with a spark in her brown eyes that Nell had chosen to ignore.

So far, however, all went well. A blue, cloudless sky arched overhead, and the early May sun shone warmly down upon their little picnic by the side of the highway

"Great sandwiches," Dan told her.

"Safeway deli," she admitted.

He grinned. "Well, they're great. You are an amazing woman."

"Because I can choose good sandwiches at the grocery store?"

"No, because you even bothered to tell me they were from the deli."

"What does it matter?"

"It doesn't matter. But ninety percent of the women I've been with—"

"That number being? . . ." she prompted with lifted brows.

"I'll never tell. But back to my point, ninety percent of them would have let me believe they had slaved into the wee hours of the morning to make us lunch. It wouldn't occur to you to lie, would it?"

"Sure." She gave him an impish grin. "But if you're going to lie, lie about the important stuff. For instance, once I hit forty, I fully intend to lie about my age."

"Evil."

"And I almost always lie about my weight."

"Bad through and through."

"Not nearly as bad as you, Prince of Lies."

He gave her an alarmed look. "Gotcha!" she said lightly, just to let him know she really wasn't all that mad. Would she be here with him if she was all that mad? "You don't really have aspirations to be a journalist, do you?"

She saw a muscle work in his jaw, and his answer took a while coming out. "Uh . . . got me."

"Then it's a good thing you're a success as a photographer."

He took a breath and gave her a long look that she didn't quite understand. Then he grinned, a lopsided, rather half-hearted grin. "Yeah. I'm a dynamite photographer. But, if you want the real truth . . ."

She arched one inquisitive brow. "Yes?"

"Uh . . ."

She provided it for him. "You pretended to be a journalist just to have a reason to hang around me, didn't you?"

He blinked, then smiled wryly. "Would any self-respecting man admit to such a thing?"

She grinned. "Admit it, you cad."

"I'll admit I'm a cad."

"And you're crazy about me."

His eyes crinkled in a teasing smile. "It's the money that catches my interest."

"Do tell."

"That and your cooking," he said around a bite of deli sandwich.

"You are a mercenary soul."

"True."

He leaned forward and brushed a few stray sandwich crumbs from her mouth, then finished the job by brushing her lips with his. The brush became a kiss, and Nell's insides turned to warm butter. Briefly he let her go and smiled just an inch from her face. "Let's see, what else attracts me to you?" He kissed her again, one hand cupping the back of her head and the other smoothing down her back, bringing her closer, so close. But she ached to get closer still. She wanted to weld herself to him so that he would never let her go, flow into him like a stream merging with the strong current of a river.

Then suddenly a cold nose pushed under her shirt and slid against bare skin, and she jumped right out of Dan's arms with a "Yipe!"

Dan sighed. "Then, of course, there's the dog. Any man would want to get close to you just so they could have the incredible dog."

Piggy's expression was the closest thing to a human smirk that Nell had ever seen on a dog's face. She caught her breath, told her heart to stop racing, and brushed her hand along Dan's cheek. "I think she wanted to remind us that we're putting on a show for the highway."

Dan managed a smile. "Considerate of her." The look he gave Piggy, however, had nothing of the smile in it.

They continued down the road, but Nell's insides maintained their melted-butter state. Life sometimes changed so fast that a person could hardly keep up with it. Once before that had happened to her, a nightmare upheaval that had left her disillusioned and shaken. Chicago. A nightmare. Now again her life careened seemingly out of control. Her familiar world had turned topsy-turvy, catapulting her into a different dimension. But this jaunt felt right to her.

This time it wasn't a nightmare. New money. New goals. New purpose. And new love. Especially the last. New love. What could be better?

That new love felt even more right when, as she rummaged through the minivan glove box for a road map, Nell happened on a treasure.

"What's this?" She held up a manila envelope.

Dan glanced over and grimaced. "Uh . . . I brought that along to show you, but now that you've outed my little deception, you can just put it back into the glove box. Or throw it out the window."

"What? Me litter?" She smiled wickedly. "I don't think so." With relish, she pulled a stack of printed pages from the envelope. "You did actually write an article about me!"

"Well . . ."

"Hush! I'm reading. Oh my!" she murmured. " 'Angel with an imp's eyes'? 'Energy all headed in the right direction'?

'Remarkable for keeping a solid grounding in the face of fairy-tale riches.'"

Her face flaming, Nell stole a glance at Dan at the same time he slid his eyes toward her. Their gazes collided in the middle and ricocheted off a surfeit of awkwardness.

Nell hastened back to the article, biting her lip as she read. This woman on the pages wasn't her. She didn't have a gentle smile, a deep connection with needy people and innocent creatures, or a natural grace that came from inner confidence.

"This is the way you see me?" Her insides melted to mush.

"Uh . . . I guess?"

"Oh, Dan. I'm so flattered. This is so complimentary." She laughed. "No one would believe it. No one should believe it."

He looked uncomfortable. "Actually, I'd have to read it again. It's been a while, and I don't remember it all."

"You're really an excellent writer. Maybe you *should* consider taking up journalism."

His laugh was rather weak, she thought. But maybe he was just embarrassed.

"You're not very complimentary to poor Piggy, though. 'Sausage with legs'? 'A sauerkraut personality'? Poor Piggy."

An indignant bark from the kennel in the back proved the dog listened to every word.

Dan let loose a genuine grin. "We journalists have to stick to the truth, you know."

Nell hit him with the rolled up manuscript. "That's for Piggy."

IF I didn't come up with a plan to shoot Cupid out of the sky soon, my money would soon be supporting this poison-pen punk in the style to which I wanted to become accustomed. Not as long as there was breath in this furry little body, I vowed.

So while I sat in my kennel on that long, boring trip, my fertile mind sorted through possibilities. Heaven knew I had nothing else to do in the cage. (Nell uses the excuse that dogs are safer traveling in kennels, but I know she stuck me in there because she didn't want dog hair on her new car upholstery. Trust me, a little dog hair just adds to the ambience.)

So I lay there in my cage and instead of snoozing, which the dog part of me wanted to do, I stayed alert and listened to their chatter. So far I had batted zero in my efforts, admittedly lame, to hit this guy out of the ballpark. But Piggy never gives up. One never knows when something simple might flip a switch in my little brain and turn the lights on some excellent plot.

For instance, I heard we were on the road to Page. Interesting. Page is the gateway to Lake Powell. Very deep, that lake is. Things dropped into those depths disappear forever. Not that I would ever be so rude as to do the villain in, even though he wrote those unjust things about me in that stupid article. No, no! Still, the thought of Dan disappearing tickled my imagination. I filed it away in my brain as Plan A. The new Plan A. The first Plan A, if you remember, proved much too gentle.

Plan B ticked in my brain with louder ticks every time I had to keep company with the studmuffin. I didn't quite know what the idea was yet, but strange familiarities arrested my eye at times— the set of the man's jaw, the line of his nose, something in his voice. Almost as if I had known him somewhere. We corgis are very sharp at such things. Honest. Corgis might look stupid, but they don't miss much.

Unfortunately, I was missing something here. But Plan B would come clear. I knew it would, given time.

Trouble was, I feared time might be in short supply, with Nell gallivanting off to Lake Powell to indulge in a little hankypanky. The poor girl thought she loved this predatory hunk. I saw it in her eyes, in her sighs. When she dreamed at night, she smiled—always a sure sign. She stared into space while sitting at her computer, and the work in front of her never rated that rapt look on her face. Mr. Studly walked into sight and she lit up like a five-hundred-watt bulb. Pathetic. Besides, Nell had prissy little goody-two-shoes written all over her. Unless I miss my guess, she wouldn't even consider crawling under the covers with some guy unless she could excuse it with love.

The little affair wouldn't have been my concern, except that Nell stood guard over MY MONEY! That money painted a target right over her heart, and Mr. Dan Gold-Digger Travis had his bowstring drawn and ready to send an arrow straight to the bull's-eye.

So as we trundled down the highway to Page and Lake Powell, I kept my mind open to Plan A, Plan B, and maybe even a Plan C. I was revving up, and Dan Travis was in big trouble. He just didn't know it yet.

Page is a little spring-up town on the very northern border of Arizona. I say spring-up because it literally did spring up to service visitors to Lake Powell, a man-made lake that is big and deep and has a lot of Arizonans fooled into thinking the state has beachfront property. If you like water and spectacular desert scenery, you'll love Lake Powell. But I never cared for water sports, even when I looked good in a swimsuit. Waterskiing requires too much energy, not to mention coordination, and sunbathing is an invitation to dry skin, sunburn, and skin cancer. Who needs it?

As a dog, I liked the water even less than I did in my former life. One would think that Welsh corgis would be natural swimmers, given that they're shaped like fat torpedoes. But the one time I tried to swim in this corgi body, I rolled over on my back like a dead fish, my feet waving helplessly in the air and my nose precariously close to the water.

So the sight of Lake Powell hulking behind the huge Glen Canyon Dam didn't thrill me. Nor was I happy to see Nell traipse off to her hospital meeting and leave me with our villain. These misguided hospital people didn't want a dog in their stupid meeting. Silly. What did they think the meeting was about?

As Nell left, Dan and I indulged in mutual glares.

"You are going to behave, right, dog?"

Right. And Lake Powell was going to freeze over, despite the ninety-five degree reading on the thermometer outside the hospital.

Eager to get on with his little tryst, Travis drove off to pick up the boat, necessarily dragging me with him. Leaving a girl's beloved dog sitting on the hot pavement in the middle of a busy parking lot is not the way to advance a seduction, and he knew it. Otherwise, I'm sure I would have been burning my butt on the asphalt.

The boat was parked, or anchored, or whatever one does to a boat, at a fancy marina that had a clubhouse, a restaurant, bar, bait shop—all the amenities that water-lovers demand. Of course, the nicer parts of the marina displayed big NO DOGS ALLOWED signs. Killjoys. I could have eaten worms for all anyone cared. That was a possibility, if the bait shop would have let me in.

But no, our villain left me kenneled in the car with the windows open while he collected the boat keys. When he finally let me out, he greeted me with a big scowl.

"No peeing on the dock," he had the nerve to say. As if I would.

He did have enough couth to find a shaded piece of dirt where I could take care of business. If only he hadn't watched so closely (rude, if you ask me.) I could have gotten a shot at his feet, which would have been classic, because he wore only sandals. But having a suspicious nature, he dodged. I got another scowl.

Then he dragged me out onto the dock—dragged, literally, because that thing dipped and wallowed with the ever-moving water, and the water splashed up all too close. Sometimes it even splashed over the dock. I could have gotten my feet wet!

He complained. "You really are a pain in the ass, you know that?"

Ditto to you, fella, I longed to say. All that came out was a sharp bark.

"Okay, dog breath, have it your way."

He picked me up and tucked me squirming beneath his arm, a difficult task, because I was no lightweight. Corgis are short, but they aren't really small. And I had packed on a couple of pounds over the past year, diet or not.

The ride didn't last long, because he was trying to haul along a cooler stuffed with food (for them, of course!) with the other arm. Poor fellow.

Did you detect my snicker there? But wait! Now the action really got fun. He set me down and gave me a stern lecture. If only I could have laughed.

"Listen, dog. You had better start cooperating, or we're going to be on this dock all night. I have a car full of stuff to unload and a boat to get ready to launch. So, do you mind?"

Yes, I minded.

We started up the dock again when I saw my golden opportunity. I walked on the villain's left, as good dogs are supposed to do. That put me in the perfect position to angle him to the right. Just a little, you understand. Just enough so that he trod the boards of the dock only about six inches from the edge.

You know what came next, don't you? Yes! Hee, hee! You're right. A slight revision of Plan A. The water here wasn't deep enough to make the jerk disappear, but a little dunking might give him second thoughts about crossing Piggy. As we walked along the dock, I cleverly managed to tangle in his feet. An innocent-looking cavort put me right where I wanted to be, and put Doofus Dan in the drink. He attempted to save himself with spectacular arm windmilling and bodily gyrations, doomed to fail. The double splash when he hit the water—one for him, one for the cooler—warmed my heart, and my howl of laughter truly came out in a howl.

Take that, you jackass. Try to move in on my trust fund, eh?

Of course, I knew he would extract a price for my little piece of fun. But how much could he do, after all? As far as he was concerned, I was just a clumsy little dog. But whatever the price, watching him rise from the murky depths like an outraged Neptune, mad as hell without anyone to shoot, kick, or pummel, convinced me that no price was too high to pay. Right at the marina, you know, the lake water is none too clean, slicked over with gasoline and oil, churned by wavelets, and inhabited by ugly carp as big as poodles. Not to mention old fish hooks and fish innards. People fish off the dock, and some of them aren't too responsible about leaving a mess behind. Shame on them! Hee, hee!

As he waded toward the dock, our villain fixed me with an evil eye. But I didn't flinch. After all, I was a heroine, and what I did, I did to protect Nell. And my money. He spat and grimaced. I don't imagine that the gasoline tasted too good.

"Hey, buddy," a passerby said. He was portly, sunburned, and wearing a silly little nautical cap. "Need some help?"

"No thank you," my victim growled.

The chubby little guy just couldn't stop being friendly. "There are better places around here to swim."

"My damned dog . . ." He scowled, then continued. "Little accident is all."

"Gotta be careful around water," Mr. Pudgy advised sagely. "A lot of accidents just waiting to happen around boats, you know. Cute dog, by the way."

He leaned down to scratch my ears, and I looked winningly doglike, innocent as could be, then slid a superior glance toward Swamp Thing, whose scowl approached thunderstorm level.

Everything about the poor man squished as he heaved himself onto the dock. Something slimy had plastered itself to his shirt and a strand of something unpleasantly green hung from one ear. He pointed a finger at me. "You!"

Moi?

"You, you . . ." he stuttered with anger. Having to endure a lecture from a sunburned Pillsbury Doughboy might have been the last straw for Studly Dan.

"You did that deliberately, you little snot."

I've been called worse.

"And you're going to pay." He advanced ominously, or I'm

sure he intended to be ominous. It's hard to be taken seriously
when you squish.

"Even rich dogs can be turned over someone's knee to have
their little butts tanned, dog."

You and whose army, buster?

I was thinking of ways to trip him yet again—corgis are
good at such things, when he was saved by the entrance upon
the scene of none other than Nell.

"Hi, you two. I got a taxi ride after . . . omigod! What is going on here?" Laughter bubbled in her voice, but Dan wasn't in
a laughing mood.

"Your dog pushed me off the dock."

Circumstantial evidence.

"Are you all right?"

"I'm wet, slimy, and I smell like a carp. Other than that, I'm
fine."

I whined pathetically and took refuge behind Nell's legs.
"What's wrong, Piggy?" Nell was all sympathy.

"There's nothing wrong with her that a two-by-four
wouldn't solve," the villain groused.

She didn't take him seriously. Too bad. A man who would
beat an innocent little dog would never make it to first base
with Nell, studmuffin or not.

I gave Nell the woebegone dog look and clung to her leg like a
leech. He abused me! my eyes told her. Insulted me! He just
threatened to beat me!

"What's wrong, Piggy? Did Dan scare you by falling into the
lake?"

It was all I could do to keep from smirking.

"She dumped me into the lake, the little miscreant. Deliberately."

"Oh, Dan. It wasn't deliberate. Dogs don't do things like
that."

"You should have seen the look on her face."

"Corgis just naturally look smirky. They can't help it."

I peeked around Nell's legs and did my best to stick out my

tongue at him. He made a sound halfway between a growl and a snort.

"You have this strange idea that she doesn't like you, but she's just a little standoffish to some people. Dogs don't conspire or plot. They don't hold grudges or scheme to get revenge for some imagined slight. That," she said brightly, "is why they're so much easier to be around than most people."

Heh, heh! Did she ever have it wrong!

THE COOLER was in the lake, and while Dan resigned himself to jumping back into the water and retrieving it, the contents were fish food.

"You're already wet," Nell reasoned. "And we can't leave it down there to trash up the lake."

He went willingly enough, but still gave Piggy an extra glare. She replied with a big corgi smile.

While Dan dove down to retrieve the cooler, Nell gave Piggy a knowing look. "Two dunkings for the price of one, eh? You little demon seed."

Piggy's ears perked up. If Nell didn't know better, she would have thought the dog looked guilty. Logically, she knew that she had told Dan the truth. Dogs did not conspire, or plot, or indulge in mischievous pranks. But this dog . . . this dog sometimes seemed more than a dog.

"All right then, Piggy," she said, feeling rather silly. "You've had your fun. So now cut it out. Or I'll revoke your therapy dog license."

Nell left Piggy in Dan's care once again while she drove to a grocery store to replace the cooler's food. Maybe if dog and man were simply thrown together enough, they would learn to like each other. It could happen, she told herself. Piggy, in spite of having a peculiar twist to her personality, was easy to love. What corgi wasn't? And Dan—well, she could fill a volume with why Dan was lovable. The thought put a smile on her face that made the check-out clerk smile in return.

"It's a beautiful day, isn't it?" Nell said, her heart light.

The clerk nodded. "I guess it is. You have a good day, ma'am."

By the time they had loaded the boat and Dan had drilled Nell in water safety, cautioned her at least ten times to not swim when the boat motor was idling—people died every season from inhaling carbon monoxide—and fitted her with one of the Mae Wests stowed under a bench on the deck, the sun rode low in the sky.

"You know," Nell said after the third time she had donned the lifejacket and proved she knew back from front and which strap went where, "sometimes you're still every bit a cop."

He grinned. "Just don't make me get out the handcuffs, sweetheart."

"Oh, now you're scaring me."

He just laughed. His good humor had returned once he had washed the gasoline and lake slime from himself and changed into dry clothes.

They cruised to an out-of-the-way beach—most of the beaches were out-of-the-way once you got beyond the marinas—and there they grilled steaks on a little hibachi and popped open a bottle of Merlot. Dessert was marsh-mallows roasted over the dying coals, accompanied by more Merlot.

By the time they pushed the boat off the sand, stars winked in the sky. Besides their own red and green running lights, the stars were the only lights they could see. The lake was their private playground, black water below, black sky above, girdled by the milky way.

"I just saw a meteor!" Nell lay in a lounge chair on the upper sundeck, her eyes fastened on the crystal-clear heavens. Dan reclined in a chair next to hers, a Budweiser in his hand. "And look! There's Orion's Belt. Or is it his knife? Whatever. There it is. And over there's the Big Dipper."

"Speaking of 'big dippers,'" Dan said, "how many glasses of wine did you have?"

"Just two."

"Ah."

"Did I mention that I'm not much of a wine drinker? It goes to my head really fast."

He chuckled. "No, you didn't mention that."

"That was awfully good Merlot."

"Yes, it was."

Nell felt bubbles of happiness go to her head. They tingled in her brain like fine champagne. Not that she'd ever had really fine champagne. She wasn't much of a champagne drinker either.

She closed her eyes, letting the gentle rolling of the boat lull her into yet deeper relaxation. This was so fine, so perfect. Obscene, really, the two of them luxuriating on a forty-six-foot houseboat complete with a deluxe kitchen and bath, two staterooms with queen-sized beds, two sundecks, and a CD sound system piped throughout the boat. Obscene, wicked, and wonderful. She could get used to living like this.

They were anchored in a little private cove well off the main lake. The warm, dry air carried the perfume of a thousand desert plants. The chair cushioned her softly, the boat rolled in a silent lullaby. Piggy curled at her feet, and nearby, very nearby, sat Dan—handsome, hunky, sometimes heroic, sometimes cranky Dan, who could, Nell had just discovered, grill a steak to a fine turn and extract a wine cork without dropping half of it into the bottle, something she had never learned to do.

Dan . . . Nell smiled, drifting with the boat, the stars, the warm night air.

· · ·

DAN SAT up and shook his head ruefully as Nell drifted off to sleep. Finally he set down his Budweiser and got up. There was no getting around it. Nell had crashed and burned, out for the night. Her breasts—those lovely, tempting breasts—rose and fell in shallow, even breaths. In the starlight, her lashes lay in soft crescents against pale, smooth cheeks.

For a moment he just looked at her, drinking her in. She made his heart turn. Made him laugh. Made him, at times, want to tear out his hair. She brought him into another world, added a new dimension to his life.

And he only had a very limited time before she found him out. Then she would go looking for pointed boots to kick him into the next county. For just this very short time he had her smiles, her kisses, her . . . well, just her. But not tonight.

She murmured but didn't wake when he picked her up and draped her over one shoulder. With the demon dog following, he carried her down the steps, through the kitchen/dining/living area, and into the bedroom, where he laid her on the bed and covered her with a quilt. Piggy jumped onto the bed and curled at Nell's feet. The dog gave him a long, pointed stare that made clear he wasn't welcome.

Wryly, Dan smiled. "This is going well."

chapter 13

NELL WOKE to warm sunlight streaming through the stateroom window. On the ceiling above her head, water reflections rippled back and forth. Muzzy from sleep, she watched the light weave and interweave, until her stomach started to weave as well.

"Uk." She propped herself up on her elbows and looked around. The stateroom dripped in decor, matching curtains and valances, built-in oak dresser and bed tables, and, of course, the comfy queen-sized bed. She lay on top of the bedspread (which matched the curtains, naturally) with a quilt thrown over her. Beneath the quilt, at the foot of the bed, a corgi-sized lump emitted mastiff-sized snores. Nell flicked back the quilt.

"Good morning to you, too, Piggy."

The dog snored on.

Nell tried to crank up her brain to normal capacity, but a headache interfered. That and a sour taste in her mouth told her she must have indulged in wine the night before. She didn't remember coming into the stateroom and putting herself to bed, which meant that Dan must have dumped her here and taken himself somewhere else.

"Great," she muttered, falling back onto the pillow. "My chance for the big love scene, and I blow it. Nice going, Nell."

In the small lavatory, she splashed cold water on her face, brushed her teeth, and fluffed her hair with her fingers. Then she followed the smell of coffee into the galley, where Dan whistled to himself while cracking eggs into a bowl. He wore nothing but swimming trunks, and his hair was damp and towel-tousled. The sight of him was almost enough to drive away Nell's headache.

When he saw her, his whistled tune ended in a wolf whistle.

"Don't be cruel." Nell grimaced at the bright light that came through the galley window.

Dan chuckled. "I don't think I've ever seen you first thing in the morning."

"Usually I'm a bit more chipper."

"You look good to me, sweetheart." He put aside the eggs and touched her cheek with one finger. "Are those circles under your eyes?"

She grimaced. "Don't let me drink wine from now on."

"A lightweight drinker. I should have guessed. Well, we'll fix you up." He handed her a cup of steaming coffee. "Eggs and bacon coming up, my lady. Just you go out on the deck, sit down, and soak up some sun."

Without argument, she complied.

Nell surprised herself by cleaning the plate of eggs and bacon that Dan brought her. The hot coffee made her feel almost human again.

"Where's the demon dog?" Dan asked between bites of toast.

"Still asleep."

"I was hoping maybe she'd fallen overboard during the night."

"No you weren't! 'Demon dog'! Poor little Piggy."

" 'Poor little Piggy,' my ass." Then he chuckled. "I have to give that dog credit, though. She has character."

Dan wouldn't let Nell wash the dishes. Instead, he offered to treat her headache.

"Just sit here." He threw a boat cushion onto the sun-drenched deck. "I'll give you the old Travis hangover cure."

She sat. "I'm probably the only person in the world who can get a hangover from just two glasses of wine."

He sat behind her on one of the cushioned benches and settled her between his knees. "Just lean back and relax."

She groaned with sheer rapture as he threaded strong fingers through her hair and gently massaged her scalp.

"Oh yes. That feels so good."

"We wouldn't want you to spend this beautiful day with a headache." His thumb found a knot in her neck that she hadn't known was there. Under his coaxing, the knot dissolved. In fact, just about every muscle in her body warmed and melted.

"There's usually a spot right here..." Fingertips converged in a mass attack on the top of her head, right in the center. It was a tender attack, gentle, but firm. Waves of bliss traveled all the way down to Nell's toes.

"Oh my..." she sighed.

"Yup," he agreed. "Right there's the spot. All our tensions and aches and pains just gather in a stream and leave through the top of our head."

Every breath was rapture. "Wonderful."

"A massage therapist in Camp Verde told me that. She works in a beauty parlor next door to my office."

"Mmm. You have an office in Camp Verde?"

"Sure. A man's gotta have an office, you know. If he doesn't have an office of some sort, he's just a bum."

She really knew very little about Dan Travis, Nell pondered, even though she had known him two months or so. One thing she did know—he had great hands. And right

222 / E M I L Y C A R M I C H A E L

now, just about anything he wanted to do with those hands was just peachy with her.

How far they might have taken that wonderful massage would remain a question, however, because a cold poke on the bottom of Nell's bare foot brought her out of paradise. She opened her eyes to meet Piggy's disapproving gaze.

"Oh dear."

"I see our chaperone woke up."

With great reluctance, Nell got up. "No doubt she needs to find a bush onshore."

"Dogs need a bush?"

"This one does."

Once Piggy's personal needs were met, they pulled up anchor and motored out of the cove. Lake Powell was a huge lake with a multitude of branches meandering miles upon miles through spectacular sandstone canyons. Even in high season, when people flocked to the lake from California, Arizona, Utah, Colorado, New Mexico, and even the Midwestern and Eastern states, the very vastness of the watery paradise made crowded water a rarity. They motored an hour without seeing another boat, put-putting through awe inspiring canyons and sticking their noses into deserted little coves that looked as if they'd never seen a trace of man.

Midmorning, they anchored again off a sandy, shallow shelf where the lake was warm and glassy green.

"You never did tell me how your meeting went," Dan noted to Nell as they lounged on the upper sundeck.

Her face lit up. "It went great. They've read the new research showing how much therapy animals help in the healing process, and they want us. Now it's a matter of finding people up here who are willing to put in the time to train their animals. We're going to offer scholarships for interested pet owners to go to the Delta Society conference later this month. That will get people motivated, I think."

"Hadn't you better form a foundation or something?"

"Mckenna's looking into that. She's the legal beagle."

He chuckled dryly. "Yeah. I can't imagine Mckenna letting anyone get away with anything. But I'm glad she's protective of you. You're too trusting, you know."

"Well, I certainly made a mistake in trusting you, didn't I?" Her merry laughter assuaged the guilt that flashed across his face. "Mr. Journalist! Journalist, indeed!"

Dan dodged a playful blow from her fist. "I think it's time for a dip," he announced just before taking himself out of range with a dive into the green water.

Nell thought the dive a bit dangerous for her taste, and watched anxiously until his head broke water. Shaking his head like a dog shedding water, he grinned up at her.

"Come on in, sissy girl. You brought a suit, didn't you?"

"I did."

"Too bad. I was hoping you might want to skinny-dip. I could lose my trunks real easily."

She laughed. "In your dreams, hotshot."

Nell donned her suit and looked at herself dubiously in the stateroom mirror before she ventured out. She would never make the cover of *Cosmo*. The two-piece suit Mckenna had talked her into buying didn't hide as much as she would have liked.

Oh well, she thought, she could hope that Dan preferred curves to angles, cushioning to bones. Nothing would spoil her good mood, not even an unwanted ten pounds.

Dan waited for her on the rear deck, dripping water onto the swim platform. He greeted her with an appreciative whistle.

"Right," she scoffed.

"Too right," he agreed. "Ready to get wet?"

"I believe in getting into the water slowly," she said primly. "One toe at a time."

"I don't think so."

Without compunction, he scooped her up and tossed her into the lake. The cool water made her shriek. In midsummer, the lake would feel like a bathtub, but not in early May.

"You snake!"

"At your service. Yee-haw!"

He took the plunge right behing her, landing cannonball-style and sending a tsunami her way. When she stopped gasping and managed to shake the water from her eyes, she sent a spray of water toward him in retaliation. "And I thought you were a grown man! You're nothing but an over-grown kid."

Laughing, he sprayed back. "Water does this to me."

Piggy stood on the swim platform watching them, or rather glaring at them.

Dan beckoned to her. "Come on in, Pig. Cool off that fat little body."

"She won't. Piggy doesn't swim worth beans. I tried to teach her to swim in Mckenna's pool, and she got so mad that she marched into the condo and peed on the living room carpet."

"The little demon."

Dan sent a little spray of water Piggy's way. The corgi backed up hastily and barked.

"Same to you, Devil Dog."

"You're going to hurt her feelings."

"Ha! I could only hope."

They swam, diving and splashing and playing like por-poises. Nell enjoyed the pleasant burn of muscles too long neglected, the cool kiss on water sliding over her skin, the slightly reckless feel of being alone with Dan Travis in a state of near undress, with the water flowing between them, connecting them, the teasing waves first pushing them to-gether, then pulling them apart. Nell had never considered swimming a sensual activity. How wrong she had been—as she discovered when she ran out of breath and took refuge by the boat, hanging onto the swim platform. Dan caught her there—as she hoped he might.

"Hi there," he said.

"Hi yourself. You swim like a selkie."

"What's a selkie?"

"A legendary creature who turned from a seal into a man at will."

He grinned and barked in a pretty good imitation of a seal. Piggy jumped forward and barked in alarm, and he laughed. "Get lost, Pig. I have a few things to say to your mom."

"You do?" Nell's heart picked up its pace.

"Well, maybe not in so many words."

He had caged her against the platform with his wonderfully muscular arms. She could escape easily enough by simply ducking beneath the water and swimming out of his little trap, but escape was the last thing on Nell's mind. Her breasts nearly touched his bare chest. Their legs, treading water, brushed against each other, tantalizing, then parting.

"You are a corker, Nell Jordan," he said quietly, closing the small gap between them. "A corker indeed."

He claimed her mouth in a kiss, and she offered it freely. The waves bounced them gently, pulling them apart, then pushing them close, until he welded them together by grasping her hips between his legs.

"A corker," she murmured when her mouth came free. "Is that good?"

"I'll say."

They kissed again, and this time his hand slipped beneath her rather flimsy bathing suit top to massage her breast. The ache this liberty inspired burned like a hot brand. She pressed herself into his hand, opened her mouth wider for his invasion, then purred with approval when he unfastened the catch of her top, flung the scrap of material onto the swim platform, then immersed himself to take her breast in his mouth.

The sweet suction made Nell catch fire. When he came up for breath, she wrapped her long legs around his hips as he tongued drops of lake water from her throat and shoulders.

Nell felt as if she were falling into a whirlpool of fire, fire that burned but didn't consume, burned with so sweet a pain. Sweet, oh so sweet. Her breasts ached with the burn where they rubbed against his hard bare chest. Where she held him between her legs, his arousal pressed against her, demanding and strong. She wanted to grind down on him, open to him, impale herself. Most unladylike.

His thumbs slid beneath what remained of her swimming suit and pushed it downward. She struggled to free one leg, and his own suit splatted onto the deck.

"Oh my," she groaned as he came up against her. Nothing stood between them now, not even their own inhibitions.

But he didn't move. Only his thumb moved against her in that most sensitive place, caressing, gentling, until her head lolled back against the deck in sensual languor.

And suddenly the whole wonderful scene broke to pieces when something sharp rapped against her skull.

"Ow!"

She twisted away from heaven to see Piggy holding her cell phone, which had been safely stowed in her briefcase, between her jaws. It was a rather large phone, as cell phones go, and made an effective head rapper in the hands—or rather the jaws—of a determined corgi.

Dan actually had the nerve to laugh. "I've heard of inopportune phone calls, but this is ridiculous."

Nell merely gaped in astonishment.

"I told you she was a devil dog."

Piggy looked very satisfied with herself, and Nell sank into the water, head and all, in pure embarrassment. When she surfaced, Dan smiled. The cell phone had disappeared, only he and Piggy knew where, and Piggy looked miffed.

"You know what?" Dan circled her bare waist with his hands and made soothing motions with his thumbs.

She couldn't speak.

"Piggy is right."

That had to be a first, she thought.

"You deserve a soft bed, flowers, music."

She let out a long, slow breath. He kissed her quickly, careful to not suck them into anything that might jump the gun on the bed, flowers, and music—or send Piggy off to hunt another blunt object. Then he grinned. "But you get no wine."

Nell laughed. A certain amount of tension dissolved.

"How about lunch?" Dan suggested.

"Geez! Do you ever stop thinking about your stomach?"

"Oh yeah." His hands roamed upward over her bare breasts. "Don't make me show you what I'm thinking about, sweetheart, or we'll never get out of the water."

Getting out of the water entailed a certain amount of awkwardness for Nell, who suffered a case of shyness. Dan seemed not at all self-conscious as he climbed the ladder onto the boat and casually stepped into the swim trunks that he had earlier so eagerly discarded. Nell did sneak a peek, then immediately felt her face burn. Actually, her whole body burned. The lake water around her should have come to a boil.

"Coming?" he asked, offering a hand to help her up the ladder.

She bit her lip. She had managed to regain the bottom half of her suit, but the top half lay on the deck out of reach.

"Nell?"

He looked at her, and she looked back, face flaming. He grinned. "Oh shoot! Dan, you grinning jackass, just hand me a towel, would you?"

His grin grew broader. "And if I don't?"

"Don't get smart, Travis. Either hand me a towel or the top to my bathing suit."

"You could get wrinkled if you stay too long in the water, you know?"

"You're being juvenile."

"It's what I do best."

"I am not coming aboard with half of me in the alto-gether." Wearing only the bottom half of her suit left about ninety-five percent of her still bare as she was born. "Dan!"

He dropped a towel over the side. "Here you go."

She wrapped the towel around her upper half and climbed aboard, to be immediately captured in Dan's arms.

"You know what?" he asked just before taking her mouth in a kiss.

"What?" she managed to respond.

"I'll make you a bet that by the time we've been on this boat another day, I'll fix it so that you can walk around these decks baby-ass naked and not think a thing of it."

He kissed her again, winding his fingers through the wet strands of her hair to hold her head still for his deep pos-session. The towel dropped, leaving her breasts to cuddle up to his bare chest. By the time he set her free, she was breathless and burning.

"I love you, Nell Jordan."

It hadn't taken the passage of a day, because Nell stood there, in the glare of the sunlight, the next thing to naked, and didn't think a thing of it. She smiled up at him and wound her arms around his lean waist.

"You know what?" she asked, using his favorite phrase. "I love you right back."

For Nell, the rest of the day floated along like a dream. One part of her expected it to end abruptly, as dreams gen-erally do. Another part of her mind refused to analyze, crit-icize, or otherwise make sense of what she was doing. Fairy tales always had a happy ending, she told herself, and this had to be a fairy tale.

Every once in a while an unwelcome question intruded into her happiness: What would Dan Travis think if he found out this fairy-tale princess had a bit of a past? Pasts had a nasty habit of screwing up the future. But she didn't want to question anything just then. She simply wanted to enjoy her days in the sun, enjoy love, and let the sensuality of Dan's smile wash over her like a warm flood.

They ate sandwiches, and Nell had to keep Dan from giving Piggy part of his.

"She looks hungry," he said.

"She's a corgi, and corgis always look hungry. It's what they do best. She's on a diet, remember? Besides," Nell reminded him with a knowing smile, "she's the devil dog."

"Even little devils need to eat."

"She gets plenty to eat."

"Just looking at those pleading eyes makes my stomach rumble."

"Then fix yourself another sandwich."

He went to the galley to do just that.

"Softie," she called after him.

"I am hard as nails, and don't you forget it, you and that dog."

She just chuckled.

They spent the rest of that lovely day poking about the lake, sunning themselves on the sundeck, watching waterskiers zipping along behind jet-fast ski boats. Nell had brought a Tony Hillerman novel to read, but she didn't so much as crack it open, too lazy to concentrate on a mystery. She reserved all her concentration for delicious anticipation of beds and flowers and music. And Dan. The important ingredient. Dan. To hell with flowers and music. To hell with a bed, even, as long as she had Dan.

When the sun sank behind the peach-colored sandstone cliffs, they grilled Italian sausages on the beach and watched the stars pop out, one by one. Then they played a game of checkers on the back deck. The battle on the board ended in a slaughter, with Nell the victor.

"You let me win," she accused.

He laughed wryly. "I never *let* anyone win anything. It's not in my nature."

"Then I really won! Woo-hooo." She gave herself a high five and strutted around the deck in a victory dance, until she ran into a hard wall that turned out to be Dan's chest.

"Don't push it, Jordan, or I'll demand a rematch and wipe up the board with your puny little men."

His eyes crinkled at the corners in the way Nell had come to love.

"Hogwash! My red guys kick butt."

He thrust his face forward. "Wanna fight?"

A sharp bolt of heat shot through her. "Bring it on."

His mouth clamped onto hers, demanding surrender. She opened to him willingly, circling his broad chest with her arms and tantalizing his back with her nails. The kiss became deeper, fiercer, warming her soul at the same time it seduced her body.

When they came up for air, she cuddled against him and smiled seductively. "I still win."

He bellowed out a laugh, and Nell found herself flying through the air to land with a humbling splash in the lake. Another splash immediately followed, and Dan's head surfaced next to hers.

"I had all my clothes on," she told him indignantly.

"I can fix that, if you want."

"In your dreams, copper." But she gave him a seductive smile that went well with the moonlight, and as she kicked away, she let her bare toes brush him seductively. If she had any luck at all, his dreams were very shortly going to come true.

They swam for a time in the moonlight, teasing, touching, laughing, and watching the waves dance in a milky sparkle of light. Once a big, slow-cruising boat motored close to their cove, sending a huge wake to bob them up and down in the water, set the houseboat to rocking, and crash upon the beach.

"We could surf!" Nell said with a laugh.

"Be my guest," he invited. "As for me, I'm a desert boy."

They let the waves carry them toward the houseboat, grabbed the ladder, and climbed aboard together. Piggy greeted them with scolding, staccato barks that told them just what she thought about their loose behavior. They ignored her.

"Want to play another game of checkers?" She beckoned him with an impish smile.

"No."

"Poker?"

"Not unless it's strip poker."

"I know!" She made her voice husky and enticing. "Monopoly! A nice, long game of Monopoly!"

He caught her around the waist. "Not a chance."

The scene was perfect—the moonlight, the warm, desert-scented air, and the two of them, delicious tension arcing between them in a silent sizzle of energy.

Or at least the scene would have been perfect if there had truly been just two of them instead of three. But there were three, and one of them rumbled with an impressive growl.

"Piggy," Dan advised. "Get a life. Your own life."

He kissed Nell on the tip of the nose and smiled down at her. "I think there's a little vase of flowers in the bedroom, and music playing on the CD system."

"Maybe we'd better go see."

"Maybe we'd better."

A throaty roar signaled the return trip of the big boat that had passed earlier, and the wake sent the houseboat cavorting. Piggy's chorus of unhappy growls ended in a surprise yip as the boat tipped her toward the gate that opened onto the swim platform—the gate Nell and Dan had left open in their preoccupation with each other. The corgi's yip ended in a loud splash as she landed in the lake.

"Omigod!" Nell cried. "Piggy! Piggy!"

Dan rushed to get the boat light, which boasted a candle

power that could stab a mile into the dark night. He soon caught Piggy in its glare.

"She can't swim! She'll drown!"

"Damn dog!"

The corgi tried to swim, but her sausage-like body turned in the water so that her stubby legs flailed uselessly in the air. Before they knew it, she sank, still flailing.

Nell started toward the swim platform, but Dan got there first. "I'll get her. Hold the light on the spot she disappeared." He dived into the center of the spot of light. After ten seconds, he surfaced without the dog. Nell moaned.

But Dan wasn't through. He took a lungful of air and dived again. This time he was down longer. A hundred images of Piggy flashed through Nell's mind. The dog had only been with her a year, but they had racked up a host of memories. Piggy curled into the bend of Nell's knees at night, keeping her legs warm. Piggy trying to raid the pantry. Piggy in the hospital with a toddler crying from too many shots. Piggy trying to push a chair toward the kitchen table to get at a roast pork. Piggy with tinsel hanging off her ears from browsing through the Christmas tree. Piggy tripping Dan and sending him into the lake.

She hadn't actually witnessed the last one, but Nell could picture exactly how it had unfolded.

"Oh, Dan!" she prayed earnestly. "Find her. Find her."

Dan surged to the surface, a wet brown dog locked under one arm. With an efficiency born of long experience, he wrapped the little victim in a towel and laid her flat on the deck with his ear to her chest.

"She's not breathing."

Nell's heart plummeted.

He turned her over and pressed down on her rib cage. Water ran from Piggy's mouth, but she didn't take a breath.

"Damn!" he said, and turned her on her back. "No heartbeat. Not breathing." Gently he pressed against an eyelid, trying for a blink reflex. And got none. "She's pretty far under."

Nell frantically pleaded, "Can't we do anything?"

Dan looked down at the dog and shook his head ruefully. "Piggy, old girl, you're going to owe me for this."

Then he circled the little muzzle with one big hand and applied his mouth to her wet, black nose, blowing gently. Her chest rose and fell. He did it again. And again. He pushed down on her sternum to massage the heart.

"CPR?" Nell asked, amazed.

"Sure thing." He seemed totally unfazed by the idea of giving mouth-to-nose resuscitation to a dog. "A cop in L.A. learns to do everything."

He continued. Nell pleaded aloud with Piggy to respond. "Don't die, Piggy. Don't go. Please!"

I WATCHED the whole drama from a seat somewhere near the upper sundeck. Except I floated rather than sat. And while part of me observed the scene as Piggy, part of me floated there as Lydia Keane—not unlike how I feel most of the time, really. Right then, however, I saw myself as Lydia, curves intact, legs so long they reached clear up to my . . . well, you know, and hair the color of an Irish setter. Irish setter? Hardly. That was the Piggy part of me butting in. The name of that particular shade was Siren Red, and I had spent a bundle on a hair stylist who could get the color just right.

Piggy hadn't taken a hike. Don't get me wrong. I did see myself as Lydia Keane once again, and I also saw myself as Piggy. Very confusing. But then, what does one expect when gazing down upon such a scene with a soul undecided whether to stay or go?

"Well, Lydia?"

Of course it was Stanley. Who else would butt in at such a delicate time?

"Or perhaps I should still call you Piggy? I see a lot of Piggy in you these days. It's an improvement, you know. Though lately you've been behaving rather badly."

I wasn't having it. "Stan, old man, are you up to your tricks again?"

"Tricks?"

"Don't act innocent. You've been amusing yourself at my expense ever since you got your clutches on me."

"Piggy, old girl, Beings in my position do not possess clutches."

"Don't change the subject. What is going on here?"

"A good question, my girl. Why don't you tell me?"

"Aren't you supposed to be watching me? I drowned. And a very unpleasant experience it was, too."

"Hm," was all the troublemaker said.

Then someone else appeared, a familiar face and twisted, crotchety smile. Except he looked younger and in much better condition than when I'd last seen him leaving his body in that hospital bed.

"Hey, Frank," I greeted him. "How you doing, buddy?"

"Can't complain too much."

For Frank, that was a grand testimonial to the afterlife. And here I thought that he'd be coming back as a poodle or some other low form of life.

"Thanks for the money, fella."

"Don't mention it. I certainly don't need it."

I threw a cross look toward Stan. "Not that I've gotten to enjoy it much."

Stanley, the worm, just smiled.

"Just thought I'd come around to say hi, little Piggy. If I'd known you were such a luscious doll, I would have left you more."

"You're sweet." Unlike some celestial bean-counters I could name.

Frank glanced down toward the scene of my demise with a particularly fond look for . . . was it for the furry, limp me, or for tearful Nell? I couldn't tell.

"Frank," the bean-counter interrupted. "Don't you have work to do? I think one of your clients in Pennsylvania just fell off her bicycle. Your beat, isn't it?"

"Sure thing, boss." He waved merrily and disappeared.

That old bugger was a guardian angel? And I got stuck in a dog suit? I told you the universe was unjust! The very thought put me in an even worse mood. I scowled at Stanley. "So, Stan, am I dead, or what?"

"We don't use that word around here, Lydia. We prefer to say someone has come home."

Hairsplitting. Stan is great at it.

"Just tell me if I'm coming or going!" My patience was wearing thin. After all, I was in the middle of a traumatic experience down on that boat.

"Do you want to come home, Piggy?"

The fact that I didn't call him on using my dog name shows that I was a bit upset.

"There are some openings you could fill."

"Like what?"

"A very deserving lady with multiple sclerosis needs a service dog and can't quite afford the fee. That would be quite a promotion for you. I could outfit you as a golden retriever. Would you like that?"

I grimaced. "Another dog suit?"

"Didn't you know that all service dogs and guide dogs for the blind are sent down from my department?"

I did, on some level, but those particular angels had to work too hard for my taste.

"Or there's an opening in my personnel office."

Me, a bean-counter? I don't think so.

"Mr. Travis down there seems to be working very hard to make sure you stay on earth."

"Of course he's working hard," I snapped. "If I go, so goes all that lovely money that he wants to get his hands on."

"I'm not sure he's interested in your money, Piggy."

Stan was clueless. But I had known that a long time.

Go or stay? Go or stay?

This was quite a decision. I looked down at the scene below. The indignity of it all for poor Piggy, with Dan blowing into her nose and treating her chest like a pump handle. The upside was, Dan couldn't be liking it that much, either.

Go or stay? Go or stay?

Nell was pretty frantic, and I did sort of like her. She was a boob, but a well-meaning boob, for all that. And she was very vulnerable right then.

Go or stay?

Life as a dog abounded with hassles. No refrigerator privileges. No private bathroom. And the diet Nell had me on! It sucked all the joy from living.

Go or stay?

On the other hand, there was all that money. And soft beds. I would miss my friends. Titi was amusing, for a cat. Idaho was fun to tease. And there were my friends from Colorado—Amy and Dr. Doofus, Joey and Ben. I would miss seeing them again.

And of course, again, all that money . . .

Go or stay?

"Well, Piggy? We can't hover here all night. I'm a busy Being, you know."

"Okay, Stan," I said. "Give me some clues here. Dan down there is pretty much a villain, isn't he?"

"Is he?"

"He's hooked up with Nell to get my money, right?"

"Is that what you think?"

"You could at least be of some help, you know? I know you arranged this whole situation as some sort of a lesson. You're going to pull the rug out from under me at the last minute, aren't you? I'm never going to enjoy any of my money."

Stan just looked inscrutable. He does inscrutable very well.

His lack of cooperation, familiar as it was, got me in a huff. "Well, if you're going to be that way, no help at all, then I'd better get back down there and take charge of the situation. Nell can't manage without me, obviously. And what would the

Hearts of Gold group do if I wasn't there to hold them together? I'm staying, and I don't care what you think about it."

This time his smile seemed genuine. "Piggy, dear, you do have a heart of gold, you know. Try to use it."

That's Stan for you. Always lecturing.

Then it hit me. Seeing Frank without the ravages of age lit a bright bulb of clarity in my brain. No wonder Dan Travis had seemed familiar sometimes—his face, his smile, his voice. They were Frank Cramer's face, smile, and voice with fifty years stripped away.

Now wasn't that interesting!

"DON'T DIE, Piggy! Don't go. Please!"

Dan pulled back from the limp body and shook his head. "She's gone, Nell. I'm sorry."

Then Piggy stirred, coughed, took a rasping, shallow breath. Dan bent over once again and massaged her chest.

"Come on, Piggy girl. Give it all you've got."

She struggled to take a breath on her own. Her eyes creaked open and connected with Dan's, connected with a fierce glare that was nearly human. Then she coughed up a fountain of foul water—right into her savior's face.

chapter 14

"DAN, YOU'RE a miracle worker."

Dan rinsed the soap from his face and reached for a towel. "That's me," he agreed with a twisted smile. "Just call me Saint Dan. How is our little furry water nymph doing?"

"She's great. It's amazing. You'd think that nothing ever happened."

"Good for her. Dog of iron. Swims like she's made of iron, too."

Nell closed her eyes. "I don't even want to think about it. I was so scared. Just thinking about it makes me want to . . . want to . . ." She opened her eyes and smiled. "Makes me want to kiss you."

"Be my guest," he invited, opening his arms.

"My hero." She planted one on his mouth, then surrendered as his arms went around her and he deepened the kiss. A familiar heat curled inside her.

"Was that my reward?" he teased.

"No," she said languidly. "No. I think it was my reward."

He kissed the tip of her nose, the center of her forehead,

and then settled again on her mouth. "Is Piggy out of our hair for a while?" he whispered against her mouth.

"She's curled up on her bed."

"That's an excellent idea. We could follow suit."

"We could," she agreed quietly.

He smoothed back her hair with his hands and gave her a look that made her knees turn to water. "Nell," he said softly. "All teasing aside, sweetheart, you've got to know that I invited you onto this boat with every intention of spending the whole four days making love to you."

"Then we've wasted a whole day."

He touched her cheek with his thumb, and his eyes crinkled into a smile. "I do love you. But I don't want you to do anything you don't want to do."

"Like I would."

"If ever a doubt comes into your mind, for whatever reason, I want you to believe that I love you."

"Dan Travis, you are the best thing that's ever come into my life. Now kiss me."

He did, with an urgency that left her breathless.

"I really think you should get out of those wet clothes."

Nell was surprised they were still wet. Those kisses should have steamed them dry. She smiled coyly. "Maybe I'm shy."

"Maybe," he suggested with a chuckle, "you need help."

A skitter of corgi nails across the deck signaled trouble, and just as Dan reached for the top button of Nell's shirt, a wet, furry torpedo knocked them both off balance. This time, however, Dan had no patience with corgi tricks. He scooped up the dog under one arm, grabbed the dog bed with the other hand, and deposited them both in the small second stateroom. When Nell opened her mouth to protest, he closed it with his own.

"I saved her pudgy little life," he explained after nearly driving the problem of Piggy from her mind. "She owes me big. And now she can just step aside for a while and let her mother get some attention for a change."

Nell couldn't disagree with that, because his fingers were already cleverly opening the buttons of her damp shirt, and with every button he opened, he traced a little fire onto her flesh.

"Do you know," he said with a smile, gently pushing her back to lean against the bulkhead, "that a wet shirt like this one here shows off every one of your delicious curves." He smoothed his palm over a particularly generous curve, then bent to take a cotton-covered nipple in his mouth.

The warmth curling inside Nell burst into flames. How wise she had been not to wear a bra.

"I like the way you take your time at things," she breathed, letting her head loll back against the bulkhead.

"I aim to please."

"But . . ." She groaned as he pushed aside the flimsy cloth and pressed his warm mouth against bare flesh. "But there are times," she gasped, "when getting to the point is a good thing."

"No, no." Another button fell to his fingers. Then another. "Shows how much you know, sweetheart. Patience brings great rewards."

He licked a warm, lazy line around the heretofore neglected breast, and as simply as that, sent her tumbling off the edge of ecstasy in a way that she hadn't guessed possible.

The damp shirt dropped to the floor, and he went on to the challenge of her shorts, cutoff jeans, loose in the waist and snug at the hips. He didn't even have to pop the button to slip his hands inside the waistband and run teasing fingers over the silky nylon of her panties.

But Nell was impatient. "Just let me get out of—"

"Sssssshhhh!" he soothed. "I'm doing the work here."

"But—"

He stifled further protest with a kiss, a tactic he employed to perfection. And while his mouth was busy, his fingers deftly unfastened, one by tantalizing one, the metal buttons of her cutoffs.

"I'm going to explode," she warned him when his fingers went exploring warm and intimate places.

"Be my guest."

She did. She did several times, in fact, during the process of getting out of her shorts. Dan made peeling off a woman's clothes a sensual art form.

When they finally got to the bed, Nell scarcely knew how they came to be there. On the bed table sat a little glass vase with limp wildflowers Dan had apparently managed to collect, and vintage Paul McCartney played over the sound system. Flowers and music, just as he'd promised. But he didn't give her much time to appreciate the amenities. He was too busy appreciating her.

And vice versa. Nell had never known that uninhibited lovemaking could be so intense, like a tidal wave carrying everything before it, flooding both body and mind with such urgency that response wasn't considered, or chosen, but just happened. She hadn't guessed she could be jaybird naked with a man and feel totally unselfconscious about any part of her body. That she could feel worshiped, admired, adored, without wondering if the adoration was some kind of an act.

Nor would she have believed that she could have explored every beautiful inch of a nude male body without a hint of embarrassment. That she could revel in his blatant response to her. That she could tease, tantalize, and enjoy driving a man to the edge of desperation.

Then she finally understood, when they had both driven the other to the limit, when Dan smoothly, but rather breathlessly, groped in the bedside table drawer for protection, then settled himself between her legs and gave her what her body craved: She understood that everything coiled together in the end, desire and emotion, sex and love, heart and body. Lacking one aspect, all others were incomplete.

He took her deep and hard, and she loved it. Loved him. His possession touched not only her body, but her soul, making her feel complete. They truly came together, and she no longer walked alone. If she could have kept him inside her forever, she would have.

And had it been possible, she thought he would have stayed.

HOW ABOUT that? I came back to this lousy planet, volunteered for more duty in dog fur—totally selflessly, mind you, to help Nell and save her from you know who—and what did I get? Tossed into a closet while they cavorted behind closed doors. You know what I'm going to say. Unfair. Totally, shamelessly, unfair.

You'd think that someone who had just come back from the dead might have rated a little more attention, right? You'd think those two could have forgotten their own little games to comfort the traumatized dog, right?

But no! Without a second thought, Nell threw me over for the studmuffin who was trying to get his oversized paws on my money. MY money. I got pushed into a cold, lonely closet while they had their fun and Studly Dan claimed his victory. I was miffed, to put it mildly.

Actually, I wasn't just miffed. I was livid, because now I had an inkling of the identity of our villain. His resemblance to my late benefactor Frank Cramer couldn't have been coincidence. No indeed. Dan Travis was part of Frank's disinherited family. Cousin, grandson, nephew—the exact pedigree didn't matter. What did matter was the certainty that the man had nefarious designs even beyond fortune hunting. Who knew what the villain intended?

There are some who might think I shouldn't have assumed the worst, that I should have been grateful to the guy for pulling me from the drink and saving my furry little life. But I knew he'd played the hero for less than heroic motives. If I had decided to go, all that lovely money would have landed right back in Jared Johansen's lap, to be doled out to the heir-in-waiting, whoever that was, and most probably the heir-in-waiting wouldn't have shared with Dan. Oh no. Nell could be manipulated, but had I gone, Nell wouldn't have had my trust fund waiting in the wings, and Dan would have been fresh out of heiresses to court. So of course he labored long and hard to bring me back to life.

And, of course, his efforts impressed the knickers right off of Nell. She flew into his arms as if someone had launched her from a catapult. Not that she hadn't been headed there already. Who would have thought that the girl had so little restraint when it came to men? Up until now, she'd been a modest and mousy little do-gooder. Boring, but predictable. Enter Dan Travis and she suddenly becomes a dirty dancer. Silly girl. Lucky for her that she had me to straighten her out. Now that I had solid, damning information the proved the studmuffin's deception, I simply had to convey that information to Nell. Easy, you think? You have never been a dog.

So I lay on the stateroom's queen-sized bed thinking of ways to accomplish my mission. Yes, a queen-sized bed. Did you think I was going to settle for that little dog bed when a nice, big, pillowtop mattress was available?

Okay. I confess. This wasn't cold, lonely closet they stuck me in. It was a stateroom with all the appointments. Plus the temperature hovered around seventy-five, and moonlight streamed through the window to make things cozy. Still, Nell should have made a fuss over me instead of that snake in the grass. I exaggerated a bit to make a point, something Stanley is always dinging me for.

So I languished in my comfortable prison, alternately napping (another corgi habit) and plotting—plotting trouble for Dan, liberation for Nell, and for me, ways to apply for a platinum VISA card without anyone knowing I was a dog.

• • •

DAWN HAD just begun to gray the sky when Dan opened the door to the second stateroom. Piggy curled in the middle of the bed, and the glare she sent him could have boiled water for morning coffee.

He grinned. "I was about to say 'no hard feelings, kiddo,' but I see that there are."

The corgi didn't move.

"I'm guessing you have to make a little trip ashore, princess." He held up her leash and collar. "And I don't trust you for one minute."

The dog rumbled when he slipped on the collar, but Dan knew her well enough by now to dismiss the empty threat.

"Just shut your little yap," he advised amiably. "Your mom's asleep, and she'd probably like to stay that way."

For some reason, he was coming to like the perverse little canine snot. Which just went to show that getting high on a woman turned a man's brain to mush.

With the dog beneath his arm, Dan waded though chest-high water to get to the beach. Piggy squirmed and whined objection.

"Don't want to get your paws wet, princess? If you don't settle down, you're going to get more than those little feet wet."

She promptly froze still as a statue, but the look she gave Dan sent a thousand knives his way.

"I have to give you credit, dog. You've got more personality than a lot of people I know. I'm not saying it's a good personality, but you are a distinct character." He set her down on the beach and made shooing motions. "Now go find your bush."

Piggy took her time, glancing back at Dan resentfully while sniffing for just the right place. Dan had plenty of time to cruise along on the wave of his good mood. Good moods didn't come to him that often, and he intended to enjoy this one while it lasted.

It would last, he told himself, as long as Nell Jordan smiled upon him. Some embarrassing situation for a tough guy, letting a female wriggle her way so far under his skin. But then, even a guy with a bum knee and bad attitude deserved a break once in a while. And Nell was a break. Any man in his right mind would walk barefoot over hot coals to have a woman like Nell. Bright, sunny, good-natured, with a truly good heart—that's what she was. And gorgeous, in his eyes at least. He wouldn't give a plugged nickel for some honey with bony hips and xylophone ribs, but he'd give everything he had for Nell. She had curves where a woman should have curves, curves enough to send a man straight to heaven, and nerve enough to go right along with him.

Yes indeed! Why shouldn't he be in a great mood? Nell had made a convert of him, baptized him with fire of the best sort. No more scoffing at love or romance. One good woman had made him see the light, and for better or worse, Dan had become a true believer.

His stomach rumbled. "Are you going to go, or what?"

Piggy just stared at him. If Dan didn't know better, he would have thought that baleful look had meaning.

"Don't tell me, princess. You need your privacy."

Her almost nonexistent stub of a tail wagged once, and only once.

"I don't believe it. Nell's dog insanity is infectious." He turned around. "I've still got the end of the leash, your highness, so don't get any ideas."

Yessir, he mused smugly while Piggy rustled around behind him. Why shouldn't he be in a great mood? Then he remembered the obvious answer, and his smugness took a hike. There was the little detail of him stringing Nell along with lies while trying to find something to blacken her character. She might not like that when she found out. And there was the other detail about him having a vested interest in her losing that fortune she intended to put to such good use. She might not like that either.

He had, Dan admitted, taken advantage of Nell in the worst sort of way. That certainly hadn't been his intention. He had tried, really tried, to avoid getting in this deep. He had tried to keep his hands to himself. But seeing Nell almost every day rivaled waving a shot glass of whiskey beneath an alcoholic's nose. How the hell did a man resist?

Besides, dammit, he had genuine feelings for the woman. More than that. He had never felt this way about a woman, even when he had been a young and infatuated fool thinking Cathy just had to be the centerpiece of his life. Nell made his heart lighter. Nell made him feel younger, stronger, and gave him the desire to be a better man.

So he had violated the most intimate trust between a man and a woman because she made him want to be a better man? That made sense. Oh yeah.

A spray of sand needled into his bare calves from behind, and he turned to find Piggy turning the beach into a missile launcher with furious kicks of her rear legs.

"I take it you're through," he said sarcastically.

Once back on the boat, Dan's good mood tentatively returned. The smell of bacon and eggs floated from the galley along with Nell's voice singing an old Barry Manilow song. Barry Manilow left Dan cold, but Nell certainly didn't, even though she couldn't carry a tune in a bucket. He loved the sound of her voice, its cheerful inflection, its hint of laughter. The sound brought to mind bright green eyes, soft blonde curls, and a man-killer smile that could light up a room.

This day they would bask in the sun, swim in the clear, cool water, and ... do other things. Maybe when Nell learned what an ass he was, she would find enough love in her heart to forgive him. Maybe she would understand why, in the beginning, he had taken her for a scheming, fortune-hunting bimbo. Maybe she would appreciate the pressures that kept him in the deception even after he'd come to love her. Uh-huh. Or maybe she would bury him in sand and call out an army of ants.

That was likely. But he didn't want to think about it.

So for the rest of this lake interlude, at least, Dan convinced himself that everything would work out. For the next two days they enjoyed the beautiful weather, the refreshing lake, and each other. Mostly each other—in the bedroom, in the galley (he would never see a dinette table in quite the same way), and in the water. After her first plunge into intimacy with him, Nell participated with uninhibited enthusiasm. She loved as she did everything else in her life, wholeheartedly. Her unabashed trust fed his guilt, but Dan refused to let his conscience cloud these jewellike days.

The time to pay the piper would come soon enough.

WHILE NELL and Dan played in the sun, Natalie and Jared combed through a dim and deserted house.

"Man oh man, does this house hold some fine memories!"

Natalie agreed wholeheartedly with Jared, but she wasn't about to admit it. That would open the door to rehashing the old times, giving in to sentiment, what-if musings, and the uncomfortable feeling of being so much more worn and old than she had been when they had loved together, laughed together, and thought that the world was their oyster.

Now they were older, perhaps wiser, and she, at least, no longer believed the world held a pearl just waiting for her to find it.

"I haven't been here since we moved my father to Springdale. He refused to rent this place out, so it's been empty ever since, with just a caretaker in the guest house."

Jared wandered into the airy great room and took in the

panoramic view through the floor-to-ceiling windows. "I wondered when you would get around to coming up here. The place is yours now. Or at least it will be after probate."

"I've only come to look through my father's papers. What on earth would I do with a house this huge?"

"I know what you mean. But we had some great times here."

Natalie had to smile as memories paraded through her mind. When she and Jared had been at NAU her father had lived in California and occupied the Sedona house only occasionally. Natalie had a key, and she and Jared had used it often. The house had been their own luxurious getaway, a borrowed love nest, a dream of a lifestyle yet to come—they had hoped.

Dreams and hopes—those had fueled those days of youthful vigor. Jared still had that vigor. Natalie could see it in every step he took, every quiet smile. Too often since they had renewed their acquaintance, that vigor had tempted her, drawn her like bait on a hook, reminding her of why she had loved him—his honesty, his quiet courage, his gentle selflessness. Those qualities still shone in his eyes.

Sometimes, especially when she and Jared were together, Natalie felt once again like that fresh girl—the girl she had been over thirty years before. Softening toward temptation would have been so easy.

She almost had to punch herself to get her mind back to the business at hand. Once something was dead, like the romance between her and Jared, it didn't come back to life without some kind of miracle. And believing in miracles was for suckers. Suckers who hadn't been burned.

"What exactly are you looking for?" Jared asked. "Maybe I can help."

"I don't know exactly what I'm looking for, though I know that probably sounds strange."

He shook his head. "Not really. Not under the circumstances."

When her father had moved to Springdale Nursing Home, Natalie had put all his vital papers in a safe deposit box, leaving only books, magazines, some old checkbooks, old financial records, and Frank's numerous beginnings to the novel he had sworn to write when he retired. She had thought he might ask for the manuscripts in Springdale, but he never had.

After the old man's death, she had told Jared to bring her father's belongings back here, to the home had had once loved. Until now she hadn't felt up to sorting through the stuff. But she couldn't put it off forever.

In a way, she would have liked to do this alone—touch and look at her father's things. But she had invited Jared to come along as insurance against anyone (like Nell Jordan, for example) accusing her of making off with anything from the estate that wasn't hers. Or perhaps she had asked him along because she wanted his company. These days her heart did such a push-pull act that she didn't know what she wanted as far as Jared was concerned.

Nor was she sure what he wanted from her.

"I put all the things from his room in the den, on the cabinet below the bookshelves—just to get them out of the way."

The den was immaculate. No dust marred the oak desk or matching bookshelves. The little fireplace wasn't marred by a single ash. The caretaker was doing a good job. Natalie sat at the big polished desk, feeling like a child pretending to be grown-up enough to sit in her father's chair.

Jared set a box of Frank's personal belongings on the desk. "He didn't keep much around. You know your father. He was spare in his tastes."

Laid neatly in the box—among other things—were toothpaste, toothbrush, razor, and three plastic bottles of prescription medications.

Natalie chuckled. "You didn't throw anything away, did you?"

"That's your job."

She disposed of the toiletries into the wastebasket, along with a comb, hairbrush, toothpicks, and a storage case for dentures. A stack of paperback novels caught her attention. The titles surprised her. Natalie hadn't known that her father had been a mystery fan, much less a reader of science fiction. She hadn't been enough a part of the last years of her father's life to know such things.

"Your dad was a big Hillerman fan," Jared told her. "Heinlein, too, strangely enough."

Jared had known her father better than Natalie had. The realization made her ashamed.

"I should have seen him more often."

Jared didn't answer, and the tacit agreement hurt. But then, honesty was one of his qualities she loved. Had loved—past tense.

"He could be so difficult to be around."

"You're right about that."

She sighed, remembering the verbal battles. Frank had always known better than anyone else, in his opinion, and he hadn't hesitated to tell everyone within earshot.

"Nat, quit beating yourself up over your father. He loved you. You loved him. It's just that a lot of things got in the way. Most of them he put there himself."

Something inside her softened. Jared understood. Even years ago he had possessed an intuitive perception of what went on in her mind. It was another of the things she had loved about him, and he still had it.

She was about to comment when her eye fell on several letters in the bottom of the box. One was brown with age. It was from her Aunt Judy, who had passed away three years earlier. Another was from . . . Taylor Investigative Services, Phoenix, Arizona? What the heck?

An intuition of her own hit.

"Jared, could I bother you for some water from the refrigerator?"

"Sure thing."

When Jared was gone, Natalie opened the envelope and scanned the contents.

"What do you know?" she breathed. "The old man had his girlfriend investigated."

The report was brief. Apparently, Frank had ordered the economy investigation.

Family: widowed mother, financially secure. Education: journalism, bachelor of arts at NAU. No bad reports. Employment: part-time work during college, then full-time position with *The Chicago World News*. Left abruptly.

Natalie's eyes widened. Her heart quickened as she read the dry account. The investigators drew no conclusions from the reports in the Chicago newspapers, other than the certainty that this was not a straightforward matter. The truth would require further investigation at a price that raised Natalie's brows.

Yet her father had still left Nell, or her dog anyway, the money. But it worked out the same. The trusting old idiot. Had he been so desperately in need of attention that... No. She wouldn't go there.

"Water, my lady."

Hastily, Natalie stuffed the report back in its envelope. "Thank you, Jared. I'll take it with me. I think I found what I need."

She could have given the report to Jared. He might have done something with it. But she couldn't be sure. Jared actually seemed to like Nell Jordan.

And Natalie had her own investigative resources. Her son had started to like the Jordan woman as well, but now he would see that Natalie had been right all along.

•　　•　　•

ON THE drive home, Nell suffered from a touch of sunburn, a hint of weariness that resulted from too much time in bed but not nearly enough sleep, and a soreness in certain places where one did not usually get sore. But total, unconditional happiness made her feel lighter than a kite skimming the wind.

This was silly, Nell knew. A mature, experienced woman didn't get all light-headed and giddy just because she decided that love had finally come her way, just because she'd found a man who made her heart swell with warmth and her body sing with desire. But perhaps she was not a mature, experienced woman. She was simply a woman who had decided to trust, and to give, and to risk her heart in commitment with nothing held back.

Well, maybe she held back a teensy bit. Dan had no need to hear all about her past, its ups and downs, its little, insignificant secrets. They could let the present, the glorious present, be their mutual fortress.

She leaned her head back against the seat and breathed out a contented sigh.

"You look like the proverbial cat with canary feathers hanging out of its mouth," Dan observed with a grin.

"That's exactly how I feel," she admitted. "Do you still love me?"

"That's a woman for you. One declaration wasn't enough? Even two?"

"Don't you know anything about women? We want to hear those words every day of our lives, for as long as we have someone in our lives we care to have say them."

"Is that the truth?"

"It is." She arched a meaningful brow.

"Okay. Then here it is. I love you, Nell Jordan, with all my heart, my soul, and whatever else still works after the weekend we just had. But you'll have to save that in a permanent file, because it's not going to change, and once we're back in civilization, a macho guy like me can't go around spouting romance on demand."

She laughed. "You're bad."

"Damn right I am."

"But I love you anyway. You can save that in a permanent file as well."

He gave her a look she couldn't quite interpret, but then his smile wiped away any confusion. "You bet I will."

"And furthermore, I want to know about your children."

"My children? Does this follow logically in this conversation?"

"Of course it does. I love you. Your children are a big part of you. I can't believe I've known you over two months and still haven't met your kids."

He grimaced. "Unfortunately, they're not with me that often." A fond smile warmed his eyes. "Marta is eight. She's a little drama queen. Everything that happens to her is either the end of the world or the beginning of a huge adventure. There isn't any in between. She's smart, though. She's already reading big books—you know, horse books—"

"*The Black Stallion* series, I'll bet."

"How did you know?"

"Because I devoured those when I was a kid. Only I was older than eight when I started reading them."

He beamed with pride. "And James is six. James has a fetish with Disneyland right now. Disneyland, Disney World, Pooh, Tigger, Aladdin, even Beauty and the Beast. I had to tell him that *Beauty and the Beast* is a girly story. He should stick to *Aladdin*."

"You didn't!"

"Well, someone had to. That wimp my wife married, Mr. Sensitivity, would have him playing with dolls and watching those stupid Powerpuff Girls cartoons, just so he'll grow up to relate better to 'women's issues.'" He pronounced the last two words as if they left a bad taste in his mouth, but his grin sparkled with mischief.

"Shame on you!"

"Someone's got to teach the boy to be macho!"

"He doesn't have to be macho! He's six!"

Dan just laughed, a sound full of warmth. His face glowed when he talked about his kids. Nell liked that. A man who loved his kids, in her opinion, was the sexiest man alive.

"And you moved out here to be close to them?"

"Yeah. Cathy came out here and got married again, so I figured someone had to keep an eye on them. When I left the police force, I followed. It wasn't like I had a big future in L.A."

"It is so lame that you had to leave the police force because you got shot in the knee!"

"I didn't have to leave, exactly. I could have sat at a desk and shuffled papers. But that's not my style."

"So you left it all to become a photographer. I like that, Dan. You're a free spirit."

The ensuing moments of silence held a trace of uneasiness. She guessed "free spirit" didn't go well with his macho image.

"What about you?" he asked abruptly.

"I don't have kids."

"I know that. But you know the highlights of my sordid life. What about your sordid life?"

A sudden pang of guilt made her catch her breath. If he ever learned about Chicago, what would he say?

His smile teased. "You hesitate. You *do* have something sordid in your past."

"No!" Then more calmly. "No. Unless you count getting tipsy at a sorority party in college, my life has been completely uninteresting."

"Tell that to the reporters I've been holding at bay."

She shook her head, reminded of his chutzpah. "I don't believe you convinced me that you were a journalist. I was obviously blinded by your charm."

"It gets to women all the time."

She laughed. "You have such nerve."

"It takes nerve to get anywhere in the world these days. And now back to your sordid past. Excuse me, 'uninteresting' past."

"Born in Phoenix, raised in the burbs, went to NAU, graduated—with honors, mind you."

He seemed suitably impressed.

"Went to the big city to work—Chicago, to be exact. Didn't like it. Came back poor but happy." True as far as it went. "And here I am."

"Rich and happy."

"Yes. Well, that was an accident."

"Rich, happy, and totally under the spell of a handsome bum."

"Photographer. You could never be a bum."

He smiled wryly. "Everyone can be a bum at times. It shouldn't make us less lovable. Remember that."

chapter 15

MONDAYS IN Natalie's interior-design showroom always swept along in busy chaos, especially in May. Just as Mondays brought out customers who wanted to start off the week doing something constructive, springtime made people want to sweep the house clean and start over with new stuff. So business boomed, and Natalie scarcely had a moment to herself.

All the same, she happily took time out to talk to Dan when he came by. She'd been calling him for the last day and a half, ever since her discovery at her father's house. But Dan's message machine always picked up the phone, not Dan. Very annoying.

"It's about time you let me know you're still alive," she scolded.

"I've been out of town." He leaned over her cluttered desk and pecked her on the cheek.

"My word! He's reformed! A voluntary kiss for his mother!"

She feigned amazement, but truly he caught her by surprise. Not that Dan was an unaffectionate son. But the meat grinder of life had cut him up a bit, making him the strong silent type, not the sensitive demonstrative type. Something, she suspected, was up.

"Come on. You act as if I never kiss you."

"Christmas 1988."

"What?"

"That's the last time you spontaneously and voluntarily kissed your loving mother."

"You remember things like that?"

"I'm a mother. Family is important to me."

"You're insane."

"There are some who say that insanity is a prerequisite for bearing a child. Now, I have something to talk to you about. But you first. You don't just drop by without a reason."

He dropped heavily into the metal folding chair that faced her desk. "I came by to talk about this situation with Nell Jordan."

"Excellent. That's the very thing I want to talk about."

"The thing is . . ."

"What? What did you find?"

He took a breath. "I think you're off base in your theories about this girl, Mother. I don't want to be a part of this anymore."

"Really."

While she strove for calm, he barged ahead. "Nell isn't what you think she is. Granddad set up that trust fund because he liked Nell and her dog, and maybe because he wanted to spit in the eye of a family who never did what he wanted them to do and didn't give him the attention he needed."

The spit in the eye part was true, as far as it went, and struck once again that chord of partly guilt, partly regret. And of course her father had liked Nell. What doddering old man wouldn't like a young hottie who fawned all over him?

"I've followed the woman around for the last two months, Mom. I've talked to people who knew her years ago. I've met her friends, seen what she's done with the cash Granddad left her in that payable-upon-death account. Nell Jordan is a hell of a lady."

Her own son had so little family loyalty that he had let his head be turned by a pretty face and practiced charm. He hadn't tried very hard to find the truth, or he would have stumbled onto the Chicago thing. He had chosen to be reeled in by that temptress rather than listen to his mother.

"It is incomprehensible to me," she said in calm, precise words, "that the men in my life insist upon lining up on the side of this woman. Is testosterone so strong that it numbs the mind, blinds the eyes?"

"Mom, don't get dramatic. All I'm saying is that I'm bowing out of this investigation. It was okay that you wanted to find out if Nell took advantage of Granddad, but now I'm telling you that didn't happen. I'm sure of it."

"Did she seduce you?"

By the stain of red that blossomed beneath the collar of his shirt, Natalie knew she'd hit the mark.

"I thought you had more taste, Dan."

"She didn't seduce me. I like Nell Jordan a lot, and that's all I'm going to say about it. If you start harassing her, I'm going to have to come down on her side. So don't make me choose, okay?"

Obviously, Dan had already chosen.

He got up, looking unhappy, then gave her a weak smile.

"By the way. I've got the kids this week. Cathy and Mike went to Hawaii, or Jamaica, or some such place. If you want to see them, drop by. James wants to beat you at canasta again."

"Maybe I will." She opened her desk drawer and took out the report that would prove a nasty dose of reality for her son. She almost felt sorry for him. "You might want to read this before building a pedestal for the Jordan woman." She handed it to him. "Then we'll talk again."

"What's this?"

She gave him a thin smile. "Just read it."

Natalie stared at the door that closed behind him, overwhelmed by a sudden sense of isolation. Why was she the only one who could see through the Jordan woman's act? Didn't any of the men in her life have a brain to call his own? Did they all have a case of testosterone poisoning? Dan, her own son, all too ready to betray his family and pant after that woman's fake charm. Jared, once her lover, who claimed to be her friend, blind as any other man when dazzled by female pulchritude.

It was all too depressing.

Natalie picked up a pencil and tapped it on the pile of sales receipts in front of her. She should have made a copy of the report for Sal Steiger, her lawyer. In fact, she should call Sal right now. But she didn't want to. The person she really wanted to call was Jared Johansen.

He couldn't help her, Natalie told herself. Just because Dan's visit had sent her spirits plunging, Jared didn't have a Band-Aid to put on her heart. Just the same, she wanted to hear his familiar voice, the voice that so often had a smile in it.

Calling Jared would be a weakness, Natalie chided herself. She didn't need to run to a man for comfort every time the world started to close in.

To hell with it, she thought, and picked up the phone.

AN HOUR later Natalie put her finger to the doorbell at Jared's front door. Her hand trembled. She took the finger away, shook her hand hard to make the trembling stop, and told herself to be sensible. Accepting Jared's invitation to come over for coffee didn't mean a thing. She needed a friendly, familiar face, and Jared had the best face she knew.

She felt a small twinge of guilt about not letting him know about the fresh ammunition she had against the Jordan woman. That revelation (and subsequent apology, she trusted) could wait until Dan had followed the lead to its end and ferreted out the whole nasty truth of the matter, which she was sure he would do once he realized that he'd been duped. For now, Natalie simply wanted to sit with Jared and feel less like the only sane island awash in rising waters of insanity.

She put her finger to the doorbell once again, steady this time, under control, a control that flew into pieces when Jared opened the door.

"Natalie! Hey! You're looking good!"

She took a breath. "Jared."

"Come on in. You haven't ever seen my place, have you?"

"No." She remembered his off-campus apartment in Flagstaff, long ago when they had both been at the university. During the cold Flagstaff winter, he could have made ice in the kitchen without bothering to use the freezer. But they had made their own heat in that dingy little place, in the cramped bedroom, on a creaky, uncomfortable bed that had been their paradise.

She certainly didn't want to think about that!

He led her into a warm and airy great room decorated in expensive Southwest art and furnished in casual leather and rustic wood—a man's room, surely, but welcoming and stylish. The unpolished wood and comfortable leather fit him, Natalie decided. She wondered if his bedroom fit him as well.

Shame on her!

"The view here is breathtaking," she said. And indeed it was. Floor-to-ceiling windows gave them a vista to the south, where a pantheon of noble red rock monuments marched down to mesquite-covered hills. In the distance rose the pine-clad heights of Mingus Mountain. It was the kind of view that people paid a million bucks to own. Jared, she guessed, was doing all right.

"Let me get you a drink," he offered. "Do you still like margaritas?"

How lovely that he remembered such details. "I thought we were drinking coffee."

"It's a warm day. Something cool would go better, wouldn't it?"

She smiled. "I've never been able to resist a good margarita, as you know."

"Well, I make a mean margarita, if I do say so myself."

While he mixed their drinks, she sat upon the sofa. The upholstery was butter-soft and surrounded her with the clean, sharp scent unique to well-tanned leather. She had always associated that scent with Jared. So many of her memories of him involved leather. The leather jacket that he had worn whenever he rode his stupid motorcycle. She had loved to bury her face in that jacket, especially when he wore it. But she had hated the motorcycle, because she feared he might crash it.

And leather hiking boots. They had hiked a lot back in those golden days, and Jared had worn the heaviest, most imposing boots Natalie had ever seen. They probably had weighed ten pounds apiece. Pure leather. And he had tended them as if they were treasures, cleaning them with saddle soap after every hike and resealing them against moisture. Natalie wouldn't be surprised if he still had the things. Jared took good care of his possessions. He had taken good care of her, when she had been his. Very good care, indeed. But she had been too young to appreciate how rarely such caring came along in life.

"Here you are." He smiled broadly as he handed her a margarita on the rocks. Salt caked the rim of the glass, just as she liked it. "Now taste and tell me that I haven't lost my touch."

She sipped, then nodded. "You haven't lost a bit of your touch, Jared."

Halfway through the margarita, Natalie realized exactly why she had come. The flash of insight shocked her a bit. But why should she be shocked? Natalie asked herself. She had need of Jared's warmth, his companionship, his strength, and perhaps the reassurance that he didn't see her as old and as worn as she sometimes felt. She had need of something more basic than that, also. Other women thought nothing of turning sex into casual recreation. Why should she be different?

She drained the last of her glass quickly—perhaps too quickly—while they talked of trivialities: the weather, the latest spat among city council members, the most recent highway construction mess. She sensed him waiting, waiting for her to hint at what brought her here.

He could have more than a hint, Natalie decided, feeling reckless. "This is an exquisite room, Jared. Is your bedroom as well done?"

His jaw dropped a bit, but overall, he kept his cool. "Uh ... would you like a tour?"

"I would." She cocked her head flirtatiously. "I would indeed like ... a tour."

She didn't need to ask twice. He took her glass, set it down with his on the end table, and then took her elbow.

"These are all local artists," he said of the watercolors that decorated the hallway.

She just smiled. "I adore your taste in art, but ..."

"But?"

They stepped through the door of his bedroom. "But right now I would just like to adore you. For a few hours. If you don't mind."

Fire lit his eyes, but he measured his words with a restraint the younger Jared would never have achieved. "Natalie ..." He touched her cheek. "Do I dare ask why?"

She told the truth. "I need you, Jared. It's as simple as that. Right now, I need you."

For a moment of pure terror, she thought he might refuse her. Perhaps she had mistaken the spark in his eye, the warmth in his smile. But no. His hand moved from her cheek to stroke down the slim column of her neck, his thumb playing with her collarbone.

"Are you sure, Nat?"

Nat. He had called her by that shortened version of her name when they had been together so long ago. An ugly nickname, Nat. But from him she had loved it.

"Quite sure," she said firmly, glad that the trembling inside didn't show up in her voice.

Or did it? Because he smiled very gently, then just as gently, lowered his mouth to hers.

Jared had learned to undress women with finesse, Natalie discovered. Years past, their youthful passion had sent clothes flying, sometimes minus buttons. Now he paid attention to detail. Clothes were not so much an obstacle to be banished as a tantalizing prelude, a part of sensual seduction. The knot of her designer scarf yielded to his hands, and the silk slid sensuously over her neck. Then Jared's wonderful big hand smoothed lightly over her soft knit shell, over her breasts, before catching the hem of the shell and easing it over her head.

Then, of course, he kissed her again.

No stranger to the game of one-upmanship, Natalie insisted upon taking turns. Jared wore casual jeans and a cotton shirt. The snowy white T-shirt beneath caressed her fingers with its softness as she smoothed it over the hard, solid chest below, then worked it up over his head to discard onto the floor. Jared had kept himself in fine shape. The broad shoulders hadn't stooped a bit. The lean strength of his physique had not surrendered to age or gravity.

"You are still the most beautiful man I've ever known," she told him.

He laughed. "So much for my manly image."

"You know what I mean," she said with a swat to his bare chest.

He made a sensual dance out of the task of removing her lacy bra, and then managed to turn her knees to water by attending to her breasts, his mouth teasing and caressing first one, then the other. She caught his hands when he reached for the clasp of her slacks, however.

"My turn now."

Off came his jeans, one button at a time, and Natalie discovered that she hadn't misremembered the strength and size of him. "You come to attention just as quickly as you used to," she teased.

"When I have the inspiration. Come here, you."

The bed welcomed them, and the rest of their clothing flew off just as it had so many years before. Their coming together might not possess quite the same fiery urgency, but for Natalie, the loving improved for being more gentle, thorough, and considerate. Doubts about her own body made her self-conscious at first. Time and gravity weighed upon women more harshly than men, and Natalie had borne two children. The last time she had cavorted naked with Jared, no stretch marks had marred her taut abdomen, and her breasts had been perky as well as full and soft. The breasts still filled Jared's hands, full and soft, but perky had disappeared with her first pregnancy. And so had the taut abdomen.

Self-consciousness couldn't win, however, when the glow in Jared's eyes told her he saw beauty through the marks of age. Time had done nothing to dim passion, and harsh lessons had taught her that joy and desire should be grasped and appreciated without reserve, for they didn't last.

Afterward, passion spent, but warmth still simmering inside, they lay in Jared's rumpled bed. Sunlight from huge windows made tattoos of light on their bare, entwined legs, on Jared's hand where it rested on her breast.

"This room needs skylights," Natalie commented.

He chuckled. "Only an interior designer . . ."

"When you've just spent as much time looking at the ceiling as I did, you notice such things."

His hand moved on her breast, caressing. "You were so bored you had to count cracks in the ceiling?"

She laughed. "Hardly. You have improved with age, Jared. Not that the younger you wasn't wonderful, but the current version is incredible."

"You make me blush."

"After what we just did, I'd wager that nothing makes you blush."

He leaned over her for a kiss, a kiss born of affection more than passion. "I'm so glad you came. I'm so glad you're here."

The intensity vibrating in his voice scared her, because it echoed the vibrations of her own heart, and the heart often led where wise women shouldn't follow. So she gave him an airy smile. "I'm glad that I'm here also, Jared. This is a nice way to spend an afternoon."

A tiny crease appeared between his brows. "This is more than a way to spend a casual afternoon, Natalie. Don't pretend it isn't."

She sighed and rose onto one elbow to look down at him. "Jared, please. Don't make this out to be something it isn't."

"What isn't it?"

"It isn't the beginning of a love affair. It isn't a commitment to love and cherish. It isn't even a date."

He stretched, then settled with his hands behind his head on the pillow. "Really."

"Really." Natalie tried hard not to let his tantalizing

torso distract her. Someone in this bed had to be sensible, after all. "Really, Jared. It's just sex. Wonderful sex between old friends. Don't spoil the fun by trying to make it something else."

He regarded her calmly. "You're scared as hell, aren't you?"

The bolt shot home all too well. "Afraid? Me? What could I possibly be afraid of?"

"Feelings. Emotional investment. The possibility of hanging your heart out there once again and getting it stomped on."

"Now you're just being ridiculous." She got out of bed, dragging the sheet with her as a drape, because suddenly self-consciousness flooded back. "I'm a grown woman, and much too old for that sort of nonsense."

"What sort of nonsense? Love?"

"Love, romance—for heaven's sake, Jared. We're both old enough to know better."

He looked damnably relaxed, propped up on the pillow with hands behind his head, the sheet covering just enough of his nakedness to fire the imagination. The dark brown eyes remained calm, the smile unruffled. "Natalie, you're the one who needs to learn better. A person never gets too old for love."

"Pish! Where did you get that—off a greeting card?" She turned her back on him and donned her slacks without putting on her pantyhose. She refused to engage in the struggle of bulges versus nylon while Jared watched.

"Natalie, you don't need to be afraid of me."

His voice sounded sad. Pitying, even, and it made her furious. Slacks securely buttoned—at last—she whipped around to face him. "No, Jared, I am not afraid. I am realistic. I have not had a lot of luck with emotional investment in men, and I've come to the point in my life where I'm very happy with my independence. Any romance in my soul died years ago, and it would take a miracle to revive it. And I no longer believe in miracles."

He merely raised a brow, looking at her as one might regard a child throwing a tantrum.

She decided to divest him of his illusions. "Do you know why I came here this afternoon? I just endured an unpleasant visit with my son, who has fallen prey to Nell Jordan, the same as every other man in this world, it seems. I wanted you to cheer me up, make me forget that this world is not reasonable, sensible, or fair.

"So that's why I called you, Jared. You were a distraction. I'm sorry to disappoint you, but that's all there is."

He didn't swallow the fib. "Natalie," he said gently. "That's not why you called."

She scowled.

"And that's not why you're here in this house, in this bedroom. But I can see you have to figure that out for yourself. When you do, call me. I'll probably still be here."

She opened her mouth for a cutting reply, but a mere shake of his head silenced her.

"You see, I'm not William. I don't let love go so easily. You never left my heart, you know. That doesn't take anything away from what I felt for my Sara. But you never left my heart."

She grabbed her shell and yanked it on, then knotted it with a jerk that endangered her throat. "Thank you for a nice afternoon, Jared."

"Wait." He swung out of bed, totally unheeding of his nakedness. At her pointed glare, he smiled and stepped into his jeans. "I can see you're in high temper—about me, Frank, Dan, Nell, and probably even poor little Piggy, so before you go and make a fool of yourself, I think you should read something."

He led her into his home office, where he got a folder out of his top desk drawer.

"I wasn't supposed to do this, but I don't think Frank anticipated how wounded you would be."

He put the folder in her hand.

THREE DAYS had passed since Dan had deposited Nell and Piggy on her trailer-house doorstep and said good-bye. Actually, the good-bye hadn't been that abrupt. It hadn't been abrupt at all. In fact, it had taken about two hours, and Nell had needed to change the sheets afterward. Not to mention release a sullen Piggy from the bathroom.

"He's gone," Nell had told the dog. "Are you satisfied?"

With an indignant woof, the corgi turned and trundled toward the dog door.

"Get used to him," Nell called after the dog, as Piggy's furry butt disappeared out the door. "He's going to be around a lot. I hope."

Except that Dan hadn't come around in the past three days. Neither had he called. He had his kids for a week or so, he had told her when he left, and he didn't know when he could break away. Nell didn't interpret the excuse as a brush-off. She knew the look in his eyes simmered with love. He had said right out that he loved her, and Dan Travis was an honest man. The little mystery about him had been settled, and it was nothing. Pretending to be a journalist so he could dog her steps. How silly! How ... almost sweet. She could only smile when she thought of his hijinks.

"Like I said before," she had warned Piggy when the dog came back into the house. "Get used to Dan. When a girl lands a catch like him, she doesn't throw him back. Don't be jealous, little girl. There's plenty of room in my heart for both of you."

The corgi stuck out her tongue and made an odd, undoglike sound. If Nell didn't know better, she would have thought she'd just gotten a canine raspberry.

After four days of being in Dan's constant company, Nell acutely felt his absence. The glow that he'd lit inside her didn't dim, but it was pale comfort without the pleasure of his company. The little trailer house seemed empty in a way it never had before. Loneliness chilled her bed.

Not that Nell spent these few days pining like some sort of trailer-house version of the Shakespearean Juliet. She stayed busy. Two deadlines for articles loomed, and she hadn't the time to do much pining. The sudden appearance of money in her life sometimes tempted her to quit work, but she had been writing one thing or another since she was old enough to pick up a pencil, and she figured that writing materials would go with her when she finally got thrown into a nursing home.

So she worked, cleaned house, worked, wondered what Dan was doing, walked Piggy, worked, thought about calling Dan (and didn't), did her hospital visit, worked—and, oh yes, plotted. Sometime during that hedonistic interlude at Lake Powell, Dan had let slip the fact that this third week of May was his birthday. This Wednesday, to be exact. Nell planned to surprise him with a fancy cake. They would have a party. She would get to meet his children. And she would see the light of love in his eyes once again and be reassured.

Not that she needed reassurance. But it wouldn't hurt.

When Wednesday arrived, she sailed through the morning hours lighthearted with anticipation. She could hardly wait to see the look on his face when he saw his cake. If the kids hadn't been with him, his surprise would have been a lot more interesting than a mere cake, but they were, so the grown-ups had to behave. Having a good time with Dan didn't require bed play, though. That, among other things, made Nell feel right about their relationship.

Noon came. Nell picked up the cake at the bakery, set it carefully on Mel's passenger seat, and started for Page Springs. The minivan had more room for the big cake box, but the minivan didn't have Mel's personality. Mel had found Dan for her, that day more than two months ago, so Mel deserved to be in on the party.

When Nell knocked on the motor-home door, she prepared to belt out a cheery rendition of "Happy Birthday," but she stopped short when the door opened and an angelic little face surrounded by blonde curls gazed up at her with big blue eyes. "Hello," the little angel said seriously.

Nell instantly fell in love. "Hi."

A female bellow from the rear of the motor home interrupted this interesting conversation. "James! You better get your little butt back here before I have to come get you!"

The little angel turned his face toward the back and bellowed back with a volume that no six-year-old should own. "Somebody's here!"

"James, you—! Oh!" A tawny-haired teen goddess appeared. Nell guessed teenaged because no woman past twenty could keep that sleek figure. Hip-hugging, skintight shorts and a stretchy bosom-hugging crop top displayed her figure to great advantage. "Whatever you're selling," the goddess said, "we're not interested."

THERE NELL went, running off to throw herself at a con man who was reeling her in like a fish on a line. Frustrating, especially since I knew the guy was a fake, a dispossessed relative of the late, generous, dog-loving Frank Cramer.

I had no intention of sitting there like a boob and letting that two-bit fortune hunter cut me out. Frank wanted me to have that money and lead a life of luxury. There were still things to be bought—like that fancy cookie jar I saw in the hospital gift shop the other day—full of cookies, of course. (Nell ignored me when I pointed it out with my nose.) Or the gross of beefy bones in the new dog catalog that arrived in the mail.

Fortunately, I had finally come up with one of my brilliant, creative ideas, a way to let Nell know there was a rotten apple in

paradise, and she was about to bite. You understand, commu-
nication is one of a dog's great challenges. Barking only gets
you tossed into the backyard. Whining might earn you a trip to
the vet to find out what hurts. Dogs are masters at getting
across concepts like "Is it dinnertime?" or "I need to pee," or
"How about a piece of that pizza?" but for something like "Your
boyfriend is a con man who's playing you like a fiddle"—well,
that's more difficult. But when has a challenge ever stood in
my way?

When the spoken word fails, the written word steps in. It
took me a while to figure this out. The idea hit me as I lay
watching Nell work at her computer, her busy little fingers tap,
tap, tapping on the keys.

Bingo!

So when Nell waltzed out the door to deliver her cake, I
struck. It wasn't easy, mind you. You would have to be a dog to
truly understand the disadvantage of not having fingers. But as
always, I managed. Fortunately, I didn't need the computer,
which I couldn't quite manage to turn on. Nell kept an old electric typewriter—it had once been her mother's, I think—on her
worktable. And in the bottom drawer of her desk were a couple
of pedigree forms leftover from the time she had tried to trace
my pedigree.

Pedigree—family. Get it? Was I clever or what? All I needed
to do was jog the girl's brain into the right groove.

I won't bore you with the details of my struggle to get the
form out of the drawer, into the typewriter, and then press the
right keys with my toe. Dogs are simply not designed to be typ-
ists. Not to mention that the office chair kept rolling out from
beneath me, causing several tumbles. But if you've read my
other adventures, you know that Piggy does not let obstacles
stand in her way. I ended up sitting on the table itself and depressing the keys with my nose.

The results were a bit sloppy, but it would get the job done—
I hoped. My last task was to shove my message in with the pile

of mail on the table. It would look as if some anonymous tipster had slipped it in her mail.

I deserved a medal for cleverness.

CAUGHT OFF guard by surprise, Nell could only say "Uh..."

"Unless you're selling cosmetics," the teen said. "I might look at cosmetics. Are you an Avon lady or something?"

Nell recovered herself somewhat. "I'm not selling anything. I'm a friend of Dan's."

The goddess unknit her brows. "Oh cool. But Dan isn't here."

"Ah." The sunlight dimmed. Birds no longer sang. "I... uh... just dropped by to bring him a birthday cake."

"It's his birthday? Bitchin'!" The girl's eyes lit up.

This little future *Cosmo* model certainly wasn't Dan's daughter! And she couldn't be... surely not... impossible... If Dan was seeing another woman, surely that woman would at least be over twenty.

Another angel, a little girl with Dan's black hair and gray eyes, appeared from behind the goddess's lissome body.

"She knocked on the door," little James informed his sister in a tone that suggested knocking on the door rated a jail sentence.

"Who are you?" the second angel piped.

"I'm Nell."

"I'm Julie," the teenager said. "Baby-sitter."

Of course. Nell hadn't been suspicious for a single moment.

"I'm Marta!" the little girl declared.

"Listen," Julie continued. "I have an idea. Dan just ran down to the drugstore to get something for Marta's sniffles."

"I have sniffles!" The child demonstrated graphically.

"He asked me to watch the kids while he's gone, but now

that you're here, you know, maybe you could keep an eye on them. I'm just dying to see this flick over in Sedona, so, you know, that way you could surprise him with the cake and everything when he gets home."

"She could be a kidnapper!" Marta declared suspiciously.

"She's not a kidnapper," Julie assured the girl. "She's a friend of your dad's."

"I'm James." The little blond angel tugged at Nell's shorts. "Do you want to see my *Beauty and the Beast* action figures?"

"*Beauty and the Beast* has action figures?"

"Everything has action figures." Julie tousled the boy's silky curls. "So?" she prompted Nell. "Is it a plan?"

"Sure. I don't mind."

"Dan will be back in a flash." She bounced out the door, all smiles. " 'Bye kids. Mind your manners for Nell."

Marta still regarded Nell suspiciously. "We don't have manners. That's what our dad says."

"Do you want to see my *Beauty and the Beast* action figures?" James's volume was growing.

Nell rethought her first impression of angels. Little demons in angel suits, more likely. But she was still in love.

"What's in the box?" James demanded, attention diverted from action figures.

"This is a birthday cake for your dad."

"Does it have sugar?" Marta asked. "My mom won't let me have sugar."

Nell took the cake from the box and set it on the dining table. "It probably has about a ton of sugar," she admitted.

"Well!" Marta eyed the piles of icing. "Maybe just this once I could have sugar."

"What's that?" James pointed a plump little finger to the top of the cake.

"That's a sugar houseboat."

"Why?"

"Because your dad likes boats."

"Oh. I like boats. What's a houseboat?"

This could go on forever, Nell deduced, but Marta answered her little brother's question.

"It's a boat with a house on it, stupid."

"I'm not stupid."

"Yes you are."

"Whoa!" Nell said. "Let's put the candles on the cake. Will you help me?"

She had to be careful that their help didn't destroy the cake, but Nell had to admit that the kids showed more creativity than she would have about how to arrange thirty-one candles. Their chatter, even their little spats, which occurred every two or three minutes, warmed her heart. She had always wanted children, but not having a husband had put a crimp into that ambition.

"Since you're not a kidnapper," Marta decided. "Maybe you should take us on a picnic."

"Uh . . . well, we could probably do that. And your dad would want to come as well."

"Yeah, he could come."

Nell pictured the four of them somewhere picturesque, a blanket laid out on the ground, sandwiches in a picnic basket. Just like a family. Her heart turned to mush. "We could go to Slide Rock. That's a perfect place for a picnic."

"Promise!" Marta demanded. "We're going to Slide Rock."

"Your dad has to agree."

James joined in. "When? When?"

"Maybe on Sunday. What would you think of that?"

"Sunday is weeks away!"

"Only days away. Just three days."

Marta's mouth twisted into a grimace. "Okay. Promise."

"I promise. If your dad says yes."

How easily they wound her around their little fingers.

"What's that?" James's attention took a sharp turn back

toward the cake. His finger pointed to the icing decorations around the rim.

"That's a camera. All those things are little sugar cameras." The bakery clerk had looked at her strangely when she had outlined the plan of decoration, but heck, a photographer should have cameras on his cake. The houseboat—well, he would know why the houseboat.

"My dad has a camera," James said proudly.

"I know he does. He has a very good camera, because he's a photographer."

Marta gave her a look reserved for the very ignorant. "My dad isn't a photographer. He's a stupid P.I."

Something inside Nell turned to ice. "He's a what?"

"My mom says only little boys who never grow up get to be stupid P.I.s. But my dad's grown-up, you know. He says it's not stupid. He says it pays the rent and buys the hamburger."

"A . . . a P.I."

"Private investigator." Marta said the big words very proudly. "Do you know what that is?"

The rest of Nell turned to ice. "I do." She swallowed hard. "Maybe he once was a P.I. and now he's a photographer."

"Nope," Marta said confidently. "Sometimes he tells us about his cases, and sometimes he says it's none of our business. Mostly it's none of our business." She gave Nell a sage look. "Maybe he told you he's a photographer because he thinks it's none of your business."

"Mom won't let us watch detective shows on TV," James added indignantly.

Nell felt like dropping her head into her hands as her bright new world crashed in upon her. She felt as though someone had just pounded her with a baseball bat. Her hands shook. Her stomach hurt. Her lungs ached almost too much to draw breath. But she couldn't melt into a puddle of misery right there in front of two kids. Somehow she would have to hold together until she got home.

Just then the sound of the Jeep sent the kids jumping and hollering as if their father had been gone a year. "Daddy's home!" they yelled in unison. "Daddy's home, Daddy's home, Daddy's home."

"Daddy's home," Nell muttered to herself.

The sound of the engine died, and Dan's slightly off-key whistling came toward the motor-home door. Numb, Nell got up to fetch the cake. His birthday cake. His goddamned birthday cake with the goddamned cameras.

The door opened. "Hi kids! Where's Ju— Nell!"

He sounded shocked to see her, the worm, the piece of scum, the slimy rat.

"Nell! What a great surprise! Did you? . . ." He halted midsentence, apparently seeing something in her smile he didn't like. Of course he would be smart that way. He was a goddamned detective.

"I brought you a cake," Nell said sweetly. "Happy birthday, Detective Travis."

Before his mouth could open, she upended the cake over his head and walked out the door.

chapter 16

DAN SKIDDED the Jeep to a halt in a spray of dirt and gravel, slammed the door shut as he jumped out, then stormed through Nell's front gate and banged it shut behind him. Bits of sticky icing still clung to his hair and face. He didn't care. His temper still clanged in his head. He didn't care. He and Nell would have this out right now. She had nerve slapping him with a goddamned cake when she should have been pleading for a chance to explain the report that smashed her goddamned squeaky-clean image all to pieces. She would cough up the truth if he had to hog-tie her and hold her down with one foot to make her talk.

She had the cojones to be mad at *him*?

The front window curtain moved as he marched up the front walk, and just for a moment he glimpsed Nell's pale face. At windowsill level a black nose pressed against the windowpane just below two dark beady little eyes.

Damned dog. Damned kids. Kids were too goddamned honest. Teach them deceit is wrong, and what do they do? They listen to you, goddamn it. Blowing his cover like that. Dammit! He'd like this confrontation a lot better if he were the only one with something to be mad about. To think he had been laboring for weeks to come up with a way to set the record straight between them. What a joke! He would have spilled his guts and groveled, and all the time Nell had Mr. Oliver Jones to explain. Had she come clean, Ms. Wholesome Innocent Girl Scout? No, she hadn't!

Nell had better have a goddamned good explanation for Chicago, or he would...would...what would he do? Could he stop loving her? Could he believe, after knowing her as he had, that she was truly as venal as those stories made her appear? Damn!

Mouth thinned to a determined line, brows beetled, Dan pounded on the trailer-house door. It flew open, and there was Nell, staring at him with a look of disgust on her face.

"We need to talk!" The door shut in his face.

Nell's voice came through the barrier. "I only opened the door so I could slam it again. I hope your face is flat!"

Something told Dan that Nell wasn't in a talking mood. Well too frigging bad!

"Nell! Open this door right now!"

"Go jump in Lake Powell. Right in front of a ski boat going forty miles an hour!"

Vindictive little brat.

"I have a good explanation!"

That was a cop-out, but it got the door open again. She stared at him with knives flying from glacial green eyes. "How could you possibly have an explanation that paints you as anything but the lowest form of scum-dwelling troll?"

He crossed the threshold before she could slam the door on him again. "Is that what I am? A scum-dwelling troll? Then what the hell are you?"

"What?"

He reached into his jeans pocket, unfolded the *Chicago Tribune* article he had downloaded from the Internet the day before, and handed it to her. She looked at the header and turned pale. Her reaction should have given Dan satisfaction, but he only felt more acid pour into his stomach.

"This isn't what it sounds like."

"Really?" He grabbed the article from her and read. Not that he needed to read. Over the past day he had memorized every damning word.

"Oliver Jones, CEO of Worldwide Industries and probable candidate for the state legislature, alleged Monday at a press conference that *The Chicago World News* reporter Nell Jordan had threatened to print false allegations about irregularities in his corporation's pension funds. The threat, he claimed, was an attempt to prevent him from ending his brief romantic relationship with Miss Jordan.

"Mr. Jones refused to speculate on any legal action he might take, and instead joked that 'Some women just won't take no for an answer.'

"Oliver Jones assumed the leadership of Worldwide in 1995 and worked hard to correct the tax and legal difficulties that had pursued the corporation before he came on board. He extended an invitation to state and city authorities to examine his books. Mr. Jones is noted for his generosity to countless civic and arts funds.

"Nell Jordan, a staff reporter at the sensationalist *Chicago World News*, has kept company with Mr. Jones for the past three months. The *World News* had no comment on Mr. Jones's assertions other than a denial that they had printed anything about Oliver Jones, his corporation, or his pension fund. Editorial policy, the *World News* claimed, required every story they printed to be thoroughly checked for accuracy."

In the silence that followed, the ticking of the little clock on top of the television seemed loud.

"You have quite a record with men, sweetheart."

Nell bit her lip and took a deep breath. "You believe that?"

"I'm waiting for an explanation."

That seemed to frost her. Instead of giving excuses for that ugly article, she went to the little kitchen table and picked up a printed form. "Well, Mr. Clean, while you wait for me to beg your understanding and absolution, maybe you'd like to explain this."

She handed him the page, which bore a labyrinth of lines which defied understanding. Typed over lines on the top of the page was his grandfather's name—with a few strikeovers. Below and to the side was his own name.

"What the hell is this?"

"It's a pedigree form. The placement of your name along with Frank Cramer's implies that you carry the same bloodlines. Someone put it in my mailbox to imply that fibbing about that stupid feature article you were supposedly writing isn't the only secret you're harboring."

"Who sent this?"

"I have no idea. I know tons of dog people who use this exact same form. I have some myself."

"Whoever it is certainly doesn't type very well."

Nell sputtered. "Is that all you have to say?"

He gritted his teeth. Busted. Busted but good. "I guess neither of us holds the high ground, then. If I listen to your excuses for—what would it be? Extortion? Blackmail? Then you agree to listen to my excuse for being an underhanded jerk."

The atmosphere inside the house had turned cold with a chill not due to the little window air conditioner that labored to fight the warm May air. Piggy regarded him from the sofa, the canine version of a hanging judge. Nell propped herself against the doorframe that led to her little office, arms crossed militantly on her chest.

"All right. Talk fast. You have five minutes before I throw your butt out."

"Okay, here it is in a nutshell." Suddenly he was a lot madder at himself than at her. "When I pulled you out of the bug, you got under my skin right off. I wanted to be with you so badly it scared the hell out of me. When you said you would go out with me, I thought maybe my luck with women had changed."

Her eyes narrowed.

"Then my mother told me that Granddad had left a fortune to you-know-who over there on the couch."

Piggy growled.

"And she guilted me into starting an investigation."

Nell's face drained of any color it possessed. "Your mother? Your grandfather?"

A sudden silence turned the air so heavy Dan could scarcely breathe.

"Frank Cramer was your actual grandfather?"

"Uh . . ."

"Natalie Donner is your mother?"

The tone of her voice was steadily rising. He was in deep shit.

"Well . . . yes." He continued quickly, before she could get worked into more of a lather. "That was how Mother played the guilt card. The old man and I didn't get along well, but I didn't like the idea of some bimbo gold digger taking advantage of him. After all, he was family."

" 'Bimbo gold digger'?"

He grimaced. "My mother's words, actually."

Nell actually growled. Piggy smirked.

The best defense, as they say, is a good offense. "Okay, if you're not a bimbo gold digger, what about this thing in Chicago?" He slapped the article copy with his hand. "Threatening some big-shot rich guy so you can keep reaping the bennies of his attention?"

She came erect and stalked toward him, one index finger

pointing to the middle of his chest like a pistol ready to fire a fatal shot. " 'Bimbo gold digger'? Hah! Maybe I just don't think I owe an explanation to you, you deceiving, low-down, self-serving, amoral, son of a bitch! You lied and lied and lied."

Dan retreated straight into the sofa, which caught the back of his knees. He sat down hard right next to Piggy, who curled lips back from her teeth.

"Don't bother, Piggy," Nell told the dog. "Leave the bastard to me."

He held up a hand, palm outward. "Nell, okay. Okay. I'm slime. I'm worm-turds. I'm the biggest jerk on the face of the planet. But what about you? You don't owe me an explanation, or you don't have one?"

"I can't believe I fell for your line. You deliberately deceived me! Even at . . . at . . ." Her colorless face turned pink. "Even at Lake Powell. Even . . . oh!"

She seemed to have lost all her words, which could have given Dan an opening for a lethal counterattack, but the sudden image of Lake Powell insidiously softened the self-righteous anger he labored to maintain.

"Get this straight, Nell. I never deceived you at Lake Powell."

"How can you say that?"

"I loved you. I meant that. By the time we hit Lake Powell, I thought you were the most perfect woman that ever walked into my life."

Her face was stone. Her lips sealed tightly, she stared at the floor instead of into his eyes.

"But you're not perfect, are you? Although I admit any complaint along those lines is the pot calling the kettle black."

He wasn't as angry as he should be. The fury he had managed to work up had mostly drained away, fading to sadness. He had loved Nell. Hell, when he sorted through the emotions ricocheting around his head, he probably would still love her. He just couldn't reconcile the Nell he had come to love with the blackmailing bitch Oliver Jones said "wouldn't take no."

"Maybe we both need to back off and bring some common sense into this," Dan ventured. "No one's perfect, and maybe no one should be casting stones."

Her mouth opened on a retort, but she snapped it shut with a scowl. She didn't appear all that anxious to open the door to common sense.

"You promised my kids a picnic at Slide Rock on Sunday. We could let them play around in the creek while we talk things out—after we've both had a chance to simmer down."

She shook her head. "I'd be too tempted to hold your head beneath the water until bubbles stop coming up."

He managed a faint smile. "I think I can protect myself. Unless you have another cake, that is. Your trick with the cake was a real audience-pleaser—at least with my kids."

Her lips twitched.

"We'll pick you up at noon."

"No. I don't want to see you again. Really."

"I'll pick you up," he insisted. "We had something, and we can't just leave it here, like this."

On that bit of wisdom, Dan turned to make an exit— and immediately stumbled over the ankle-high living ottoman who had slunk silently into his path. With a curse he normally wouldn't have used in front of a lady, he tumbled tail over teacup out the door, to land spread-eagled on the concrete patio slab. He raised his head, and two images of a grinning Piggy swam in his vision, finally merging into one very satisfied dog.

DAN MARCHED into his office with Marta and James marching along in his wake. BJ took one look at his face and didn't even bother with his usual cheery hello.

"You know, Dan the Man, I remember one time, it might have been a year or so ago, you came here in a good mood. So I know it's possible."

"Don't start," Dan warned.

"Is that a lump on your skull, or are you simply trying out the lopsided look today?"

"He fell!" Marta proclaimed tragically.

"He did? Oh my! And you must be little Marta."

"Big Marta," the girl insisted.

"Big Marta, then. And little James."

"Is my dad your boss?" James inquired.

"I'm the one who keeps things going around here." BJ slipped a meaningful look Dan's way. "But your dad claims to be the boss."

"My dad's everybody's boss."

"Well, sometimes he tries to be."

Dan snorted. "Very funny, both of you. I just need to pick up my binoculars. The kids and I are going bird-watching."

"Bird-watching?" BJ chortled.

"That's what I said. Bird-watching is both fun and educational."

"Of course," BJ agreed. "Enjoying Mother Nature is good for the soul. And hopefully, for the state of mind."

"Why are you here on a Wednesday, anyway? Shouldn't you be in class?"

"Dan, it's almost the end of May. I graduated."

"Oh. That's right."

"And thank you for the graduation gift." His tone grew serious. "The set of Agatha Christie is a treasure."

"You're welcome. And as long as you're here, you can do something for me." He dug the infamous and much folded *Chicago Tribune* article from his pocket and slapped it down on BJ's desk. "Sleuth around the Internet and find out whatever you can related to this."

BJ brightened. "Sleuth around. I like that image."

"So use it in your book. But find out what you can. And I'd like to know what kind of fellow this Oliver Jones character is." His scowl softened. "I'd appreciate it as a favor, BJ. You're better on the Internet than I am."

BJ looked pleased. "You got it, Boss-Man. And oh yes, before I forget, your mother called. The note's on your desk."

Dan closed his eyes in pain. "My mother. Of course. Watch the kids while I call her back, will you?"

Dan closed the office door behind him, sat down at his desk, and stared at the wall for a moment to gather his strength. He'd had a very bad day so far. Talking to his mom could only make it worse.

She answered the phone promptly. "Dan, dear."

"It's that caller ID thing again, isn't it?"

"Yes, dear. I never pick up a phone without it. But thank you for calling back. I wanted to apologize."

His brows shot up. "You're kidding."

"No, of course I'm not kidding. You think I would kid about something so painful? I don't apologize easily."

"I never remember you apologizing at all."

"Well, I am."

"What for?"

"I . . . perhaps I shouldn't have said some of the things I said when you came to my showroom Monday. I realize now that you're probably genuinely fond of Nell Jordan."

She still couldn't pronounce Nell's name without making it sound like poison.

"And you believed in her innocence."

"Yes." Dan saw no reason to fill his mother in on the depressing state of his love life. Former love life, that is.

"I do hope you're looking into that letter I gave you from those investigators your grandfather hired. But I won't push. You're old enough to make up your own mind."

"Thank you, Mother."

"And by the way, happy birthday. I don't suppose you'd like to have dinner out?"

"Thanks anyway." He made himself sound as if he were smiling, even though he wasn't. After all, his mom was trying to be nice. "I've had a bit of a tough day. Besides, the kids and I are about to go bird-watching down by the river."

"Well . . . That's very nice."

There was something else. Dan could tell there was something else. The awkward silence was filled with it.

"I . . . need to tell you something, Dan."

They were making progress. "Yes?"

"I visited with Jared Monday after you left."

Something interesting colored her voice there, Dan noted.

"He imparted some information I believe you should have."

"Okay. What?"

Natalie told him, and suddenly the whole complex mess of his life got a lot more complicated and a lot more messy.

PERFECT! IT was perfect! I wish I could have been there in the fur to see Nell crown the studmuffin with that cake, but she gave me a blow-by-blow account when she got home. Oh was she mad! And upset, of course. Humiliated. Of course she was, the poor dear. And I felt sorry for her. Even to the point of cuddling with her on the couch.

But it's not like she wasn't asking for trouble.

Of course I iced the cake (a pun, there, in case you didn't catch it) with my clever ploy of leaving that pedigree where Nell couldn't help but find it. That gave her even more ammunition, compliments of yours truly. This double deception put Dudly Dan in the enemy camp without a doubt. So I could hardly believe my eyes when the jackass had the chutzpah to show up on our doorstep when my poor girl still had tears running down her face. Like Nell needed to forgive him! I don't think so! I thought Nell held her own fairly well during the tiff. He deserved no mercy, in my opinion.

Unfortunately, Dudly Dan had some ammunition of his own. I didn't understand what Chicago had to do with the battle, but apparently our Nell has a bit of a past, a fact that inspired a sympathetic warmth in my little heart. We girls with a questionable history have to stick together, you know. Still, the villain managed to score a few points on our girl. I came to the rescue, naturally, and while I couldn't recover all the ground Nell lost, at least I pulled off a touchdown at the end. All's well that ends well, and Dan's little farewell tumble out our door made a fitting end to his schemes. His exit would have been even more special had I thought to lay a few canine mines on the concrete patio to cushion his fall, but Nell gets very prissy about keeping the place picked up.

And just in case my puckered-up probation officer Stan was watching, the whole thing happened purely by accident. Certainly no one could prove otherwise. I simply moved into the right place at the right time. I couldn't have been more innocent.

Almost poetic in its justice, though, wasn't it? That'll teach the slimeball to try moving in on MY money.

Well, I thought the caper had come to an end, that Nell—and my money—were safe, that I had once again saved the day. Nell apologized profusely for having doubted my canine instincts about the villain and tried to make things right with multiple hugs, which benefited her more than me, I have to say. A few extra tidbits came my way also. Small thanks for my efforts, but welcome just the same.

I got to rest on my laurels for three whole days. Then Sunday rolled around, and imagine our surprise when the villain showed up once again on our doorstep. He had the kids in tow, but if he thought that would sway my Nell, he needed to think again. Her fretting and fuming hadn't let up in the three days that had passed. Time might calm her down, but not days. More like years.

I did have to give him credit for trying, though. You have to admire a man who sails along on pure guts.

But anyway, Nell opened the door before the studmuffin even knocked. He had wisely left the kids in his Jeep, but they gaily waved to her from there.

"Hi, Nell!" they piped in cute little voices coming out of cute little faces.

That got me worried. Nell played the sucker for almost anything, and cute kids made powerful sucker bait.

Nell waved back with a smile pasted on her face, but when she looked at Dan, the smile flattened.

"We have a date," was his opening punch.

She blocked. "Sorry. I'm busy."

He feinted with an earnest look. "Nell, you wouldn't disappoint the kids. They're really looking forward to a picnic at Slide Rock."

"Then take them. You don't need me along."

A good blow, I thought. Solidly landed. But of course he came back with a roundhouse punch.

"We need to talk about this, Nell, not fight about it. And the kids are expecting you to come. They give their affection so easily. Don't disappoint them."

"Yes, well, I gave my affection very easily as well, didn't I? And I'm learning to live with disappointment. With a father like you, so will they." She closed the door in his face.

Knockout! Terrific. If I could have, I would have done a victory dance. But all I could do was let loose with a joyous woo-woo of congratulations.

Nell cried, though. She collapsed on the sofa and cried as if her heart had broken into pieces. My little heart, cynical as it was, went out to her. So I crawled into her arms and muzzled her with my wet nose. She squeezed me hard, crying even harder. But I could take it.

I was, after all, a celebrated therapy dog.

     •   •   •

NELL PLUNKED herself down in an overstuffed chair in the hospital lobby, waiting for Jane, with whom she planned to share a hospital visit. Jane and Idaho would take half the hospital, and Nell and Piggy the other half. But Jane was late, as usual. Business at her boarding kennel kept her jumping in a way that never let her get anywhere on time.

Piggy, decked out in her green therapy dog vest, jumped into Nell's lap, where she promptly bestowed a doggie toothpaste-scented kiss on her cheek. Nell scratched the corgi's ears and mused on the amazing ability of dogs to sense a special need for comfort and love. Since D-Day—Disaster Day, as Nell thought of the previous Wednesday—Piggy had drawn closer than she ever had before. Maybe all the weeping and breast-beating gave the dog a clue, Nell thought wryly. She hadn't exactly borne her misery in silence. Even now, five days later, she indulged herself in fits of sniveling. Just the day before, after she and Piggy had slammed the door in Dan's deceitful face, Nell had cried for hours. Well, maybe not hours. But certainly a good long time. She didn't sleep much. Her appetite had cratered. And she couldn't work up much enthusiasm for anything. She, who usually shrugged off bills, empty bank accounts, cranky editors, and a nonexistent love life, had folded over a bit of bad luck.

Some bit of bad luck. Not only did she find out the man she loved was a double-crossing turd, but he had found out about Oliver Jones. Oliver Jones, whom she had thought she loved until she had found out about his hanky-panky with his employees' pension fund. How stupid had she been, warning the guy ahead of time that she intended to turn the light on his crime? So quickly it made her head whirl, he had covered his tracks, destroyed her credibility, and killed her career. Now Oliver had reached clear over to Arizona to destroy what she had here as well.

For that, Nell didn't know whether to cry for her losses,

or laugh at the ridiculous roller-coaster ride of her up-and-down fortunes. First Oliver Jones. Now Dan Travis. What was it about double-dealing men that lured her into their web?

She gave Piggy a hug and sighed.

"Hey there!" Jane greeted them as she walked through the automatic glass door with Idaho. "You look like hell."

"Thank you."

"Feeling low, are you?"

"It's stupid. I know."

Jane dropped into the chair beside her. "It's not stupid. You got quite a kick in the guts, and that hurts."

Nell bit her lip. "I keep telling myself I'll feel better soon. And I will. I will."

Jane patted her hand, a rare display of affection from a woman who had once claimed she had a rawhide soul. "You're better off without the creep."

"Of course I am. Much better off."

"And you learned something, right?"

Nell grimaced. "Look before you leap, I guess. Mckenna was right all along about not being able to trust people."

"Give me a good dog any time," Jane said with a grin. "You can always trust a dog. A dog doesn't tell lies, doesn't sniff after your money, and it's content with the foot of a bed—usually." She gave Idaho a meaningful look.

"You're right." Nell tried to chuckle, but it was a poor attempt.

"Nell..."

"Oh, ignore me. I'm just being stupid. He just... well, he filled a part of me I didn't know needed filling, and now that he's gone, that part seems emptier than ever."

"You know," Jane said, resuming her usual no-nonsense stance, "if you're that upset, you shouldn't be visiting the hospital. The patients don't need someone with a case of the blues coming into their rooms. Blues are contagious, you know."

"I'll forget all about it once I start working. Promise."

"Okay, then." She got up and straightened Idaho's therapy vest. "Where do you want to go?"

"I'll take Critical Care and Surgery. There's nothing like a visit to Critical Care to put a person's troubles in perspective."

"You have a point. See you later. I'm off."

Nell had spoken the truth about a visit to Critical Care. By the time the nurses had told her what rooms she couldn't visit and why, her own troubles seemed small.

"The guy in fourteen is pretty critical," Stephanie told her, "but I think he would enjoy seeing Piggy. And certainly his wife would. She's having a hard time. The guy doesn't have much of a chance."

Nell felt herself go pale.

"Oh don't worry," Steph assured her. "He's not going to die on you. Not this morning, at least."

"And the woman in nine has a huge abdominal incision. Make sure Piggy doesn't put one of her fat little feet on the patient's stomach."

True to her promise, the minute Nell greeted the first patient, she forgot about Dan Travis. Well, almost forgot.

She had been in the unit about twenty minutes when Stephanie caught her between rooms. "There's a kid in twelve. I wasn't going to send you in there, because the little boy's in a coma, but the mom wants the dog to visit. Put on a stiff upper lip, because this one's a tearjerker. The boy hasn't been conscious since his dad rammed the family car into a semi truck. The dad's okay, but the kid won't wake up, and the docs aren't quite sure why."

Nell bit her lip.

"Up to it?" Steph asked. "The mom would appreciate it."

The boy's name was Stevie, and he looked like a pale little wraith against the white sheets of the hospital bed. Dark red curls lay against the pillow like a bloodstain, and his face was white as the bed linen—with the exception of a blue-and-purple bruise near his temple.

"Oh, thank you for coming," the mom said when Nell introduced herself and Piggy. "I'm Karen, and this is ... is my son, Stevie. Stevie adores dogs. I thought ... I thought ..." Karen couldn't continue. Tears overflowed her eyes and ran down cheeks that were almost as pale as her son's.

This was a toughie.

Nell kept her voice light. "Piggy would love to say hi to him."

She lifted Piggy onto the boy's bed, and the corgi immediately wedged her little nose between Stevie's cheek and the pillow, nuzzling gently.

"Oh," Karen cried. "She is so sweet!"

"She's a good girl," Nell acknowledged, her heart aching for both boy and mother.

"Stevie loves dogs so much, and his dad promised he could have a dog when he turned eight and grew big enough to take care of one. He was seven three weeks ago."

Karen needed to talk, Nell guessed.

"He wants a golden retriever, and that's such a big dog. But they're gentle, aren't they?"

"We have a wonderful golden retriever who visits here. His name is Fred. I'll tell Fred's mom to be sure and drop by."

"Oh, would you?"

Piggy settled between Stevie's arm and chest, her nose resting in the curve of his neck.

"His dad ..." She bit hard on her lip. "His dad can't bear to look at him. I think he wishes he himself had died in that accident. But it wasn't his fault."

There wasn't much Nell could say, but Karen wasn't expecting a response. She concentrated on watching her son.

"He knows Piggy's there. He does."

Stevie hadn't moved. Not so much as a twitch. But Nell did think that perhaps his breathing was a little easier.

"I can see it in his face. He knows she's there. Please,

could you come in every day while he's here? It would help. I'm sure it would help. Maybe he'll come back to us if there's a little dog asking him to."

Nell didn't want to give false hope. "Piggy's not exactly a miracle worker."

"I think she might be."

Nell could only nod. "We'll try to come in as often as we can. And I'll tell the other people in our group to stop by as well. If they move Stevie, leave word with the nurse to tell me where he goes. And we'll do our best."

"You're in that Hearts of Gold group, aren't you? Stevie went wild when he saw your dogs in the St. Patrick's Day parade."

"Well, now he gets to meet the dogs up close and personal."

Karen reached out a hand. "Thank you. Thank you."

When she left the room, Nell had truly forgotten her own troubles. But they came back to slap her with amazing speed when she encountered a familiar face in the hallway, a face showing the same surprise as Nell's and headed her way.

Natalie Donner.

CALMING HERSELF after seeing the Jordan woman in the hallway, Natalie tentatively pushed aside the curtain that blocked the doorway to Stevie Crenshaw's room in the Critical Care Unit. The rooms in this area didn't have solid doors. They had glass walls with a wide sliding-glass door that seldom closed when a patient was in the room. Nurses kept ever alert eyes on the critically ill or injured patients, and only a curtain gave the patient privacy.

"Karen?"

"Oh, hi, Natalie."

"How are things going?"

Karen shrugged. In the bed, her son Stevie lay pale and

unmoving. Natalie's heart cried. How would she have felt, she wondered, if Dan or Emma had ever been struck down like this? Would she have been as brave as Karen? She suspected not.

"He looks better," Natalie lied.

"That's because he just had a visit from the hospital visiting dog."

In spite of sympathy, Natalie was miffed. "I just saw that Jordan woman and her dog in the hallway. They were here?"

"Yes. Isn't it great? Stevie loves animals of all kinds, and Piggy got right up on the bed with him and cuddled. He knew she was there. I know he did."

Poor Karen. She would grab on to any straw in the storm. She would be better off not entertaining false hopes. "That's just silly, Karen. He's in a coma."

"No one knows what coma patients know or don't know about what's going on around them, Natalie. I think he knows. The dog is good for him."

"That dog is the one that my father left almost his entire fortune to."

Karen looked surprised. "Really? I didn't know she was the one. You must admit she's very sweet."

Natalie dropped the subject, because Karen had enough stress without worrying about Natalie's problems and prejudices. So Natalie offered to read to Stevie, since Karen's voice was growing hoarse from her constant attempts to communicate with her son.

Natalie admired her friend's spirit and determination. The young woman had once been Natalie's client, and now she played an active role on the Sedona Chamber of Commerce, where they had discovered that in spite of the age difference—Natalie in her fifties and Karen in her thirties—they had much in common. But Karen's relative youth showed in her stubborn belief that miracles could happen, that anyone who refused to give up hope eventually had prayers answered.

Natalie knew better. Life had taught her that the harder you hoped, the more painful the final fall. Smart people avoided hoping for something that would never happen.

"I think Stevie has more color," Karen commented wistfully. "Don't you?"

Natalie merely continued to read.

chapter 17

DAN MADE a mental note. Next time the blues got hold of him, he shouldn't regard the local animal shelter as a cure. How could a person visit one of these places and not walk out with every single animal in tow? He wanted to, and he wasn't even a creature freak like Nell and her buddies.

"How do you work here?" he asked the volunteer who escorted him around the kennels.

She gave him a look the devout reserve for the uninitiated. "Someone has to. This is just a drop in the bucket, you know. We put hundreds of animals to sleep every year, and more poor unwanted puppies and kittens are born every day."

He'd heard the lecture from the woman who sat at the desk up front, and desperately wanted to avoid a second one. "If those puppies and kittens are unwanted, why did someone arrange for them to be born?"

She sniffed indignantly. "To let some idiot's kids watch the miracle of birth. To let some unfortunate female have at least one litter of puppies. Or because someone thinks that spaying is cruel, or some guy"—she cocked a brow his direction, as if he were the guilty party—"has to cross his legs whenever someone suggests he neuter his male."

He flung up a hand as if taking an oath. "Not me! In fact, I've never had a dog."

Instantly suspicious, she scowled. "Then why do you want one now?"

Because he had the idiot idea that a dog would help him slide back into Nell's good graces, so she could explain away Chicago, he could explain that he wasn't quite as big a jerk as he seemed, and things could go from there.

Not that he was sucker enough to let that Chicago business slide, but he would like to hear what she said about it. He could hardly get an explanation worthy of forgiveness if the forgivee wouldn't speak to him.

Oh hell. Why didn't he just admit it to himself? In spite of that show of meteoric indignation, he was still a sucker and an idiot. An idiot in love.

That was why he wanted a dog. But probably none of those reasons would go over very well with this keeper of the dog keys.

"I . . . uh . . . I've always wanted a dog," he fibbed. "My mother would never let me have one."

Of course, he had just celebrated his thirty-first birthday—with a beautiful cake over his head, no less—and he'd been out from beneath his mother's thumb since he was eighteen. The volunteer just looked at him with pity in her eyes and didn't bother to point out the discrepancy. Maybe she thought a man of his ripe years shouldn't still be kowtowing to his mother.

And maybe, Dan mused darkly, he had hit upon something that was close to the truth. But he had enough to depress him right now. He refused to think about that little gem.

"Look around," the volunteer invited. "There are lots of dogs here who could use a good home."

She understated, Dan discovered as he walked up and down the rows of cages. Big dogs, small dogs, shaggy and smooth dogs. Feisty dogs, quiet dogs, beautiful or ugly. About half could have boasted a purebred pedigree. One short-legged, pointy-eared little corgi brought Piggy to mind, only this one didn't look quite as Machiavellian. Would Nell choke if he showed up with a corgi? He almost laughed, but he didn't, because the little dog turned her big brown eyes upon him and made him want to cry.

Another cage held a big yellow Labrador retriever. The Lab gave him a goofy dog smile as he walked past his kennel. Dan couldn't resist stopping to visit.

"Hi, there, big fella."

The dog smushed his face against the chain-link fence to get closer.

"He's a love," the volunteer said, "but he's almost been here too long. Everybody stops to visit, but then they say he's too big, and he'll eat too much or stuff like that. Poor boy, I'd take him home myself, but I already have six."

Dan pictured the big Lab in the motor home. Neither he nor the dog would have room to turn around. "How long does he have before he goes over to Death Row?"

"A couple of days, maybe. The director likes him, so she might cut him some slack."

BJ lived in a big old house down by the Verde River. He could use a great big dog, Dan decided. "I know someone who would love this dog, and I'm going to send him over here today." BJ would be here if Dan had to march him here at gunpoint. "So don't let anyone get antsy and gas him."

For the first time, the volunteer smiled. "You can count on it."

In the last kennel in the third row, Dan found what he was looking for. Well, maybe he hadn't been looking exactly for this dog. Who would have? It had to be the funniest-looking dog ever born. But the dog definitely knew he belonged with Dan. Something in the big brown eyes told him so.

"Now this one," he declared to his escort, "is a dog!"

"This one?"

"How'd such a cute little guy get into a place like this?"

"Cute?"

"Yeah. Cute."

"He's a stray. Someone picked him up behind Wal-Mart. Apparently he was being terrorized by a cat."

The dog looked positively shamefaced. Dan grinned. "Yeah, dog, I'd be embarrassed, too. Can I take him for a walk?"

"Be my guest."

Five minutes later Dan walked down the dirt road on the other side of the humane society being dragged along by a twenty pound mutt who looked like a thistle come to life. The little guy had no manners, but he did turn around to check on Dan with touching regularity, and every few minutes he stopped pulling and trotted back to solicit a pet or two.

"You're a perfect candidate for Jane Connor's school for wayward dogs," Dan informed the little creature. "And if you can reel me in Jane's assistant, I'll see you in dog food and soft beds for the rest of your life."

The dog wagged his tail in agreement. Actually, he wagged his whole body in appreciation.

"It's a deal, then." Dan squatted down, took the little refugee's leg, and gave him a gentle high five. "That's the spirit. You and me, we're both going to be lucky dogs."

"I'M NOT generally a sucker for kids," Mckenna said. "But this kid would break a stone's heart."

Mckenna, Titi, Nell, and Piggy sat on a bench and watched the cars straggling into the parking lot of Jane's kennel. A new basic obedience class began tonight.

"Can you imagine how hard it is for Stevie's mom to sit there day after day and watch him just lie there?" Nell said. "And the doctors can't tell her much of anything."

"It's bad enough for her. What about the dad? He was driving the car."

"He hasn't been in once. Karen says he'll hardly even talk."

Mckenna shook her head. "Sometimes I'm really glad I don't have family. Actually, most of the time I'm glad I don't have family, except for Titi." She gave the cat a squeeze. The cat replied with a bored yawn. "You invest your heart in people, then they die, or leave, or double-cross you."

A week ago, Nell would have argued the point. But exactly a week ago, she had discovered, for the second time in her life, the perils of getting too close to the wrong person. But she didn't want to talk about that.

"Visiting Stevie and Karen really puts a person's own small troubles in perspective," Nell observed.

"True enough."

Nell sighed. "And speaking of troubles, Monday when I visited the hospital, none other than Natalie Donner confronted me in the hall right outside Stevie's room. Turns out Karen is a friend of hers, or a client, or something."

"Ouch! You know, we should be able to get an injunction against her harassing you. I'll talk to—"

"No, Mckenna. Not every annoyance in life requires legal action."

"Well, it was a thought."

"She didn't harass, just stuck her nose in the air and looked at me like I dripped bog slime. The chill around that woman could have cooled the whole hospital, even in ninety-degree heat."

Mckenna put a hand on Nell's shoulder in genuine sympathy. "I'm sorry, sweetie. You don't deserve that."

"Life used to be so simple."

"Money does tend to complicate things," Mckenna said with a sigh. Then she grinned. "So do men. But at least money is worth the trouble."

"I guess." Nell sighed and glanced at the crowd gathering

in the yard. "This is a big class for a Wednesday night."
Twelve people had bouncing, barking, whining dogs under
varying degrees of control, most approaching zero.

"It'll whittle down," Mckenna predicted. "Forty percent
of these people are quitters."

"You are such a cynic."

"Comes with being an attorney. We get to deal with the
scum of the earth."

"You're an attorney in Sedona," Nell reminded her. "Sedona doesn't have any scum of the earth."

"That's what you think." Mckenna grinned wickedly.

Nell dismissed her with a wave of one arm. "I'm going to
work. Keep an eye on Piggy, would you?"

Jane had already finished her opening spiel about training techniques and class policies when yet another student
showed up. Nell took one look at the Jeep CJ-7 and could
hardly believe her eyes. The man who stepped out of the
Jeep looked like Dan, and the vehicle certainly looked
like his, but this man carried a scruffy little dog beneath
one arm.

"Is that Dan?" Nell's stomach sank.

Jane grimaced. "Looks like it, doesn't it?"

Even Mckenna had stood to see who it was.

"It is Dan," Nell moaned. "Oh, Jane! You let *him* register
for class?"

"He used another name. Robert Travis. How was I supposed to know he was your Travis?"

"He's not *my* Travis!"

Jane shrugged. "I didn't think your Travis had a dog."

Mckenna had strolled up beside them. "Are you sure
that's a dog?"

"Hi there," Dan said as he came through the gate. "Sorry
I'm late. This is Weed."

"Appropriate name," Mckenna noted. "The creature
looks like a cross between a terrier and a tumbleweed."

"Mckenna," Jane said in the voice that controlled rot-tweilers. "Go sit. And stay."

"Yes, ma'am."

"Mr. Travis, from now on, I'd appreciate it if you were on time. We wouldn't want you to miss anything. And put that dog down. It has legs of its own, doesn't it?"

"Uh . . . sure."

"Then it should learn to walk on them."

Nell turned away, gritting her teeth. She thought of leaving: scooping up Piggy from her perch on the bench, climbing into the minivan, and getting the hell away from here. But that would be retreat, and Dan Travis should be the one retreating, not her.

Jane settled Nell's battle with indecision. "Nell, go over there and help the poor man with the malamute. The dog seems to be giving the orders there."

Nell sighed and echoed Mckenna. "Yes, ma'am."

She did her best to pretend that Dan was not there, but she couldn't help but notice his antics with that ridiculous little dog. If Weed had come with any other student, she would have thought the dog cute. With Dan, the poor creature couldn't rise above ridiculous in her mind. And Dan—Dan the bogus hero, the one who knew all the moves with everything, including gullible women, Dan bumbled and stumbled, all thumbs when it came to training a dog. The dog managed to tangle him in the leash until he almost fell on his face. His heeling made the other students look good, difficult to do in a first-week beginning class. Weed spent more time bouncing up and down in front of Dan like some sort of Weed-in-the-box toy than trotting at his left side in the proper heel position.

Even the man with the bossy malamute did better.

"The dog is cute," Jane muttered in an aside to Nell. "And together, those two are a stitch. You have to admit that."

"No I don't," Nell said sullenly. "Dan is a louse and the

dog should have preferred staying in the animal shelter to going with him."

Jane just smiled. "That is one of the nice things about dogs. They're capable of loving even a louse."

Class ended, finally, and Nell hastily retreated toward the house, but not before Dan caught up with her. Jane pointedly left them in privacy, and she cut off Mckenna before she could ride to the rescue.

"Let them take care of it," Nell heard Jane say to Mckenna before she took her arm and dragged her in the other direction—just as Dan took Nell's arm to stop her flight.

She didn't wait for him to speak before launching the first volley. "What the hell do you think you're doing?" She yanked her arm from his grip. "You think this is funny? Are you getting a good chuckle out of it?"

"Nell, settle down."

The command in his voice made her even angrier. He sounded as if *she* was the one being unreasonable, as if *she* was the one in the wrong. The jerk!

"I will not settle down," she growled. "Why are you here? And don't tell me you came to train that dust-bunny disguised as a dog. You don't even like dogs!"

"I like Weed. And yes, I came here to give him some training. Didn't you once tell me that dogs are happier if they know their limits and if they have to do some work to earn their keep?"

She gritted her teeth.

"But you're basically right. Mostly I came here to see you." He took a quick glance around, then pushed her toward Jane's covered porch, where they would have more privacy from the departing students. "Nell, I want you to listen to me. We need to talk. I know I screwed up. And you have some explaining to do as well, you know. I'm going to keep after you until we straighten this out. Because I think maybe we have something worth saving. What we began at

Lake Powell is worth saving. I said I loved you, and I meant it. You said you loved me, and I don't think you're a person who takes love lightly. You don't get over love, even when someone hits you in the teeth with it."

"Yes I do! I might have been duped by your practiced charm, but I've come to my senses."

" 'Practiced charm'? Me?"

"Yes, you worm! Practiced, empty, meaningless, deceitful charm. I wised up fast enough when I learned the truth. So just back off and leave me alone!"

He shook his head, unmoved by her tirade. "If I'm willing to listen to you, why can't you listen to me?"

She wanted to kick him, but that would have been just too childish. "Do you think I'm stupid? What are you after now? Still looking for dirty little secrets? Haven't you discovered enough to break your grandfather's will, or maybe you've figured out an easier way to get your finger in the pie of your grandfather's money."

He scowled. "I never wanted any part of my grandfather's money. He offered me a great job with Cramer Electronics when I left the police force. It would have made me rich. But I turned him down, because the old man always attached strings to anything he offered. He thought he knew how everyone should live his life, and he damned well tried to make sure everyone lived life his way. He always, always wanted to pull the strings."

He gave her a penetrating look. "Whether or not you angled for the money you got, how many strings is Frank Cramer still pulling in your life, Nell?"

Perhaps he hit a little too close to the truth with that statement. Frank Cramer had indeed changed her life, but the change was for the good, wasn't it? How often he had chided her about living in a trailer house in a "podunk town," as he had called Cottonwood. "Life is a rat race," he'd told her time and time again. "But it's a race that makes the blood pump and brain keep firing. You should join in, girl. Get organized. Get moving. Get some ambition."

His bequest to Piggy didn't have anything to do with strings or manipulation, did it? She remained the same, basically, in spite of the investment counselor, financial strategies, new car, soon-to-be new house, a service that screened her callers, and a schedule so busy she scarcely had time to write.

Uneasiness settled heavily in her stomach. How dare this jerk, this lying, underhanded jerk, deliberately throw another monkey wrench into a life that already had become too complicated? The mother tried to convince her with one cold look that she was the scum of the earth, and now the son wouldn't leave her alone to mend the heart he had shattered into pieces. Damn him! And damn the whole Cramer family while you're at it!

Furious, she pointed toward the gate. "Leave, Dan! Just leave! And take my advice: give up! I don't love you! I'm not interested in your excuses, and I'm not going to give you any for a bunch of lies told about me in Chicago."

"So you say it was all lies."

"Leave!" she shouted.

"Okay for now, but I'll be around. I don't give up easily." He grinned. "And poor little Weed here wants to be a therapy dog. He's going to need a lot of training."

She gritted her teeth to hold back a scream, but at least he left, his ridiculous little dog tucked beneath his arm.

"And put that dog down!" Nell shouted as a parting shot. "He's got legs!"

DAN TRIED to keep his cool as he headed for the gate. As he'd told Nell, a mule had nothing on him when it came to stubbornness. Giving up just didn't figure in his character. Unfortunately, Nell appeared to be blessed with the same determination. And she was mad. Oh yes, she was mad.

"Hey, guy." Jane detached herself from a group of lingering students and gave him a smile—one of the few he had seen that evening. "Trying to make water run uphill over there?" She jerked her head in Nell's direction.

He answered with a morose grunt.

"Give her time, okay? Nell's got a lot on her plate right now, and you certainly didn't help with that low trick you pulled."

"Yeah, well, I never meant to be a lying piece of shit. It just turned out that way."

Jane laughed. "I do like a man who's not afraid to call crap by its proper name."

"So why are you talking to me?"

She shrugged. "I make a living seeing through bullshit. The students bullshit me that they can't do what I tell them to do. The dogs bullshit me that sitting, staying, and heeling are going to kill them. But that's all just surface garbage.

"Now you, on the other hand . . ." She grinned. "Could be I see a champion beneath that pit bull exterior of yours. Might be that you just need a little training, a bit of discipline, a couple of little pops on the collar to make you behave."

"Didn't I just hear you tell the class that jerking a dog around by its collar doesn't accomplish anything?"

"With you I might make an exception."

"If you handed the end of the leash to Nell, I'm sure she would give new meaning to the term 'choke collar.'"

Jane laughed. "Give her time, Mr. Pit Bull. Give her time. Sooner or later she'll remember that everyone deserves his day in court." She gave him a pointed, narrow look. "As long as you remember she deserves one, too." She paused. "That bit in Chicago was bullshit, you know?"

With a slow nod, Dan answered. "So she claims. But she won't trust me with the details."

"She doesn't like to talk about it."

"That's bullshit, too."

Jane gave him a half-grin. "Maybe you should tell her that. It just so happens that she's moving into her new house this coming weekend. Mckenna and I are helping, of course, but I'm sure we could use some muscled help."

A slow smile lifted his mouth.

"You look like you work out a bit," Jane said with a lift of one brow. "Put those muscles to good use carrying some furniture. You know where the house is. The truck should get there around ten."

Without waiting for an answer, she turned and went back to her students. Then she turned and scolded. "And put that poor dog down on the ground. You're going to make him think he's a Pomeranian."

Next morning, Dan still clung to optimism. He forced himself to get to his office early, and when he found a note from BJ on his desk saying two potential new clients had called, he felt the tide of events turning his way. Bad luck and good luck came in waves, he had always found. Seemingly unrelated things plunged or rose according to the same hidden forces. For the past week, his luck had stayed in a trough. But the lift of the next swell loomed just ahead.

"All right!" He rubbed his hands together. "A couple of jobs. Maybe I can pay the office rent next month."

Then he read BJ's next note and the bottom dropped out once again.

Boss—

Checked out your Chicago Tribune *article. See attached related stories. Just call me Sherlock.*

By the way, thanks for the tip on Moose. That's what I named him. I finally have a companion in bed who doesn't expect me to give up watching the midnight mystery movie.

Dan had to smile at the thought of that big yellow Lab from the humane society lolling across BJ's bed. But the smile flattened as he looked through the newspaper articles BJ had copied off the Internet, along with some biographical information on Oliver Jones. Amazing what information one could find in cyberspace. As Dan skimmed the printed words, he was seized by an urge to meet with Mr. Jones and share a knuckle sandwich.

NELL LOOKED at the boxes piled on the front porch, which had once seemed so huge. They had already made two trips with Jane's van, and there was more to come. "How could I have so much stuff? I've been living all this time in a tiny trailer house. Where did all this come from?"

"Stuff multiplies when you move," Mckenna told her. In designer jeans and an expensive knit crop top, she didn't look ready to tackle an army of dusty boxes. Supervising was her talent.

Jane grinned as she slit open a box. "All your stuff secretly reproduces when you're not looking. These are recipe books? You actually cook?"

"Occasionally. Oh no. Here comes the truck with the new furniture, and I haven't decided where to put anything. Moving has to be the world's biggest pain."

"No," Mckenna said. "Men are the world's biggest pain." She sat on a box and fanned herself with one hand to combat the late May heat. "Do you believe that Tom Markham asked me out on a date yesterday?"

"Tom Markham, the hunky cowboy?" Nell asked.

"Ex-cowboy," Jane reminded her. "I'm surprised he waited this long."

"What?"

"I could see he had eyes for you way back on St. Paddy's Day. I wondered when you two would get together."

"We are not together. The idea is ridiculous."

"Nell grinned. 'Methinks the lady doth protest too much,' or something Shakespearean along those lines."

"Oh please! Worse than being a cowboy and liking country-western music, he's a do-gooder who still thinks the law is about who's right and who's wrong rather than who has the most pull."

"Fancy that," Jane snorted. "What a concept."

Mckenna frowned suspiciously. "What's that supposed to mean?"

"He struck me as a nice guy. Why don't you give him a chance?"

Mckenna crossed her legs primly. "Even if I wanted to—and I don't—he works for me."

"Poor guy," Nell said sympathetically.

"I thought you attorney types were all sort of independent." This from Jane.

"Well, we are, but I'm a VP, and in charge of this branch office, so technically he works for me. I can't believe he had the nerve to throw out a line and expect me to bite. Men can be such a hassle."

"So you skewered him on the sharp spear of your disdain," Nell supplied.

"I wouldn't put it so crudely. I was polite. Besides, I'm almost engaged to Adam."

"Is Adam the hottie in Denver?" Jane asked.

"That's him."

"And why isn't Adam a hassle?"

"Probably," Nell told Jane wryly, "because Adam is in Denver."

Nell and Jane both smiled. Mckenna pointedly ignored them.

"If some guy ever did to me what Dan Travis did to you, Nell, I'd have his balls on a skewer."

"Ouch!" Nell gave Mckenna a pained look.

"You were very wise to send that jerk packing."

Jane looked uneasy. "Uh . . . about that, Nell."

"About what?" Nell asked cautiously. Whenever the

subject of Dan came up, which it did too often, she still got that sinking feeling.

"He does seem like kind of a nice guy."

Mckenna gave a sharp bark of laughter. "Aside from underhandedly trying to set her up for a fall and lying to her about who he was."

Jane shrugged. "That sucks. But I can see where it might happen. He works as a private eye. There's nothing so bad about that. And he had no way of knowing that Nell wasn't what that dreadful Donner woman says she is."

"The Donner woman is his mother," Nell growled. "I told you, didn't I, what she did to me in the hospital outside Stevie's room?"

"Yes," Jane said. "But we're talking about Dan. I can see where things might have been awkward for him when he started to like you. You might at least listen to what he has to say."

"Phooey," Mckenna said. "He deserves to be stuffed into someone's trash can and have the lid locked down upon him."

"Everyone deserves a second chance," Jane insisted. "You said he knows about the Chicago fiasco, but he seems willing to give you a second chance."

"Oh please!" Mckenna griped. "The man never even came clean. His kids told her. He didn't have the guts."

"I'll bet he would have."

"As if you know so much about men? When was the last time you slept with anything besides a dog?"

Jane gave Mckenna a steely-eyed glare. "Insight into human nature—specifically men's nature—does not require promiscuity."

"No," Mckenna answered flippantly, "but it helps."

Nell intervened. "Okay, you two. Break it up before I have to fetch a hose to get you apart. That truck is coming down the road, and no one is here yet to help. Jane, didn't you say that you called that moving service to hire a couple of guys for the day?"

"Well, I did say that." Jane appeared uncomfortable again, noticeable because Jane rarely looked uneasy about anything. Someone who told Doberman pinchers and bull terriers what to do couldn't afford to lack confidence.

Nell was instantly suspicious. "Jane, what have you done?"

"Why hire guys at seventy bucks an hour when I've got plenty of muscle?"

"And? . . ." Mckenna joined in the third degree.

"And I'll have plenty of help."

"Not us," Mckenna said sharply. "I don't do things that require sweat, and Nell needs to supervise the furniture arrangement, not make like a stevedore."

"Not you," Jane conceded. "Him."

She pointed down the road, where behind the furniture truck came a Jeep. The canvas top was down, letting the sun shine full on the two occupants—one a dust-colored shaggy dog, and the other a fine-looking private eye with a grin on his face.

chapter 18

NELL TRIED to ignore Dan's Jeep as the furniture truck pulled into her driveway. The big diesel Main Street Furniture van pulled to a stop with a squeak of brakes, and a burly driver with a row of silver rings in each earlobe climbed down from the cab. The driver was the only burly guy, unfortunately. Jane had cancelled the two others who were supposed to be with him.

The driver strutted up to the three women with a clipboard full of paperwork. Men with rings in their ears, Nell had often observed, couldn't move in anything but a strut.

"Which one of you is Nell Jordan?"

"That would be me," Nell confessed. From the corner of her eye, she watched Dan's Jeep pull in beside the truck. The jackass blithely jumped out, lifted Weed from the passenger seat, and sent the dog into the high grass beside the irrigation ditch to do dog business. The scruffy little creature blended in so well with the weeds he could scarcely be seen.

"Sign here," the burly one instructed. "We gotta unload fast, 'cause I have two more deliveries today."

As she obediently signed for the delivery, Nell spared a stern glance for Jane, who merely smiled.

"You got help?" the driver asked. "I was supposed to bring two guys, but they got cancelled."

Mckenna drawled sarcastically. "If only it were so easy to cancel other men as well." She looked straight at Dan, who leaned on his Jeep with arms crossed over a chest impressively displayed by a worn T-shirt.

The driver gave Mckenna a wary look.

"I'm the help," Dan declared amiably.

The truck driver gave Dan an assessing look that burly men reserve for other burly men. "You'll do, I guess," he concluded.

Nell muttered an aside to Jane. "I'm going to get you for this."

As the driver opened the back of the truck and set up a ramp, Dan ambled courageously within Nell's striking distance. He didn't look at all afraid, probably because he knew by now that in spite of her threats and name-calling, she was basically a wimp.

"I don't suppose I could persuade you to leave," she said in a tone bordering upon hopeless.

"You wouldn't send away the only muscle you have, would you?" A positively infuriating smile slanted his mouth as he surveyed the mountain of boxes on the porch and the jumble of furniture and boxes in the truck. "Why didn't you hire a moving company?"

"I didn't think of it."

He shook his head sympathetically. "Sweetheart, you need to get used to having money."

Mckenna jumped in to snipe. "Spoken like a man who wishes he had some." Then she turned on Jane. "You told him Nell was moving today."

"Ladies!" Dan held up a hand like a referee telling two boxers to back off. "I'm a private eye. I can find out things for myself."

Mckenna merely sniffed.

Letting the hostility roll off him, Dan went to work with the driver to unload the truck. Weed trotted into the house with the women, greeting Piggy with a furiously wagging tail and an offer to play. Piggy turned up her nose, of course.

An hour later, Mckenna had the furniture arrangement sketched out, with Nell's blessing, and Jane and Nell had a good start on unloading the kitchen boxes. The living room furniture sat in the front yard and a bedroom set, computer desk, and bookcases crowded the driveway.

As they all stood on the porch and watched the truck drive away, Dan stretched out his back and wiped the sweat from his face with the bottom of his T-shirt, immodestly leaving an impressive set of abs exposed to Nell's view. In spite of her determined disdain, a herd of butterflies took off in her stomach and her pulse began to pound. Lake Powell nights—starry, warm, and passionate—rested too heavily in her memory for her body to have forgotten.

"Stop that!" she objected.

"Stop what?"

"Put your shirt down, you exhibitionist. You did that deliberately."

He looked at the wad of shirt still in his hand, then down at the expanse of bronze skin. With no sign of embarrassment, he let the shirt drop back into place. "I didn't," he said with a smile. "But if I'd known it would bring that rosy color to your cheeks, I would have."

"Jerk."

He ignored the cut. "Where do you want this chair?"

"Living room. Across from the pellet stove."

She made no offer to help when he hefted the old overstuffed chair and walked it through the front door, or rather, limped it through the front door. Nell staved off guilt. He didn't have to be here, after all. In fact, she didn't want him here.

"Stupid man's going to hurt his bad knee," she said under her breath. But Jane heard her. Jane had ears like a bat.

"He looks fit enough to me. And anyway, do you care?"

"Of course not."

Jane just smiled.

Jane helped Dan with the dining room table as Mckenna called Nell into the kitchen to solve the problem of where to stash the pots and pans. When Nell finally emerged from the kitchen, the living room sported a full set of furniture and both Jane and Dan panted like bulldogs.

"Gee, Jane," Nell said. "Thanks." She handed her friend a glass of cold water, then gave Dan a bland look. "This hanging around and trying to be a nice guy isn't going to do you any good." Though she did hand him the other glass of water.

He grinned and wiped his face. "Hope springs eternal."

"Only if you're a moron."

"Tch. You've grown into a harsh and bitter woman, Nell Jordan."

"Look to yourself, you lying sack of dog poop."

Of course he ignored her. "You'll be glad to know I've decided to forgive you for not telling me about Chicago."

She responded to that bit of news with a decidedly ungrateful snort. "Chicago is no one's business but my own. There's nothing for you to forgive."

"Could be. When you look at it that way, I guess my family connections and job aren't really anyone else's business, either. And by the way, I didn't lie about being a photographer. I am a photographer. I just don't use photography to pay the rent."

"You are so full of bullshit."

And so went the rest of the day.

Nell's new grandfather clock—she had always wanted one, and Mckenna had talked her into splurging—struck a sonorous five before Jane and Mckenna left. When they drove off, Nell stood in the living room and looked around at a fairly organized house. Of course, weeks would pass before she could find anything, and the kitchen still showed signs of disarray, but a bone-deep weariness discouraged any attempt to lift one more finger in labor, at least today.

"How about we order pizza?"

Nell turned to find Dan coming through the kitchen door, wiping his face on a paper towel.

"You're still here?"

"I expect at least a pizza for all the work I've done today."

"I didn't ask you to come."

"You're glad I came. Admit it."

"You are delusional." She had to turn her face away, though, to hide a reluctant smile. She had to give him credit for sheer, unadulterated nerve.

"So you're going to toss me out, eh?"

"You and your little dog, too. And speaking of Weed, where are the dogs?"

"Playing out back. Weed finally persuaded Piggy to play chase."

"If she's chasing him, he'd better pray she doesn't catch him. She can be a cranky girl."

"Like her mother?"

Nell gave him a disgusted look. "Aren't you in deep enough? Why don't you just get your dog and leave before you make an even bigger ass of yourself?"

He shrugged, then bellowed. "Weed!"

Ten seconds later, the little bundle of wiry hair, who had added a few small sticks and strawlike Bermuda grass to his coiffure, bounced into the room.

"See," his proud papa said, "he already knows how to come. What a dog!"

"Right. Then you won't have to come back to class, will you."

Dan smiled. "Don't count on it."

"I'm counting on your leaving any second now."

Finally he gave up, and the sound of the Jeep engine coughing to a start left Nell feeling unexpectedly lonely.

"Piggy!" she called. Nothing cured loneliness like a nice cuddle with a corgi.

No ticking of toenails on the floor answered her call.

"Piggy!"

The little fatso had to be tired if she had chased poor Weed around the backyard. She probably had taken refuge in the middle of the new queen-sized bed.

"Piggy!"

She wasn't in the bedroom, or lying on the cool tile in either of the bathrooms. Nell began to feel some concern.

"Piggy!"

She searched the dining room. None of the boxes still lying about hid a corgi. Next came the kitchen.

Nell found her there, of course. Piggy loved the kitchen. Nell laughed and realized she should have searched there first. Then the dog's appearance struck her. At the corgi's feet lay an empty sixteen-ounce tub of raisins—or at least the tub had once been full of raisins. A massacred jumbo package of beef jerky lay nearby. Apparently, soda crackers had served as dessert, because pieces of the saltine box littered the floor.

Piggy herself looked entirely satisfied. Her stomach dragged the floor, a contented corgi grin softened her foxy face, and as Nell stood there in horror, the dog loosed a nearly volcanic burp.

"Omigod! Piggy! What have you done? Shoot! Phone! Phone! I have to call the vet. Where's the goddamned phone?"

But of course the phone hadn't yet been installed, so she had to find her cell phone. She did, finally, and got the vet's recorded message. The office had closed at noon. The day was Saturday, of course. Emergencies never occurred on a weekday! Nell left a frantic message on the vet's pager and said she would meet her at the clinic as soon as she could get there. Then she grabbed a bemused Piggy and rushed to the big detached garage. Only Mel waited there. The minivan was in the shop. Nell stuffed Piggy into the backseat and started the engine.

But the engine didn't start. The click, click, click of the starter shouted dead battery.

"How could your battery be dead? I just drove you over here this morning!"

Mel didn't answer, and Nell didn't have time to argue. She was dialing Jane on her cell phone when she noticed that Dan's Jeep was just then rolling down the front driveway. Without a second's hesitation, she flew from Mel and frantically waved her arms.

"Stop! Stop!"

Weed barked, and Dan stuck his head out the window. He had been delayed putting up the canvas top, just in case the lowering clouds fulfilled their promise of rain.

"Stop, please!" she panted.

He grinned. "Changed your mind already?"

"It's Piggy. She got into some food that wasn't put away. Her stomach is dragging the ground. She could bloat," she sobbed, "and raisins can be poison to dogs. And Mel won't start. I've got to . . . got to . . ."

He wasted no time. "Where is she?" he asked, springing from the Jeep.

"In Mel's backseat."

IT WAS an absolutely lovely day until Dan the Dud intervened and dragged me to the vet just as I happily settled in to digest the best meal I'd had in months. Raisins and beef jerky topped off with saltines. Ummmm! Maybe not a gourmet's delight, but to my palate—heaven! I was doing very well enjoying the warm pleasure of an overstuffed stomach when Nell rushed in and panicked. I suppose she had my welfare at heart, but she just doesn't understand the seductive power of food. I would *have survived just fine if she had simply let me take a nice long nap on the bed. At least I think I would have survived.*

Not until we got to the clinic did I start to feel really bad, and being at the dreaded vet clinic caused that, I'm sure. I tell you, things go on in those places that would make you shudder to hear about. Veterinarians have no sympathy for dog sensibilities. Even the simple act of getting a temperature taken is pure humiliation.

Anyway, I won't horrify you with a detailed account of what happened there. Trust me that it wasn't fun. Supermodels would love to get their hands on whatever substance the vet gave me. With that stuff at hand, they could eat all they wanted and get rid of it in one great big ugly eruption. It takes all the joy from eating, let me tell you.

After my stomach shrank to the vet's idea of a proper size, she shut me into one of those cold stainless-steel cages with just a blanket for comfort. Some comfort! Did this doctor know, I wonder, just who I was? After all, I was not simply some ordinary flea-bag canine. I was rich. And I think I deserved better treatment. She wouldn't even give me a drink, much less a dog cookie to replace the rich meal she had just made me lose.

Things took a turn for the worse when Ms. Sadist, DVM, came back laden with tubes and needles. She made me look like a pincushion with tubes attached. Well, maybe I exaggerate. But I'll bet she had to cheat to pass her vet school class in setting IVs. She was not delicate about it.

So there I sat, one lousy blanket between me and cold stainless steel, and heaven knows what dripping into my veins through a very uncomfortable needle. Where, I ask, was the therapy dog to ease MY distress?

IN DR. Taylor's waiting room, Nell cried on Dan's willing shoulder, completely forgetting for the moment that he was a no-good jerk. She desperately needed someone's shoulder, and his was available—available, broad, and tempting.

"Poor Piggy," she sobbed. "I should have been more careful. I *know* how she is around food. I should have made sure all the food was out of reach before I did anything else."

He pressed her into his shoulder and rubbed her back. "You're way too hard on yourself, sweetheart. You couldn't be everywhere at once, and moving is chaos that requires your full attention. So don't beat yourself up."

"If she dies it'll be my fault. Poor little corgi. She's such a sweetie."

Dan chuckled. "Now you're just being ridiculous. That little girl has spunk, smarts, guts, and entirely too much personality. But she's not by any stretch of the imagination sweet."

"The patients at the hospital think she's sweet."

"They're sick. What do they know?"

Nell smiled faintly and wiped her eyes. "This might seem silly, I know. It's just that . . . you can get so bonded to a dog. I guess you find that hard to believe."

Weed looked up from where he lay curled at Dan's feet, and Dan scratched his ear. "I'm beginning to know what you mean."

Nell regarded the four-footed tumbleweed with soft eyes. "He is sort of cute. I have to admit it."

"Don't let him hear you call him 'cute.' We guys don't relate to 'cute.' We're handsome, or macho, studly, or just plain cool."

She managed a laugh. "I'm sorry, but Weed is none of those things. Cute is as far as I'll go."

Dan shook his head. "She's a stubborn one, Weed, but give her time. Eventually she'll see past the flaws on the outside to the quality inside."

Nell turned her head away, not wanting to go there. She knew very well he wasn't talking about the dog.

"Piggy has been quite a heroine in her life, you know."

"Piggy?" he scoffed. "A heroine?"

"More than once. She saved my friend Amy from a guy who did his best to kill her. And then later, when Amy left her with a friend for a while, Piggy saved a whole bunch of people from getting blown to pieces by a bomb. Then she ran down the bomber."

"Piggy?"

"She's an exceptional dog, I tell you."

He smiled. "And now she just uses all that talent to trip me off of docks and send me flying out your front door."

"She tried to save me from you," Nell said darkly. "Piggy knew you were playing games."

"No. Piggy was jealous. She wanted you all to herself."

"Nonsense."

The vet's entrance forestalled any argument. Dr. Taylor wiped her hands on a towel as she came into the waiting room. She sported a new set of scratches on her forearm and something disgusting spotted her formerly white lab coat. "Piggy's still got a lot of spunk," she told Nell with a smile. "Poor girl didn't like those raisins and saltines coming up as much as she did going down."

"Is she going to be okay?"

"I think so. I put in an IV drip—she didn't like that much, either. And I want to watch her tonight and Sunday. There will be a vet tech on duty, and I'll come in and check on her a couple of times myself. Raisins can actually be a serious problem for a dog, especially in that quantity. And also the salt in the saltines. We need to watch her blood chemistry for a while, so its best that she stay here. But I think she'll weather this with little more than a tummy ache."

Nell took her first easy breath since she had discovered Piggy's illicit banquet. "Thank you so much for coming down here after hours."

The vet smiled wearily. "We need to teach these dogs to do these things only between eight and five. Eight and noon on Saturdays. And by the way, congratulations on your good fortune. I understand the patient in there now has the financial resources to live like the princess she's always thought she was. The whole office talked about it for days after we heard." She grinned. "We thought of hitting Piggy up for a new wing, or at least a new X-ray machine."

"I'm sure the emergency fees for this little escapade will go a ways toward one of those goals," Nell said with a smile. "I'll call you tomorrow afternoon to see how she's doing."

Nell left the clinic in much higher spirits than she'd entered. In fact, her spirits climbed so high that she let Dan talk her into dinner.

"These last few hours have left you looking like a stranded fish gasping for breath," he said. "You need something to eat."

" 'A fish gasping for breath,' " she echoed wryly. "Thank you so much."

"I always did have a way with words."

"Like the phony words you wrote in that phony article about me?" She couldn't resist the snipe as she climbed into the Jeep's passenger seat. Weed insisted upon settling into her lap.

"Those weren't exactly my words," he confessed with a grimace. "My assistant put that together. He's a good writer, don't you think? He wants to be a famous mystery author."

Nell sighed. "Is there anything you ever told me that is true?"

His tone grew serious. "It was God's honest truth when I said that I love you."

Something in her actually wanted to believe him, but she pushed that something aside. "Weed ought to be strapped into the back," she said as Dan started the Jeep.

"Lighten up, sweetheart. We're only going around the corner to the Sonic."

"We're eating at the Sonic Drive-in?"

"You got it. Not all of us are guardian to the world's richest dog, you know."

Actually, Nell liked the Sonic. Ordering a hamburger and fries from the drive-in speaker made her almost believe she'd gone back in time to the fifties. She didn't know if life actually had been simpler back then, but from the perspective of her life in the twenty-first century, it was comforting to think so. How had her life gotten so complicated?

Also, she discovered that one couldn't really stay seriously angry at someone while sitting next to them in a car, munching a hamburger and thinking about ordering a cherry shake.

"So tell me about the P.I. business," she suggested.

"It's a living. Barely."

"Is it exciting—other than digging up dirt on perfectly innocent women and lying your way into their confidence, that is?"

A brow lifted. " 'Perfectly innocent'?"

She grimaced. "Mostly innocent."

The silence strung tight as he waited for more. Finally, Nell threw him a tidbit. Because Piggy had survived, she felt generous. "My biggest mistake in Chicago was naive stupidity—and bad taste in men. I tried to do what was right and got outflanked by a pro. A sleazy dirtball, but still a pro. I got so angry when I found out that Oliver was a— well, wasn't the man I thought he was. I told him that I was going to expose him, and stupidly thought he would sit around with his head in his hands, waiting for me to do it. Stupid, stupid, stupid."

"I believe you."

"You do?"

"I do. I confess to doing a bit more digging into your past associations. See? I'm being painfully truthful. I asked BJ to research some pertinent facts about your sleazy dirtball. Did you know your Mr. Jones got in trouble with the unions a year ago—about none other than the employee pension fund?"

Nell gasped. "No kidding?"

"No kidding. The case never got to court. The man has some sharp lawyers on his side. But you're not the only one who has pointed a finger his way. I would say that most everyone, if anyone besides you still thinks about it, would have to admit that you were the one falsely accused, not Jones. I doubt it would convince my mother that you're not the arch-slut. It would take nothing less than a miracle to do that. But I wouldn't worry about any court thinking that you have a lurid history."

The weight of more than three years' brooding lifted from Nell's shoulders. It felt so good she could hardly breathe. "I don't care what your mother thinks," she said. "Believe it or not, it wouldn't kill me even if she managed to break Frank's will." She closed her eyes and smiled. "But it feels good to be exonerated at least in some small way."

"If I had half a brain, I would have known you couldn't have done what he said. Every instinct told me that you were not that person."

"Oh, Dan! Thank you! Thank you, thank you, thank you." She threw her arms around him and kissed him, spilling her fries and earning herself a ketchup smear on her blouse.

"Whoa! Mm! Does this mean I'm forgiven?"

She took a napkin to a ketchup smear on his cheek. "Maybe."

"What? It seems to me this P.I. business of mine has done you more favors than harm."

"I don't know. Why didn't you tell me about this earlier?"

"Why didn't you trust me with an explanation earlier?"

She made a face. "Okay. I was a bit stubborn."

"And how was I supposed to know you didn't know about your friend Oliver's comeuppance?"

"Well . . ."

"I rest my case—I think. Now, could we get back to the kissing part?"

"I'll give it serious thought." But she knew her smile was

transparent. "Geez, Perry Mason! Have you ever thought of becoming a lawyer?"

"Oh hell yes. I set out to go to law school."

"Really?"

"Actually survived a year of it before marriage and a baby drove me to actually making money instead of spending it."

"I can see you as a lawyer."

He put up a hand to ward off the next remark. "Yeah, yeah. I know. Lowest form of life and all that. I heard all the lawyer jokes in law school. I imagine you'd be willing to put me into almost all of them."

"I've got nothing against lawyers," Nell said with a shrug. "Mckenna is a lawyer."

"And that's a recommendation?"

"Oh, now, Mckenna has her moments. She's not nearly as much of a bitch as she pretends."

"I'll take your word for it."

"She's just rude because she thinks you're a jerk."

"That's comforting."

Nell laughed. "So, you were a law student, then a cop, and now a P.I. Anything else?"

"Oh sure. I was a cook in a pizza place once. And for a while at the university I studied accounting. That didn't last long. Let's see, what else. Oh yes, I actually have sold photos to a couple of magazines. One is in *Arizona Highways*. So I guess that makes me a photographer. And summers when I was at UCLA I worked at a riding stable."

"Oh! You ride?"

He tipped an imaginary Stetson. "Yippee-ki-yi-yay."

"Is there anything you haven't been?"

"A journalist." He grinned.

She caught her breath, then smiled. The thought of his perfidy didn't bother her quite as much as before, probably because Piggy's near suicidal gluttony had made other traumas seem minor in comparison to losing such an important part of her life.

She contemplated the depths of her Diet Coke and sighed as her mind moved back to the evening's disaster. "Poor Piggy."

"I have a feeling she's going to be all right. That dog is tough as nails."

Nell made a face, then looked out the window at the bright expanse of stars. "Do you think after people die, they still care about what goes on down here?"

"Now there's a question that could lead into an hours-long discussion."

"I suppose so." She sighed and fixed her eyes on a particularly bright star. "Frank, if you're up there, and if you have any influence at all, put in a good word for Piggy, would you? Make sure she's all right. You liked her a lot, and so do a lot of other people. Even though sometimes she can be a little snot."

"If Granddad's up there, I'm sure he has tons of influence," Dan said with a sad smile. "He made sure he had influence wherever he went."

"Do you think prayers work?"

She felt his eyes upon her, resting on her face with a strange intensity.

"I hope they do."

After they'd had their fill of hamburgers and fries, Dan drove her back to the house. When he didn't turn at her old street, she started in surprise.

"Forget where you live?" Dan asked with a smile.

"It's been a hard day," she explained.

Dan followed her through the front door of her new home. Nell wearily dropped down upon the sofa and looked around. She liked this house, this spacious, clean place with no neighbors who collected junk cars, with bedrooms bigger than her old living room, with a backyard big enough to rate a safari. But this house didn't yet give her the secure, cozy feeling of Home. Home with a capital H, that no matter how shabby, enveloped her with welcome, with memories, with comfort for her bumps and bruises, both physical and emotional. Right now the only memories in this place weren't that great, and the jumble of boxes, packing paper, pictures waiting to be hung, and furniture that hadn't quite found its place kept comfort at bay.

The upshot of all this, Nell discovered, was that she really didn't want to be alone.

"You could stay for coffee," Nell suggested to Dan.

"You can find the coffeemaker?"

"The kitchen is fairly organized, believe it or not. Mckenna was in charge there, and she doesn't leave things half-done."

"Except for leaving food within corgi reach."

"Yes, well, she's a cat person. Just about everything is within a cat's reach, so Mckenna doesn't think about such things."

"I would like some coffee." He smiled that winning smile that crinkled his eyes and warmed his face. "I'll even make it."

Weed jumped onto the couch beside Nell when Dan went into the kitchen, pressing against her leg in a warm, tangled offer of comfort. The little stray could someday be a good therapy dog, she mused, if Dan really did have intentions in that direction.

Be careful, Nell told herself. She was seriously weakening toward the man, and did she really want to go there again? But he did, after all, deserve some credit. Helping Piggy hadn't really been in Dan's best interests. If Piggy died, her trust fund reverted back to the next-in-line named in Frank's will, and whoever that next-in-line was, Dan's mother no doubt would have been happier.

And less important than helping Piggy, but important nonetheless—Dan had set her free of the cloud that had hung over her head for three years. Instead of walking out as soon as he found out about her past, he'd taken the trouble to find the truth.

All in all, he had given her a fairer trial than she had given him.

But Mckenna's voice still spoke in her head, persuasive as only an attorney can be. No one except Jared Johansen knew who Frank had named as next in line. He might have left the trust fund to the Verde Valley Model Ts, or to the Save the Sparrow Foundation. As long as Dan had a chance to get to that money through Nell, he would be sweet as pie, Mckenna reminded her. Don't give the scuz too much credit.

Nell told Mckenna's voice to go away. Tired, displaced, and still worried about Piggy, she didn't want to deal with such complexities. Right now, Dan offered much needed comfort and companionship. For just a few hours, she could forget her ambivalence.

"Coffee's on," he said, coming out of the kitchen. "I see Weed has made himself comfortable."

"He knows a dog-friendly couch when he sees one."

Dan picked the dog up and put him on the floor. "There's only room for one of us on the sofa, buddy, so you lose."

Nell couldn't very well object to Dan sitting so close to her. Boxes occupied every other possible place to sit, and this little love seat didn't have room for him to keep his distance. How tempting it was to bask in the warmth of his presence. This day really had been a bad one. It had shredded her resolve to limp ribbons.

"I guess I have to thank you for being such a help tonight."

"Don't mention it. Do you think I'm a big enough jerk to let poor Piggy suffer?" He thought for a heartbeat. "Maybe you shouldn't answer that."

Nell sighed. "I don't know what to think anymore. Sometimes just not thinking is a great temptation."

He took advantage of her waffling. "I've missed you, Nell."

"I've missed you, too." The confession just sort of came out of her mouth.

"I don't suppose we could kiss and make up."

"Don't be ridiculous, Dan. What's happened between us—on both our parts, I guess—isn't something you just make up from."

"Nell, I never meant to be unfair to you. Not about the things that really matter."

His nearness pressed upon her resolve. She remembered so well the scent of him—soap and Mennen musk deodorant and just a hint of something very male. And the feel of his skin against hers. A woman didn't forget such things. And now he sat so close, his arm lying along the back of the couch behind her, his side against hers, hard and warm. She needed that kiss. She really, really needed that kiss.

"Coffee's done," he announced. "I'll get it. Do you take anything in yours?"

"I like mine black."

"A woman after my own heart."

He left to get the coffee, and the house felt suddenly cold, even though the temperature outside still held above seventy. Outside these unfamiliar windows, dark night loomed.

She needed more than one dog, Nell decided. One little Piggy-sized dog couldn't fill up the emptiness in this new house. She needed . . . she needed . . .

Don't even go there, a cautionary voice warned. *You do not, repeat, do not need Dan Travis. And since when has your life seemed empty?*

Since she found out Dan Travis wasn't quite the hero she thought he was.

On the other hand, maybe a man didn't have to be a

hero, didn't have to be perfect, for her to love him. Was she perfect?

"Coffee, black, just as ordered," he said, putting the cup on the table in front of the sofa.

"You'd make a good waiter. Prompt and obsequious."

"I've done that, too. Obsequious isn't my thing, though."

"I could have guessed that." She blew the steam off her coffee and took a sip. "Good. Hot." She set it back on the table beside his. Then abruptly she turned and kissed him on the cheek. "That wasn't a kiss-and-make-up. That was just thanks for the coffee."

You just couldn't stand not having your lips on him, you ninny.

"That wasn't really a kiss." He shook his head sadly. "You need a reminder, Nell, of what a kiss really is."

Before she knew it, he took her in his arms. Fingers threaded through her hair, capturing her for his descending mouth, but she made no resistance. Gently he played with her lips, until she took the initiative to deepen the kiss. Opening her mouth, she invited him in. Sweet, so sweet. Blessed possession. The beginning of passion threading through her veins.

Then they broke apart, panting. One kiss didn't nearly satisfy the need pounding inside her. Ten kisses, sweet as they were, couldn't satisfy that need.

"Nell, I love you."

She closed her eyes. When his warm hand pushed up her T-shirt, a sigh of utter bliss escaped her mouth. She knew exactly where they were headed, and she didn't have the will to resist. At this point, she didn't even want to resist.

"I shouldn't be doing this," she told him as his mouth found her breast. She leaned back to give him better access.

"Mm," was his only response.

"We could go into the bedroom," she suggested. "I do have a brand-new queen-sized bed."

"Now there's an idea," he whispered against her damp skin. His voice had that husky quality she loved, a slight hoarseness that came from the heat of desire.

Nell took his face in her hands and forced him to look into her eyes. "This doesn't mean we're back together, Dan. It's only sex."

"With you and me," he said softly, "it will never *only* be sex."

This time he told the truth and she lied, Nell reflected, but need for him drove out all desire to think further upon it, or to think at all. She made no objection when he easily picked her up and carried her to the bedroom.

chapter 19

NATALIE DIDN'T mind solitary evenings. A woman her age with grown children and no husband got used to being alone. She had friends, of course, but most of her friends were casual acquaintances—satisfied clients, or other members of the Chamber of Commerce. They had spouses to occupy their time, and children as well. Most of them even had the blessing of grandchildren.

Natalie, on the other hand, had only a childless daughter in California and a son who lived in a motor home—of all things!—and saw her only when she bludgeoned him with filial duty.

Not that she minded all that much. When one got used to solitude, it became a friend. What did she want with a husband or lover cluttering up her life? After years of struggling to raise two children on her own, always putting their good ahead of hers, she deserved the blessing of privacy and independence. Natalie loved her life. She wouldn't change it one bit.

As much as she enjoyed her solitude, however, she didn't let it turn her into a homebody. The pleasant pastimes of

Sedona ensured she didn't stay in her condo drinking tea and eating frozen dinners. This lovely evening, the last Saturday in May, she strolled about Old Sedona, looking into the familiar shops, making notes in her mind about artwork that might tickle the fancy of this client or that client, and allowing herself a small gloat that her establishment still put most others in the shadow when it came to class.

As the sun went behind Sedona's famous red buttes, Natalie found herself looking up the unique enclosed staircase that led up to Oaxaca, her favorite Mexican restaurant. Why not? she asked herself. She could almost hear their Red Rock Enchilada call to her.

The hostess greeted her with warm familiarity and led her to a window table where she had the best view of the spectacular cliffs that rose above the town. She ordered a margarita and munched on chips and salsa while waiting for her enchilada. Oaxaca made a wonderful margarita, but not as good as the one made by... but she didn't want to think about him. Why ruin a lovely evening?

The restaurant hopped with their usual Saturday evening business. In Sedona, of course, just about every evening filled the restaurants and motels. Natalie suspected that she had bumped someone's reservation to get this lovely window table, but told herself that regular patrons ought to have some privileges, after all.

Then she spied another regular patron sitting in the corner under the huge ficus plant. Jared. The margarita-maker that she didn't want to think about. And with him was a very attractive woman, a brunette beauty who looked at him with frank adoration in her eyes. The hair color, Natalie thought, had to be from a bottle, and the makeup was too artful and a bit heavy for Natalie's taste. But then, Natalie's opinion didn't matter all that much. She wasn't the one sitting with the woman, laughing, and apparently having the time of his life.

As if attracted by her stare, Jared took his eyes from his

companion to meet her gaze full on. Embarrassed, Natalie quickly looked away. She didn't look back, at least not so blatantly. But the couple was still visible out of the corner of her eye. Even when she concentrated on her enchilada or gazed out the window at the spectacular sunset, they distracted her. Their laughter carried to her table. How could it not? They certainly weren't subtle about enjoying each other's company. When she couldn't see their smiles, she imagined them. Their eyes glowed for each other. She just knew it.

The pain that settled in the region of her heart had to be heartburn, of course. Natalie had rejected him, after all. Why shouldn't Jared get on with his life? He had told her during their last encounter—the one she so didn't want to think about—that the next move belonged to her, if she wanted to make it. He had lobbed the ball into her court, and if she didn't return it, fine. Fine, fine, fine. And she certainly didn't intend to call him, or knock on his door, or any of the other things she tried hard not to think about. Jared Johansen spelled complication, and she certainly didn't need any more complications in her life.

So Jared should get on with his life, and she would get on with hers, and everything would be just hunky-dory.

But the Red Rock Enchilada tasted a bit off tonight, and Natalie didn't think the flavor came from the sour cream.

Natalie paid her bill and left without giving Jared and his bimbo a glance. She shouldn't think in those terms of Jared's friend, though. Probably she was a perfectly nice bimbo. Woman. A perfectly nice woman.

She didn't make it two shops up the street before Jared caught up to her. The woman clung to his arm with a proprietary grip.

"Nat!"

Lord, how she hated that nickname. Except that she hadn't hated it when they had been . . . but she wasn't going to think about that.

"Nat! Hello. I wanted to come over and say 'hi' in the restaurant, but you left before I got a chance."

Sure he had wanted to come over. Right. Natalie put a smile on her stiff face. "Hello, Jared. I saw you in Oaxaca, but you seemed to be enjoying yourself so much that I didn't want to disturb you."

Jared gave his companion a warm smile that made rocks grind in Natalie's stomach. "Nat, this is Cherry. Cherry, meet my friend Natalie Donner. Nat and I go way back."

"I'm so happy to meet you, Natalie. Jared has told me so much about you."

"Has he?" Natalie didn't know how much longer she could hold the smile. "Cherry. What a unique name."

"It's a family name, believe it or not."

"Cherry is my cousin from Duluth. She was in Phoenix on business and decided to drive up the hill to pay her hick cousin a visit."

The rocks in Natalie's stomach turned into butterflies. A cousin. How about that? "How nice. Now that you mention it, I do see a resemblance between you and Jared."

Cherry laughed. "We grew up together, and all the time people thought we were brother and sister. When I let my hair go natural, it's the exact shade of Jared's." She gave her cousin a playful nudge on the shoulder. "Except that his has much more gray."

"Well, I'm very happy to meet you."

Jared whisked his cousin away to a production of Shakespeare Sedona and gave Natalie a friendly wave good-bye. His manner reeked of impersonal friendship. The fire in his eyes no longer burned. Or had it simply been banked?

Why should she care? Natalie chided herself. And shame on her for getting so worked up over that woman, and feeling as if she had a new lease on happiness when Cherry turned out to be Jared's cousin. First cousin? she wondered suddenly, then mentally kicked herself. What did it matter? Natalie didn't want Jared. Did she?

• • •

MONDAY MORNING, Nell woke late to see the sun laying a pattern of warm light on her bedcovers. Her bedroom was a delightfully warm room—not the uncomfortable warmth that an Arizona spring and summer could bring, but a light, airy warmth that penetrated the spirit and made the world seem a better place. And the lump in the bed beside her definitely made the world feel like a better place.

Nell grinned and gave the lump a playful swat. "Wake up, slug. Don't you ever work?"

Dan's tousled head appeared from beneath the covers. "What?"

"Slug! Look at the time. Normal men have donned their suits and ties and started slaving at their desks an hour ago."

"Men who wear suits and ties are not normal," he countered. "And I put at least three hours of work in yesterday, returning client calls. And the day was Sunday, so it counts as twice the work."

She laughed and sprang out of bed.

"Hey," Dan objected. He rose on one elbow, causing the covers to fall back and reveal a nicely sculpted chest. "Come back here. Don't you know that guys like to . . . uh, cuddle first thing in the morning."

"Cuddle is not what guys like to do first thing in the morning," Nell shot back, pulling on shorts and a T-shirt. While she brushed her hair, she glanced toward the bed to enjoy the sight of broad shoulders, taut pecs, and appealingly mussed black hair. "Believe me, I'd like nothing better than to crawl under those warm covers and give a whole new meaning to the word 'cuddle' but it's Monday, and I need to pick Piggy up."

Dan collapsed back against the pillows. "Ah. Piggy."

The day before, Dr. Taylor had called Nell's cell phone and assured her that Piggy was recovering nicely. Long-term ill effects from the eating binge didn't seem likely, and Piggy could come home on Monday—today.

Dan had dropped by early in the evening to ask about Piggy's condition—or at least he had used that as an excuse. Talking about Piggy had led to talking about other things, which had led to calling out for pizza. Of course he had offered to stay and help wash both of the dishes they had dirtied—such a big job. And then he had offered to drive her to the vet clinic on Monday. And to save gas, he had simply stayed the night.

Dan was a great one for excuses, even the most transparent, to justify what he wanted to do. Nell had laughed at him. He had kissed her, and the next thing she knew, she was waking up to the morning sunshine and the tousled magnificence of Dan's naked body in her bed.

"Are you going to get up and drive me to the vet's?"

"Piggy can't wait another thirty minutes?"

Nell coaxed. "I can't wait another thirty minutes. I miss the little snot."

Reluctantly, Dan climbed out of bed and headed into the bathroom. Seconds later, Nell heard the shower go on, and in ten minutes, he emerged with combed damp hair and a good-humored smile. That smile so warmed Nell's heart that she considered the advantages of turning these "make-up" sessions into a more permanent arrangement. His mother would probably put out a contract on her life.

"Ready?" she asked.

"Is every bit of food behind corgi-proof doors?"

"It is."

"Then let's go."

When they walked into the vet-clinic waiting room, the place was in an uproar—not unusual for a Monday morning. Nell didn't worry until Kate, the receptionist, greeted her with a cry. "There you are! We've been trying to get hold of you all morning. Don't you ever leave your cell phone on?"

A bolt of fear struck Nell right in the stomach. Something

had happened to Piggy. She just knew it. "What? Why? What's wrong."

Kate bit her lip, a very bad sign. "Let me put you in a room so you can talk privately to Dr. Taylor."

Dr. Taylor came into the exam room looking very grim. Nell had dragged Dan into the room with her, and now she crushed his hand in an agony of suspense.

"I'll cut right to the chase," the vet said. "Piggy has gone missing, I'm afraid."

"What?" Nell cried. "What happened? Did she slip her leash? Did someone leave her kennel door open?"

Dr. Taylor grimaced and pinched the bridge of her nose. "Worse. Well, actually not worse, I suppose, because we know where she is, sort of. And I'd guess she's quite all right for now."

"What?"

Dan had gone narrow-eyed. "You want to explain more clearly, Doc?"

Dr. Taylor sighed. "We found this note in her cage this morning."

Nell swiftly read the scrawled script, hardly believing her eyes.

One million dollars, small unmarked bills, will get the dog back. Otherwise the pooch is coyote bait. Will call clinic to arrange an exchange. Be careful. No tricks.

She nearly choked. "I don't believe it! This is ridiculous."

Dan read over her shoulder. "Not so ridiculous when you consider the amount of money Piggy is worth."

"Our new vet tech is missing as well. He was on duty last night, and there's no doubt that this is his writing. I don't think he even cares if we know who he is. No doubt as soon as he gets the money, he'll head for the Mexican border."

"A million dollars," Nell groaned. "I would pay it, but I

can't lay hands on that amount of money, not in a lump sum, even after Frank's will goes through probate."

"I've called the police," Dr. Taylor told them, "and they should be here soon. If you like, Nell, you can wait in my office until they show up."

In the privacy of the vet's office, Nell let the tears flow. "I don't believe this," she choked out. "This is crazy! Absolutely crazy. I don't know what to do!"

Dan took her in his arms. "Take it easy. We'll get Piggy back. Talk to the police and see what they have to say. I'd say this dognapper isn't too smart. An amateur at best. The police can probably track him down in no time."

"Oh I hope so!"

"And if I know Piggy, she's probably making life a living hell for him."

Nell buried her face in his shirt. "Poor Piggy," she said through more tears.

The police came, they questioned, they raised eyebrows, and one nearly snickered. "Don't think I've ever seen a case like this before."

"Don't make light of it," Dan warned. "This dog is very valuable."

"Oh, we wouldn't make light of it. I checked on that name you gave me, Dr. Taylor, and your tech has a record. He did some time for armed robbery. And there's an outstanding warrant in New Mexico."

Dr. Taylor flushed. "Great. Now I need to do a background check before hiring staff. What's the use of living in a small town anymore?"

"Well, small towns get their share of bad apples as well as the big towns. Travis here can tell you all about that. He's dealt with a rotten one or two in the time he's been working here, haven't you, Dan?"

"Let's get back to the bad apple at hand," Dan advised. "He's going to hole up somewhere, and the longer it takes us to get after him, the harder he'll be to find. And we don't know how well he'll treat the dog."

Nell groaned.

"We'll send out bulletins to look for the guy's car or a—what did you say the dog was? A Labrador retriever?"

"A corgi!" Nell all but shouted.

"A fat, little, short-legged dog with no tail," Dan offered. "She looks like a fat sausage with a foxy face."

"Well, that shouldn't be hard to spot," the officer admitted. "If he still has her."

"What?" Nell asked frantically. "What do you mean, 'if he still has her'? He wants a million dollars for her!"

"Yeah, well, it would be real easy to kill a dog and dump the body in the broken-up hills and ravines around here. Killing a dog isn't exactly a federal crime, and if the guy's clever, he could still get his money."

Nell gasped. Dan put a hand on her back and gently rubbed.

"Gotta be realistic about this. We'll do the best we can, of course."

Left unsaid was a huge "but" that made Nell want to cry again.

"This is ridiculous," Dan growled as the police officers left. "What we need here is a competent private eye."

I DIDN'T deserve this, getting dragged off to the clinic to be abused and stuck in a cold, comfortless cage just because I indulged in a little snack. Then worse, a guy in a lab coat—you know, one of those cute little veterinary lab coats covered with puppies and kittens—got very disrespectful and cranky. Those lab smocks are a fashion nightmare, by the way. If I had a job that forced me to wear such a hideous thing, I'd be cranky, too, I suppose.

But this tech carried crankiness to criminal lengths. He woke me at a ridiculous hour of the morning, slapped a muzzle on my face, and stuffed me into a dirty dog crate in the back of his beat-up Ford Taurus station wagon. Can you believe it? Me! In a muzzle! The crate stank of stuff I don't even want to mention. And the car was none too clean, either. I was dealing with a real loser here.

Do you think Stanley came to my rescue? Or even made an appearance to comfort me in my distress? No! Of course not. He had only made one appearance since this whole Arizona adventure began, and then he mostly twiddled his otherworldly thumbs and smirked. I had a whole list of complaints to lay upon him next time he appeared.

Does it seem to you that I complain a lot? It's true, I'll admit. But I have so much to complain about! Dogs are supposed to be kept at home and coddled, shielded from the harsh world of work and worry. Especially me. Piggy the corgi heroine deserved a vacation. And what did I get? Shuffled from one person to another like some unfortunate foster child—first Amy, then Joey, then Nell, and now this dreadful dognapper. For all I knew, this might be a permanent change in my personal situation. Stan isn't above a trick like that.

So you see, I had a lot to complain about.

To make things worse, the villainous dognapper picked up yet another low-life criminal before we headed down the highway into the rising sun. They both guzzled beer at an alarming rate until the Taurus finally bumped to a stop at a ramshackle cabin. They let me out of the crate to do dog business, and I took a look around. The dognapper—Arnold was his name— had definitely headed for the high country, because the cabin sat smack in the middle of a pine forest. The pines and cooler air tipped me off that we had arrived somewhere in the vicinity of Flagstaff.

"She's cute!" the newcomer said. "And she's little. I can't believe you're such a wimp that you had to muzzle a fat roly-poly little dog like that."

"Watch your mouth, Jack. Take the muzzle off if you're so brave."

Jack did just that. I gave him a grateful kiss on the finger. That muzzle had really annoyed my whiskers, not to mention the indignity of the thing.

The little kiss really won old Jack over. "You thought this was a vicious dog?" he chortled at his friend's expense.

I sat at Jack's side and leaned on his leg, a sure heartwarmer. Not that I liked the guy, you understand. But a girl sometimes has to play up to slime to get what she wants.

So on Jack's say-so, I got the run of the house, but these guys weren't stupid enough to let me outside unsupervised. I paid them back by leaving a doggie gift on Arnold's bunk. I don't know why he made such a fuss. The covers were already filthy. Jack just laughed. The man had a laugh like the bray of a donkey. He's lucky I didn't leave him a pile as well.

They wisely stuck me back in the dirty crate when they settled down for naps. Poor fellows. Arnold had been up all night at the clinic, and Jack, I guess, was just naturally lazy. So they set out to snore the afternoon away while I languished in a disgusting prison.

Just as they both drifted off into pleasant slumber, I pulled out one of the most basic dog tricks—rattling my cage. The metal grate door made a most satisfactory racket when pawed at by little feet, and of course I added an accompaniment of barking.

"Shut up, mutt!" Arnold shouted.

That just made me work harder.

"She doesn't like to be locked up," Jack said.

"Tough," Arnold growled.

"Let her out. She's a puny little dog. What can she do?"

Obviously, Jack didn't have a lot of experience with corgis. He got up and let me out of the crate. I rewarded this positive behavior with a melting look of gratitude, and the dumb cluck totally fell for it.

"Go to sleep, pooch."

I obligingly curled up in a corner and closed my eyes, but only until the two villains started sawing logs in their respective bunks. Then I got up and went to work. Dognap me, would they? Shove me in a smelly old crate. Drag me off to heaven only knew where. And the worst thing: they hadn't even fed me!

I had no trouble getting out the door. This rustic little cabin had a latch, not a knob. If the door had been fitted with a regular doorknob and lock, the task would have taken me a bit longer, but with the latch, all I had to do was stand on my hind feet, tip the bar with my nose, and walk out of the stinking place.

My first thought, of course, was to escape. I certainly didn't want to hitch my wagon to Arnold and Jack, and besides, all that money awaited me back home. If I could find my way home. But where was home? Which direction was the freeway? How far? I needed a map. Except, of course, I didn't have hands to hold one. The lack of hands never ceases to annoy me.

Then I noticed Arnold's old station wagon parked beneath the trees. Being stranded at this stupid cabin might put a crimp in the villains' plans, I decided. Nell would certainly have the police out looking for me. After all, I am an heiress.

Stranding the jerks was easier said than done, unfortunately. But I got the job done. I always do, one way or another. Luckily for me, the Taurus window was open. I made the jump after only four tries. Looking at a corgi—any corgi—you wouldn't think we could jump. But our short little hamhocks are just like springs. There's not a corgi born who can't jump onto a bed or sofa by the time it's barely out of housetraining. A car window is a lot higher than a sofa, but I had determination on my side. Like I said, I made it on the fourth try.

Once in the driver's seat, releasing the brake and leaning on the gearshift until it dropped into drive—drive forward, that is—posed no problem. Since the car was pointed a bit downhill, it eased forward. Before it gathered any speed, I jumped out, and then I watched as the old Taurus bounced and swerved about a hundred feet to the edge of a ravine, rolled halfway down, and came to rest against a pine tree. I smiled a very corgish smile. That front grill would never be the same.

• • •

THIS MONDAY had lived up to every dreadful thing anyone had ever said about Mondays. The police had called midafternoon to report that Arnold Cruz had given his employer a false address. No big surprise there. They would continue to work on the case, the police promised. The sheriff's department and the state police had been alerted as well.

Dan had the cops beat by a mile, though. A half hour before Officer Davies called Nell to tell her of the false address, Dan had called with the real address.

"Arnie's house number and street were false," he told Nell. "But the phone number was real. I traced the billing address, and bingo. This guy isn't too smart, that's for sure."

"He wouldn't just take Piggy to his home," Nell said. "Would he?"

"I doubt he's that dumb. He'll have holed up someplace he thinks is safe. Want to go out to his house in Cornville and take a look around? We might turn up something that points the way."

"Is that legal?"

"Definitely not."

"You're going to do it whether or not I come along, aren't you?"

"You got that right."

"Then I'll come." In that moment Nell's heart warmed toward Dan. How could she have ever been so unforgiving as to believe he was really a villain? Right then she wanted to name him a hero.

They had to bump down a poorly maintained dirt road to get to Arnold's house, which was an older single-wide mobile home set on a half-acre of cactus and scrub grass. The trailer had once had a covered patio, but the roof apparently had fallen victim to one of the summer monsoon winds. It still lay against a barbed-wire fence, probably where it had blown, and the four by four timbers that had held it up stood at the corners of the patio like skeletal fingers sticking up from the ground.

"Lovely place," Nell said as they pulled up to the gate.

Rutted tracks led from the gate to the house. An old truck propped up on cinder blocks sat in front. Paint peeled off the exterior of the mobile, and one of the steps leading to the front door had partially caved in.

The little town of Cornville included some very upscale neighborhoods, but this wasn't one of them.

"Maybe you'd better stay with the car while I go knock on the door," Dan suggested.

"I'm coming with you," Nell insisted. Then less certainly. "You don't think he's here, do you?"

"It never hurts to be careful."

Nell went with Dan to the door. No one answered his knock. The door was locked, but that proved no impediment to Dan, who took only seconds to slide a credit card past the lock and get it open.

"I'll bet they didn't teach you that in cop school," Nell said.

"Hell, I learned that in junior high. In cop school they taught us just to break the door down."

This was a side to Dan that Nell had never seen. As he advanced warily through the trailer, eyes and ears missing nothing, firmly holding her in back of him, Nell reflected that they could be acting a scene on a television police drama.

"Nobody here, hiding, drunk, unconscious, or otherwise." He relaxed his grip on her. "You take the kitchen and look for addresses or names scrawled by the phone. I'll look for a desk or at least a drawer where he keeps personal items."

Dan took only minutes to find Arnold's address book. Nell was amazed that he had one.

"Even low-life scumbag dognappers have family and friends. They send Christmas cards, too, you know."

She gave him a look. "What are you going to do with an address book?"

"Hopefully, find out where Arnie goes when he wants to be alone."

They returned to Nell's place and, with BJ's help, spent the night phoning every single name in Arnold's little book. They didn't finish until close to midnight, when BJ wearily left and Nell and Dan fell into bed together, merely holding each other, and quickly fell asleep. Dan did the holding. Nell needed to be held. The house echoed with the absence of a fat little corgi, and Nell thanked heaven that she didn't have to sleep there alone.

The next morning they called a seven o'clock powwow that included Nell, Jane, Dan, BJ and Jared Johansen. Mckenna had wanted to be there, but she was tied up in court. They met at Randall's Restaurant in Cottonwood. Randall's served the best breakfasts in town, not to mention good, strong coffee. Right then, Nell and Dan needed caffeine just about as much as they needed air.

"Okay," Dan said over a plate of bacon and eggs, "these are the possibilities. Last night we talked to everyone from Arnold's girlfriend to his grandmother."

Nell still had a hard time believing that bad guys had grandmothers.

"One of Arnold's friends disappeared with him: a guy by the name of Jack Morrison, who lives with his mother. She says a friend picked him up either Sunday night or early Monday morning. When she woke up Monday he was gone. So my guess is, we're dealing with two of the slugs."

BJ grinned. "The plot thickens."

Nell glared at him. She didn't see anything amusing in the situation. With the miniscule amount of sleep she'd gotten the night before, she didn't see humor in just about anything.

"An ex-girlfriend gave us a couple of ideas about where they might be holed up. And a couple of his friends—he doesn't have that many, by the way; seems to be pretty much of a loner—anyway, a couple of his friends threw some other ideas into the pot." Dan smiled a rather unpleasant smile. "None of these people seem particularly loyal to poor Arnold. They all seem to be on the side of the dog."

"Kidnapping a dog is as bad as kidnapping a kid," Jane said in disgust.

"Yeah." Dan grinned wryly. "In kidnapping this particular dog, these lowlifes may have bitten off more than they can chew. If I know Piggy, she's not making life easy for them."

"Okay," Jared said. "What do you plan to do?"

"I'm going to make the rounds of the four most likely places where we might find these characters. BJ, I'd like you to check out a couple of others. I don't think they're there, but it never hurts to be sure. And I'd appreciate it if you deliver this list to the police and tell them what we've done. You might leave out the breaking-and-entering part."

"Sure thing," BJ said with a grin.

"Jane, do you know the local animal shelters pretty well?"

"Too well. I used to work for the county as an animal control officer."

"Great. Would you go around to the shelters and give them a description of Piggy? Just in case the little imp escapes and gets picked up. I don't think our Piggy would appreciate being thrown in the slammer with the 'common' dogs."

Jane chuckled. "Too right."

"Our Piggy," Dan had said. Nell's heart warmed a bit at the plural possessive. It implied they were family.

Dan continued. "Nell, you stay by the phone. And Jared, I just wanted you in on what's happening, since you're the one dealing with the probate. If this doesn't work, we're going to have to find some money somewhere, to draw these yokels out."

Jared took a sip of coffee and gave Dan a long, considering look over the rim of his cup. "Before you launch this dog hunt, Dan, I'd like a word with you in private."

Dan balked. "I need to get going, Jared."

"Perhaps you aren't the most appropriate person to be charging to the rescue," Jared chided.

Obviously he expected Dan to understand his meaning. Nell certainly didn't. She thought Dan was the ideal man to be charging to the rescue.

Dan scowled. "This is me, going." He got up and picked up his bill from the table, but Jared forestalled him with a hand on his arm.

With obvious reluctance, the lawyer asked, "What if things don't work out? What are people going to think when they learn that you're the one who gets the remainder of the trust if Piggy dies or in some other way leaves the picture?"

Nell gasped in surprise.

"This was supposed to be confidential information," Jared told them. "But the situation has gotten complex beyond Frank Cramer's expectations. Beyond anyone's expectations. Dan, if Piggy dies or disappears, everyone, including the court, will suspect foul play on your part if you're involved in any way. Let someone else go to the rescue."

"I don't give a goddamn about the money!" Dan growled. "I'm the best person to find her, and I'm going."

"Wait just one minute!" Nell's head reverberated with the impact of Jared's words. Dan would get all that money if Piggy died? How long had he known? Once again she felt betrayed. Just hours ago he had promised she could trust him, and now . . . She felt the blood rush to her face.

"You knew this?" she demanded.

"Well . . ." His expression painted his guilt.

"Fine! Just fine!" She grabbed the list of possible hideaways from his hand. "I'll do the rounds. I'll find my dog." She pushed her chair back so abruptly it almost toppled as she got up.

"Nell," Dan objected. "Don't—"

"You're fired!"

"You never hired me!"

Ignoring him, she walked out the door and toward Mel, who now had a brand-new battery. Jane went after her, but Dan pulled her back.

"Let me," he said.

She gave him a narrow look. "I generally believe in letting dogs settle tiffs on their own, as long as they're not going to kill each other."

"I'm not going to kill her, but I can't promise she won't put a few holes in me."

"You'd better get it right this time, Fido. Next time I'm coming out with a choke chain." Then she grinned. "Good luck."

Dan caught up to Nell at her house, where she hurried to throw together water, a map of northern Arizona, a flashlight, a canister of pepper spray, and a few snack bars into a backpack.

He cornered her in the kitchen filling a water bottle. "You can't do this, Nell."

"You lied! Again, you lied! I was such an idiot to believe all that talk about love and trust."

"Nell, I didn't lie. I didn't know this until a few days ago when my mother told me. She thought it might get me back on her side, but it didn't. It didn't. I don't care about the goddamned money."

"Oh sure! A trust fund that earns over a million in interest, and you don't care about it. I believe that! Were you charging to the rescue, Dan, or charging out there to help these guys get rid of a four-legged inconvenience?"

"That's a low blow. Get real."

She pushed the water bottle into her backpack and yanked the drawstrings so hard they nearly snapped. "Just why should I trust you? You've been underhanded from the first. I can't believe I let you back into my life . . ." She bit a lip, hard. "Back into my life after I found out what a low-life, lying sack of manure you are."

His pewter-gray eyes turned to steel as his expression hardened. "Are you going to dredge that up as ammunition everytime there's the least little doubt in your mind about something I do?"

"*Little* doubt?"

"How is your assumption that I would screw you and Piggy over for a ton of money any different than my mother assuming you took advantage of my grandfather for the same ton of money?"

"Because you should have told me—"

"And you should have told me about Oliver Jones and Chicago. But you didn't."

That brought her up short.

"Nell, even before I found out Jones got brought up on charges, I had decided you wouldn't do such a thing, even though it was in goddamned print in almost every Chicago newspaper that existed at the time. When you know someone, and especially when you love that someone, you trust on faith. You keep faith even when things seem to point to that trust being wrong."

She opened her mouth, then shut it as she grasped only too clearly the parallel to his own situation.

"Now!" He poked a finger in her direction. "I don't want the goddamn money. Okay? I'm going to get that moron dog of yours back, and when I do, you, me, and Miss Piggy are going to live happily ever after. Together. And Weed, too. And if you want to give Frank's money away, I don't care. If you want to use it to build a monument to dog therapy, I don't care. I just want you waking up beside me in the morning for the next seventy years or so. Understand?"

Her mouth still hung open, so he took advantage by drawing her in for a kiss. The kiss demanded love, possession, loyalty, and trust through conquering lips and a heart that beat a steady pulse against her body. It robbed her of resistance and at the same time gave her the gift of assurance, desire, and endless love.

They parted, breathless. The first to find voice, Nell hastened to say what she needed to say, what she longed to say. "I love you, Dan."

"I know."

"I've been as big an ass as you have."

"That makes us even."

A smile pulled at both of their mouths, and he gave her another quick kiss.

"I'm going. I'll come back with Piggy."

"I'm going with you."

"No, you're not. These characters might be nasty, and I don't want to have to worry about your safety."

"I can take care of myself, tough guy."

"I don't think so."

"It's my decision."

"I won't have you putting yourself in danger."

"I'm going! Piggy is my kid. If you won't take me, I'll follow."

He grinned and held up a short length of wire. "Coil wire from Mel's engine."

"You jackass!"

"Remember, you just said that you loved me. Stay here by the phone. I'll bring Piggy back. And then we'll do something about your having to regard a fat, snotty little dog as your only child." He smirked as he walked out the door. "Did I tell you I want more kids?"

She sputtered after him. "This is politically incorrect!

Men no longer gallop off to the rescue and leave the women behind. It's very nineteenth century!"

"That's the kind of guy I am." He waved cheerfully and climbed into the Jeep. "Call my cell if anything comes up that I should know about. I love you!"

Nell sighed as he spun his wheels leaving the driveway. "And I love you. Jackass."

chapter 20

BY TUESDAY morning, the cretin kidnappers weren't giving me much trouble. One had suffered a concussion the evening before, poor man. A little accident on some veggie oil I spilled when I got back from my station wagon caper. Yes, I raided their cupboards while they still snoozed in the bedroom—that's corgi standard operating procedure. And in my exploring the cupboards, I found a treasure. Someone had stored a full bottle of canola oil where I could get to it. Loosening the cap didn't pose a problem—teeth come in handy that way.

So when Arnold dragged his lazy butt out of bed to investigate the racket (the racket primarily resulted from my battle with a box of graham crackers, not the vegetable oil), the poor man slipped on the oil and hit his tiny-brained head on the corner of the kitchen table. His buddy Jack found him sprawled on the kitchen floor. Tch, tch. Ever since then Arnold had laid in bed, occasionally groaning and a bit confused. He got up only to stumble to the bathroom and toss his cookies. Heh, heh!

As for Jack, he busied himself trying to extract the station wagon from the ravine—a hopeless task, if you ask me. But I suppose the man had to have something to occupy his time.

The soft-headed idiot didn't have the heart to shut me back in the crate. He thought the oil spill was an accident, natural canine curiosity gone awry. And he didn't give me enough credit for brains to lay the fate of the Taurus at my feet. He thought Arnold had forgotten to set the parking brake, and poor Arnold wasn't in any shape to defend himself.

Poor fellows. I almost felt sorry for them. But not quite. I couldn't forget that they had dragged me out to that dump in the middle of the forest. What's more, they hadn't fed me. The graham crackers hadn't been their idea.

Why didn't I just leave? you ask. I could have, if I'd been a total fool. I've never been fond of the outback, you know. It's full of scolding squirrels and ill-tempered birds, dirt, sharp rocks, odd scents, and pine needles that pricked my little feet. There's a reason those things are called needles. Worse, who knew what lurked in that dark pine forest? Maybe some insane "save the wildlife" activist had released wolves up here. You never know. At the very least coyotes prowled about, looking for small morsels such as I to provide them with a snack. Not to mention skunks, snorting javalinas, slithery snakes, and even deer. That Bambi movie was a piece of deer propaganda, you know. Deer aren't nearly as cute and cuddly as they would have you think, especially to someone who looks and smells like a predator. Yes, I do look like a predator. The run of the mill human might get a chuckle out of a corgi's appearance, but to a deer, I spelled danger, and that's when sharp hooves and horns might come into the picture.

So anyway, I didn't fancy trekking through the forest on my own. And even if I had made it back to the freeway and some soft-hearted person picked me up, how was I supposed to give directions back to Nell's place? (My place actually. It was purchased with MY money.) So I stayed put and kept a watchful eye on what developed.

I didn't resign myself to being helpless, however. I am never helpless, even though Stanley stuck me in a dog suit with no hands and a brain that kept getting distracted by dog stuff, like *gorging on graham crackers and sniffing out squirrel trails. My kidnappers paid me no mind. One occupied himself groaning and barfing, and the other puzzled over the physics of moving the car. So I helped myself to the phone.*

Using the phone is tough for a dog, but no tougher than plinking keys on Nell's electric typewriter. With strong enough motivation, I can figure out how to do almost anything.

I pushed a chair to the kitchen counter and climbed aboard. Once on the counter, grabbing the wall phone by the refrigerator was child's play, though the thought of opening the fridge instead of working on the phone did distract me a bit—the dog brain interfering again. But I managed to stay on task. All I had to do was dial 9-1-1, and the location of this place would automatically come up on the operator's screen. Thank heaven for modern technology, I say. If the cops were on their toes, someone would trundle out here to investigate.

If you know what's good for you, never mess with a corgi.

WHEN HIS cell phone rang, Dan was driving away from the second place he had checked out. The first had involved a cranky bartender in Arnold's favorite watering hole. The man hadn't wanted to disclose who might be in his back room, and he got real offended by Dan even asking. Dan normally considered himself a nonviolent sort of guy, but a two-hundred-fifty pounder coming his way with fists swinging called for a little self-defense. His knuckles still smarted.

These things had been a lot easier when he was a cop. And thank heaven he was friends with most of the police officers and sheriff's deputies in the Verde Valley. They had jumped right on to the scene. Dan had to grade them an A for efficiency. He had been waved on his way and the bartender lectured about his temper. What's more, considering the Piggy situation, the cops had led the way into the back room in question, only to find it occupied by nothing more than mice, spiders, and one lonely scorpion.

The second stop—a camping trailer that an ex-roommate of Arnold's had parked in a campground in Oak Creek Canyon—had been less of a confrontation, but just as futile. The trailer inhabitant had some interesting opinions about Arnold's ancestry, intelligence, and choices of entertainment. Apparently, the two had not parted friends.

"Hell, man, he lifted two hundred bucks from my wallet when he took off six months ago. What's more, he was fuckin' my girlfriend. If you find him, tell him that after the cops are through with him, it's my turn."

He had invited Dan into the trailer to look around, just to prove what an upstanding fellow he was. The camper had no place to hide a man of Arnold's size, for sure, and since the little built-in couch sported no dog hair, Dan concluded that Piggy had never been there. That dog left hair wherever she went.

"I hope you find the motherfucker and screw him good," the ex-friend called after Dan as he left.

"I intend to." Though not literally, of course.

When his cell phone rang, he was heading back south toward Sedona on 89-A.

"Yeah?" he said into the phone.

"It's Nell."

"I love you, Nell."

"I love you, too. What's happening?"

"So far, nothing." The fight with the bartender didn't count. "But I'll find her."

"A detective from Flagstaff called. There was a very strange 9-1-1 call from a place that matches one of the possibilities on our list. The cabin south of Flagstaff out by Mormon Lake. There was no voice on the phone, just sort of a heavy breathing."

"Bingo!" He swerved over to the shoulder and stopped. "Is there even a remote possibility that Piggy is clever enough to use the phone?"

"I wouldn't put anything past Piggy."

"I was going to check that place last, because it's the far-thest. But I'll go there now. Is Flagstaff sending anyone?"

"Probably. The Flagstaff guys are talking to our guys. It's a different county, different jurisdiction, which complicates things. Our guys are trying to get Flagstaff not to rush in there and scare Arnold into grabbing Piggy and making a run for it."

"I'll get there before they do, with any luck, and believe me, Arnold isn't going to run so fast that I can't catch him. He's got my back up."

"You have the map?"

"I've got the map. I just hope that ex-girlfriend of Arnold's gave us the right directions."

"Dan, be careful."

"I'm always careful."

Dan did a one-eighty and headed north, punching in a new number on his phone as the Jeep climbed well above the speed limit.

"Detective Howard," said the voice in the phone.

"Hey, Howie. This is the guy who beat you for three straight weeks on the shooting range."

"Hey, Travis. How's it hanging?"

"Not too bad. But I need a favor." Dan knew the Flagstaff police as well as he did the Verde Valley guys.

Howie and two uniforms met Dan a mile east of 89-A at the beginnings of a rutted dirt road that disappeared into the trees.

"So this dog is worth a million dollars, eh?" Howie shook his head. The uniforms grinned at such a notion.

"The dog's worth a lot more than that to the lady who owns it," Dan replied.

"Well, if this guy Arnold is up there in the cabin, like you think he is, we have a stake in this. Did you know the guy's wanted in New Mexico for two counts of assault and rob-bery under an alias?"

"Nice fella. You guys can do whatever you want to do to

pry him out of that hole, but I want a chance to get the dog out first."

"I can't believe I'm delaying an operation because of a dog."

Dan grinned. "That's what friends are for, Howie."

"You've got thirty minutes."

"That's not long, considering I'm going to walk. A car coming up the road might scare them off."

"Okay. Let's all walk. We'll wait out of sight while you do your thing. But if this thing turns to crap, man, I'm gonna blame it on you."

Dan chuckled ruefully. "What else is new?"

Fifteen minutes later, all four of them peered through the trees at a sizeable but shabby log cabin. The phone and electricity lines running into the place spoiled whatever rustic appeal it might have had. They had passed other cabins on their way in—summer cabins not yet occupied for the season.

"You sure this is the place?" a uniform asked. "There's no car."

"Maybe someone went into town to get groceries," Howie suggested.

"Or maybe it's a false lead," Dan said with a sinking heart. "It can't be. The coincidence is too great. Give me fifteen minutes."

A clear area immediately surrounded the cabin, so Dan made a fast dash for a corner, out of view of any windows. No one seemed to be around.

Then he spied the car in the ravine several hundred feet away. Now that he had come closer, the faint sound of cursing reached his ears from the same direction, and low groans issued from inside the cabin. He almost laughed. He would bet his last dollar that a fat little corgi had something to do with the apparently less than happy state of her kidnappers.

Then the little miscreant herself wandered out onto the

front porch looking nearly as stuffed as she had when he and Nell had rushed her to the vet clinic. Her stomach didn't drag along the porch floor, but she definitely waddled. Piggy greeted him with an admonitory woof and a clear "It's about time you got here" expression.

This time he did laugh. "Piggy, old girl. Remind me to stay on your good side from now on."

SO THERE you have it: my great adventure. The long arm of the law carted off Arnold and Jack to face the wrath of justice, and I hoped that Arnold got thrown in a cell with a pack of cranky rottweilers. Jack wasn't too bad a guy, for all that he kept rotten company. Not real smart, but a bit of a softie.

Back to the point, though. The villains were marched off in handcuffs, and Dan claimed credit for the rescue. Never mind that I did all the work of subduing the bad guys. I didn't begrudge him credit, though. At least he had come after me, surprising after the things I'd put him through—taking an unwilling dive off a marina dock, stumbling out of Nell's front door and kissing the hard concrete, among others. When he tucked me under his arm and carried me out of those dreadful woods toward his Jeep, I felt positively warmhearted toward him, even though I suspected he carried me not to spare my tender feet, but to make sure I didn't get away before he presented me like a canine trophy to Nell.

My reunion with Nell brought tears to her eyes. I had to endure an eternity of hugs and kisses, but Dan's presence saved me from being absolutely overloaded, because Nell wanted to kiss him more than she wanted to kiss me. This didn't make me all that happy, you understand. But making some colorful canine objection to their romance would have been in poor taste after Dan had just pulled my little hamhocks out of the fire. Besides, all my efforts to keep those two apart seemed destined to fail. Even after the man had shot himself in the foot, metaphorically speaking, Nell had taken him back. She'd seen him at his sneaky, scheming worst, and still she loved him. I didn't under-stand it, but for once Stanley had thrown me a curveball I couldn't hit. I was just certain I needed to save Nell, and my money, from this bum, but at that point I simply threw up paws and said to hell with it.

So imagine my surprise when my corgi ears, perked toward a phone conversation between Nell and Mckenna, heard that Frank Cramer had named his grandson next in line after me. That piece of information blew me away. Even knowing that I stood between him and having a fortune for himself, our stalwart P.I. had charged into the forest to rescue me from the bad guys.

My little heart melted when I reflected upon it. Somewhere deep inside, I must have always known the studmuffin for hero material. I did him a favor by providing a chance to prove it to his lady love.

Under the circumstances, I decided that I could put up with Dan. And Weed, too. That scruffy excuse for a dog wouldn't give me any trouble. Never in either of my lives have I had trouble handling males. They're putty in my paws.

NELL KNOCKED on the closed door of the room in the Transcare unit, where the hospital had recently moved little Stevie.

Stevie's mom Karen answered. "Come in."

Nell peeked around the door to find Karen reading Dr. Seuss to her still-unconscious son. "Can Piggy say hi to Ste-vie?"

"Oh, Nell! Of course!" She laid the book aside. "I'm sure Stevie would like nothing better. I heard about Piggy. Is she okay?"

"She's fine. She even managed to cop a few snacks while the dognappers had her. Now she needs to take off another two or three pounds."

"Poor Piggy." But her eyes were on Stevie's face. "They're moving us to the care facility across the street tomorrow, because the hospital is short of beds. Can you imagine my poor little boy lying in that place?"

"It's a very nice facility," Nell said. "We visit there all the time."

"But it's mostly an old folks' care center. Stevie doesn't belong there. But we can't afford private care."

Piggy nudged the boy's bony little shoulder and looked intently at his face.

"Look at that sweet little dog," Karen said with a sigh. "It almost looks as though she's willing him back to us, doesn't it?"

The moment shattered when Natalie Donner walked in. Startled, Nell had to will herself not to retreat from Stevie's bedside.

"Good morning, Karen," Natalie said. Then with added icicles, "Miss Jordan."

"Hi, Natalie," Karen replied evenly. "Stevie has a furry little visitor."

"So I see. Are you sure it's good for Stevie to have that dog up on the bed? Think where those dog feet might have been, or what might be in the fur."

"Stevie loves Piggy," Karen told her.

Natalie dropped the subject, but Nell could feel her disapproval and dislike beating upon her. She was thinking of excuses to leave when Karen shrieked. "He moved a finger! Did you see that?"

Piggy's little pink tongue flicked out to kiss the boy's nose. Stevie's eyes blinked open. His hand moved very shakily to Piggy's ruff, and in a hoarse little voice, he whispered "Hi."

The corgi nuzzled his ear. He actually giggled.

Karen flew to the bed to hover over her son. "Stevie!"

"Mom?" he croaked.

"Oh, Stevie!"

Natalie had the presence of mind to ring for the nurse while Karen and Nell made a fuss over Stevie and Piggy.

"How do you feel?" Karen asked her son.

"Pretty bad," Stevie confessed. Then he looked straight at Piggy. "But the dog called me back. I had to wake up to see the dog."

NATALIE SAT in the crowded cafeteria, sipped strong coffee, and stared fixedly at the plain white surface of the table. She felt as though a giant hole had opened beneath her and sucked her down, down to a place where her firm notions of right, wrong, smart, and proper didn't apply.

She had invested a lot of emotion in the certainty that Nell Jordan was a mercenary fraud, but obviously she had been wrong. Not only had she been wrong, but she had been unnecessarily cruel. Never had she pictured herself as cruel. Practical, realistic, perhaps a bit sharp and cynical, but life did that to a woman alone.

But how did cynicism stand in the face of a miracle? How could Natalie continue to despise someone who had hugged Karen and cried with her for the recovery of that dear little boy? She knew honest emotion when she saw it. The Nell Jordan she encountered this morning had nothing counterfeit about her.

Natalie wasn't accustomed to being wrong, and she didn't like the feeling. What else had she been wrong about? She had never really believed in miracles. Her credo urged her to good sense and realism. She didn't invest heroic efforts in things she knew were impossible. In fact, with great sympathy, she had urged her friend Karen to accept the horror of Stevie's fate and not pin her hopes on something that probably wouldn't happen.

But look what had happened. Karen had refused to give up on her son. She had ignored the odds and kept trying. Now Stevie was giving a dog hugs and wanting to know when he could have his favorite food—barbeque-flavored potato chips. The doctor himself had gone to hunt some up for him.

Natalie had to wonder. The universe had provided a miracle for Karen and Stevie. Because they had tried. Karen had tried. The dog had tried. And yes, even Nell Jordan had tried.

Natalie had given up trying years ago, she admitted. She had given up on her life, accepted what she had and refused to try for better. Might the universe give her a miracle if she let down her defenses and actually fought for what she wanted? The miracle of bringing her heart, long dead, back to life.

Stevie's drama had brought home to her just how unpredictable life was. Nothing lasted forever. Nothing was secure, no matter how hard a person battled to make it secure. Disaster reached into a life when least expected. And so did miracles. But miracles didn't come to those who stood fast on the status quo, Natalie suspected.

The urge to step out of line and take a chance grew stronger—frighteningly strong. A thrill of fear coursed through Natalie at the very thought of stepping out from behind her protective barriers, of leaving herself open to the kind of hurt she had sworn to leave behind so many years ago. But life was short and capricious. Stevie's near brush had taught her that. And miracles could happen, if a person tried hard enough. Stevie had taught her that also. She had just been slow in picking up the message.

"Look!" a little girl at the next table told her mom. "There's a dog in the hospital!"

Natalie looked up in time to see Nell and Piggy walk past the cafeteria door. Natalie steeled herself. Apologies had always curdled her stomach, and this one in particular would leave a sour taste in her mouth. But she had to do what she had to do. She hastily discarded her trash, put her dirty plate in the tray provided, and dashed out into the hall. "Miss Jordan!"

Nell turned. A rosy flush of exhilaration still colored her face, but her eyes filled with dread. Natalie suffered a pang of regret.

"Miss Jordan. Might I have just a moment?" Across the hallway from the cafeteria, a glass sliding door led into one of the hospital's outdoor "meditation gardens," where patients sometimes sat to get a dose of fresh air. Natalie gestured toward the door. Looking as if she marched to a firing squad, Nell followed her to a bench under a riotously blooming plum tree. Natalie motioned Nell to sit beside her, and as Nell cautiously settled herself, the dog gave Natalie a look that made her suspect that the fur-bearing part of this team would be the most difficult to deal with. No matter, Natalie told herself. She had wronged even the dog, and if clearing the slate required a bit of groveling to a canine, she supposed she could do it.

"Miss Jordan, I'm unsure how to begin, because I don't often find myself apologizing. But it appears I've done you—" She cleared her throat awkwardly. "You, and the ... uh ... dog, a grievous wrong. I jumped to the conclusion that you were the worst sort of opportunist. I set my son to pry into your life, and even when he presented evidence that you are not the villainess I thought you to be, I refused to believe him. I was terribly wrong, and I apologize."

Nell's jaw dropped. "My goodness!"

"After the time I've given you about my father's will, a mere apology is inadequate, I know. But it's the best I can do. You must think me a terribly selfish and vindictive woman."

"Well ..." Nell blushed. "Actually, I did think that, yes."

Piggy woofed in agreement.

"But since you have the courage to admit you were wrong, I guess I'll have to revise my opinion."

Natalie breathed easier. Her stomach hadn't curdled nearly as much as expected. "I thank you for that. I heard one of the nurses say that you are trying to extend animal services to other facilities, and sometimes meeting resistance. After what I just saw you do with little Stevie, I would like to offer help in your quest. Being on the board of the medical center in Sedona, I have influence elsewhere as well. Maybe in that way I could make up, in some small measure, for the injustice I did you."

A light came into Nell's eyes. "That sort of help would be very welcome."

"And of course any plans I might have had to protest my father's will are now cancelled. Hopefully that will smooth the road out of probate and give you and...uh...what's the little dog's name?"

"Piggy."

"Piggy. How appropriate. Well, I suspect that you two really do plan to put your earnings from the trust fund to good use, as long as it lasts. If I can be of help facilitating that, you will let me know, won't you?"

"You can count on it."

The dog gave her hand a nudge where it rested on the bench. Gingerly, Natalie stroked her head. "Does this mean the dog forgives me, too?"

Nell laughed. "With Piggy, you never can tell. But I think so."

As Natalie rose to leave, Dan waved at them through the glass door. "There you are!" He smiled cautiously as he stepped into the garden. "Hello, Mother."

"Hello, son."

"Nell's late for our lunch date, so I tracked her down here."

Nell chuckled. "Don't look as if you need to don a flak jacket, Dan. Your mother and I have made up. We were having a very civil conversation."

"No kidding?" He visibly relaxed. "Did Nell tell you that you're going to be a mother-in-law?"

Natalie's eyes narrowed slightly. This was a bit much, truthfully, but she supposed she could handle it.

"Congratulations, you two," she said as gamely as she could. She would absolutely *not* be suspicious of Nell's motives in snagging the man who would get Piggy's trust find once Piggy passed on. She would not. Absolutely. She was turning over a new leaf.

Piggy woofed, obviously miffed at not being the center of attention.

"Hey, Pig." Dan rumpled the corgi's ears. "Every nurse on the floor is buzzing about your latest victory. Good work, Fatso."

"If you don't stop calling her that, she's going to disown you," Nell warned. "Then you won't be able to go to law school."

"Nah. Her mom will talk her out of it, because she loves me so much."

Natalie interrupted. "Dan? You're going back to law school?"

"I'm going to apply at U of A." He grinned. "I'm afraid if I just lie around enjoying being rich, Nell will put me to work cleaning house, or cleaning up the yard, or, heaven forbid, becoming secretary in charge of everything for her dog therapy group."

"I . . . that's wonderful. I always thought you had more potential in the courts than on the streets. It seems I have something else to thank Nell for."

"How about you ladies come out to lunch over at Randall's? They have fish and chips on special."

In spite of the fact that she had just eaten, Natalie found herself wanting to join them. She liked the way her son glowed when he looked at Nell, and she actually had an urge to know the woman better. But first, she had an important call to make.

"I'll catch up to you two," she said. "Save me a place."

They left already looking like a family, arms about each other, Piggy trotting stolidly at Nell's side. Natalie felt her heart thaw a bit as she watched them go.

When they disappeared down the hall, Natalie took a deep breath, called up all her courage, and pulled out her cell phone. Then she punched in Jared Johansen's phone number—to take a chance, and trust in small miracles.

Just call, he had said. *I'll be here. Just call.*

author's note

Many of the animal therapy scenes included in this story are fictionalized anecdotes based upon my own experiences and the experiences of other therapy handlers to whom I have spoken. If you are interested in the benefits that gentle, loving animals can bring to people in need of healing, or if you are interested in registering your own pet as a therapy animal, go to the Delta Society website at *www.deltasociety.org*.

about the author

EMILY CARMICHAEL, the award-winning author of more than twenty novels and novellas, has won praise for both her historical and contemporary romances. She currently lives in her native state of Arizona with her husband and a houseful of dogs.

Read on for a preview of
the next outrageous romance by

EMILY CARMICHAEL

The Cat's Meow

on sale fall 2004

The Cat's Meow

on sale fall 2004

MCKENNA WRIGHT looked up from her work to find the devil regarding her from her office doorway. The devil wore cowboy boots and a know-it-all grin, and had sandy-colored hair that curled around his battered Stetson.

"What the hell are you doing here?" Mckenna grumbled.

The grin widened. "Fine welcome."

Mckenna met him eye to eye. Her staff knew better than to disturb her when she was poring over a case, barricaded in the citadel of her office and enthroned at her desk. But her staff had left two hours ago.

"I knew I would find you here on a Friday night," the devil said. "Everyone else is out partying, or spending time with the family, or vegging in front of the tube. But not Mckenna. She's hard at work for the firm, brow furrowed, mind focused, giving it all for good old Bradner, Kelly, and Bolin."

Mckenna leaned back in her chair with a sigh. *The State v. Todd Harmon* was going nowhere as long as Tom Markham, temptation personified, stood in her doorway. He couldn't come within sight of her without irritating, distracting, provoking, and otherwise tempting her to think about him rather than the work at hand.

"Okay, cowboy, so you found me hard at work when I should be out partying. I'm sure any hole in the party world is diligently being filled by your colleagues at the District Attorney's office. After all, being on the government payroll means you aren't caught dead working after hours, right? We wouldn't want the taxpayers to get more than their money's worth, would we?"

He shook his head—a handsome head in spite of the too-long hair and cowboy hat. "You need to go out and have some fun once in a while, Mac. Then maybe you wouldn't be such a grouch."

"Spare me the lecture. Are you here for a reason, cowboy, or is your idea of a Friday night party coming over here to needle me?"

His long, lean frame lounged against the door. A relaxed smile showed total unconcern with her annoyance. Tom Markham had always shown total unconcern for Mckenna's annoyance, even during the year he had worked for Bradner, Kelly, and Bolin. The fact that *her* name plate boasted the title "Vice President" and *he* barely even rated a name plate hadn't intimidated him in the least.

But then, a man who had ridden bulls for a living before taking on law school might not regard a mere law firm vice president as intimidating, even one who cultivated a sharp tongue and an edgy temper.

"I *am* here to needle you," Tom admitted with an insouciant grin.

"Like I didn't know that?"

"And—believe it or not—I'm also here in an official capacity."

"Really," she drawled skeptically.

"Semi-official. It is Friday night, after all. Want to go somewhere for a drink?"

She had to laugh. "You're asking me out?"

"Oh no. Would I be so bold, after the last time?"

He would, Mckenna thought. Tom Markham's boldness knew no limits. If his boldness had been aimed at his work with BKB, he would have soared to the top, as Mckenna had done. But Tom Markham was bolder with bulls and women than with the law. Thus his current fate at the D.A.'s office, stuck as a middle-class public servant, taking his revenge by being a thorn in Mckenna's side.

"Nope," he assured her in his cowboy drawl. "You don't have to worry about me takin' liberties, ma'am. You made yourself pretty clear on that score a long time ago, and I'm not a man to beat a dead horse. Actually, I want to talk to you about work. Nose to the grindstone sort of woman that you are, you should appreciate that."

"Work," she echoed. "What work?"

"The Harmon case."

The Harmon case was the last thing Mckenna wanted to discuss with anyone from the D.A.'s office right then, especially sharp-eyed, sharp-eared Tom.

"I just thought, this being the beginning of the weekend and all, that music and maybe a little liquor could make the discussion a little more amiable."

Stuffing the file on her desk into a briefcase, Mckenna grimaced. "You're not going to give up and go away, are you?"

"Not a chance."

"All right, cowboy. I'll give you an hour. After that I have to put that nose back to the grindstone. I have a ton of work waiting for me."

She insisted upon taking separate cars. No way would she cede a driver's seat to Tom. He led the way to the Rainbow's End, a steakhouse and bar in an historic stagecoach stop on the western edge of Sedona. Almost everything in Sedona, Arizona, qualified as picturesque—from southwestern cowboy quaint to New Age kooky. But the Rainbow's End boasted the best margaritas in town to go with the atmosphere.

The place also grilled the best steak in town, a reputation Tom tested by ordering a huge New York Strip, juicy rare, with a baked potato soaked in butter.

"I thought we were here for a quiet drink and legal talk."

"A man's gotta eat," he said, stabbing a near raw hunk of steak and blissfully forking it into his mouth.

Dinner, caveman style. Mckenna contemplated throwing up. Her idea of a tasty meal was perhaps salad greens and a few slices of tomato. The closest she generally came to meat was opening a can of food for Nefertiti, her cat.

"You should weigh five hundred pounds, eating like that."

Tom swallowed a bite and answered cheerfully. "Just doing my part as top of the food chain. Nothing wrong with real food, Mac. You should try it some time. You're thin as a rail."

Regarding him sourly over the salted rim of her margarita, Mckenna said, "I like being thin as a rail. It's healthy." Not to mention elegant, fashionable, and sexy— three qualities which boosted any woman's career. It wasn't fair that dumpy and plain were usually fatal to a female seeking professional advancement, but that was the way the world worked. "That's just disgusting." Mckenna grimaced at Tom's steak. "Now that you're not battling bulls in the rodeo arena, you've decided to eat them?"

"Nothing better in this world than a good steak. And a good buttered potato. Mmmm."

Mckenna took a cleansing sip of margarita just to drive the notion of all that fat from her palate. "Can we get down to business, Tom? You did drag me here to do something more interesting than watch you drool over a dead cow, right?"

He grinned engagingly, showing white, straight teeth. "I could think of a number of more interesting things to do."

Mckenna skewered him with a glare.

"How's that boyfriend of yours?"

That caught her by surprise. "Adam?"

"Yeah, Adam. I heard he was quite the hotshot attorney

in Denver. The word is out that you two are planning to tie the knot."

"He is a hotshot attorney, and the rest is rumor."

"Ah. Rumor. You can tell me. Is BKB going to lose its best attorney to matrimony?"

She gave him a superior smile. "Don't get your hopes up, cowboy. My career is never going to take second place to matrimony. I'll be here to whip your ass in court for the foreseeable future."

He chuckled in acknowledgment that he'd been bested. Her answer to his question hadn't told him what he wanted to know, which was none of his business and he knew it. She didn't want to talk to Tom Markham about Adam.

"And just what about the Harmon case did you bring me here to discuss?"

"Ah, Mac, you never relax a minute, do you?"

Of all her friends and acquaintances, Tom was the only one with the nerve to call her Mac.

Annoyed, she scowled. "Not that it's any of your concern, but yes, I do take time to relax. In certain circles, in fact, I'm considered a fun person."

"Yeah, I know. When you take that uppity cat of yours to visit the hospital, the patients think you're a barrel of fun. Of course, considering other stuff on a hospital agenda, their standards may be pretty low."

Mckenna set her glass on the table and whipped the napkin from her lap. Now he had the nerve to insult her cat. "I'm outta here." Even a good margarita wasn't worth this.

"Whoa!" he commanded as she stood. "Wait!"

"Why? So I can waste time with this nonsense?"

"I do want to talk about Todd Harmon."

"Then get to it, cowboy." Huffily, she sat. "What do we need to discuss about Todd Harmon, other than the fact that the D.A.'s office and the bumbling Keystone Cops in the sheriff's office are targeting an innocent man simply because he's a high profile celebrity?"

"Mac, if we wanted to target high profile celebrities around here, we could drag half of Sedona to the station to get fingerprinted. This is a town full of celebrities."

"Sure. Artists, writers, a movie icon or two. But Todd Harmon is a rock star. He's the lead singer of a group that dresses nasty, acts nasty, and sings about dickhead cops, slutty women, and the joys of violence. So you just assume he's heavy into drugs."

"I know he's heavy into drugs. Not only doing drugs, but pushing them. Right here in the fair little town of Sedona."

"Bullshit," she said airily.

"I have witnesses."

"All of whom were snockered to the gills at the time of the alleged drug transaction. I'll rip them to pieces on the witness stand."

He waved a forkful of steak at her. "The stupid shit tried to sell coke to a police officer, for chrissakes!"

She answered with a superior smile. "Entrapment. I'll get it thrown out. The jury will never hear it. Besides, Todd thought it was a joke his buddies were playing on him."

Tom gave her a stern look. "Cut the defense attorney song and dance, Mac. You're not impressing a jury here. This is me. Your client is guilty as sin of both possession and selling, but to save the taxpayers money, we're willing to do a deal, because for all his money and worshipping fans, Todd Harmon is a small fish in a big, scummy pond. If he tells us who the big fish are and turns state's evidence when the time comes, we'll let him plead guilty to the lesser charge of possession. He'll get an abbreviated sentence, along with rehab, and before too long, he's back to wowing 'em on stage singing about killing cops and laying whores."

Mckenna shook her head, but she did throw him a bone. "I'll talk to him, but he won't go for it. He knows you've got holes in your case, and he also knows he has the best defense attorney in the state on his side. I can kill you in court, cowboy."

"The truth has nothing to do with it, eh?"

"You know better than that. Right and wrong, true and false, don't exist in a court of criminal law, only proving something beyond a reasonable doubt, and a jury can see reasonable doubt in something as small as a defendant's charming smile or the prosecutor's ugly tie. Hell, don't tell me you still believe in the law as a tool for righting the wrongs of society."

His smile twisted wryly. "Cynicism. It sounds so wrong coming from that angel's face of yours. Don't you ever get tired of not believing in anything, Mac?"

She prayed for patience. Angel's face, indeed! The way Tom Markham often looked at her—as if she were some kind of ripe fruit waiting to be picked—never failed to muddle her brain, though she wouldn't in a million years let him know that. So she shot him a look that no one, not even Tom Markham, could call angelic.

"I'm not in the business of tilting at windmills, cowboy. And realism isn't cynicism. I owe Todd Harmon the very best defense I can give him, because that's what the law says he deserves, whether he's a bum off the streets or a rock star. Everybody has the right to the best possible defense against eager-beaver prosecutors like you. So quit angling for me to hand you my client on a skewer."

He gave her a long, hard state that she met head on without a flinch. Tom Markham was an idealist, and he was not going to make her feel guilty about this, because everything she had said was right. Idealists screwed up the world, not realists.

"Okay," he finally said, giving up on the stare. "Talk to Harmon, and think about it, Mac. Think about the greater good for a change."

She rolled her eyes as he pushed back his chair, slapped his Stetson onto his head, and stood up. "I'll get the bill."

"Never mind," she told him. "I wouldn't want the taxpayers to get stuck for that steak. My expense account is fatter than yours, I'm sure."

"The taxpayers won't be buying my steak." He grinned

wickedly. "But I'll let you buy it with that fat expense account, if you insist. I'm outta here for the weekend. You'll be nose to the grindstone for BKB, right? But I'm spending the weekend on a pair of water skis at Canyon Lake. Call me Monday. We'll talk."

Mckenna stared into her glass while Tom disappeared out the door—just to show herself that she really had no desire to watch his butt as he walked away in those snug jeans. Then she smiled to herself. Like hell she didn't want to watch his butt. It was a supremely superior butt, as men's butts went, and she didn't have to buy the product just because she admired the packaging.

Water skiing, eh? Skiing double, no doubt. She wondered who would be sharing the lake with him. Some "fun" honey with more boobs than brains, probably. Not that she cared. In fact, she totally didn't care. Tom had made his play for her when he worked for BKB, and she'd given him the cold shoulder for a host of reasons. She had been his boss, for heaven's sake. Like that would have worked out? She didn't think so. Besides, an ex rodeo cowboy wasn't even close to her type. That down-home drawl and stupid Stetson reeked of cowboy bars and country music. Mckenna preferred four-star restaurants and Mozart when she had time to indulge in such frivolities, which wasn't often.

She needed another margarita, Mckenna decided, and motioned to the waiter. From across the room he pointed to her glass with a questioning lift of a brow, and she nodded. They knew her entirely too well here.

The office with its pile of work on her desk beckoned her to return, but she really did need this second drink. Tom Markham. What a pain. He had left BKB on the pretext of wanting to practice the kind of law that helped the community rather than pandered to wealthy clients. Mckenna snorted at the very thought. The man needed to grow up.

But he was no slouch when it came to the law. You didn't get away with much when Tom prosecuted a case. He was going to rake her over the coals Monday when she told him about the witness he didn't know about in the Harmon case. She had to tell him about it. No way around it. That was what she had told Todd Harmon that afternoon when she had tried to get him to do the very thing Tom wanted him to do—take a plea bargain.

But damn, it was tempting to keep the whole thing under wraps.

"Mckenna!"

The hearty greeting came from a tall, almost skeletal fellow in an expensive gray suit and equally expensive blond toupee.

"Toby!" She put on her professional smile. "Having dinner here?"

"Just finished. Was that our noble prosecuting attorney who just walked out?"

"Tom Markham. He's a good man."

Toby's smile was cool to that notion—understandable, since he was Todd Harmon's agent, and Harmon was the man's bread and butter. "Frankly, I'd just as soon he were an incompetent bum. But we have the best attorney in the state on our side, right? Todd's not worried."

Todd should be worried, but Mckenna wasn't going to discuss the case with Toby Ryan just because he was her client's nosy agent. Ryan and his superstar client had a peculiar relationship, with Ryan pulling the strings that made the rock star talk and move, or so it seemed to Mckenna. And while Mckenna frequently found Todd Harmon less than charming, Toby reminded her of a snake.

Her half-finished margarita had lost its taste. She looped her handbag strap over her shoulder and pushed back her chair. "Got to run, Toby. Work is waiting at the office. Try one of their margaritas. They're good."

"I'll do that. Don't work too hard."

The tone sounded friendly, but the smile chilled. Mckenna felt his eyes on her back as she walked out the door.

In spite of her declared intention to go back to work,

Mckenna gunned her BMW sports model right past the adobe office complex that housed, among other upscale offices, Bradner, Kelly, and Bolin. She had the mother of all headaches, and the very expensive little house she had just bought in Oak Creek Canyon beckoned with its comforts of Tylenol, a warm furry cat, and a soft bed. Damn Todd Harmon anyway. She could almost feel her blood pressure rise at the thought of this afternoon's conversation.

"Todd," she had said in a matter of fact, professional voice. "Maria Oranto's testimony is going to kill you. We need to do a deal."

"Maria won't testify," he'd assured her.

"Maria *will* testify. I've already interviewed her. She doesn't want to testify, but she won't have a choice."

He had laughed in the bad-boy tone he used on stage between screaming out the words to some song—to use the term loosely—that only his whacked out fans could understand. But then, perhaps Mckenna was the wrong generation to appreciate his style of "music."

"Maria," he had continued with a smirk, "is gone."

Mckenna had instantly leapt to the worst possible conclusion. "What do you mean, gone?"

"Just gone. Back to Mexico. She was a wetback, babe! I did my part for the immigrant problem, set her up with some money for her family, and sent her on her way. No way that stupid fuckin' D.A.'s gonna find her."

Todd had such a way with words.

Mckenna's head pounded harder as she thought about the sheer arrogant audacity of the man. But she had kept her cool. BKB would not have approved of her taking such a prized client's head and bashing it through the drywall of his multimillion-dollar house.

"Todd," she had said in a very reasonable—she thought—tone of voice. "I am required by law to tell the D.A. that there's another witness. I won't tell him you sent her out of town, because that is protected by attorney-client confidentiality, but I have to tell him that Maria has relevant testimony and I know pretty much where to find her."

He had uttered a word Mckenna didn't use even on her worst days. "No, you fuckin' don't! You don't tell the fuckin' D.A. a thing, and you get me a verdict of not guilty. Or you're screwed, lady lawyer."

"Mr. Harmon, the law states—"

"Fuck the law! The law is stupid! If you say one thing to the D.A., I'll find me another law firm is what I'll do, and then you'll lose your fuckin' job!"

Unlikely, but the loss of a high profile multimillionaire client, jerk though he was, certainly would add lead weights to the rising balloon of her career.

That was why she hadn't yet told Tom Markham about Maria, the housemaid who had with her own eyes seen about a ton of stuff that could get Harmon an all expense paid visit to the big house, compliments of the state of Arizona. A wicked, evil, unprincipled part of her brain told her to consider the situation until Monday. After all, Harmon had a point. Maria was unavailable to testify, and finding her in Mexico would be like finding a needle in a haystack for someone who didn't know where she was. Unfortunately for her defense case, when Mckenna had talked to the timid little maid, Maria had mentioned her family in a small town in Sonora. Knowing the name of that small town, how hard could it be to bring her back? The Mexican government would cooperate. They wouldn't want to make trouble over such a small thing.

But as things stood now, the prosecution didn't know about Maria. There was no hard testimony except from witnesses that Mckenna could blow out of the courtroom with one hand tied behind her back. She could win this case, be the darling of BKB and the media that would flock to the courtroom. Her career would soar.

But the law said she had to tell the prosecution. Damn! Tom would jump on the girl's testimony. Unless Harmon did a plea deal, which would happen when hell started serving frozen daiquiris, the rock star and his stupid not guilty plea would go down the river, no doubt screaming about stupid laws, injustice, and incompetent defense attorneys. And Misters Bradner, Kelly, and Bolin would exact revenge by keeping Mckenna in Sedona, in this tiny offshoot office two hours from a proper shopping mall and just as far removed from a chance to make a name for herself. That was if they were in a generous mood and didn't demote her to legal assistant.

Sheesh! No wonder her head pounded. Had she remembered to take her blood pressure meds that morning? Her doctor just a few months ago had warned her to cool her jets or her heart was going to send blood rocketing through the top of her skull. That was happening now, if her headache gave a clue. Tears gathered in her eyes and made the road in front of her blur.

Even in daylight and seen through non-swimming eyes, the road winding through the canyon required close attention. Picturesque during the day, Oak Creek Canyon was damned dark at night. The stream tumbled through rocks and trees on Mckenna's left, and the towering cliff wall rose on her right. She squinted to see the pavement markings in the BMW's headlights, and that made her head hurt even more. Oh man, she needed a warm bath, a bottle of Tylenol, and a conversation with Titi, who even if she didn't understand a word Mckenna said, at least never talked back. Or if she did, the backtalk came out as a cute little meow. Cats never had a problem with things like doing the right thing versus doing the expedient thing. Nope. Cats were always out for themselves.

Temptation returned. Mckenna could be out for herself as well. Who would it hurt? Ethics or career advancement? Right or . . . wrong? Was it wrong to get ahead? One more minor drug conviction in a world gone wild with drugs, violence, anger, and cheating. What difference would that one little conviction make?

Ethics countered with a body block. Damn, how could

she even think such a thing? She was almost as bad as that jerk Harmon. Cleaner language, better manners, and better sense of style, but almost as disgusting.

Her interview notes on Maria Oranto seemed to burn a hole through the file folder, the briefcase, and right into Mckenna's brain. Tell or don't tell? Be good or be smart? Back and forth, back and forth. Temptation and ethics.

The road ahead curved sharply. A white light exploded in front of Mckenna's eyes. The world spun out of control, then came up to smash her flat.

TIME PASSED, many hours, and she finally woke. But she didn't remember the white blaze that had blinded her. She didn't remember the screech of brakes, the world rising up to hit her. In fact, she didn't remember much of anything.

The world was dark when she woke, and that was good. Darkness comforted. Darkness somehow made wrestling with who, what, and where unnecessary. So floating in nothingness, drifting, sinking once again toward sleep, she ignored the murmurs around her, the gentle touches, and refused to open her eyes . . . until a weight landed rudely on her sternum, an awful pressure that made breathing hard labor.

Disgruntled, she surrendered any hope of peace and opened her eyes to find a yellow-eyed monster sitting on her chest.

No, not a monster. A cat. A cat the color of mink with a baseball size head and two implacable eyes staring straight into hers.

And then the cat said, "Welcome back, Mckenna."

Before she was a therapy dog,
Piggy was already working miracles.
Don't miss her other adventures in . . .

Finding Mr. Right

and

Diamond in the Ruff